T0313538

THE
LAST DAYS
OF KIRA
MULLAN

NICCI FRENCH

THE LAST DAYS OF KIRA MULLAN

**SIMON &
SCHUSTER**

London · New York · Amsterdam/Antwerp · Sydney · Toronto · New Delhi

First published in Great Britain by Simon & Schuster UK Ltd, 2025

1 3 5 7 9 10 8 6 4 2

Simon & Schuster UK Ltd
1st Floor
222 Gray's Inn Road
London WC1X 8HB

Simon & Schuster Australia, Sydney
Simon & Schuster India, New Delhi

www.simonandschuster.co.uk
www.simonandschuster.com.au
www.simonandschuster.co.in

A CIP catalogue record for this book
is available from the British Library

Hardback ISBN: 978-1-3985-2413-2
Trade Paperback ISBN: 978-1-3985-2414-9
eBook ISBN: 978-1-3985-2415-6
Audio ISBN: 978-1-3985-2416-3

Typeset in Sabon by M Rules
Printed and Bound in the UK using 100% Renewable
Electricity at CPI Group (UK) Ltd

MIX
Paper | Supporting
responsible forestry
FSC
www.fsc.org
FSC® C171272

To Jasper, Arlie and Elias

PART ONE

ONE

The journey into darkness began with the move, although for Nancy North moving felt more like an ending. The wreckage of the past lay behind her and she couldn't see into the future or imagine what it would be.

'We'll come back,' she said determinedly, wrapping glasses in newspaper to keep them safe, placing them into the large box at her feet.

Felix smiled across at her.

'Of course,' he said.

'And soon.'

'Soon,' he echoed, but Nancy knew he was just humouring her.

He taped his box shut and labelled it with a marker pen. Nancy watched him. Her packing was impatient and slapdash; his was calm and methodical.

They were moving from a flat that she loved into a smaller and cheaper one she hadn't seen, and from a patch of East London where she knew every shop, every alley, to an area she had never set foot in. She'd had to look at a map to find out where it was. West London: it was travelling to a different continent.

'Harlesden,' she said. 'What's it like then?'

Felix straightened up and pushed his fingers through his blonde hair. He looked tired, and Nancy felt a familiar stab of guilt. She had done that to him. All of this was her fault, and he hadn't complained once.

'Interesting,' he answered. 'Diverse. I think you'll like it.'

It sounded like he was reading from a guidebook. There was an anxious, almost pleading note in his voice. Nancy crossed the room and put her arms around him.

'It'll be an adventure. While we plan what comes next,' she said, and kissed him.

An adventure. If she allowed herself to think about it, which she tried not to, it felt more like a failure and a humiliating re-treat. Eleven months ago, she had opened a tiny restaurant in Stoke Newington, the fulfilment of a dream she had had since she was a teenager. It had taken most of her twenties to save up the money for the deposit, working long hours in shitty jobs while friends became lawyers and teachers and management consultants, whatever they were, or travelled for months at a time, posting photos of themselves from beaches and jungles. At last, she managed to get a bank loan with scary repayments, and then had to find the premises, to equip it, to get the right person to be waiter and bar tender. A year and a half ago, just before she turned thirty-two, she had opened the restaurant. She had never worked so hard or with such intensity: in the kitchen before most people's day began, home very late, and even then, she would lie in bed and think about the tasks that hadn't been completed and the things that she could do better. It was like being an accountant and an artist at the same time. She even dreamed about menus. She barely saw Felix in those feverish months, or friends, unless they came to eat in the res-taurant. She never took days off or went on holiday. But she was happy, if happiness means joyful immersion in a task. She was also, she realised now when it was too late, scared that it was too good to be true and couldn't last.

It couldn't.

Four months ago, on a Sunday in the hot middle of July when she was making raspberry sorbet, a voice had whispered to her, 'It's coming.'

Nancy had looked around. The kitchen was empty.

She pushed an escaped lock of hair back inside her cap and returned to her task.

'It's coming,' said the voice again, nasty, menacing, making her heart beat faster.

There was still no one there. Perhaps she had been talking to herself. She often talked to herself, giving herself instructions, admonitions. 'Get out of the bath, Nancy North,' she would say, or she would tell herself where she was putting her keys so that she wouldn't forget them. She talked in her sleep as well. Felix would gently shake her awake and tell her she had been shouting out, asking for help.

That sinister voice was the last thing she remembered. Everything that happened after was a blur: yells and screams, leering faces and pinching fingers, a hurtling sense of terror and she knew she had to get away but there was no place to hide, no safety anywhere. She did have a few clear and shaming memories. One was of urgently taking her friend Bridie by the arm and making her run, shouting at her all the while to go faster, trying to take her away from danger. When they had at last come to a gasping stop, Bridie had stared at her in such horror that Nancy had crouched on the ground and covered her face with her hands. The other was of Felix crying, his mouth wide open and fat tears streaming down his cheeks, into his stubble. She had never seen him cry before, nor since. She promised herself she would never make him cry like that again.

She had been sectioned, drugged, talked to as if she was a small child, made to put food in her mouth. In the psychiatric ward she had lost all sense of time. She had learned to talk about what had happened to her as a psychotic breakdown, the result of working so hard and with such a feverish passion. Her voices had been externalisations: the self warning the self of its danger. She had come to understand that she had often heard the voices before, though they had never seemed violently threatening.

When she was released from hospital, back into a world where the light seemed too bright and the sky like a bruise, she had lost almost everything she cared about: her beloved little restaurant, several of her friends who were embarrassed and appalled by what she had been like in those wild weeks, her self-respect, her self-belief, her joy. The shame was intense: there were days when it took all her courage to meet someone's gaze. She wanted to hide, to cover her eyes, be swallowed up in darkness and forgetfulness.

Felix had saved her. He had been calm and steadfast and tender, and Nancy, who hated being looked after by anyone, let herself be looked after by him. It was Felix who had dealt with all the bureaucracy of the fall-out, faced up to the fact that they could no longer afford the flat they were living in, found the new place which a friend of his was moving out of and which he'd often visited, organised the removal men, and done the lion's share of packing.

'Felix,' said Nancy.

'Yes?'

'This teapot has a crack. Keep or chuck?'

He lifted it in his broad, competent hands and examined it.

'Keep until we buy a new one.'

'And Felix.'

He looked round at her.

'Have I ever told you how fab you are?'

He grinned.

'Rather a lot recently.'

In her late teens and twenties, she would have overlooked Felix, or dismissed him as boring. He wasn't reckless, charismatic, unreliable, unpredictable or downright self-harming; not thin and stubbly and carelessly dressed. No sharp cheekbones or tattoos or piercings. He didn't take drugs, except the occasional spliff; he paid bills on time. He was solid, blonde, sensible and good-looking in a way that was easy to ignore. He was only two years older than Nancy, but sometimes, she thought, they seemed to belong to different generations.

'Remember our first meeting?'

He had come, with a mutual friend, to the restaurant where she worked before she opened her own. She hadn't fallen for him at once, but she had rather liked the way he looked, the way he listened, his modesty, his composure, his lack of irony, the way he ate his food slowly and thoughtfully, giving it his full attention. He wasn't neurotic or troubled. He was, well, nice. And he adored her. It was almost absurd how much he adored her.

'Do you remember what you ate?'

He lifted knives from their magnetic strip and folded them in tea towels before saying, 'No, but I remember you came out of the kitchen in white trousers and a funny little cap on your head with some of your hair escaping from it and there were freckles on the bridge of your nose. I thought you very fetching.'

'Fetching?'

'Yes.'

'You had tagliatelle with wild mushrooms and parmesan and lots of black pepper.'

'That sounds pretty good.'

'We should have that as our anniversary meal.'

'It's a plan.'

He was pulling pots and pans out of the cupboards.

'I'm going to start cooking again soon.'

'Only when you're ready.'

'I miss it.'

'Don't forget what your doctor said. One step at a time.'

Nancy felt a pulse of irritation. She wanted to say that of course she wouldn't forget, and that Felix didn't need to incessantly remind her: he wasn't her doctor or her carer, but her partner. But she held her tongue.

'It's about three steps to the bedroom,' she said instead. 'A goodbye fuck.'

'Nancy, we have to get everything packed and we've barely started.'

But he was smiling and moving towards her, frying pan still in one hand. She put her arms around him, and he pushed her long, pale brown hair away from her face before kissing her.

Everything will be all right, Nancy told herself, putting her fingers in his soft hair, feeling the graze of his cheek. She would take her drugs, see her therapist, take things step by step and day by day. But there was a sinister tingling in her brain, like pins and needles. The objects in the room came in and out of focus and she closed her eyes to stop the world from wavering. I will make it all right.

On the other side of London, in a small flat in Harlesden, twenty-three-year-old Kira Mullan was saying goodbye to the man she had spent the afternoon in bed with. He was called Ollie and she liked him. She really liked him. It had been a long time since she had fallen like this for someone: maybe, she thought giddily, not since her first real boyfriend when she was sixteen and a half and thought that love would last for ever, but then he had left her for one of the mean girls in her class. She could still remember the heartbreak, how she had cried for days until her eyes were red and her whole face puffy with luxurious weeping.

But then what about Davey, who she'd gone out with when she was nineteen? Or Serge, who had overlapped with Davey, which wasn't something she usually did, or Angus with the lovely voice and the drug habit that got out of control. Since she'd arrived in London, there had just been a handful of un-satisfactory hook-ups that she had tried to pretend to herself were more pleasurable than they actually were. A few of them had been scary and some were a tipsy blur. Sometimes she wondered if she had made a mistake coming here. London was exciting, but also monstrously huge and sprawling, and she didn't understand how to belong to it, how to meet people who wanted to be friends with her. She did her best to sparkle and be fun and show her best face, but there were days when loneliness swamped her normal buoyant optimism. Not today, though. Today she was brimful of hope.

Ollie pulled his jacket on. Kira was wrapped in a flimsy robe and her hair was a tangle; her lips were chapped. Happiness and sex had made her young face glow.

'I don't want to go,' he said.

'I've got to get to work. I'll be late as it is.'

He ran a thumb against her lower lip, pressed his lips to her jaw.

'I've been wanting you for weeks,' he said. 'Ever since I saw you in the bar.'

'Really?'

'You're beautiful,' he said, his mouth in her hair, hands on the small of her back. 'Gorgeous.'

She leaned into him, feeling his warmth.

'You're not so bad yourself.'
'I'll call you when I get back.'
'When will that be?'
'Six days.'
'I'll be waiting.'
It was the last time he would see her.

Two

Early the next morning, Felix left to pick up the van he had rented. It was a Saturday in mid-November, cold and grey and threatening rain. Nancy, alone in the flat full of boxes and bulging cases, walked from room to room. She was saying goodbye and readying herself for the next stage.

She checked her shoulder bag. Her passport was in there, her make-up bag, the drugs prescribed by Dr Lowe that she needed to take at regular times through the day but which dried out her mouth. She sometimes felt that her edges were being rubbed away, all the sharp and unexpected bits of her. But she would go on taking them, and go on checking in with Helena, her therapist.

'Never again,' she said aloud to the room.

'What's that?' a voice called.

'That was quick.'

Felix came into the room, jangling a key in his hand.

'I'll take the heavy stuff,' he said.

As the van filled up, Nancy thought how much and yet how little they had. There were all the flimsy bits and pieces of a life — the plates and glasses and cutlery; the bed linen and towels; the laptops and chargers; the cases of clothes and splitting bin bags of shoes; the things they didn't really want but couldn't bring themselves to throw away — and yet they possessed barely any furniture and certainly no possibility of a place of their own.

She put a large pot plant near the back of the van and shut the door.

'Ready?' Felix asked.

She nodded.

'You don't want to check one last time?'

'You do it,' she said.

Her keys were on the table. She needed to be gone.

London rolled by, first familiar and then strange. The sky was tea-bag brown and it was starting to rain. The windscreen wipers swept back and forth, trailing shreds of loose rubber which made a squeaking sound. It was a long, slow journey. Nancy's head buzzed.

'Okay?' Felix asked.

'Fine.'

'You're sure? You seem a bit quiet.'

'I'm fine.'

'Just say if you aren't.'

'I will. Tell me about the other people in the house. Do you know all of them?'

'I only really know the guys in the basement flat. Barney and Seamus.'

'What are they like?'

'Good guys,' Felix said.

'What do they do?'

'Seamus is some kind of fitness instructor. I'm not sure about Barney.'

'Old? Young?'

'Maybe our age or a bit younger. Early thirties, anyway.'

'Friendly? Shy?'

'Barney's a bit shy.'

Nancy gave up.

'You don't know the other people?'

'I've no idea who lives opposite. I've met the woman on the ground floor in passing.'

'What's she like?'

'She seems nice.' Felix turned left. They were driving along-side a road, one side of which was residential, and on the other was a whole system of railway tracks. Beyond those, there were cranes, industrial buildings, storage tanks. A freight train rat-tled past in the opposite direction. 'You mustn't worry,' he said.

'I wasn't worrying. I was wondering. What about the flat?'

'It's quite small,' he said cautiously. 'But you're about to see it.'

The house in Fielding Road was from the late nineteenth cen-tury. A few feet of gravel pathway led to the communal front door with four buzzers in a vertical row to its left. A metal staircase led down to the basement flat.

Felix fumbled in his pocket for keys and opened the door. Nancy stepped into a dark hall, cracked tiles on the floor and a naked bulb hanging from the ceiling. There was a door to the right and on the other side a staircase carpeted with a fraying runner.

'First floor,' said Felix, and they mounted the stairs in silence.

There was a high wailing noise that grew louder as they ap-proached the first floor. At first Nancy thought it was an alarm, but then she realised it came from a crying baby.

Felix opened the door to their flat and then shut it behind them, but even with the door closed the noise was piercing.

'Don't worry,' said Nancy, seeing his anxious expression. 'It's bound to stop soon.'

She looked around the flat. Felix had been right to call it

small. The door led directly into a square living room, furnished with basic pine furniture, leading into a tiny, doorless galley kitchen with a door that led down a flight of rickety steps into the far end of the narrow, untended garden. To the right of the living room was a bedroom with just enough room for a double bed, a wardrobe and a chest of drawers. To the left was a bathroom.

'What do you think?'

The walls were stained and peeling. The room smelt of damp, the windows weren't big enough to let in much light – although perhaps it would be better when it wasn't grey and wet outside. She thought of the bright, airy flat they had just left. She thought of her modest, satisfying little restaurant with its whitewashed walls and sturdy wooden tables. She made herself smile.

'We can make it feel homely,' she said. 'Once our things are in here, pictures on the walls, throws.'

Felix nodded gratefully.

'I'll start unloading,' he said. 'Then I need to get the van back.'

Kira heard people going up and down the stairs, carrying things. She thought of offering to help, but she was still in her pyjamas even though it was early afternoon. She wasn't working today, and she had spent the morning lying in bed with a mug of coffee and toast and honey, looking at her phone, half dozing and then waking up in a state of voluptuous drowsiness. She felt like a cat curled up in its own warmth.

Eventually she made herself get up. There was the party this evening, and she'd seen a dress in town that she wanted to buy. A beautiful green sequined sheath. She imagined herself wearing it.

As she left, she met Olga from upstairs in the hall. Olga

was small and thin, and she was holding her baby, who was enormous and red-faced, with a huge open mouth from which came frightful howls.

'Sorry for the noise.'

'You look exhausted.'

'I am. How do other mothers do it? Perhaps,' she added, 'their husbands help more.'

Kira thought of her own mother, who'd done it all alone. She would rush in from work and start cooking their tea before she'd even taken her coat off. Kira's father had left just after her younger sister was born. Her mouth tightened: she didn't like thinking of him. He was a thin, querulous, complaining man who had abandoned his family and then felt sorry for himself. Sometimes he called her in the middle of the night, when he'd drunk too much, to tell her how nobody understood him and how life had let him down.

'Let me babysit one night,' she said impulsively to Olga. 'You and Harry can go out together.'

'You would do that?'

'Of course. I'd like to.'

Felix left and Nancy sat on a packing box and stared around. The baby was still screaming. If anything, it was louder than ever. She wanted tea, but which box contained the tea bags, which the mugs? She pulled a strip of masking tape off the nearest box and levered it open. Pots and pans. She lifted one out, a heavy cast-iron saucepan that she hadn't been able to resist. She held it on her lap for a few moments and then began to weep. Everything was wrong.

The dress was still there. Kira took it into the changing room, stripped off her jeans and sweatshirt, and inched herself into it, the silky, chinking material cool against her flesh. She looked at herself in the mirror, turning this way and that, glancing back at herself over her shoulder. She took off her socks with their balding heels and stood on tiptoe. It made her look both slim and voluptuous, she thought: the stretch of it over her hips and her breasts, and she imagined herself wearing it when Ollie came back. She smiled at her reflection. I'm pretty, she thought; I'm sexy. Only five days, she told herself.

Kira bought her dress, though she couldn't really afford it. Almost all of her money went on paying the rent for the nasty little flat which smelt of damp and had silverfish in the bathroom. She should move, find a flat share so when she got up in the morning there would be someone to chat to over a mug of tea, and when she came home at night, it wouldn't be to an empty room, the freight trains rumbling by and making the windows rattle.

She walked back in the strengthening rain. On the street, she ran into Michelle Strauss, the woman who lived next door. Michelle was middle-aged and plump, with round glasses that made her look like an owl and a smile that always seemed ironic. She usually wore baggy linen clothes. She had always been very friendly to Kira, and once invited her for supper, but the way she would look at Kira with speculative curiosity made her uneasy, and the way her husband, Dylan, looked at her made her flinch.

'Hello, Kira,' said Michelle. She looked at the bag Kira was clutching. 'Been shopping?'

'I bought a dress. I shouldn't have. It was stupidly expensive. But I couldn't resist.'

'Show me.'

Kira brought the garment out of the bag and for a moment, in spite of the rain, held it against herself.

'Wow!' Michelle said.

'I'm going to wear it to Seamus and Barney's party tonight.'

'Have fun.'

'Seamus invited me to their party tonight,' said Felix as he came back into the flat, having delivered the van.

'Party?'

'In the downstairs flat. He said it was a last-minute thing. Shall we go?'

Nancy's heart was jumping in her chest and her pulse was fluttering in her temple. She didn't feel quite right.

'You go,' she said.

'Don't you want to come? Just for a bit?'

'I'm a bit tired.'

'I'll stay here too. It's our first evening.'

'Don't. It would be good to go. After all, they're our new neighbours.'

'I'll just pop in for a few minutes after supper. I thought I'd get us a takeaway.'

'Stay as long as you like.'

Kira ate a bag of crisps slowly, licking the salt off her fingers. She dried her hair and tied it loosely back at the nape of her neck. She painted her nails, put on a necklace, some dangling earrings, several thin silver bangles. She applied make-up carefully: dramatic eyes and red lips. Then she stepped into her new green dress. It was like a second skin. She smiled and her looking-glass self smiled back. Her eyes shone.

Nancy lay in bed and listened to the sounds of the party. It was two floors down, but the floors were thin, and the whole house seemed to reverberate with the noise. Good music, she thought. She loved dancing, but she couldn't remember the last time she had danced.

She was glad Felix had gone to the party. Since coming out of hospital, she had rarely been alone. It was as if he didn't quite trust her yet; as if he thought she might unravel again if he didn't keep an eye on her. It was good to lie in bed, music pounding below her and trains rattling by outside the window, and let thoughts drift through her. Everything was strange to her: the breakdown, the move, this flat, her future. She felt small and naked in the world.

She woke briefly when Felix climbed into bed beside her.

'Good party?' she mumbled.

'I didn't mean to wake you.'

His breath smelt of beer.

'What time is it?'

'Go to sleep now.'

Three

Nancy's real feeling of dread began the next day, with a small patch of damp on the wall. The wallpaper was the coarse, cheap kind that landlords used to cover up cracks. It had little chips on it like the chickenpox pimples on skin. She raised her hand and pushed it against the patch. The paper had come away from the wall behind. She thought of the moisture oozing out of the body of the house.

She looked around the room and remembered the old saying: a place for everything and everything in its place. Just at the moment, here in this new flat, there was a place for nothing and nothing was in its place. The walls were bare, except the pale rectangles where pictures had once hung. A light socket dangled from the centre of the ceiling with no light bulb in it. The previous tenant had taken the pictures and taken the light bulbs.

Cardboard packing cases covered the floor. One of them had split, showing the paperback books inside. It was their whole life, stacked in front of her. In Stoke Newington it had looked hopeful and now here in Harlesden, ten miles to the west and a whole world away, it looked lost and defeated.

In the next couple of days the boxes would be unloaded and the contents distributed and arranged and hung and stowed, and it might almost look like a home again.

But that stain would still be there, even if they could cover it with a picture.

As she looked at it, she suddenly felt as if the building was alive and it was suffering from a wound and was exuding some blood or awful liquid. The wall had tried to contain it but it was trying to force its way through.

Nancy heard a rumble and felt it too, beneath her feet. Water was running through pipes under the floorboards. Probably the heating was switching itself on or off, or someone in the flat next door was emptying a sink. She felt the building was alive and the pipes were its veins and arteries. The house was trying to tell her something. She could hear the whispers, but she couldn't make out the words.

She had taken her pills, but she knew the signs and knew she needed to be in the fresh air, not looking at that damp, dark stain any longer. She picked up her worn leather jacket – as comforting as an ancient teddy bear – and pulled it on. She looked instinctively at the mirror on the wall to check her appearance, to see that her long, pale brown hair wasn't too disordered, but there wasn't a mirror on the wall. Not yet.

Felix was out of sight in the galley kitchen. He would be installing something, doing something practical.

'I'm going out,' she said in a raised voice. 'I have to . . .'

She couldn't think of anything that she had to do, but she hoped it would be enough.

'Can you get something for me?'

Nancy didn't want to talk, and she didn't want to have to remember anything. She felt that she was being held underwater by an irresistible force and that she was about to open her mouth and breathe in the water and drown. The muttering around her increased and she tried to ignore it. Maybe it would go away.

She heard a horrible sound and at first, she couldn't tell what it was or where it was coming from, whether it was inside the house or outside the house. She opened the door to the flat and stepped out into the common passageway, where the sound at once became clearer and more defined. Of course, it was the crying baby in the flat opposite. She knew that the crying didn't mean anything except that the baby was hungry or tired, but it felt like a drill, except the drill was inside her skull.

She hurried down the stairs and stepped out onto the path. A few stumbling paces later she was on the pavement. She took deep breaths in the cold air. She had made it.

It was a Sunday afternoon in mid-November, and it was as if the day was already preparing for evening. Windows glowed up and down one side of Fielding Road. Every minute a train, a caterpillar of lights, rumbled past and disappeared. She didn't know the area and she had nowhere to get to except away from where she had been, so she just started walking.

One day the road would be familiar, the street where she lived, but now it felt as if she had been dropped there and abandoned. A young man in a heavy jacket and a woolly hat was walking towards her. She avoided meeting his gaze, but as he passed her, he said something. She couldn't make out the words, but they sounded like a threat. *You can't get away from me.* Nancy speeded up her walk. The important thing was not to respond, not to engage.

Suddenly there were people everywhere, as the houses became shops: pound stores, furniture warehouses with sofas wrapped in thick polythene piled outside on the pavement, fish shops that also sold meat, barbers and charity shops. It felt like an area for people like her, who were exiles from another part of London or another part of the world. They were there because they didn't have the money to live anywhere else. She walked along a motley storefront of mops and bins and plastic flowers and crates of energy drinks and found herself in a market. Parsnips and carrots, flecked with the earth they'd been pulled from. Meat hanging from hooks, glistening pink and with a smell that caught in the back of her throat. There was a pyramid of over-ripe mangoes, flesh oozing out of split skin. Christmas trees standing in a row. They would be dead long before Christmas.

Something spun her round. A woman shouted. A finger jabbed her. She heard spiteful laughter. Where was it coming from? It seemed all around her, bubbles of sound.

Up close was a face, jowly, spittle on the chin. Reek of cigarettes and garlic. So many smells, so many sounds, and it was as if she could smell and hear them all.

'Cry baby.'

'What?' Nancy stepped back.

'Escape,' said another voice, close at hand. 'Get away.'

There were bodies closing in all around her and she was trapped by them, trapped by the voices that were asking her for something, telling her something, but she couldn't hear what. A figure reeled towards her, face blotchy and discoloured, with staring eyes, like an upright corpse. So much fear and distress.

Nancy ran a hand over her face, she pressed her fingers to her mouth. Her skin pricked and itched, as if there was an army of stinging ants marching across her.

'It's okay,' she said out loud because sometimes talking to herself in the third person helped.

Her feet slid on wet, slimy leaves. It hasn't been a good idea to come out. She was less safe here than in the flat. She had to go home. But home is where the heart is. She put her hand flat against her chest to feel her heart hammering away. Distress signals.

She turned. Someone spat at her. No. Not spit, rain. Fat clean drops of rain on her hot cheek.

She walked back slowly, one foot in front of the other. What was that marching rhyme from her childhood, walking in the mud and chill of a winter Sunday afternoon with her father chivvying her? Left, left, you had a good home and you left; right, right, it serves you jolly well right.

The crowds abruptly fell away. A bike light wavered towards her, gleaming on the damp road, and then passed.

The house was just a few yards away. She could do this.

Four

She reached the path and a shape erupted out of the gloom and barreled into her shoulder, a bag flying through the air, spilling its contents. A woman's cracked voice. Nancy could feel a distress like a scratching on her skin. The woman was very young, almost a girl. Her face was pale in the dusk and framed by a matted tangle of curls, her mouth drawn back in a grimace and her huge grey eyes glittering. Streaks of mascara ran like tears down her cheeks. She smelt of drink, weed, sweat, fear.

'It's all right,' Nancy said in a whisper.

She was talking to herself. She was talking to the woman. Perhaps there was no difference. All she knew was that the distraught woman was asking her for something or telling her something. The whole unsettled day had been leading her to this one moment of connection.

The woman gave a hoarse laugh that sounded like fabric tearing, and that turned into a sob. 'It's not all right. But please.' Her voice crumbled. Nancy couldn't make out the words properly. 'No more,' she heard the woman said. 'Get away,' she said. 'No.'

'Let me help,' said Nancy.

To help the woman, even in the smallest way, was a way of helping herself: to lay a healing hand on chaos. There was a thread out of the labyrinth, she thought. She just had to follow it, carefully feeling her way out of the darkness and violence towards the light.

She knelt to pick up the things that lay scattered on the path with clumsy fingers. A toothbrush and toothpaste, deodorant, a few pieces of underwear. The woman was wearing dark green leather boots with bright yellow laces.

'Take care,' she said.

The woman stared at her.

'You too.'

Nancy stumbled up the stairs, fumbled open the door to the flat and slammed the door behind her. She leaned against it, breathing heavily. She pressed her hands against her face, which felt rubbery and unnatural. Gradually her heart stopped beating so fast. She listened. The flat was silent, just the uneven drip of the tap from the kitchen.

'Hello,' she called. 'Felix? I'm back.'

There was no reply. She was glad he wasn't here to see her like this. She headed straight for the bedroom, which was full of opened packing boxes, bin bags of towels and jumpers, a knot of cables on the floor, pictures leaning against the wall. At least there was a made-up bed. Nancy pulled off her jacket and let it slide to the floor, kicked off her boots, hauled herself onto the bed, and pulled the covers over her head. Silent, dark, warm, like the lair of a wounded animal. Wait it out.

In the flat beneath her, Kira Mullan was dying.

She tried to shout, but the rope round her neck was too tight. She tried to lift her hands to her throat, but they were held pinioned; to thrash but her body wouldn't budge under the weight. She tried to fight, she tried to beg for mercy, but a small crackle of distress came from her.

A train rumbled past outside.

She was too young, Kira thought. It wasn't fair. A black tide was sweeping over her. Her body was a scream of fear and pain.

A memory, bright as a jewel, came to her: she was eleven or twelve, on the brink of adolescence, her body changing, and she was wearing a new denim skirt and a blouse with little green sprigs on a white background, her nails were painted a pearly pink, and she was delighted with herself. She could feel the sun on her face. Life flowed through her, abundant. She could almost fly with the pleasure of it. What a fragile gift life is. How had she not understood? She could see her feet kicking in the green boots with yellow laces, but less frantically now. The blood-dark mist was rising all round her. The rope creaked. She wanted her mother. She wanted.

FIVE

Nancy lurched awake from a dream where someone was shouting. She had difficulty in remembering where she was. She thought she was back in her old flat. But when she sat up, fully dressed and confused from her afternoon sleep, and saw the mess all around her, it came back to her. The voices, the faces, the ill wind blowing. But that was over: she felt better, clearer-headed. It was like a fading dream.

She peered at her phone and saw it was past five o'clock. She'd slept for nearly two hours.

She climbed out of bed, negotiated her way round the boxes and bags, and pulled open the door. The blinds were pulled down in the living room and there was a bunch of scruffy purple chrysanthemums on top of one of the packing boxes. Her old green sofa, the only item of furniture they had brought with them, had been pulled to the side of the room. She smelt frying garlic and heard music, the sort of jazz that Felix listened to when she wasn't around. Through the open door Nancy could see him standing at the stove, blonde, stocky, unruffled, serene. He was meditatively stirring something. A heavily bearded man was seated on a wooden crate beside him, drinking beer out of a can and looking at his phone.

They both turned to her as she came in. Felix lifted the wooden spoon in greeting.

'We didn't want to wake you,' he said.

'You didn't.'

'You remember Gary.'

Did she?

She put out a hand. 'I don't think we've met.'

He stood up and shook it, his fingers cold and soft against her palm.

'We have,' he said. 'Several times.'

'Really?'

'We went for a drink up the road,' said Felix.

'Good.'

'I should go.'

Gary picked up his duffle coat. He seemed in a hurry to leave. Felix saw him out, then touched her on the shoulder.

'You seem a bit, you know . . .'

'I'm fine,' she said.

'Because if . . .'

'I'm *fine*. What are you cooking?'

'Just a spicy tomato sauce. I thought we could have pasta after they've all gone.' He gestured. 'I even found the salt and pepper pots.'

'After who's gone?'

'I thought I said. I invited Seamus and Barney for a drink when I dropped in on their party last night.'

'I remember the party, anyway,' Nancy said. 'I woke up at six and it was still going on. Was it fun? I forgot to ask this morning.'

'It was crowded. You'd have liked it more than me.'

'Did you stay long?' she asked.

'I was too tired. I just thought I'd show my face.'

'Right.'

'I invited the couple opposite as well. I bumped into the woman in the hall and helped her carry the buggy upstairs. I think she's called Olga, but that might be the baby. Funny little thing. The baby, I mean. And I knocked on Kira's door, the woman who lives in the ground-floor flat, but she must be out.'

'Do we have anything to drink?'

'I got some beer and some wine and some crisps. Why don't you have a bath before they come?'

'A bath?'

'You seem . . .'

He scratched his head. Nancy felt trapped by his solicitous gaze.

'I don't want a bath, Felix. I'll have a quick shower.'

He came over to her, pushing boxes away, put his arm around her and it took all her willpower not to push it off.

'It's all right,' he said.

Seamus Tyrell arrived first. He was tall and bulked out, with curly dark hair, pale eyes and a cleft in his chin, and was good-looking in a way that was almost comic, like a cartoon of a handsome man. He was in his mid-thirties, but already becoming bulky. He clapped Felix on the shoulder and kissed Nancy on one cheek, then the next, a bit too close to her lips. She could smell his perfume and his sweat.

'You're an improvement,' he said.

'On what?'

He stood back and looked at her appraisingly. She had washed her hair and dug out her moss-green cashmere jumper which had moth holes in the sleeves but was soft and familiar against her skin.

'On the guy who lived here before.'

'Drink?' Felix asked. 'Wine? Beer?'

'Beer. Hair of the dog. Long night. You should have come,' he said to Nancy.

'Next time.'

There was a rattle of knocks on the door, like an announcement.

'Am I late or early?' asked the young man who almost fell in through the door when Felix pulled it open. He was small and blue-eyed, with a slightly doughy face, an uneven beard, brown hair that already showed specks of grey, although he looked young, barely out of his twenties. His clothes looked like they'd been slept in. 'My phone's run out of battery and I've lost the charger. When I woke up it was dark, and Seamus wasn't there.'

He pulled a woebegone face.

'This is my flatmate, Barney,' said Seamus. 'He's feeling a bit delicate today. Barney, this here's Nancy. Felix's ...' He hesitated. 'What's the word?'

'Girlfriend,' said Felix, just as Nancy said, 'Partner'.

Barney groaned and laid himself along the sofa, pushing crisps into his mouth, chomping on them.

There was another rap on the door, this one single and assertive. A man with sandy hair and freckles came in, holding a bottle of wine.

'I'm Harry from opposite,' he said, pushing the bottle into Felix's hands. 'Olga said you'd invited us round. But I'm afraid it's just me. It's the baby's bedtime.'

As if on cue there was a long, high wail. Harry winced.

'You must be cursing us.'

'It's fine,' said Felix.

'Worse for you,' said Nancy. 'Is it always this loud?'

'She.'

'What?'

'It's a she. The health visitor said that some babies just cry and that she would probably be better by nine months.'

'How old is she now?'

'Three months.'

'Babies,' put in Barney thickly through a mouthful of crisps. 'Who'd have them?'

Harry glowered at him for a moment. His face was very pale, as if he hadn't been outside for weeks, and there were dark smudges under his eyes.

'Your party was louder than our baby ever is. We barely slept. And I'm on nights this week.'

Seamus, holding up his hands in apology. Everything about him, thought Nancy, seemed slightly exaggerated, slightly fraudulent. 'Sorry about that, mate. What can you do? This house has walls like fucking paper.'

'What do you do?' Nancy still felt slightly dazed.

'I'm a doctor. You know, the overworked, underpaid junior doctors you see on the news. Only with a crying baby,' he added. 'And a roof that leaks.'

'I'd like to be a doctor,' said Barney, who was still lying on the sofa, his eyes half closed and a can of beer tipping dangerously from his outstretched hand, its spume of froth at the opening. 'It sounds pretty good compared to what I do?'

There was a silence until they realised that someone was meant to ask what he did.

'What do you do?' Felix asked.

'Consumer research,' he said. 'Freelance. But it's not as glamorous as it sounds. And it's zero hours.'

'And our boiler's died,' said Seamus. 'I'd swap your roof for our boiler.'

'So we win,' said Barney, sitting up.

'I can have a look at it if you want,' said Felix.

'Are you a plumber?' said Barney.

'I'm an insurance claims manager.'

'That sounds a bit fucking grown up. How does anyone get to be something like that?'

'I like maths. I like helping people.'

'Is it boring?'

'Sometimes,' said Felix mildly. 'And sometimes it's interesting.'

'The landlord should help,' said Harry stubbornly, still thinking about the boiler. 'That's in the contract.' He took a long gulp of beer. His pale face had angry spots of colour at the cheeks now. 'But William Goddard is a bastard, so does he? No, he doesn't. I ask about the roof: he doesn't reply. I ask about the cracked glass: he doesn't reply. I ask about the dripping taps. Drip drip drip; the baby cries and the tap drips.'

He seemed intent on driving himself into a rage.

'Your friend who lived here before probably didn't mention the mice.'

'As long as they're mice, not rats,' said Nancy.

'I knew someone who had a rat come out of his toilet,' said Barney. 'While he was sitting on it.'

'Before you ask.' Seamus moved closer to Nancy while Felix opened another bag of crisps. 'I'm a fitness instructor.'

'That sounds good,' said Nancy.

Harry was now pointing towards their ceiling.

'That's been freshly painted to conceal the damp.'

'I can give you some private lessons if you want,' Seamus continued.

Nancy tried to think of a polite way of saying that she would rather die.

'Nancy likes to do her exercise outside,' said Felix, coming over. 'Don't you, Nancy?'

'And what do you do, Nancy?' asked Seamus, lingering on her name as if he was tasting it.

'At the moment I'm helping out a friend.'

'How?'

'I write about products she's selling on her website.'

'Cool.'

'It isn't. But I'll soon go back to doing what I was doing before.'

'Who wants wine?' Felix asked, pushing himself between the two of them. 'Beer? More crisps?'

'What was that?' Seamus asked.

'Nancy's just working out what she wants to do next, aren't you, Nancy?'

'I ran a little restaurant,' said Nancy.

'She had to step back from it.'

Felix put a hand on her shoulder and squeezed it reassuringly.

'I'll return to it,' Nancy continued.

'There's no rush,' said Felix. It wasn't clear whether he was saying this to Seamus or to Nancy herself.

'I could murder a curry,' said Barney, who had lain down again and put his feet on the arm rest. 'What's your signature dish?'

She was saved from answering by a knock at the door.

'Maybe it's Kira, after all,' said Felix.

It wasn't Kira. It was a middle-aged couple, the woman holding a large bunch of flowers wrapped in brown paper, and the man a bottle of champagne. She was short and plump, with cropped greying hair and round glasses and wearing baggy linen trousers and a loose jacket. He was tall and burly, with hair that came to the collar and a bullish way of jutting his head forward. He had a fresh scratch on his nose that he kept touching with the tip of one finger.

'We're your neighbours from 101,' said the woman. 'We didn't realise you'd have guests.'

'Dylan,' said the man. 'Dylan Strauss.'

'And I'm Michelle.

'I'm Nancy. They're beautiful flowers. Thank you.'

'Welcome to the neighbourhood, Nancy. I hope you're going to be very happy.'

An hour later, they'd all gone. Felix cooked the pasta and Nancy rummaged through boxes to find plates and cutlery. The events of the day had receded. Now they were just a nasty haze – a passing fever dream of disaster.

'Let's see if I've got them straight,' she said. 'Seamus is a fitness instructor and thinks he's God's gift.'

'Seamus is all right,' said Felix.

'If you're a man, maybe. Barney is a freelance in ... what was it?'

'Consumer research,' said Felix.

'You've been paying attention. Harry from across the corridor is a doctor who hasn't slept for months and has a glazed look. He's angry. What's his partner called?'

'Olga.'

'Olga, who had to stay home with their yelling baby. Then there's Michelle from the big house next door and her husband is Dylan, with the big jaw – what does he do?'

'He's retired,' said Felix. 'But Seamus said it wasn't his choice. Apparently, he was something in retail.'

'Had you met them before?'

'Just to nod at over the wall.'

'Which only leaves Kira, who never turned up but who you described as friendly.'

'Or bubbly,' said Felix.

'That's a very male way of describing a woman.'

He smiled down at her where she crouched over the boxes.

'You're obviously feeling better.'

'I wasn't feeling bad.'

'You were. I always know.'

'It's not a good idea to tell me what I'm feeling.'

'I wasn't telling you. I was just noticing.'

'What does she look like?'

'Kira?'

'Yes.'

'I've never really looked properly. Here, pasta's ready.'

Through the thin adjoining wall, the baby started to cry again. From the basement, music started up, the bass notes throbbing.

A few feet beneath where they sat, Kira swung from a rope, her open eyes staring at nothing.

Six

'Is one spoonful enough? Or do you want two?'

Nancy looked at the saucepan filled with glistening porridge. Felix cooked it on a low heat in the oven overnight. He said it made all the difference. He was standing poised with a spoon: not a normal soup spoon. It was more like the sort you'd use for stirring a giant casserole. None, Nancy felt like saying: none at all.

'One will be fine.'

He emptied a large, heaped spoon of stodgy porridge into the bowl in front of her.

'Would you like some milk or some cream or brown sugar?'

'Not this morning. I'll just have it as it is. I'm not super hungry.'

'I'm ravenous,' said Felix. He tipped the rest of the porridge into his own bowl. He sprinkled brown sugar on top and poured milk over it. He stirred it so the sugar formed a brown spiral and took a mouthful. He started to say something and then stopped for a few seconds because his mouth was still full.

Nancy put a tiny amount of porridge into her mouth. It felt slimy and reminded her of frog spawn. Felix got up and poured coffee from the cafetière. He put one of the mugs in front of her.

'Can I get you some orange juice or half a grapefruit?'

Nancy looked at her mug. This morning, in the after-math of the episode in the market, everything seemed too sharply in focus. Each sound felt so distinct and precise that it almost hurt.

'Just coffee will be fine,' she said.

He was opposite her. Although she was looking down at her porridge bowl, she could feel his gaze on her.

'You know I hate to say this . . .' he began.

'Then don't.'

'I don't want you to feel like I'm policing you. But I worry that when you're stressed, you just don't eat. And you're not eating.'

Nancy gestured at her bowl.

'I'm having a hearty breakfast,' she said.

'That wouldn't feed a mouse. And you're just moving it around in your bowl anyway. But I shouldn't have said anything.'

Nancy took a spoonful of the porridge, a proper spoonful, and put it in her mouth and swallowed with an immense effort.

'You know I'm not really a breakfast person,' she said. 'My ideal breakfast is coffee.'

'It's just that I worry about you. You know, with everything.'

Nancy did know and she understood why Felix was doing what he was doing and she understood how he felt awkward and embarrassed saying it. It was something they should probably talk about, but just now that was completely out of the question. It was like having a discussion while she was in a burning building.

'Have you got lots of work today?' Felix asked, standing up and pulling on his thick coat.

Nancy pushed the bowl away and leaned back.

'Today I'm writing about Easter. How many ways can you

think of to describe milk chocolate?' She held up a finger. 'Velvety. Smooth. Rich. Silky. Irresistible. Decadent.'

'My friend went out of his way to get you this little job,' said Felix a little stiffly.

'I'm grateful. Of course I'm grateful.' She stood up and put her arms around his neck. Buttery, she thought. Melting. Creamy, Addictive. Warm. Earthy. 'Stop looking so anxious. I'm going to be fine. Go to work.' She kissed him on the mouth and felt his lips smile beneath hers.

'If you're sure you really—'

'Felix.' She put her hand on the small of his back and gave him a push. 'Shoo.'

When Felix left, she waited and listened for his footsteps on the stairs, the door to the street opening and then closing. She took a deep breath. The quiet and stillness was an immense relief and she almost told herself that this would be enough. But she knew it wasn't enough.

Then she made the call.

'Can I come in this morning? Straight away. Is it possible?'

She waited for her request to be passed on. Yes, it was possible.

She would like to have gone by bike, but she didn't ride her bike anymore. She would like to have walked, but it would take too long and after yesterday she wasn't sure that walking was a good idea. The underground was impossible for her with the noise and the heat and the crowds and the lack of space, above all the sense of being in a metal tube underground. But there was one good side to being in this new, strange part of north-west London. A train clattered past almost as a reminder. Willesden Junction. The overground. She looked at her phone. She could get there on time.

*

The walls of Dr Roland Lowe's consulting room were an unequivocal white, like a laboratory. There was nothing on the wall but framed degrees and there was a blue rug on the floor of the sort designed to be easy to scrub clean.

Dr Lowe looked at her with an appraising expression. He was a gaunt, angular figure, bald with grey hair close-cropped on the sides of his head. Nancy always felt that for him she wasn't so much a patient to be cured as a problem to be solved.

'You said it was urgent,' he said.

'I think I need to make some adjustments.'

'Are you having a problem with side-effects?'

'I'm having a problem with my brain. I think I may need to up the dose a bit.'

'Has something happened?'

'Yesterday I had a bit of a – well, a recurrence, I guess.'

Dr Lowe seemed to consider this for a moment. It was as if Nancy was at a garage, and she was telling the mechanic that her car was making a rattling sound. She quite liked that: it felt practical.

'All right,' said Dr Lowe. He reached across his desk for a pad of paper. He took a pen from his pocket, removed the cap and wrote something at the top that Nancy couldn't see. 'You probably know the drill by now, Ms North,' he said.

'Nancy. Please call me Nancy. You sound like you're talking to a body on a slab.'

It took only five minutes for Nancy to describe her experience yesterday, which had felt like a frail echo of her previous psychotic attack. Dr Lowe didn't respond. He simply opened his drawer and took out a prescription pad. He wrote on it and then tore off the page.

'I'm increasing the dose by a milligram. That should help. If it doesn't improve after a few days, come back and we'll try another milligram.' He handed the prescription to Nancy. 'This should do the trick.'

One hour after she had left Dr Lowe's consulting room, Nancy was sitting in a room on the second floor of a Victorian house. Its walls were painted sage green, and it had two large, comfortable armchairs facing each other in the centre of the room. One was a mustard yellow, the other scuffed brown leather.

Nancy sat in the yellow chair, as she had always done. She looked at the picture of trees on the wall opposite that she had looked at the last time she was here, two months ago. Everything was exactly the same. The same vase with a single sprig of rosemary, the same rug on the floor, the same view out of the window – except the last time, the tree had been in blossom and now only a few brown leaves clung to its swaying branches.

She wanted to cry in relief.

'Hello, Nancy,' said the woman who sat opposite her, in the leather chair: soft white hair and brown watching eyes, her hands folded together in the pleats of her grey skirt. 'How are you?'

'You said I should call you if I ever felt the need.'

'What's up?'

Nancy looked out of the window once more, at the birds perched in the branches and beyond them the low, grey sky, thinking, readying herself to speak.

'It happened again. I heard voices talking to me and even though I knew they weren't real, they felt horribly real. I've been doing well. I've been obedient. I've taken the drugs. I've tried to live on an even keel, which goes against my grain. I've been careful. I'm all right today. It was very brief, but I know I have to take it seriously and deal with it. Nip it in the bud. I've been to Dr Lowe and he's upped the drugs, and I felt it would be helpful to talk to you. I don't want to tell Felix. I want him to see me as the woman he fell in love with. Not a patient, a problem, a burden.'

Fifty minutes later, Nancy was walking down the broad, tree-lined street, on her way back to Harlesden. She felt satisfied with her morning's work. She had dealt with things in a proper way. Nobody would ever have to know.

SEVEN

It was dusk and the flat was silent. No baby was crying, no TV blaring, no music pounding. Just the shiver of trains passing. Nancy found the trains almost restful, like the flow of a river. From the window, she could see a fox stretched out like a peaceful dog in Dylan and Michelle's garden, which was full of terracotta pots of herbs, pruned shrubs and raked gravel. It was very unlike the bedraggled patch of wilderness she and Felix had, which was reached by metal steps, or the yard that Seamus, Barney and Kira all had access to.

She glimpsed Dylan standing at his lit kitchen window, eating what looked like a bagel. He wasn't wearing a shirt and his naked torso was quiveringly large and pink. He looked up and their eyes locked for an uncomfortable stretch of time. He raised his half-eaten bagel in a kind of greeting and she raised her hand.

She made herself another mug of coffee, wrapped a blanket round her and, sitting on the sofa, opened her laptop. For the past three months, ever since she had emerged from her breakdown into the wreckage of her old world, Nancy had been employed part time to write copy for the website: sprightly descriptions to entice people to buy egg timers, singing birthday candles, wonky glasses, cheap lockets, silk flowers, nutcrackers with grinning faces, personalised mugs. In the summer, she had been busy on the Christmas catalogue. Last month there'd been a Valentine theme, now she was working on Easter. She gazed disgustedly at what she had already written. *Bring spring to your garden!* Her fingers hovered over the keys. Now what?

She got up, went to the kitchen and opened the fridge. She cut herself a slice of blue cheese and ate it slowly. It was salty and crumbly and comforting.

There were sounds from downstairs, footsteps, voices. She tried to ignore them. Doors opening and closing. A yell. Was that Felix's voice?

Nancy opened the door. The voices were louder. She ran down the stairs two at a time. At the foot of the stairs, she came to an abrupt halt. A group of people were crowded round the door of the ground-floor flat, which stood half open. She recognised Michelle, Seamus. Felix was there as well. He looked at her in alarm.

'Stay where you are.'

She ignored him and pushed past, reached the door. She looked through.

A pair of boots. But they were floating in the air.

Green boots with bright yellow laces.

Someone was shouting. Hands roughly pulling at her, yanking.

'Come away,' said Felix urgently.

Nancy could only see the lower half of the body. She needed to see the face. She tried to get nearer.

'Stop,' said Felix, laying his hand on her.

'Let go,' Nancy hissed. 'I have to.'

'Oh no, you don't.'

Now Felix had one of her arms and someone else had the other. They were taking her away, bundling her back up the stairs while she struggled to get free of them. They were crushed together on the narrow staircase.

'She's not been well,' said Felix to the other man, who turned out to be Dylan and whose fingers pressed into her flesh like pincers. 'She mustn't be upset.'

'I saw her,' said Nancy. 'She warned me.'

'Steady on,' said Dylan, as if she was a bucking horse.

'She's been ill,' repeated Felix. 'She's still not quite herself.'

Nancy kicked him hard in the shin.

'Darling,' he said.

EIGHT

Detective Inspector Maud O'Connor was very late to leave work. It was Monday evening, and the cells in the basement of the station were already full. They were more than full. There was a young man who had been threatening suicide in the street. He should have been in hospital, but he had been brought here. There was a man whose trial was due to start today, but it had been postponed at the last minute. There were four remand prisoners who should be in prison. Now three young gang members had been involved in a serious affray and there was nowhere to put them, and Maud had spent the last hour ringing round trying to find places where people could be shifted to: a hospital, a prison, another police station.

On top of this, the case she had been working on looked as if it was about to collapse. The young woman whose partner had beaten her so badly that when she had turned up at the station last week, she had barely been able to utter words from her split and swollen lips, was now saying she wanted to withdraw all charges. She had a broken rib, a broken nose, her face discoloured, but she said she had made a mistake. She had fallen down the stairs.

Maud put on her leather jacket and picked up her backpack. As she opened her door, she heard voices in the corridor.

'So young,' said a woman's voice.

'Yeah.' A man answered. 'It's usually the young men, not the women, who top themselves.'

'Will you write the initial report for Kemp, or shall I?'

'You do it. It's pretty straightforward. She obviously looped the rope over the beam, tied a noose, stepped off that stool. End of story.'

'I wonder why, though?'

'We'll never know.'

'Drink?'

'I need one after that.'

The voices faded, and Maud left her room, pulling on her woollen hat and tucking in the stray tendrils of blonde hair.

A young woman had taken her own life. The male officer was probably right when he said they would never know why. The woman and her individual tragedy would remain a mystery, a small entry in the filing system. So often, she and her colleagues just scratched the surface of a case. If they were lucky, they found an answer to a crime: they followed a formula, wrote notes up in triplicate, dotted the i's and crossed the t's, made things that were savage, incoherent and incomprehensible seem neat, moved on to the next case.

Maybe it was the only way to do this job, thought Maud, although it wasn't her way. You could go mad if you looked too closely at what lay beneath the surface. A young woman had died. As the officer had said: end of story.

NINE

The next morning, Felix had a meeting on the other side of London, and he left early, hovering on the threshold to tell her yet again to take care of herself, to call him if she felt agitated. At last Nancy heard his footsteps on the stairs, the main door slamming shut.

She had barely slept, but had lain next to Felix, hearing the rumble of trains, the cry of the baby. Now she was tired, but her mind was still full of images that she couldn't chase away, a dread that clung like a smell.

She needed to do something physical. She looked around at the chaos in the living room. Life is so fragile: you think you've got it all ordered and arranged but then, almost in a moment, you take it apart and put it in boxes and it just looks like rubbish, like junk. Easy to take apart, harder to put back together again: could these half-open boxes, piles of books, random pieces of furniture, ever be assembled into something that would look like a home and a life?

She fetched a knife from the kitchen and began to slice the masking tape that held the nearest packing case shut. It was marked 'odds and ends' in Felix's handwriting, and that's just what it was. She lifted out a sieve, a glass vase wrapped in a tea towel, a cookery book, a puncture repair kit, several wooden spoons, some insect repellant. She sat back on her heels, at a loss for where to put them. It was a relief when there was a knock on the door.

She opened it to a woman she didn't know. The woman looked as if she was in her mid-fifties, with shoulder-length grey-streaked hair. She was wearing dark slacks and a dark sweater and there was something strange about her face. It looked bleached, as if it had been squeezed out. Nancy saw the fine lines at the corners of her eyes and her mouth.

'My name's Ruth Mullan.' Nancy's puzzlement must have been obvious. 'I'm Kira's mother. I've just been in her flat.'

Nancy felt a lurch of panic and pity.

'I'm so sorry,' she said in a rush. 'So very, very sorry.'

The woman raised both her hands as if she were warding off a blow. She shook her head slowly. Her lips were tightly shut. Nancy could see that she didn't trust herself to speak. Then she brought her hands together as if in prayer and put them over her nose and mouth.

'Come in,' Nancy said, and she reached out and took the woman by her arm and led her into her main room. She asked if she would like some coffee or tea and the woman nodded. Nancy steered Ruth Mullan into a chair and then went to the kitchen. Coffee would be quickest. By the time the water had boiled, she had ground the beans. She stirred the cafetière vigorously and then immediately poured the coffee into two mugs and returned to the living room. She handed one of them to Ruth Mullan.

'I don't know if you want milk or sugar,' she said, but Ruth didn't seem to hear, just cradled the mug in her hands as if they needed warming. Nancy pulled a wooden chair across so that the two women were more or less facing each other. Ruth was staring in front of her but Nancy felt she was look-ing through her or past her. Her eyes suddenly focused and she looked down at her untouched mug of coffee and then at Nancy.

'Would you take this?' she said. 'Because I've got nowhere to put it down and I think I'm about to drop it.'

Nancy leaned forward and took the mug.

Ruth took two deep breaths and then a howl seemed to come up from her chest and through her throat and into her mouth and then to spill out. It wasn't like crying. It was like a huge, drawn-out moan of pain from an animal. Fluid ran down her face, from her eyes and her nose and her mouth. The moans came and went, as if they were being breathed out from her lungs.

Nancy stood for a moment, holding a coffee mug in each hand, transfixed. She walked to the kitchen, put the mugs into the sink and came back with a kitchen roll. She tore off two sheets and handed them to Ruth who buried her face in them, muffling the bestial sound. She blew her nose loudly and wiped her face and scrunched up the paper and stowed it in the side pocket of her jacket.

She started to talk. She spoke in a numbed tone, describing everything that had happened since she had taken the call, while out walking with her dog in the park: what the female officer had said on the phone, the neighbours she had left the dog with, the long journey from Derbyshire through heavy traffic and – as if it was just another part of the itinerary – how she had been taken to identify the body of her daughter. Her beloved daughter, who had been the sweetest daughter anyone ever had, her heart on her sleeve, so eager, and what would she do now, what would she ever do? It was a terrible dream, and she would wake up from it, but she knew it wasn't a dream, she had seen the body, the neck with the ghastly red groove on it.

Nancy felt helpless. She nodded and murmured her sympathy, made small sounds of meaningless comfort. At last Ruth paused, took the sheets of kitchen roll from her pocket and blew her nose again. She shook her head slowly.

'She was looking for a new job and she was all excited about it. She was coming home for a visit at Christmas. She was going to see friends.'

Nancy thought of her own parents and their reaction – or non-reaction – when she had her breakdown. Even now, they pretended it hadn't really happened.

'I'm so sorry,' she said. 'It's hard to know what people are feeling, even when you're close to them.'

Ruth's flushed, damp face crumpled. Nancy could see all the lines and furrows she would have when she was old.

'I am her mother; I should have known. She told me she was happy. She kept saying not to worry about her, everything was good. I wanted to believe her, so I believed her.'

'I can't imagine what you are going through,' said Nancy feebly.

'Perhaps she wanted to protect me. But I'm her *mother*. I should have protected her.'

Her shoulders began to shake again. Nancy cautiously put out an arm and touched the woman's arm and waited. Gradually the fresh burst of sobbing subsided and Ruth sat up straighter, wiping the slime of snot and tears from her face.

'I've got things to do,' said Ruth. 'Things that a mother shouldn't ever ...' She paused and took more deep breaths, visibly preventing herself from breaking down once more. 'Certificates and clearing her things. It's a nasty little flat. She told me it was fine, but it isn't. It's falling apart. I wanted to talk to people who knew my daughter, her neighbours, the people who lived with her. I know it's too late, but I thought I could make some kind of sense of it all.'

Nancy had been waiting for this. All the time, while listening to Ruth's outpouring of grief, she had felt something of a fraud. She should have stopped Ruth and told her the truth, but she couldn't find the right time.

'Ruth,' she began. 'Is it okay if I call you Ruth?' The woman nodded. Nancy gestured around the room. 'As you can see, we've only just moved in. We're still unpacking. I'm probably not so useful for you to talk to. There are other people here who've been here a long time.'

'Did you never meet my daughter then?'

Nancy thought of that terrible day, walking through the market, being harassed by the voices and the encounter as she returned. She thought of the green boots with their yellow laces that she'd glimpsed in the frame of the door.

'Do you have a photo of her?'

'A photo?'

Ruth took her mobile out of her pocket and started scrolling through images.

'This is a nice one,' she said, her voice thick with tears again.

Nancy looked at the face on the screen, pale and freckled, tawny hair, large eyes, a full mouth that was smiling; she looked radiant.

'She looks lovely,' she said.

'She was lovely.' Ruth Mullan's voice filled up with tears, and her sore, bloodshot eyes started streaming again, tears falling unchecked. 'Everyone loved her. There was no side to her. Maybe that's what got her into trouble. Too trusting. I told her to be careful, but who wants to be careful when they're young?'

'I did meet her,' Nancy said slowly. 'Just once. Very briefly. It was the day before yesterday. I met her when I was coming in and we had a sort of conversation.'

'What do you mean, "a sort of conversation"? What does that mean?'

Nancy found this question difficult to answer.

'I wasn't feeling very well,' she said. 'I had a sort of fever.'

'I'm sorry,' said Ruth woodenly.

'No, no,' said Nancy quickly. 'It was nothing. That's not the point. The point is, I can't remember very clearly.'

'But you did talk to my daughter just before she died?'

'Yes. On my way in.'

'And you spoke to each other.'

'Kind of. I actually bumped into her. She dropped her stuff. I helped her pick it up and we just said a few words to each other.'

'How did she seem?'

Nancy tried to remember it. It was like looking into a fog full of murky shapes and blinding lights. It was hard to separate what was real and solid. She looked at Ruth. Should she try and soften it for this harrowed woman? She decided that she couldn't; she deserved the truth, whatever that was.

'I don't know what she was normally like. But she didn't seem in a good way. I can't remember her exact words, but she said something bad was happening to her, and she was going to do something about it.' Nancy concentrated so much that it hurt, trying to remember. 'I think I offered to help, and she said I couldn't. But maybe she was only talking about the things I'd knocked onto the floor.'

Ruth's face looked if anything paler than before.

'Are you saying you met my daughter when she was about to kill herself?'

'I don't know. I suppose I did.'

'Perhaps you were the last person to see her alive.'

TEN

A second knock at the door came towards the end of the afternoon, as Nancy sat with her laptop on her knees, tapping out inane descriptions of objects that would help people peel garlic or thread a needle or label the seeds they were planting. It was Seamus. He gave a loose, wide smile and jerked his hand in a greeting. His gaze was unfocused. Nancy wondered what he was on.

'Am I disturbing you? I am. I can see you're working.'

'Trying to.'

'It's hard to concentrate on anything, isn't it? I don't have any more training sessions till this evening, and I've been mooching around and thinking. Thinking about poor Kira.'

Poor Kira was going to be her name from now on, thought Nancy. Poor Kira and a solemn expression.

'Can I come in?' asked Seamus.

Nancy thought of her work waiting for her – and Felix had been right when he said his friend had gone out of his way to give it to her. An act of charity. She looked at Seamus's handsome, expectant face. She gave an inward sigh.

'Do you want a mug of tea or something?'

Seamus's face broke into a grin, showing strong white teeth and a charming dimple in his left cheek.

'That would be terrific.'

*

She made him a mug of tea but didn't have one herself. Seamus sat astride a chair and took several sips, making appreciative little groans with each one. He set the mug down on the coffee table.

'You're probably wondering why I've pushed myself in like this.'

'Yes.'

'I like that. You don't mince words.' Not everyone liked that about her, thought Nancy. 'But you've got a kind face.'

Nancy didn't know what to say to this. She waited.

'I know I can talk to you. You're new, a stranger. You didn't meet Kira, so I can tell you things, things I couldn't talk about to Barney or anyone else. I definitely couldn't say it to the police officers. It was bad enough having them in our flat.'

'Did you talk to the police?'

'Everyone did.'

'We didn't.'

'She was so great,' he said. 'Game for anything. She didn't take life too seriously, not like some women, if you know what I mean.'

Nancy winced. She wanted him to stop. She *needed* him to stop.

'We had a thing. Just a few days, a week or two. It was just good fun. Great sex.'

Don't tell me about the sex, thought Nancy.

'But it didn't mean anything,' Seamus continued. 'I ended it, moved on. And at the party, I hooked up with this other woman.' Seamus's face was damp with sweat; his movements were twitchy. 'I thought I knew Kira wouldn't mind. Then the next day she kills herself.'

'You think she did it because of you,' said Nancy, who was considering walking out of the flat – but then, he would still be inside.

'What am I meant to think?' Seamus didn't really want her to answer. He dropped his face into his large, strong hands and began to cry. At first, Nancy thought he was putting on an act, but real tears were rolling down his cheeks.

'Sorry,' he said. 'I just can't—'

And then he launched himself off the chair and fell forward against her, burying his head against her breast and wrapping his arms tightly around her, like a great spider.

She sat quite still while his body shuddered against hers and the crying gradually came to a halt.

'Sorry,' he said. 'Sorry, Nancy. I'm just so sad.' He lifted his face. 'God, but you're lovely.'

And then his mouth was pressed against hers like a limpet and the smell of his sweat was in her nostrils. One hand was on her breast and the other at the back of her head.

Nancy violently jolted back at the same time as the flat door opened.

'Hello,' called Felix. Then he saw the two of them there, Seamus still half holding her. 'Hello,' he repeated in an entirely different voice.

'I was upset,' said Seamus. 'Nancy was comforting me.'

Nancy pushed him away from her and stood up.

'Get the fuck out of here.'

ELEVEN

The door closed behind him. Felix and Nancy stared at each other and he dropped his gaze first.

'There's one neighbour I won't be spending time with.'

'Do you want to tell me what happened?' His voice was cold.

'What happened? You saw what happened.'

'I mean, when he said you were comforting him ...' He stopped.

'What are you asking?' She looked at his wretched face and took pity on him. 'He told me he and Kira had had a fling and he thought that's why she killed herself.' Nancy snorted. 'Anyway, he cried, and then he came on to me while he was still crying.'

Felix took his heavy, rain-speckled coat off and sank into the sofa.

'This flat isn't working out very well, is it?'

'You mean because one neighbour killed herself and another tried to get me into bed?'

'I wanted to give you a safe place.'

'Don't take everything on yourself.' She sat on the sofa beside him and sighed. 'We have to do things together.'

'Of course.'

'Seamus said the rest of the house have all talked to the police. Why haven't they talked to us?'

'They have.'

'What?'

'They talked to me.'

'But I was here the whole evening.'

'I went down to them and said you shouldn't be bothered. I could speak for us both. They seemed to understand.'

Nancy wasn't sure how to respond to this.

'After all, you didn't have anything to say,' Felix continued.

'How do you know?'

'What do you mean?'

'Maybe I've got things to say.'

'You want to go to the police.' He spoke warily. 'About Kira.'

'Yes.'

'Why is that, Nancy?'

She flinched at his exaggeratedly polite tone.

'Because I've been thinking, maybe her death isn't so straightforward.'

Felix stared at her.

'What makes you say that?'

'Because her mother said she'd been happy and excited about the future.'

'You've met Kira's mother?'

'She came here.'

'But you didn't know her.'

'I gave her coffee. She sat at the table and cried. Screamed. I've never heard anyone make a noise like that before.'

'That's awful.'

'Her daughter had died.'

'It's terrible, but why would you want to talk to the police?'

'Her mother said she was happy.'

'Her mother can tell that to the police. Not you. You've never even met her.'

'I did meet her.'

'You met Kira? When?'

'The day after we moved in. Sunday.'

'You never said.'

Nancy shrugged. 'I bumped into her as I was coming home in the afternoon. She seemed scared or in some kind of trouble.'

'Why didn't you tell me this?'

Nancy went and stood by the window. In the darkness, people moved like shadows through the carpet of slippery leaves; cars sent up arcs of water from puddles as they sped past.

'I didn't take it seriously,' she said.

'There you are then. Look, it's very natural that seeing her mother like this has . . .'

'No. Listen. I'd had a bit of a bad afternoon.' She felt rather than saw him stiffen. 'That's why I went for a walk.'

'What do you mean, a bad afternoon?'

'Just a bad afternoon.'

'Do you mean the old trouble?'

'It was barely anything and it didn't last long.'

He walked across and took her by the shoulder, turned her so that they were looking at each other.

'It started happening again and you didn't tell me?'

'I've got it under control.'

'What does that even mean?'

'I went to see the doctor yesterday and he's increased the dose a bit. He always said these drugs need micro-managing. So we've micro-managed them.'

'Yesterday?'

'And my old therapist fitted me in for a top-up session.'

'You did all this yesterday?'

'Yes.'

'I don't know what to say.'

'You should be pleased. You're always telling me to take it seriously. I took it seriously.'

'Were you ever going to tell me?'

'I'm telling you now.'

'Only because this new idea has popped into your head, and you needed to come clean about meeting Kira.'

'Going to see my doctor is not some kind of dirty little secret.'

'You're making it seem like a dirty little secret.'

'I didn't want to worry you,' she said, her voice tight. 'I didn't want it to be like this.'

'It's only like this because you did it behind my back.'

'This isn't about you. Or me. It's about a woman who's died.'

'Did you actually see her, or was she part of your episode? That's why you didn't tell me. Because you didn't know if it was real or not.'

Nancy hesitated. Felix was right. She hadn't been sure, but she was sure now.

'When it happened,' she said at last, feeling her way cautiously, 'it's true that I mixed her up with the other voices and faces.'

'Exactly. And then when Kira died, you made all these false connections to give external reality to something that was just inside your head.'

'I saw her shoes.'

'What? Her shoes?'

'I know I saw them. Boots, rather. Green with yellow laces. That's why I was so freaked out when I got a glimpse of her hanging in the doorway. It was the same green boots. I know.'

'Don't you see what you're doing?'

'Then I asked Ruth – Kira's mother – to show me a photo,

and I know it was the same woman and she thought she was
in danger. Or I was. Or something.'

She stopped as she saw the look on his normally calm and
pleasing face.

'Let me get this right,' he said, speaking loudly and distinctly
as if she was hard of hearing or had only just started to learn
the language. 'You have a psychotic episode. You hear voices.
One of those voices belonged to a woman. You come back
home and say nothing about it. You go to your psychiatrist the
next day and to your therapist as well. Then when you see poor
Kira hanging there and you meet her mother, suddenly all the
things you heard and saw two days ago come together and you
decide the voice belonged to the dead woman and that she was
telling you she was in danger – or you were.'

'You're putting it in an unfair way,' said Nancy, trying to
keep her voice calm.

'And now you want to talk to the police about it.'

'Yes,' said Nancy.

'Think carefully about this, Nancy, very carefully.'

'Don't talk like that. I'm not a child. I need to talk to the
police and tell them what Kira said to me just before she died.'

'Right,' said Felix. 'If that's what you want.'

He strode from the room. Nancy subsided onto the sofa.
Rage was draining away from her, leaving her feeling slightly
restless. She looked around the room. Perhaps they should get
a cat. A cat made a place seem more homely. It would lie on
her chest and purr when she was feeling stressed, dig its claws
in and out of her skin.

'I think we should get a cat,' she said as Felix strode back
in, no change in pace as if he had tramped a vigorous circle
round the flat and was now on his second lap. He was clearly
still steaming with anger.

'I called them,' he announced as he came to an abrupt halt in front of her.

'What?'

'I called the police.'

'Why on earth would you do that?'

'First you want me to and then you're cross because I have.'

'I was going to call them myself, obviously.'

'Now you don't have to.'

'That's not the point.'

'An officer will be here soon.'

'You're joking.'

'Have you changed your mind?'

'I didn't think it would happen so quickly.'

'But it's urgent,' he said. 'A woman has died.'

He sounded sarcastic and angry.

'Felix,' she said.

'What?'

'This is horrible.'

He nodded stiffly.

'I'm sorry I didn't tell you. It wasn't right.'

She waited. He puffed his cheeks, then let out a deep breath.

'I shouldn't have lost my temper,' he said eventually.

'But there are some things I need to do by myself. You can't speak for me. I am not obliged to tell you every single thing that happens in my head. I can't live like that. You do see that, don't you?'

'Yes,' he said. 'I just worry.'

'I know you do.'

Twelve

The police officer sat on the wooden chair and Nancy sat on the sofa. She was several inches lower and felt at a disadvantage. Felix was in the kitchen and could hear most of what was being said, even though Nancy tried to keep her voice low.

Nancy told her story. It took a long time – not because there was much to say, but because the woman was laboriously writing it down, and she kept interrupting, asking her to repeat or clarify.

At the end, the officer frowned at her notebook. She seemed embarrassed.

'We're not actually treating the death of Kira Mullan as suspicious,' she said eventually.

'I thought you should know what she said to me.'

'We're grateful to you, of course,' said the officer, not sounding grateful at all. 'But you say here . . .' She turned a few pages back, searching. 'That she appeared upset. Which seems to support our view that she took her own life.'

'I said she seemed scared. If she was scared, then what was the reason? That's what we need to know.'

'You didn't mention this earlier.'

'I'm telling you now. I'm a witness to her state of mind shortly before she died.'

The woman gave a little cough.

'I understand you were in a bit of a state yourself.'

Nancy felt herself go cold. The lights in the room suddenly seemed horribly bright.

'What have you been told about me?'

'Just about some medical issues. Issues that might be relevant to your evidence.'

Nancy couldn't stop herself. She looked towards the kitchen. There was no sound from Felix, but he would be listening. She knew who had told the police about her psychiatric problems. She looked back at the officer.

'I saw what I saw.'

'Yes. But still, you must see the difficulty.'

A heavy silence filled the room. At last Nancy broke it.

'It is true I was having a bad day on Sunday.' She looked accusingly towards the little kitchen and as if in answer, there was a chink of cutlery. 'But even if some of the things I saw and heard were not quite real, that doesn't mean Kira didn't speak to me.'

She knew this was useless. The officer's face was wearily and almost contemptuously patient, hearing her out but knowing her to be the very epitome of an unreliable witness: a deluded woman who heard voices, saw what wasn't there, conjured terrors and conspiracies from the random mess of life.

'You're just going to ignore me, aren't you?'

'We will take everything into account.'

She stood up.

'I want to speak to someone else,' said Nancy. 'Someone senior. Who's in charge of this case?'

'That would be DI Kemp. But he is already satisfied that Kira Mullan tragically took her own life.'

'Tell DI Kemp I want to see him.'

Felix came out of the kitchen, clutching a handful of forks.

'Nancy,' he said warningly.

'Stay out of it,' said Nancy. 'You've done enough already.'

'Nancy is understandably upset,' said Felix to the officer and she nodded at him. Nancy felt anger crackle through her and she balled her fists.

'I am not upset, I'm quite calm and rational and I want to see this DI Kemp.'

'I will convey your feelings to him.'

'That's not good enough.'

'I'm afraid he's very busy. And he's about to take annual leave.'

'But he's in charge of the case.'

'There is no case. It's closed.'

'Open it!'

Felix and the officer slid each other a glance. Nancy bit back a yell.

'Ms North,' said the officer sternly. 'A horrible thing happened and unfortunately you saw the aftermath. But a young woman has died. Her family is devastated. It will not help them in their grief if you start throwing suspicions around like this. The matter is in our hands.'

'Oh, and that's meant to be reassuring?'

'Nancy!'

'Good evening.'

The door clicked. Nancy and Felix looked at each other.

'That was fun,' said Felix.

He subsided onto the sofa and closed his eyes.

'This isn't the end of it,' said Nancy.

'Of course it is. You've had your say, for what it was worth.'

'Yes, well, you saw to that, telling her in advance about my history.'

'You were in a disturbed state that Sunday. Were you going to keep it secret?'

'Not saying something isn't the same as keeping it secret.'

'Debatable.' Felix opened his eyes. 'It's done now, anyway. Let's put it behind us. I don't want to argue; I only want you to be all right.'

Nancy was tired of people saying that to her.

'Promise me you won't interfere any further.'

She hesitated. But a word has many meanings.

'Nancy?'

'I won't interfere,' she said.

'Good. Because honestly, Nancy, if you carry on like this, you might not get a second chance.'

Thirteen

Nancy returned very late from an evening out with a group of friends, most of whom she hadn't seen since her breakdown. Bridie had been there, but they hadn't talked properly. The ease of their relationship had gone, and now it seemed to Nancy that they performed cheerfulness and closeness, a bit hyperbolic, striking slightly the wrong note. Felix was still up, hanging pictures on the walls. She was sure he had stayed up waiting for her, like her father used to do. He looked at her reproachfully and she pretended not to notice.

She climbed into bed and when he joined her, she knew at once he wanted sex. Her body felt cold and resistant; she wanted to curl into herself and sleep and not dream. She didn't want to be touched, brought to feel pleasure, another body against her – not tonight, not after everything that had happened.

She thought about the conversations she had had with friends over the past years about inequality of desire, that treacherous grey area between frank and vigorous pleasure and explicit rejection, between wanting and not wanting. He took the book away from her and tossed it on the ground. He kissed first one breast then the other. She remembered how constant Felix had been through the terrible times, absorbing her anger and frustration, just a flicker of hurt crossing his face sometimes before he quickly extinguished it. How had he done that? She could never have managed such heroic patience, and in fact it had been his patience that had most enraged her, because it made her feel coddled and infantilised. She didn't want to be endlessly forgiven; she didn't want to be let off the hook. She needed to be held to account.

'Felix,' she said. 'It's not really—'

Then they heard, as if it was in the same room, a drawn-out coo followed by a rhythmic male grunting, getting louder.

'Oh God,' said Felix in a whisper, pulling away from Nancy. 'Is that . . . ?'

She giggled. 'Of course it is.'

'They must be able to hear *us* like that.'

'Yes.'

'Christ.'

He rolled onto his back.

There was a pause while they both lay looking at the ceiling. There was a sinister crack running across it that Nancy hadn't noticed before.

'I get it wrong sometimes,' Felix said. 'I know that. I'm sorry I called the police without telling you first.'

'That's all right.'

'I want to try to help and sometimes I go too far. I know it can be difficult for you. I'm not surprised you were angry.'

'I wasn't angry.' Nancy, still staring at the ceiling, bit back any comment. 'It's more difficult for *you*. Sometimes I need to do things for myself. Like going to the doctor.'

'I get that,' said Felix. He was stroking her hip.

Nancy closed her eyes so she wouldn't have to see the crack.

'It's like something that happened in a dream,' she said. 'I met this woman just once and just for a moment, but it was as if we recognised something in each other. I feel I let her down. I think I should probably have a few more sessions with Helena.'

'The medication is what matters.'

'Both matter.'

'Do you ever feel like you'd like to move away from all of this?'

'Move away? We've just moved here.'

'This can't be permanent, though, can it? Wouldn't you like to move to the country?'

'The country? What does that mean?'

'Somewhere with trees and fields. Without all the noise and the people.'

'I like the noise and the people. Remember, I grew up in the country and spent most of my childhood longing to escape it.'

There was a silence.

'Have you never thought that city life, all of the bustle and the chaos, might have brought your condition on?'

'No,' said Nancy firmly. 'Absolutely not.'

Fourteen

Maud walked towards the station. The nearer she got, the slower she walked. It was rush hour. The roads were clogged with traffic and the pavements thick with people on their way to work, heads down against the wind.

This part of London felt as unfamiliar to her as a foreign country. She had been born in London and lived all her life there, but she was an East Ender. She had grown up on a housing estate in Newham where her father, a roofer, still lived, as did two of her four brothers. For the past eight years she had lived in Hackney, where two years ago she and her partner had bought a tiny flat. They had been planning to start a family. But then Silas had left her. They had sold the flat and Maud had been promoted westward, a promotion that she knew was also a punishment and a warning: do what you're told, don't question your superiors, be a team player.

She saw the station ahead of her and for a moment came to a halt. It was a Victorian building in need of restoration. Its bricks were stained and its gutters leaking; there was a down-at-heel air to it. Inside, there was a public-facing desk with a metal grille across it because too many people had been drunk and aggressive to the officer on duty. Its formal priorities were to reduce violence and drugs in the area, but Maud knew that a lot of this was a tick-box exercise. Officers were encouraged to take cases they could easily solve.

'Good morning,' said a voice behind her. 'You don't look very eager to get to work.'

She turned to find Danny Kemp grinning at her.

'Hi,' she said coolly.

She wasn't keen on DI Kemp. He was a bullet-headed, barrel-chested man with protuberant blue eyes and a conceited air. He was married, but behaved like he wasn't. He had a special responsibility for domestic abuse and other 'female' crimes. 'It's a good way of meeting women,' he'd once said to her. Maud knew that he disliked her, perhaps even hated her, and that he was always bad-mouthing her to other officers, spreading scurrilous rumours. At the same time, he wanted her approval, endlessly boasting about his cases and his conquests to her. He resented her promotion, was rivalrous, wanted to humiliate her, would shaft her if he could. All the while, he pretended, in a faintly derisive way, that they were friends.

'How's it going?'

'Not great,' she said. 'The case looks like it's going to run into the sand.'

'Tough,' he said, a smile twitching at his mouth. 'Especially when you've spent so much time on it, and nothing to show for it.'

'And you?' she asked, when he showed no sign of moving away.

'Good,' he said. 'Very good. A quick result, which is what the boss likes.'

'I heard there was a young woman who killed herself.'

'That's right. Twenty-three years old. Hung herself in her flat. It's not going to take much time. Except get this, now one of her neighbours is convinced there's something suspicious about her death.'

'And you're sure there isn't?'

'It's as open and shut a case as any I've dealt with. And anyway, the neighbour's got her own problems.'

He tapped his head. Maud looked at him, raising her eyebrows slightly.

'What does that mean?'

'Hears voices. Was sectioned a few months back.'

'Have you talked to her?'

'I don't need to talk to her. I'm a DI. I delegate.' He bent towards her, his eyebrows raised questioningly. 'Do you know that word?'

'But if she has any grounds for—'

Kemp frowned, suddenly not pretending to be pleasant any longer.

'She's a fucking fantasist and this is my case, O'Connor,' he said. 'You do your job, if you can, and I'll do mine.'

FIFTEEN

'I think it's important to get to know your neighbours,' said Michelle, as she opened her dark blue front door and ushered Nancy inside.

Nancy looked around at a house that looked both familiar and unfamiliar. The two houses had been identical when they were built in the second half of the nineteenth century but Nancy shared number 99 with three other flats. Michelle and her husband lived in 101 alone.

'There's so much space,' said Nancy wonderingly. 'It makes me feel like I live in a little rabbit hutch.'

'I know,' said Michelle. 'It's unfair. When Dylan and I bought this place thirty years ago, we thought that we had finally found a bit of London where nobody wanted to live and then over the next few years prices doubled and then doubled again. I sometimes think of Harry and Olga and their baby all squeezed together in their flat.'

Nancy walked around the large front room, looking at the pictures on the wall, the books on shelves, the large sofas. It made her own existence seem chaotic and improvised. She thought of their packing cases and the possessions that she and Felix had haphazardly acquired before they met and pooled them. Everything in Michelle's house looked like it had been bought for a reason and put in the place that was perfect for it. When she sat down at the table, she rubbed her hand along it. Michelle came through carrying a tray with coffee and two mugs and a small jug of milk.

'I want all of this,' said Nancy. 'It makes me feel calm and safe.'

'You can come here any time you want. Now that the children have gone, it feels like too much for just Dylan and me.'

'Careful what you ask for. I might take you up on that.'

Michelle poured coffee from the cafetière, and Nancy took a cautious sip.

'Just as a matter of interest,' said Michelle casually, 'I saw the police car parked outside yesterday. Do you know what they were here for?'

'We called them,' said Nancy.

'Really? What about?' She held up her hands before Nancy could reply. 'Don't tell me if you don't want to. I don't want to interfere. But if it was about Kira . . .'

'They'd talked to the rest of the house, but they hadn't talked to me. I thought they needed to.'

Michelle raised her finely shaped eyebrows. Nancy realised she sounded as if she had felt left out of all the drama.

'I think they need to look into it a bit more,' she added.

There was a silence. Michelle was frowning in puzzlement.

'Why?' Michelle asked at last. 'Why should you think that? You never even met Kira.'

'I did. Shortly before you all came round for drinks. On the street. She said some things to me.'

'What things?'

'She seemed in trouble. Or troubled.'

'There you are then.'

'Where are we?'

'She seemed troubled and then she took her own life.'

'I'm not sure she seemed depressed though.'

'People who kill themselves don't always seem depressed. They may not even *be* depressed.'

'Are you a doctor?'

'Not that kind of doctor. I'm an academic and psychology is my subject. Not exactly that kind of psychology. But I still can't see why you needed to speak to the police.'

'I just felt they should know.' Nancy's coffee was tepid. She pushed it away. 'In case.'

'In case what?'

'Just in case.' Nancy looked at Michelle with a new interest. 'How well did you know Kira? Was she a friend?'

'A friend? I don't know about that. We met in the street, we said hello and chatted. She's sat where you're sitting and drunk from that cup.'

'What was she like?'

'She was a young woman who had arrived in London and was having fun. Maybe it all became too much for her.'

'Did she have a partner?'

'Nancy,' said Michelle. 'Do you think it's a good idea for you to dwell on Kira?'

She picked up her mug and held it in both hands, looking at Nancy over its rim with her bright, clever eyes.

'What do you mean?'

'Dylan told me how upset you were.'

Nancy remembered the way he'd hauled her upstairs.

'I've never seen a dead body before.' Nancy suddenly noticed something about Michelle's expression. 'Has Felix been talking about me?'

'How do you mean?'

Nancy felt a familiar tide of anger rise in her. Her cheeks burned.

'What's he said?'

'Nothing really,' said Michelle lightly. 'Just that you've been having a difficult time. Was that the word?'

'Yes,' said a voice behind Nancy. She swung round, startled, to find Dylan standing right behind her. For a big man, he was remarkably quiet on his feet. 'I think difficult was the word.'

Nancy put down her mug and stood up.

'I'm fine,' she said. 'Absolutely fine.'

'Good,' said Michelle soothingly. 'But if there's anything we can do to help you through this . . .'

'Who else has he been talking to?'

'It wasn't like that. He just has your best interests at heart.'

'Has he talked to everyone in the house?'

'No need to get so het up,' said Dylan cheerfully, and Nancy felt a spurt of pure hatred go through her.

Michelle frowned reprovingly at him, then put a hand on Nancy's arm.

'Don't take any notice of my husband.'

'I'll let myself out,' Nancy said.

Sixteen

As she returned to the house, a head popped up from below. Barney was standing on the metal steps that led down to the basement flat.

'Hello, neighbour,' he said. 'How are you doing today?'

He spoke in a gentle voice of concern. Nancy felt her skin prickle.

'Fine,' she replied.

He started to say something, but she turned away and opened the front door.

There was clatter from above her. A tiny woman was lugging a large buggy down the stairs towards the hall, her face screwed up in a grimace on concentration. Nancy realised it must be Olga.

'Can we help?' Nancy called up.

The woman put a finger to her lips in an exaggerated gesture. Nancy and Barney went up the flight of stairs and took hold of the buggy from either end. Nancy could see a portion of a baby's face peeking out of the blanket, two large ears, faintly blue lids closed over its eyes, a tiny exhalation of breath puffing out its milk-blistered lips.

The three of them manoeuvred their way down the steps and back into the narrow hall, where they gently set the buggy on the floor. The baby's eyes clicked open. Fierce blue eyes stared accusingly into Nancy's face. Its mouth puckered.

'Oh no,' said Olga.

A thin scream pierced the air.

'No, no, Lydia,' said Olga pleadingly. She had small features and an Eastern European accent. 'I am very sorry.'

'Don't apologise to me,' said Barney. 'You're the one who has to live with it.'

'Her,' said Nancy.

'Lydia,' said Olga. 'She cries too much. Harry says she is hungry. What do men know?'

She rocked the buggy rather violently and the sobs subsided and then picked up again.

'Quite,' agreed Barney.

'You are in the flat across?' Olga asked anxiously.

'Yes, I'm Nancy.'

'Do you hear her in your flat?'

'It's worse for you.'

'Your husband says you need quiet.'

'Oh, does he?' said Nancy. 'He's not actually my husband.'

She leaned into the buggy. Lydia's face was purple now, her mouth a huge 'o', her fists clenched, her entire body stiff. That amount of righteous anger seemed very impressive. She straightened up.

'Do you ever get a break?'

'Sometimes Harry looks after her for a bit and I go and drink coffee with my friend from home. Two cups of coffee and a slice of cake.'

Which was better than nothing, thought Nancy.

'I could perhaps—' she began, and Olga shrank back.

'Oh no,' she said. 'That's very kind, but I wouldn't dream, what with your . . .' Her voice faltered to a stop.

Oh fuck, thought Nancy. Her too.

Olga looked at the door they were standing next to.

'Kira said she would,' she said in a hushed voice, as if the dead could hear. 'Poor thing.'

'Would what?'

'Babysit for Olga, so that Harry and me could go on a date together.'

'That was nice of her.'

'The day before she died,' said Olga, looking at the door, her eyes big in her small face.

'The day before she died, she said she would babysit?'

'Yes. And then she went in there.' Olga pointed at the door. 'And, God forgive her, took her own life.'

Olga left the house, but Barney seemed in no hurry to go too, though he was dressed in a quilted jacket and had a messenger bag slung over his shoulder.

'Poor thing,' he said.

'Olga?'

'A baby who cries and a husband who shouts.'

'Does he shout?'

'You can hear everything in this house, even from the basement. And I have heard him shouting.'

'I hope she shouts back. What did you make of her saying that Kira was going to babysit the day before she died?'

'Make of it?'

'Isn't that odd?'

'That's Kira for you. She was just too nice to people. Always thinking the best of people, letting people take advantage of her.'

'Like Seamus, you mean.'

'Oh, you heard, did you?'

'He told me. I think he worries that he triggered the death.'

'Though Kira was the one who didn't want it to continue.'

'Really?'

'Not the impression he gave you?' He grinned with pleasure. 'That's Seamus for you.'

'You don't seem to like your flatmate very much.'

'He's okay. We've shared for too long, that's all; I know too much about his ways.'

'Right,' said Nancy. 'Back to work for me.'

'After I've bought some milk and tea bags, back to *Elden Ring*.' He saw the puzzlement in Nancy's face. 'It's a video game. Welcome to my working day.'

He smiled, but it didn't quite reach his eyes.

Seventeen

Helena was visibly shocked.

'I don't quite know what to say. What a terrible thing. The poor woman.'

'You probably think it's one of my fantasies,' said Nancy. 'You can check it online, if you want.'

'What about you? Are you all right?'

'I don't want to make this about me.'

Helena smiled at that.

'In this room it really is all about you. Have you had any more episodes?'

Nancy considered this.

'Sometimes I think there are things on the edge of my vision or my hearing. I don't know how to describe it. Then I think it might happen again. But I also try to remind myself that if I do hear or see something, I can't just run away from it.'

'That's right.'

'This is me, who I am, and it's not going to go away,' Nancy continued. 'I have to find a way to live with it and to pay attention to what the voices are saying to me. You said that to me once: talk back to them, try to make friends with them.'

'Have you managed to do that?'

'Not properly. I was so scared. I still am a bit. I'm a work in progress. That's why I need to come here. It doesn't help that everyone in the house knows.'

'Knows what?'

'Knows about me having a breakdown and that I had a recurrence. I don't know if they know I was sectioned, but they probably do.'

'How do you feel about that?'

'Angry. Ashamed. The shame's the worst. It makes me want to hide or run away. I can't bear to be looked at in that way.'

'What way is that?'

'Pity, curiosity. Felix shouldn't have told them.'

'Why do you think he did?'

'To protect me. Because he cares about me and is anxious. But it wasn't his story to tell. It's my story.'

She walked back to Fielding Road, though it was cold and damp and she had to keep checking her route on the phone as she walked along busy roads she didn't know. As she stepped into the hall, she saw that the door to Kira's flat was propped open by a plastic bucket and a woman was backing out, carrying a bucket and holding a mop under her arm. She was dressed in overalls and looked round at Nancy.

'We are cleaners. But we are finished.'

Nancy looked over the woman's shoulders and saw a companion carrying a grubby, industrial-looking vacuum cleaner in one hand and a bulging bin bag in the other. She thought she should ask some question, but she couldn't think of anything.

'Was it untidy?' she asked feebly.

The woman shook her head and laughed and made a sound that seemed to suggest that it had been very untidy.

'But better now,' she said.

'Here, let me,' said Nancy, and she held the door open as the second woman squeezed past murmuring her thanks.

The front door slammed shut. Nancy stood silently for a

moment and then looked around. Almost in surprise, she saw that she was still standing there, with the flat door open. She was about to close it, but she didn't.

All her life, Nancy had heard voices. Friendly voices, unfriendly voices. Sometimes they threatened and scared her, sometimes they were kindly and encouraging. Sometimes too encouraging. They told her to jump off that high diving board. They told her to go to that party when she felt reluctant, to say yes to that boy. And now a voice – she didn't know if it was from inside or outside her head – told her to go in.

She stepped inside and eased the door behind her so that it was almost completely shut. She was in Kira's flat alone.

Eighteen

For a moment she remained quite still, staring around her. Then she realised that she was standing in the space where Kira's body had hung, a few feet above the ground. She looked up. A steel girder ran the length of the room. A wind chime still hung from one end, near the window. Nancy took several steps further into the room.

It was cold. The heating had been turned off and the window was open. The living room was similar to the one in her and Felix's flat, and it gave on to a tiny galley kitchen. From there, a door led out onto the flat's scrap of neglected garden that was shared with the residents of the basement flat. There were two doors on the left – presumably to the bedroom and bathroom. The furniture was basic: a small pine table with a burn mark in the middle, a dark grey bench-like sofa and a dark grey wing-armed chair, a stool, a threadbare rug. Everything belonging to Kira had been removed, presumably by her family.

Nancy advanced into the centre of the room. She didn't know why she was here or what she was looking for. Olga's words were like an itch in her brain. She stepped towards the tiny kitchen, a replica of theirs. She saw that the women hadn't cleaned the oven, and they hadn't mopped the floor properly or wiped down the windowsills. Mugs were stacked on the draining board.

She heard a sound. The scraping of a key and the main door

being opened, feet on the boards. Voices in the hall outside, as clear as if the partition wall was made of card.

'Thank you. I'm just going to pop in on the new people upstairs.' It was Michelle talking. 'The woman's not in a very good way, I'm afraid. I mean, in her mind.'

Michelle was talking about her.

A male grunt of assent.

'What a terrible thing to happen in your property,' Michelle continued. 'When are you letting out the room again?'

The landlord, Nancy realised. William Goddard. She looked around desperately.

'Not long,' he said. 'The family are coming down in a few days to take the last of her stuff. I wish they'd get a move on.'

'If you're going in there, can I come and get a dish I lent to Kira?'

Nancy froze. She could see herself in the large mirror on the opposite wall, small and furtive, her pale brown hair piled up in a crazy mess, her eyes full of fear and guilt. She took a few steps towards one of the doors and yanked it open. It was Kira's bedroom. There was a shabby patchwork quilt thrown across the bed. Was she actually going to hide? She was doing nothing wrong after all, except being a bit nosy. But even as she thought this, she was very softly closing the door, pulling it fast with a soft but definite click.

'The door's open,' said Goddard. 'Bloody cleaners.'

'Did you hear something?' Michelle sounded suspicious and she also sounded horribly close. They must be inside the flat now, standing a few feet from where Nancy was cowering. 'Perhaps they're still here. The flat doesn't look like it's been deep-cleaned to me.'

'No, they left. No one's here.'

'I'm sure I heard a door shutting.'

Nancy, standing by the window, thought of hunkering down beside the bed, or even stepping into the wardrobe. But she wasn't a burglar, and if they discovered her like that then it would look infinitely worse, so instead she took a deep breath, walked across the room and opened the door. Better to reveal herself than to be discovered.

'It's only me,' she said brightly.

The two faces stared at her.

'Nancy?' Michelle sounded as though she wasn't sure if Nancy was actually real.

'Hi, Michelle,' said Nancy, trying to sound casual and friendly. 'How are you?'

'What are you doing in Kira's flat?'

'Yes, what are you doing?' asked Goddard, who was very bald and very solid, and whose face wore an unfriendly expression.

'The door was open,' explained Nancy brightly. 'I thought I'd have a look inside.'

'You were in her bedroom.'

Nancy didn't reply to this since it was self-evidently true.

'This is private property,' said the landlord, who didn't seem quite sure how angry he should be about this.

'She won't do it again,' said Michelle, as if Nancy was *her* private property.

'I was just curious,' said Nancy. She was still speaking in a cheerful tone that didn't at all suit the situation, but she couldn't find another. Her cheeks were burning and her legs shaking.

'She's not well,' Michelle said to Goddard, and she gripped Nancy by the upper arm.

'I'm perfectly well.'

'Come along.'

'What?'

'We're leaving. Shall we have coffee in your flat?'

'I've got work to do,' said Nancy as Michelle hustled her out of Kira's flat.

'Really? It didn't seem to stop you from snooping.'

'I wasn't snooping.'

'Do you have any idea what William Goddard is like?'

'No.'

Michelle went up the stairs and Nancy followed her. At the door of Nancy's flat, Michelle said, 'You don't want to get on the wrong side of him, Nancy. He's already had a run-in with Seamus and Barney this year and they didn't come out on top.'

'What happened?'

'That's not the point.'

'It's a bit messy,' said Nancy, unlocking the door and stepping inside.

She took off her thick coat, cleared some of Felix's papers away from the sofa to make space for Michelle. A shiny brochure slid out from among them and she found herself looking at a picture of a tiny red-brick house surrounded by trees. She stared at it disbelievingly, then pushed it away. She would deal with that later.

'That's okay,' said Michelle. 'Dylan's rather untidy too. He used to be much tidier when he worked; the more time he has, the untidier he gets.'

'Is he retired?'

It was strange to be exchanging small talk just after Michelle had discovered her snooping – and snooping was definitely the right description – in Kira's flat.

'He doesn't like that word. He says he is thinking about the next stage. But essentially, yes. It wasn't really his choice. He was in hotel management, and you might have noticed that the hospitality business is having a tough time.'

'I'm sorry,' Nancy said dutifully.

Michelle shrugged. 'Lots of people are going through difficult times. It's the young people I feel sorry for.'

'You want some coffee?'

'Not really.'

'But you asked . . .'

'What were you doing in there, Nancy?'

'I don't know,' said Nancy. 'I just saw the open door and went in. It wasn't planned.'

'What were you looking for?'

'Nothing.'

'You were in Kira's bedroom.'

'Why are you so bothered about it?'

'We're concerned about you.'

'We?'

'Dylan and me.'

'Don't be.'

'You're our neighbour and you are new to the area; you've seen a terrible thing; you're obviously having a hard time.'

'Not at all,' said Nancy. She felt furious, even though Michelle was looking at her with sympathy.

'You can talk to me,' said Michelle. 'I know you're angry with Felix for telling me about your problems and for asking me to keep an eye out.'

'He shouldn't have done it.'

'I agree,' said Michelle. 'And I'm sorry.'

'Thanks,' said Nancy gracelessly. She chewed her lower lip. 'Can I tell you something?'

'Of course.'

'I'm not sure about Kira's death. That's the reason I was in her room.'

Michelle briefly closed her eyes.

'I don't understand.'

'She offered to babysit.'

'And?'

'She said it to Olga the day before she died. Isn't that strange?'

'I don't know. Is it?' She paused and then her tone became more urgent. 'What are you actually saying? That Kira didn't take her own life? What does that mean?'

'I know,' said Nancy, picking at the sleeve of her jumper and looking away from Michelle's gaze. 'I understand that it sounds ridiculous.'

'It sounds,' said Michelle carefully, 'as if you are still in quite a fragile state and you need to be very, very careful about saying things like that. What if Kira's family heard?'

'Do you think I'm just making it all up?'

Michelle put a hand on Nancy's arm.

'Nancy, I have no idea why Kira did what she did, poor girl, and probably no one will ever know that. But you need to let go of your notion that there's a sinister mystery about it. Take a step back. Try and have some insight into what's going on in your head. Don't make something painful even more so; don't go believing that only you can see the truth.'

'You're probably right,' said Nancy slowly, hating the pity in Michelle's voice and the way she was looking at her, as if she could see all the mess and dread coiled up inside.

'Is there a but?'

'But what if you're not?'

Nineteen

When Michelle had left, Nancy bent down and picked up the shiny brochure from the floor. She riffled through the pile of papers and found two more. She laid them out in front of her.

Three very desirable properties, two to rent and one – in need of thoughtful renovation which was estate-agent speak for being an uninhabitable wreck – to buy. One was in Kent, another in Bedfordshire and the third in Essex. As far as Nancy could make out from the photos, two were on the edges of tiny satellite villages and one seemed to be the middle of nowhere.

She pictured herself walking across muddy fields, the wind driving into her face, a few stunted trees on the horizon and not a cafe or shop in sight and the lurch of panic that she felt made her dizzy.

She strode into the kitchen and pushed the brochures deep into the recycling bin. She tried not to think about it because thinking about it made her so angry that she couldn't bear it.

The anger took her out of the house before she could prevent herself, into the street. The wind whipped at her, slashed her hair across her cheeks, flung a few drops of rain into her face, but she was hot with her rage and it was only when she was halfway down the road that she realised she hadn't put on a coat and was only wearing a thin jumper and shoes that let in the wet. Voices clamoured in her head, imploring her not to do this, to turn back, to remember what she was risking, but she thought of Felix planning to remove her from London without even discussing it and her feet quickened.

She burst into the station, banging the door shut behind her and stomping up to the desk.

'I want to see the head detective, Kemp.' Her voice was loud and shrill. She lowered it an octave and tried to sound calmer. 'At once, please.'

'What's this about?' asked the man, regarding her with a belittling indifference.

'I have something very important to tell him about Kira Mullan and he needs to listen.'

'I'm not sure—'

'He can't just ignore me. I'll report him. Who do I report him to?'

'Name?'

'I told you. Kemp.'

'Your name.'

'Nancy North.'

She needed to keep the righteous fury alive, to bat away the knowledge that she was doing something foolish, perhaps damaging. Her heart raced.

The man picked up the phone on the desk and turned from her, speaking in a low voice so she couldn't hear the words.

'Through that door.' He pointed. 'Along the corridor and third on your left.'

'Good. Thanks.'

She marched on. Don't think, don't pause. She knocked on the door and pushed it open before the man behind it had time to tell her to come in.

He was large. His shoulders were broad, his chest was like a barrel, his trousers were slightly too tight. His muscles bulged through the shirt sleeves. I bet he works out, Nancy thought, and she pictured him and Seamus together in a gym, pumping iron, their faces glistening.

'I'm Nancy North and you never interviewed me,' she said, sitting down although he hadn't invited her to. 'I've got information. Important information.'

Kemp looked at her, taking his time, smiling slightly in a way that made her feel a bit sick.

'This is about Kira Mullan, right?'

'Of course it is.'

'That case is closed.'

'How can it be closed if you haven't interviewed me?'

'My colleague interviewed you.'

'That was a waste of time.'

'I agree. A waste of her time. We're very busy, especially at this time of year, but she took the time to come and see you. As a matter of courtesy.'

'She didn't listen to what I told her.'

'She listened very patiently.'

'Aren't you going to ask me what I believe?'

'I know what you believe, and I also know you have a history of believing things that aren't true. That are all in your head.'

'And that's it?'

'That's it. You're lucky we aren't charging you.'

'Charging me? For trying to help you?'

Kemp leaned forward. Sweat glistened on his forehead.

'Shall I spell it out?'

'What are you talking about?'

'You hear voices, don't you?'

'That's not the point.'

'It's very much the point. You were locked up because you weren't in your right mind.'

'I should have known this was no use.'

'You've wasted our time and you've tried to get in the way of our investigation.'

'No.'

'Do you know what I think? I think you just want attention. Well, you're not getting mine.'

Nancy rose to her feet. Her legs were shaking.

'You're an arsehole,' she said.

He smiled again.

'Lucky I'm in a good mood,' he said. 'You can leave now and I don't want to hear from you again.'

TWENTY

Maud left the station earlier than usual, with the sense of not enough done. As she stepped onto the pavement, a young woman rushed past her into the wind and rain. She wasn't wearing a coat, just a thin jumper. Her hair was unbrushed, her eyes were glittering, she seemed to be talking to herself.

'Are you all right?' Maud asked, but the woman didn't stop or look round.

It took Maud ten minutes to get to the underground, walking through the drizzle, all the light of the shops and flats blurred by rain, people scurrying along the streets with heads bowed, clutching bags.

It was a few stops on the underground and then a ten-minute walk until she arrived at the vast college building, with its turrets and towers. The dozens of windows glowed in the evening darkness. As she entered through the large swing doors, the building felt almost empty. During the day, it was crammed with students. In the evening it was almost abandoned, with just a few sparse groups of mainly middle-aged people making their way up the stairs and along the echoing corridors to their classes in Spanish or creative writing or, in Maud's case, law. Her colleagues would now be still at work or in the pub or back with their families. Maud was going back to school.

When she pushed open the door of lecture room C301, she saw the familiar faces seated in groups on the raked seating.

They were a strange collection of different ages, ethnicities, genders. There was a man who looked as if he was in his sixties. Hadn't he left it a bit late to train as a lawyer? There was a woman in a hijab. There was a woman who looked like a teenager. Her hair was dyed blue, and she had piercings in her ears, nose and lower lip and two full sleeves of tattoos. Maud didn't know their individual stories and motivations and she didn't really have time to know. All they really had in common was that, for one reason or another, they had to study law in the evenings. Maybe they had full-time jobs, like Maud. Maybe they had families. Maybe they had done a language and a drawing course and wanted to try something new.

Maud had her usual seat in the front row. It was always available. Probably people felt too exposed, too likely to be called on to say something. But it was the closest to the door. That was useful. She had already noticed that this adult evening class was turning into something that reminded her of being back at school. This collection of strangers was gradually turning into groups. People had their special places where they sat together and whispered to each other. At the end of the lesson, some of them would go to the pub across the road. Probably that was why some of them were taking the class in the first place. It wasn't so much that they were going to go through the hard, grim process of becoming a lawyer in two or three or four years' time. They were mainly here as a way of meeting people. But Maud was here to learn and nothing else. When the class was over, she could leave the room without having to make conversation. She had calculated that these twice-a-week sessions and the work that went into them could just about fit into her life if she was absolutely ruthless about it. It wasn't fun, but it was her escape route.

The instructor came into the room. She was a middle-aged

woman, who dressed in bright colours and flamboyant scarves. She looked like nobody's idea of a legal academic and at some other time, in some other life, like someone who could be a friend. But Maud didn't have time for another friend just now. She was finding it hard to keep up with the ones she did have. There was a bustle behind her as someone pushed through the door as the instructor was closing it and almost collided with her. The man apologised, then looked around and headed for the nearest seat, which was where Maud was sitting, so she had to move along.

She had seen him before. He was bearded, with messy brown hair, and was dressed in a dark suit, a blue tee-shirt and scuffed trainers. He looked not just as if he had left work in a hurry but as if he had got out of bed in a hurry. He rifled through his tote bag and produced a ring-backed notebook and a couple of pens, one without a top, and placed them on the desk in front of him.

'What's this one?' he said.

'What?' said Maud.

'What's today about?'

'Tort,' said Maud. 'An introduction to it.'

'Tort?' the man said doubtfully. 'I've no idea what that is.'

'Maybe that's why we're doing a class on it.'

That came out more sharply than Maud had intended, but the man just laughed.

'That's good,' he said.

Halfway through the class, Caroline, the instructor, looked at her phone and said she had to deal with something and that it would only take a minute. She stepped outside and Maud could see her through the little round window in the door talking animatedly, something about keys. Conversations started behind her. Nancy looked down at her notes.

'Now I know what tort is.'

It was the man next to her. She just gave a nod of acknowledgement.

'And it's definitely not the sort of thing I went into the law to learn.'

'What *did* you go into the law to learn?' she asked.

'It probably sounds a bit childish. I've got sick of what I was doing and thought I could do something a bit more useful. You know, be like Atticus Finch.'

'Didn't Atticus Finch's client get convicted?'

The man looked disconcerted. 'Is that right? I haven't read it since I was at school.'

'I don't think it was his fault, though.'

'I'm Stuart, by the way.'

'Maud.'

Stuart contemplated her with narrowed eyes.

'I've been trying to make you out. I think I know why most of the other people are here. Mainly it's because they messed up the first time and they're giving it a second chance. Old Jim at the back is doing it because he wanted to do something to keep himself occupied after his wife died. A few others like me weren't happy with their job. Actually, that's not quite true about me. I'm reasonably happy. I just don't seem . . .'

He couldn't think of the right word.

'Righteous,' Maud suggested.

'That's a big word,' said Stuart. 'Too big, probably. But it's something like that. But what about you?'

Before Maud could answer, the door opened and Caroline came back in and immediately started speaking. It was a dense, complicated lesson and Maud was frantically writing notes about laws of obligation and civil law and notions of rights and negligence and compensation. About the distinction between a strict tort and a specific one. They sounded like they should be the same thing, but they were different. The introductory classes on criminal law had dealt with issues that she faced every day, and she barely took a note. But this felt like learning a foreign language and by the time the class was ending, and Caroline was setting them homework, her head was reeling. She closed her notebook and put her pen in her pocket.

'Teacher,' said Stuart.

'What?' said Maud.

'As I said, I've been trying to make you out. You're a teacher, aren't you?'

'No, I'm not.'

'Teacher adjacent, then.'

'I'm not sure what you mean by that, but I think the answer is probably no.'

'Social worker?'

'No.'

He pondered this.

'You're not a doctor, are you?'

'You're right. I'm not a doctor.'

'Oh, I know,' he said. 'You're unemployed. Temporarily, I'm sure.'

'No, I'm not,' she said.

She got up, ready to leave. Stuart was frowning.

'I'm normally good at this. All right, I give up. What are you?'

'I'm a Metropolitan Police Detective,' she said.

She'd read in books about the colour draining from a character's face but she'd never actually seen it in real life, even when interviewing a suspect, even when charging them. But she saw it now. Stuart's face went pale and when he spoke it was almost with a stammer.

'I don't know what to say.'

Maud didn't know what to say either, so she picked up her notebook and headed for the door, passing the groups from the class who were heading for the pub.

TWENTY-ONE

It rained for the whole evening. As Nancy lay in the bed, Felix asleep beside her, she could hear the rain slapping against the window, the rain and the trains rumbling past. She thought of living in the countryside. Felix was probably thinking of walks across the fields on summer days or in the sharp winter sun, ending with a drink in front of the fire in a rustic pub with wooden beams and horse brasses on the wall. But what about days like this, when it was rainy and dark and cold? You wouldn't be able to go anywhere, and you wouldn't be able to do anything except stay indoors and make your own fun. She looked at the man beside her. The two of them. Making their own fun.

It was still raining as they ate breakfast the next morning.

'Suddenly I see the benefit of working from home,' said Felix. He was wearing a yellow jacket he normally wore for hiking. 'I'm not sure it'll keep the rain out.'

'At least people will be able to see you.'

'Is that a sarcastic statement? Do you think I look ridiculous?'

'It's a descriptive statement. It means people will be able to see you, which will probably be useful on a day like this.'

He found a beanie hat to wear and a pair of bulky gloves. With all of that and his maroon backpack, Nancy did think he looked a little ridiculous, but she didn't say anything. What did it matter, as long as it kept him dry?

When he was gone, she made herself more coffee and sat at

her computer. She clicked on some property sites. She wasn't looking at houses in the country. She was at looking commercial properties for rent. There were a lot of them. It was like a scene of devastation, the remnants of the restaurants and the delis and the coffee shops that had gone bust during the pandemic or gone bust after the pandemic because they couldn't find the staff. It was too early to think of starting again, of course, but in her head, she was making calculations. All she needed was some money, a business plan, a couple of people to work with and the perfect property in the perfect place.

She was happily looking at an empty site on Newington Green when there was a knock at the door. A knock on the door had started to feel alarming, like a phone call in the middle of the night. It signalled that the person was already inside the house. She opened it to be confronted by Harry, his hand held up, ready to knock again. He looked agitated, his hair unkempt, dark rings under his eyes.

'Is anything wrong?' she asked.

'I was about to ask you that. Have you had any water coming through?'

'No, why?'

'Can I come in?'

Nancy stepped aside and he stepped inside.

'Do you mind?' he said.

'Mind what?'

He looked around, seeming to orientate himself, and then walked into the bedroom. Nancy walked after him, baffled, but also embarrassed and angry. She wasn't even sure if she had made the bed. He walked to the far wall, by the window, and looked up. He reached towards the ceiling and placed his palm on the wall, running it this way and that.

'It seems dry to me.'

'Of course it's dry,' said Nancy. 'What are you talking about?'

She followed him back out of the bedroom.

'I just got back from a night shift,' he said. 'I went into our bedroom. It shares a wall with yours. What I found was rain coming through the ceiling. There was a bulge in the wallpaper on the ceiling and then it was running down the wall. It always fucking . . .' He stopped himself and took a breath. 'Sorry. It just always happens when there's heavy rain. There's a bit on the roof where the lead meets the tiles . . .' He stopped himself again. 'I won't bore you with the details.'

Nancy gestured towards her half-full cafetière.

'I'm just drinking this,' she said. 'Do you want some or will it keep you awake?'

'Nothing could keep me awake after the night I've had,' he said. 'Except water dripping onto me.'

She poured him a mug. She gestured at the milk, but he shook his head and gulped at the coffee.

'It's probably not hot enough,' she said.

'It's fine. It's coffee.' He glared in front of him. 'It's the land-lord. Have you met Goddard?'

'Kind of—'

Harry interrupted her.

'I brought in someone to look at it. He said that whoever did the job, did it wrong. It needs doing all over again. I wrote to him and told him about it. No reply.' He gulped down the rest of the coffee and put the mug down heavily on the table. 'He can reply when it suits him. One month our rent didn't go in because of a mix-up at the bank. The first we heard of it was a warning letter from his solicitors. But ask him to bring the building up to a decent standard, then suddenly he's awfully hard to track down.'

'I'm so sorry,' said Nancy. 'It must be difficult. With the baby and everything. And then Kira's death.'

His face lost its angry expression and became pensive. He nodded.

'I see things at work, people dying, all the time. But when it happens to someone you know, it feels completely different.'

'Your partner told me that she was about to babysit for you.'

He looked taken aback.

'I don't think so.'

'She said—'

'I don't think Kira would have been a suitable babysitter.'

'Why?'

'She didn't seem altogether reliable.'

'Everyone I've talked to says she was nice.'

'I didn't really know her but I'm sure she was nice. That's not the point.'

'Doesn't it seem odd, though, that she offered on the day before she took her life?'

He shook his head.

'You should see the people I see when they're brought in. When you're in that terrible state, you don't think of other people.' He turned and looked at Nancy more directly. 'I suppose you understand that more than most people.'

Nancy wondered what he would do if she started screaming.

'I meant that if she offered to look after Lydia, then she wasn't thinking of taking her life on the Saturday.'

'I don't see what you're getting at.'

'I was just thinking aloud really. And I'm afraid I've got to go,' she said. 'I actually do have a prior engagement.'

Harry started to move towards the door but then looked around.

'You're sure that no water has come through?'

'I haven't seen anything.'

'This house,' he said. 'If it's not one thing, then it's another. I sometimes think that I'd like to find out whoever did the electrics in our flat and then track him down. But if you have any problems, get in touch. I think we should deal with Goddard as a group. Strength in numbers. In fact, if you've any concerns at all, let me know. I'm a doctor as well as a neighbour. If you need to talk about anything . . .'

Nancy reached for her jacket and punched her fists into its sleeves.

'No,' she said. 'That won't be happening.'

Twenty-two

Nancy walked through the market. She passed the butcher's stalls with their rows of cow's hooves. The peppers and chilis in the greengrocers' glowed in the greyness of the day. Harlesden was like Hackney before the hipsters moved in with their sourdough bakeries and their coffee shops. She rather liked it.

She was lost in thought as she made her way back to Fielding Road, so that she crossed roads, walked through the market, turned this way and that automatically, without noticing where she was. As she approached the house, she came out of her reverie and noticed she was walking so close behind a man that she was about to bump into him.

As she stopped herself, she stumbled slightly, and the man looked round. It was Dylan Strauss from next door. She smiled and gave him a nod, but he stood in her way, so she had to stop. She could see that he was frowning. His face was flushed from the cold. She saw the livid mark on the side of his nose.

'Are you all right?' he said.

The words themselves sounded sympathetic but the tone in which he barked them, and his expression, made it sound like an accusation. Nancy didn't particularly mind showing her irritation.

'Why do you ask?'

He planted himself right in front of her, just slightly too

close. It felt like he was occupying as much of her space as possible. She took one step back.

'I know about your troubles,' he said.

He did not sound sympathetic.

'I don't know what you've heard, but what you call my "troubles" are my business. As it happens, they've been sorted and I'm fine.'

Dylan gave a grunt that managed to sound both disapproving and dissatisfied.

'Well, then,' he said, 'there's no excuse.'

Nancy felt like she was being sucked into a conversation she didn't want to have. Not with Dylan, not out in the street. She was meant to ask, excuse for what? But she wasn't going to.

She tried to move past him, but he stepped sideways, so he was still in her way. Would she actually have to push him aside? She bunched her fists.

'When I first heard about your behaviour,' he said, 'I thought it was the action of someone who was afflicted and who needed help. But either you're in some kind of denial or you need a short, sharp warning.'

'What is this?' said Nancy, now genuinely angry and not caring whether she showed it.

Dylan took on a thoughtful expression. It reminded Nancy of a head teacher giving a speech to the pupils at the end of term.

'I know you've only just moved into this street, so you don't understand things yet. We're a community here. We're more than neighbours. We're like family. We look out for each other. It's a delicate balance. Michelle told me how she found you in poor Kira's flat, how you'd broken in, like some kind of burglar.'

'That's ridiculous. I didn't break in. The door was left open, and I was curious, so I went in to have a look.'

Even as she spoke, Nancy hated herself for trying to justify herself to this man.

'You were curious?' said Dylan with heavy sarcasm. 'This is the scene of a tragic suicide, and you think you might pop in for a look, as if you were at Madame Tussaud's.'

'If you want to know, I don't think the death has been properly investigated.'

Dylan's mouth opened and closed, and his face turned a darker shade of pink.

'Are you insane?' he said. 'Well, of course, you are insane. We all know that. But what the hell do you think you're doing? You blunder into a place of . . . of . . .' He searched for the appropriately grave term. 'Of tragedy and mourning and sanctity with your delusions and your interference.'

'I'm just asking questions.'

When Dylan responded, he was spluttering and speaking so loudly that Nancy looked around to see if others were noticing.

'Just asking questions. That's what every conspiracy theorist says. I'm not an anti-vaxxer. I'm just asking questions. Don't you realise that there are real people involved? There's a grieving family.'

'I don't have to justify myself to you,' said Nancy, in as calm a voice as she could manage. 'You're not her family. You don't even live in the building.'

Dylan seemed to calm down, but Nancy disliked his calmness even more than his anger.

'I should say that my wife was very distressed by what she saw. Very distressed indeed.'

'Do you want to talk about distressing?' said Nancy. 'Kira's body. Hanging there. That's distressing.'

'What were you even doing? What were you looking for?'

'I don't know. It didn't feel right.'

'Didn't feel right,' said Dylan, again in a sarcastic tone. He took a deep breath. 'Look, young lady, let it never be said that my wife and I are unsympathetic to the terrible curse of mental illness. You were saying that you've recovered. Well, that may be true, or it may not be true. Perhaps it's not for you to judge. I don't want to go into detail, but I've heard not just about your problems but about the problems you've caused for others. If you think that people are going to stand by and let you do harm to those who are suffering and grieving, then you may need to learn a lesson.' He paused and looked down at her. 'Are you hearing me? Are you listening to me?'

'I could hardly not be hearing you,' said Nancy. 'I think everyone in the street can hear you.'

'That's good,' said Dylan. 'That's very good. I'm glad you find it amusing.'

'I don't find it amusing. I don't find it amusing at all.'

'You may not like what you've heard, and you might find it uncomfortable, but you'd better pay attention to it.'

'Will you get out of my way now,' said Nancy, 'or will I have to walk round you?'

Dylan seemed to consider whether to let her go, whether he had said enough. Then he stepped to the side and waved towards her front door in an almost theatrical gesture. Nancy walked past without looking at him.

Kemp pushed open Maud's door without knocking and glared at her out of boiled blue eyes.

'Death by her own hand,' he said.

'Sorry?

'The coroner's inquest. Kira Mullan. Death by her own hand.'

He had obviously been brooding and working himself up into a fury against her.

'Right.'

Maud returned to her work, scrolling through the various hospital reports that showed the young woman she was working with had been admitted seven times in the last three months with lacerations to the face and once a broken wrist.

'Convinced now?'

'Why do you mind what I think?'

'I don't give a shit what you think.'

'Good. We're on an equal footing then.'

The door banged shut.

Twenty-three

The following morning, a young man with wild hair and steamed-up glasses and wearing a bulky quilted jacket unlocked the metal shutters, then the cracked wooden door of a small retail unit and let Nancy and her three friends inside.

It was pouring with rain and the sky was overcast, which made the space they crowded into seem even darker and smaller than it actually was.

'They left in a bit of a hurry,' said the estate agent, pushing his hands deep into his pockets.

Nancy didn't reply. She gazed at the room, its flaking plaster, naked light bulb and trailing wires, cracked window, greasy stainless-steel counter. There was a stool lying on its side, a stack of dirty Tupperwares in one corner, signs of mice everywhere. She made her way past her friends and into the back room. A large, deep ceramic sink with brass taps that made her heart sing, an oven she didn't even want to look at, a fridge minus its door, a toilet off to one side down a narrow passageway. She didn't bother going in there. A small window furred with green algae looked over a back yard that was piled with junk.

She turned to her friends: Sam, who had worked front-of-house at her old place; Delia, who had helped out there on an ad hoc basis and who was calm and practical; Bridie, who was one of her oldest friends. Nancy had partly invited her along because she had a secret dread of seeing her and she needed to confront that. Bridie had been the person who had witnessed her spectacular descent into psychosis, and Nancy still remembered the look on her face: fear, pity, maybe even a kind of disgust.

'It's a bit grim, isn't it?' Sam poked at a heap of rags with his foot.

'It is *now*. But think of how it could be. Little mismatched tables, great lighting, painted in classy colours. We could think of opening up to the kitchen so it's almost one room. We could even think of making the yard an overflow space in summer, a little oasis. I think it's south facing, yes?'

The estate agent nodded.

'And it's a great location.'

'What was it?' asked Bridie.

'Some fast-food place that went bankrupt.'

'You'd have to begin again,' said Delia.

'That's the beauty of it.'

'Really?'

'Nancy,' said Bridie. 'Wouldn't all of this be hideously expensive?'

'That's for me to worry about. I need to do the sums, obviously. But what do you think in theory?'

'I think I like it,' said Sam.

'And I think,' said Delia as she kissed Nancy on her forehead, 'that you are fabulous.'

Nancy travelled across London on the overground. She stared out of the window into the little back gardens of Kentish Town, the glimpse of Hampstead Heath. Then back into unfamiliar West London. When she pictured the space she had just visited, she felt flickers of hope run through her. She told herself not to get too excited: she needed to think about the finances and the great task that lay ahead were she to continue. Then she thought about Felix. She hadn't told him she had arranged this viewing. She didn't want him to be anxiously disapproving, or, even worse, to pretend go along with her; nor did she want him to be obstructively sensible and rational.

Behind the particular concern lay, of course, the general one – the one that was always there like a steady drumbeat: that she and Felix weren't going to last. He had been so steadfast and tender, and the thought of separating from him made her chest ache with guilt and love. She tried to push it to one side: not now, not yet.

As she approached the house and was pushing her hand into her jacket pocket to retrieve the keys, she came to a sudden halt. The bins that stood in the tiny garden by the front door were full, and even though collection wasn't until next Tuesday, several bin bags had been left on the ground beside them: including, Nancy saw, the large black bag that one of the cleaners of Kira's flat had been carrying.

The voice in her head was telling her not to be so stupid. She looked up at the blank, unlit windows and back at the bags. She casually sauntered the last few feet to the house. She whistled a bit, looked up at the leafless trees as if she was interested in what she could see there, then knelt down beside the bins as if to tie up the laces of her shoes, even though she was wearing pull-on boots. She yanked the bag towards her.

It was tied at the top and she swiftly unknotted it and opened the bag wide.

Tissues. Face wipes. Kitchen cloths. An empty deodorant can. Official-looking empty envelopes. A madly early Christmas card from someone called Robin. Broken glass that Nancy nicked her thumb on.

She saw herself from the outside, rummaging through a bag of rubbish that had been collected from a dead woman's flat. She looked mad.

A cracked mug. A dead cyclamen in a plastic pot. A ripped cotton scarf. But what was that? Was it . . . ?

Nancy leaned in closer, screwing up her face.

She froze.

There were two feet in scuffed trainers in her narrow field of vision, two shins in sweatpants.

'Nancy?'

Nancy plunged her hand into the bag and closed it around the object. She looked up into Barney's face.

'Hi!' she said, too effusively.

Another face appeared, another pair of trainers, cleaner and nattier.

'Seamus!' she added with equal zest.

She stood up with difficulty, still beaming.

'What are you doing?' Barney's forehead was corrugated in a frown. He wasn't smiling back.

'Doing?'

'Yes.'

'Hello,' said a voice from behind her.

Nancy almost howled aloud. Instead she turned around and raised a hand, still folded around the object she had retrieved, in enthusiastic greeting.

'Michelle,' she said. 'This is all very neighbourly.'

'What were you doing?' repeated Barney stubbornly.

'You mean, going through the rubbish bag? I thought I might have thrown something away by accident. Not,' she added with a sudden burst of defiance, 'that it's really anyone's business.'

'That isn't your bin bag,' said Barney.

'What are you talking about?'

'It came from Kira's.'

'What the fuck,' said Seamus.

'Nancy?' Michelle spoke in a soft but not friendly voice. 'Is this true?'

'How do you know it came from Kira's? How would I know that, for that matter? It's just a bin bag.'

'I took it from the cleaner and put it there myself,' said Barney.

'And anyway, surely anyone can recognise when rubbish isn't theirs,' said Seamus. He pointed at the gaping bag. 'Is that your name on the envelope?'

Nancy looked from face to face. She lifted her chin.

'Okay, it's Kira's rubbish. So what? Is it a crime?'

'It's disgusting, is what it is,' said Michelle.

'Or insane,' said Seamus. He nudged Barney. 'I told you what she was like, but you didn't believe me.'

'We are all concerned about you, Nancy,' said Michelle. 'Very concerned.'

'I am doing just fine,' Nancy said.

Twenty-four

Back in the flat, Nancy uncurled her fist and stared down at the used condom. With her other hand, she opened a deep drawer full of baking trays and utensils, rifled through it, found a freezer bag and shook the sticky object into it. She put the plastic bag on a work surface and washed her hands for several minutes, using plenty of soap.

She felt slightly nauseous. She also felt scared by her actions, which were not those of a sane woman.

Then she stood at the back door and pressed her forehead to the cool glass, looking through the trickles of rain onto the drenched and neglected garden. Metal steps ran from their kitchen into the crudely partitioned-off back section. There was a rusting barbecue at the back, against a blank wall, and a couple of large pots full of leaves and water. The patch of grass was overgrown, and a dead branch lay in the middle of it.

Out of the corner of her eye, she saw a shape emerge. Dylan had come into his and Michelle's long and well-tended garden, and he was dragging something that turned out, as he came into clearer view, to be a punch bag on a stand. He was also not wearing a shirt. He positioned the punch bag, readied himself, took a swing. His pale torso rippled.

Nancy heard the flat door open and then shut again. There were footsteps.

'Felix,' she said without turning round. 'What are you doing back here? Did you forget something?'

Out in his garden, Dylan was dancing slightly and delivering a series of swift blows to the punch bag.

'Hello, Nancy.'

Nancy wheeled around.

'Michelle? How did you get in?'

'I have a key.'

'You have a key? What do you mean, you have a key?'

Michelle held up a Yale and Chubb key attached to a metal ring.

'I have a key to your flat.'

'Why? How?'

'Your husband gave me one.'

'He's not my husband.'

'Of course. Apologies. Felix gave me one, for safe keeping.'

'Why would he do that?'

'As I say, for safe keeping. We're neighbours.'

'Do we have your key?'

'Why would you have our key?'

'Well, exactly.'

'No. You don't have our key.'

'You let yourself in without knocking or ringing.'

'Yes.'

'You can't do that. You can't just walk in here.'

Michelle regarded her steadily.

'Nancy, I'm not going to lie. Felix is seriously worried about you.'

'He doesn't need to be. And if he is, that's between him and me. It's got nothing to do with you. I want you to give me the key back.'

'He's concerned for your safety. He has told me everything.'

'Give me that key.'

'Felix has asked me to keep an eye on you while he is at work, and whether you like it or not, that is what I am going to do.'

'You mean, let yourself in here whenever you feel like it.'

Nancy made a lunge for the keys; Michelle stepped back. Nancy stood glaring at her. From the garden she could hear the thwack of fists on leather.

Michelle's eyes were on her and then she saw them flicker to one side. Had she seen the condom? Nancy forced herself not to look at it, but using one hand she slid it into the deep drawer that stood open.

'I'll be on my way,' said Michelle, pocketing the keys.

'Good. If you let yourself in here without permission, I'll call the police.'

'Call the police again, you mean?'

She left on the last word and Nancy listened to her brisk footsteps going down the stairs. She took her mobile from the table and went to the recent calls.

'I need to come and see you,' she said.

Twenty-five

Helena listened without comment. Nancy didn't feel she came out of the story very well. When she had finished, there was a long silence that she didn't feel a need to fill. She could hear the traffic outside, someone shouting, the drip of rain from the gutters.

'I don't have anything to say about the tragic death of this young woman,' Helena said finally. 'We talked about that before. My concern is you: the person who's sitting in front of me.'

'What if I'm right?'

'You may be right, or you may be projecting your anxieties onto someone else. It may be that when you talk about this woman who wasn't listened to, that you're really talking about yourself.'

'That sounds too clever for me.'

'If there's something suspicious about this case, that's what we have police for.'

'What if they're not investigating properly?'

'That's not your concern. You can't do anything about that. Your concern is to get better. Nancy, I don't normally talk like this, but you've done a fine, brave job in coming back from what you've gone through. What happened to you, all that you lost, would have broken a lot of people. And now you're putting your life together, isn't that right?'

'I suppose so.'

'I've got a warning as well. I don't know about the woman who died and I'm not sure you know either. I don't know what you're actually planning to do. I don't know what you actually *can* do. But I can't help feeling that you're risking everything you've gained.'

'I'm just asking questions,' said Nancy.

'I don't like saying this, but one of the symptoms of your condition is seeing the world as a hostile place.'

'Sometimes the world really is a hostile place,' said Nancy.

'But then it's not your job to cure the world. It's your job to cure yourself. With what you've gone through, your mind is like . . .' Helena gestured with her hands, searching for the right comparison. 'It's like a beautiful, delicate piece of pottery. It got broken, shattered into a thousand pieces, and over the last months you've put it back together, piece by piece. But if it shatters again, you might not be able to put it back together so well.'

Felix came home earlier than usual. He was very wet, and he had a sombre expression on his face as he struggled out of his waterproof jacket and hung it carefully on the hook.

'Why did you give Michelle our key?' demanded Nancy as he was unlacing his shoes. 'Why did you tell her to keep an eye on me?'

He straightened up, passing a hand through his damp hair. She saw how tired he looked.

'Hang on, Nancy, before we get on to that, there's something we need to talk about.'

'What do you mean, before?'

'I heard something today.'

'What? Are you ill? What's happened?'

'No, I'm not ill.' He laid a light stress on the 'I'm' that made Nancy take a small step back.

'What is it?'

He sat down and she took the chair opposite him.

'Bridie called me.'

'Bridie?'

'She said she'd gone with you to a viewing of a potential restaurant.'

'That's right.'

'I thought we agreed we were going to trust each other.'

For a moment, Nancy thought she was going to shout at Felix. But he was right. Of course she should have told him. She looked him in the eye.

'I'm very sorry I didn't tell you,' she said. 'It was wrong. I knew it was wrong, and I feel bad about it.'

She waited. The expression on his face didn't soften.

'She said something else as well.'

'About the restaurant?'

'About you. She thought you might be ...' He hesitated, rubbed his face with his hand.

'What did she think I might be?'

'A bit hyper.'

'I was not hyper.'

'A bit ...' He searched for the word. 'Grandiose.'

'That's a horrible thing to say.'

'She's your friend. She is anxious for you.'

'I was *excited*. I thought she'd be glad for me.' Tears pricked at her eyes and she blinked them away furiously.

'She apparently warned you that it would be incredibly expensive, but you sailed right over that, as if money didn't matter.'

'It wasn't like that at all.'

'It's what she said.'

'Sam liked it. Sam thought it was a good idea.'

'Nancy, you're thinking of charging back into a highly stressful life. You don't seem to remember that you've been ill.'

She stamped her foot, feeling as powerless as a tiny child.

'I have been. I'm not now. I'm better.'

The more she said it, the more implausible it sounded.

'There's another thing.'

'Yes?'

'I ran into Seamus.'

'Arsehole.'

'He told me something.'

Nancy closed her eyes. Kira's rubbish. She waited.

'He was very awkward about it. He said that he hadn't known whether to speak to me or not.'

'What?'

'He said you'd been the one to make a pass at him.'

'What the fuck?'

'He said you seemed troubled.' Felix's voice was dull and careful; he wasn't looking at her. 'He said he felt bad for you.'

'And you believed him? You believed him rather than me? Come on, Felix, look at me. Look at me! Is that what you're saying?'

'I don't know, Nancy. I just know what he said.'

'What he said. What Bridie said. What about what I'm saying?'

'Never mind what you're saying. What do you think you're *doing*? Take a good look at yourself. You told me that being sectioned was like being in hell, remember? Do you want to be in hell again?' He leaned closer; she could see the tiny flecks of stubble under his skin and his eyes were bloodshot. 'Do, you Nancy? If it were just one person. But are you saying they're all wrong and you're right?'

TWENTY-SIX

Maud arrived late and so she had to sit at the back, next to a man who chewed gum loudly and just behind a woman with a dry, continuous cough. It was hard to concentrate. She untied her hair and pulled it back more tightly, capturing all the tendrils of hair, and bent over her notebook.

Litigant in person, she wrote, *force majeure; dilatory tactics.*

It was hot in the room and she was wearing too many layers of clothing because outside it was sleety and cold.

Someone seated near the front twisted round in his seat, scanning the rows. His eyes landed on her and for a beat he looked at her. That man from two days ago, who'd backed away from her as if she had the plague when she had said she was in the Met. Maud felt a spike of irritation. She held his gaze, not smiling, then turned back to her notes.

Avoidance, evasion, inclusion.

She needed to concentrate on the granular satisfaction of legal terminology, the way the law narrowed things down and down, until there were barely any cracks in the framework. But she kept thinking about the young woman with the destroyed face who wouldn't press charges, and about the hostility in Kemp's voice.

'And that's it,' said the lecturer, a wispy man with a wispy grey beard and hexagonal spectacles perched on the end of his narrow nose.

Maud stood up, pulling on her waterproof jacket, gathering her things. The hum of conversation around her grew louder. People were heading out into the wet night in small groups. She saw the man – what was his name? Stuart? – wrap a scarf around his neck and slide his folder into a canvas messenger bag, and as if he could feel her eyes on him, he looked up and half smiled.

She didn't smile back. Instead, she pushed against the flow of people and stood in front of him. He looked startled.

'Hello,' he said.

'It's your turn. Or rather,' she corrected herself. 'It's my turn.'

'Sorry?'

'To guess what you do, based on how you look.' She scrutinised him. 'Hair slightly too long. Beard needs a bit of a trim. Nice glasses: hipsterish, probably expensive. Baggy cords and a nice cotton shirt, though it's missing the top button, did you know? Social worker?'

He shook his head.

'Philosophy teacher at a sixth form college.'

'No.'

'Maybe you're a graphic designer. No, I forgot, it's got to be something that gives you the moral high ground. You work for an NGO, or you're a baker, a sourdough baker . . .'

'I get it. Stop.'

'No. Seriously. What do you do?'

He coughed unnecessarily, bent down to pick up a bike helmet.

'Actually, I'm in advertising.'

'Advertising?' Maud started to laugh. 'You mean, where you persuade people to buy things they don't need.'

'Sometimes they need them,' he said stiffly, but then smiled sheepishly. 'You're right. I was just startled when I found out what you did.'

'Join the queue.'

'Sorry. Do you fancy grabbing a drink?'

'Not really.'

She saw his face fall, and left before she could change her mind.

TWENTY-SEVEN

That weekend, Nancy and Felix did the sort of things that they always did, that couples were meant to do. The alarm was set an hour later than on weekdays. When it went off, Felix went out and bought some pastries. Nancy found a melon and a mango in the fridge. She sliced them up and arranged the result on a plate. They sat for an hour, drinking coffee and reading crossword clues and quiz questions to each other from their phones.

While Nancy washed up the plates and mugs, Felix packed a small bag with trainers and shorts and a bright yellow shirt. He was meeting friends for a five-a-side game.

'What are you going to do?' he said to Nancy.

'I don't know,' she said. 'I thought I might go for a walk.'

'Are you meeting anyone?'

'No.'

'Will you be okay?'

'What do you mean?'

'You know what I mean. It was when you were out, walking on your own, that you had your little episode. Will you be safe out there?'

The phrase 'little episode' made Nancy angry. It sounded like some girly quirk. But she didn't say anything.

'I'll be fine,' she said with a studied calmness. 'But thank you for asking.'

'You can come along with me to the football, if you like.'

She laughed. 'What? Just to watch?'

He flushed slightly.

'It's not so stupid. Other people bring their girlfriends.'

'I'll see you later, Felix.'

She walked down to the park. It was a cold day, threatening rain, but there were people walking dogs, parents with children. She spent a long time sitting on a wooden bench, looking at other people's lives, thoughts drifting through her mind.

When she returned to the house, she found a young man at the front door, his finger repeatedly jabbing at one of the buzzers. He turned as Nancy approached.

'I'm looking for Kira,' he said.

'Kira?'

'She's not answering her phone.'

He had a broad, open face and brown eyes like the eyes of a spaniel.

'She's not there,' said Nancy, delaying the truth. 'Are you a friend?'

'Well, kind of. I'm Ollie. We had a—' He stopped. 'Anyway, I've been away and now I can't get hold of her. Do you know when she'll be back?'

'She won't be back.'

'She's moved out?'

'No.' Nancy took a deep breath. 'She's dead.'

She watched his face. At first, nothing changed, then the colour drained from his cheeks.

'What do you mean?'

'I'm sorry. She died last Sunday.'

'But I don't understand. It's not possible. She was fine when I saw her. Fine,' he repeated. 'We were going to meet when I came back.'

'When did you see her?'

'Friday.'

'And she was all right?'

'She was—' Ollie stopped, shook his head from side to side as if to clear it. 'I don't believe it,' he said.

'I'm sorry,' Nancy repeated.

'How did she die? Did she get run over or something? Did some bastard drive into her? Was that it?'

'They say,' said Nancy slowly, 'that she took her own life.'

'What?'

'It's what the police think.'

'That's stupid. Kira wasn't like that.'

'What was she like?'

'Happy,' he said. 'She was always smiling. I used to see her in the bar where she worked and she was full of life.'

'Tell the police,' said Nancy. 'Go and see them and tell them you don't believe Kira took her own life.'

'What?'

'Don't say you met me though.'

'Sorry?'

'If you mention me, they won't believe you.'

'I don't understand.'

'Just say you know that she was happy, and it makes no sense, but leave me out of it.'

But Ollie was backing away from her with a perplexed expression on his face. Then he turned his back and walked away. Nancy gazed after him, but Kira wasn't her problem anymore.

That evening they ordered a takeaway and watched the first couple of episodes of a Spanish TV series that a friend of Felix's had recommended. While they were watching, Felix drank most of a bottle of wine. Nancy wasn't really supposed to drink, because of her medication, but she poured herself a glass and ignored his questioning look.

'What do you think?' said Felix, when the second episode finished.

'It's all right.'

'It's a bit of a commitment. I think there's four series of it. Maybe five. That would be like . . .' He considered for a moment. 'About two days of our life.'

'We can try something else,' said Nancy, knowing that they wouldn't try something else. She looked at the time. 'I might go to Frankie's party now.'

'It's nearly half past eleven, and it's the other side of London.'

'So?'

'I don't think you're up to it. Not yet.'

'That's for me to decide. I want to see my friends.'

'Your druggy friends.'

'You mean fun friends, cheerful friends,' she said. 'People who are important to me.'

'Nancy,' Felix said. 'What if I ask you, just this once, to stay home with me and have a nice evening? You're on new medication, things have been weird, and I don't think it's wise.'

Nancy was about to tell him not to ask. But she didn't. One party, one Saturday evening, didn't matter.

She was on the brink of telling Felix that it was over, finished, but held back the words. She needed to do it properly, not late on Saturday night in the middle of a disagreement.

On Sunday, they went down to Tate Modern and Nancy lost herself for two hours of blessed silence, just her and the painting in front of her. Afterwards, they walked along the river and had lunch at one of the little bistros on the South Bank. As she ate her bowl of pasta, she felt a moment of regret. Could things have been different? Isn't this what a good relationship was meant to be like? But then Felix looked around and interrupted her thoughts.

'Look,' he said.

'Look at what?'

'Look at all the waiters. Look at the cooks behind the counter. And the person at the front desk and there must be people we don't see in the background washing the dishes. Can you imagine the finance and the organisation it takes to run a place like this? And they've got all the benefits of scale. There must be about fifty branches of this restaurant, all over the country, all with the same menus, all ordering the same products in bulk. Even so, it must be a struggle.'

Nancy's regret vanished.

'Is this about me?' she said wearily.

They finished eating mainly in silence. They travelled home on the bus mainly in silence, Felix looking at his phone, Nancy staring out of the window. She could feel the words in her mouth: it's over. She could see the look on his face. She felt like a murderer.

At home, they both pottered around, seeming to find it difficult to settle on anything. In the evening, they had a meal of scrambled eggs and some leftovers from the fridge.

'Do you want to watch anything?' Felix asked.

The pressure inside her felt intolerable, as if she must explode. She took a deep calming breath. Why was this so hard? She knew it had to be done.

'Maybe we can talk,' she said.

'Sure.'

Then a message pinged onto his mobile. He glanced at it and turned away from her to answer.

'Felix.'

'Sorry. This won't take too long.'

She waited and he tapped away.

'I've got a bit of a headache,' she said at last. 'Maybe I'll go to bed.'

Felix turned to give her a sharp, inquisitive look.

'Are you okay?'

'Sometimes a headache is just a headache.'

'But it's been a good day, hasn't it? And a good weekend?'

It felt like Felix was talking about the end of something.

'Yes,' said Nancy. 'Peaceful.'

When Felix came to bed, Nancy was still awake, but she pretended to be asleep. She lay for a long time in the darkness with him tranquilly at her side, unsuspecting. Tomorrow afternoon, when he came back from work, she would tell him it was over. She should have done it long ago. His goodness and love had bound her to him, but she needed to be free.

TWENTY-EIGHT

The next morning Nancy felt that the light seemed harder, clearer, more in focus. Or was it just her mood?

It was a normal Monday morning in every way but just as Felix was opening the door to leave, he turned and looked at Nancy. She was starting to dislike that look intensely. He began to say something, then didn't speak, but stepped forward and gave Nancy a long hug. She was taken aback by this, but she didn't want to push him away. She just put her arms lightly round him and gave his back a light tap. He stepped back and nodded slightly and left.

Nancy felt a huge sense of relief. Although she had the whole day, she decided she must act immediately. She rummaged in the cupboard in the bedroom and found two bags. That would be enough. She laid them out in the living room and began to pack them. She did it slowly and systematically. She couldn't take everything, but she would need enough to last her for a couple of weeks, perhaps up to a month. She wasn't sure how Felix would react to her leaving, so she didn't want to leave behind anything she would really miss. She had to remind herself that she wasn't packing for a holiday. She was about to start her life again. As she moved back and forward, between the bedroom and the living room and the bathroom, she hummed to herself determinedly.

The bell rang and she felt a wave of panic. What if Felix had come back for some reason? She didn't want him to find her packing. She buzzed the front door open, heard the door close and then footsteps on the stairs. She opened the door and the sight that met her was so unexpected that it took a few seconds to recognise the man.

She moved back and Dr Roland Lowe stepped into the flat.

At first, she found it difficult even to speak. She had never seen him anywhere but in his office at the hospital. He was wearing a long, fawn-coloured overcoat and his pale face was flushed from the cold. He looked at his surroundings, blinking. Nancy was shocked and confused, but he seemed ill at ease as well.

She gave a nervous laugh.

'This is a surprise,' she said. 'I didn't know you made house calls. Did I forget an appointment?'

'No. Nothing like that.' He noticed the cases on the floor. 'Are you packing?'

'It's only good news,' said Nancy. 'I'm taking control of my life. I'm moving out and I'm looking to start a restaurant again.'

He responded oddly to this. He didn't nod or smile. He just looked at her in the way he did when he was deciding whether to increase her dose or reduce it.

'It all sounds a bit sudden,' he said.

She laughed again and there was an edge to her laughter.

'There's a bit of me that wants to say that that's my business rather than yours.'

Again, he didn't smile or attempt to defend himself. He just looked at her and she was struck even more strongly by the strangeness of his being there.

'I'm sorry,' she said. 'Why are you here? If you wanted to see me, why didn't you just ring me and arrange an appointment?'

He muttered something under his breath as if he was struggling to find the right words.

'I don't do this lightly,' he said. 'I mean, coming to your home. It's just that I've received some reports. Some concerning reports.'

'You mean about me?'

'Yes.'

'Who's been sending reports to you? Why would someone do that?'

Dr Lowe was fidgeting with his coat and Nancy noticed that he had done up the buttons wrongly so that the edges of the coat at the bottom didn't join properly.

'Sometimes,' he said, speaking slowly and deliberately, 'someone can be in a crisis and what is needed is a quiet time, a controlled time, in which the crisis can be assessed and dealt with.'

'I don't know what that has to do with me,' said Nancy. 'I'm not in a crisis. I'm feeling much better and I'm getting on with my life.'

Dr Lowe looked down at the half-packed bags.

'Or upending your life.'

'You can call it what you like, but it's my life. I still don't get what you're doing in my flat.' She heard the note of panic in her own voice. 'I don't get what this is about. I came to see you after my brief episode. You increased my dosage very slightly and it worked.'

He frowned. 'Nancy, is it true that you broke into a neighbour's flat, that flat where a woman had recently taken her own life?'

'What are you talking about? What's that got to do with you?' She took a deep breath. 'All right, I'll explain. I walked past the door of the flat and saw that the cleaners had left it open and I stepped inside to look.'

'You were also found rummaging through her garbage.'

'Is that fucking Barney or was it Dylan? Or Michelle? Did they somehow find you?'

'Who got in touch with me is not the issue. Is it true?'

'And did you hear that another neighbour said I'd come on to him. Did you hear that?'

Dr Lowe paused and seemed to consider this.

'No,' he said. 'No, I hadn't heard that.'

'It's not important anyway. None of it's important.'

'Everything's important,' said Dr Lowe, 'and it's severely worrying, when seen as a whole.'

There was a long silence. Dr Lowe was still staring at her. She felt like an animal in a zoo.

'Nancy.' His voice was severe and quiet, as if he was a judge delivering a sentence. 'It is my considered opinion that you are in need of medical help. Will you accept my recommendation that you should voluntarily spend some time in hospital to recover?'

'What the fuck!' Dread washed through her. 'Hospital? No! No, of course I won't.'

'That's what I thought.'

'Then you were right,' said Nancy. 'And I think you should leave now and if you don't leave I will call the police.'

'A moment, please,' said Dr Lowe, taking his phone from his pocket. He held it in front of his face and tapped at it like someone confronted with an unfamiliar device.

'If you're calling an Uber, you can do it from the street. Fuck off and I never, ever, ever want to see you again.'

Dr Lowe replaced his phone and stood there, apparently lost in thought.

'I said leave! You have no rights.'

The doorbell rang, making Nancy start. He walked towards

the door but instead of opening it and leaving, he looked at the control box and jabbed the two buttons.

'Which is the one that opens the street door?' he said.

'What are you talking about? I said you should leave.'

There were footsteps on the stairs, multiple footsteps getting louder. Dr Lowe opened the door and a man and a woman stepped in. Behind them, Nancy could see just the tops of the heads of two other people. But they stayed outside and Dr Lowe pushed the door to without closing it completely.

The man and the woman were both dressed for the cold outdoors, the man in a grey donkey jacket and the woman in a long brown coat that reached almost to her ankles. Nancy looked at them in bemusement and they looked at her with curiosity and almost, Nancy thought, tenderness. That was worse than anything. She put both hands up as if to ward them off.

They were both about her own age and seemed like the sort of people who could have been her friends. The man was kind-looking with floppy brown hair and a wispy beard. The woman was tall, with her dirty blonde hair tied up in a bun, as if it had been done in a hurry.

'No,' said Nancy. 'No no no no.'

'Nancy, I am Imogen Boyce,' said the woman in a soft, clear voice. 'I'm a GP at the Green Park practice, where you're registered.'

'You've never met me.'

'I'm very sorry,' said Dr Boyce. 'I know this must be distressing for you.'

'No,' said Nancy. 'Go away. All of you go away. I'm packing, can't you see. I'm going to begin my new life.'

'I'm Steve McDonnell.' The man took a step forward. 'I am an accredited mental health professional.'

'You don't need to be here. None of you need to be here. It's a mistake.' Her growing sense of terror was hot inside her chest; she tried to speak more calmly, to appear rational, but her legs were shaking so much she almost fell over, and Imogen Boyce put an arm out to steady her, which she shook off.

'This is my home, and I'm going to have to ask you to leave. If there's anything you want to talk about, we can arrange an appointment in your office at the hospital.'

Dr Lowe glanced at the doctor and the social worker, then he looked at her once more with a more resolute, more dispassionate expression. When he spoke, it was like he was reciting a prepared speech.

'Out of concern for your welfare and safety and the welfare and safety of others, I am recommending that you need to be admitted to hospital under section two of the Mental Health Act.'

'You can't do that. I know my rights. I know you can't do this. It's a violation, an abuse. You can only do this if I'm a risk to myself or to others. And I'm not. You can't say I am.'

'Nancy,' said Steve Mc Donnell. 'You have the right to put your case, and I am here to see that the right decision is made once I have the evidence. Nobody wants you to be detained against your will if it isn't necessary.'

'Just let me go then,' said Nancy. 'You'll never hear from me again.'

'There have been various concerns. You seem to have become convinced that the young woman who took her life died in suspicious circumstances. You told the police this, and also your neighbours.'

'That doesn't mean I'm mad. I mean, what if I'm right?'

She saw at once from the melancholy expression on McDonnell's face that she had said the wrong thing.

'You have been acting in a wild and irrational way, according to friends.'

'What friends?'

'And your neighbour Michelle Strauss has reported your last encounter.'

'Michelle? Why has she got anything to do with this? When I first moved in she was all neighbourly, wanting to be helpful, and then just as suddenly she turned against me. She and her unpleasant husband.'

'Is that why you told her you were going to kill her? Or kill yourself?'

'What?' said Nancy, stunned. 'Kill? I never said anything like that.'

'You didn't have words with her?'

'I had words with her. I had lots of words. But not that. Is that what she said?'

'Are you saying it's untrue?'

'Of course it's untrue. Why would she say that?' Nancy felt suddenly nauseous and dizzy. The room swam. She stared from face to face. 'She's trying to put me away so I don't make trouble. You have to believe me. You have to. She's lying and I know why she's lying.'

She turned to the GP; surely this woman with a nice, tired face would see she was telling the truth.

'You believe me, don't you?'

'Please,' said McDonnell, holding up his hand, but she plunged on.

'It proves I was right all along. Michelle wants to silence me, which means she must know something. She knows who killed Kira.'

She stopped. The room was silent.

'You'll get better in hospital,' said McDonnell with a terrible gentleness.

'I can't go into hospital again,' said Nancy. 'I can't. I just can't. I'll do anything but don't send me there. Please don't send me there.'

'You'll be safe. You can get better.'

'You can't make me. I'm an adult. I've got a right to refuse treatment.'

'If you are detained under section two of the Mental Health Act, you have no choice in the matter, although once in hospital you do have a right of appeal.'

'Felix will tell you,' said Nancy desperately. 'He'll tell you I'm not a risk. Call Felix.'

'He's actually outside,' said Dr Lowe. 'Waiting.'

'What do you mean, waiting?' She suddenly felt horribly cold, as if winter was pressing in on her, thinning her blood and shaking her limbs. 'Why?'

But she knew. Even before Felix came in and she saw how he couldn't look at her and how his cheeks were wet with tears, she knew.

'It was you,' she said. 'You did this? You?'

'Darling Nancy.' He held his hands out imploringly.

'You,' she repeated.

'If you could just . . .'

'Don't speak to me. Don't touch me. Nobody. I say no.' She looked around and reached for her jacket. 'You all tell me I have no choice. Well, you just try and make me. I'm leaving now.'

She pushed past Dr Lowe and past Felix and made for the door. As she pulled it open, she found herself confronted by two men dressed in green scrubs.

'Don't even try,' she said, her voice guttural. 'I'm warning you.'

But as she pushed herself between them, she was gripped hard by both arms and almost lifted off her feet as she was dragged back into her room and onto her sofa. Even there they held her in position, kneeling on the sofa on either side of her. She tried to wriggle herself free, but they were holding her rigid. She tried to butt at them with her head and to kick at them. She started to shout and scream and swear. Maybe someone outside, even in the street, would hear her and call the police.

One of the men, his large pink face apologetic, put his free hand over her mouth. She tried to bite it.

'Careful,' said Dr Lowe. 'Don't choke her.' He leaned down towards her. 'Nancy, you are coming with us to hospital. If you won't come, you will be forcibly restrained and transported. If you keep screaming like this, you will be sedated. Do you understand?'

He nodded at the man, who lifted his hand.

'You fucking fuck off,' she shouted. 'Get off me. You can't do this to me.' Then she was half shouting, half crying and the hand was once more spread over her mouth. But she didn't stop shouting and she didn't stop wriggling. She had to stop this somehow. She wasn't going to co-operate. She wasn't going to give in.

Her vision was blurred by her tears and perhaps also by her rage. She saw the outline of Dr Lowe retreat, get smaller and then it got larger again. She felt a coldness against the soft skin of her arm, and then the coldness spread along the arm. Everything went soft and blurry. The weight that was on her mouth softened and she tried to scream but she couldn't manage it. There was a soft moan that seemed to come from another person, somewhere far away in another world.

Dimly, this body that didn't fully belong to her anymore was lifted up. She was still making the hopeless effort to resist. She wouldn't walk. She made her body a dead weight. They would have to drag her.

She didn't know how or who was doing it but her feet were held and lifted. She still tried to fight against it, moaning like a dying animal. Her head cracked on something. She somehow, through a fog, realised it was the doorframe. She was tipping forward and she heard heavy footsteps on the stairs and then felt the cold air of the street.

There was a pause and then somehow, out of that fog, that fog that was like a dream or another world, she saw the face of Michelle looking down at her. It was the last moment of clarity, like a gap in the clouds that shows a glimpse of the moon, and in that moment, she saw what looked like an expression of triumph.

And then everything turned to grey and then to black.

PART TWO

Twenty-nine

She was in a dream she couldn't wake up from. Huge forms moving softly around her, lunging soundlessly towards her. Cold white hands touching her. The earth was full of slimy things that writhed and clung to her.

Waves of pain in her skull, cresting and crashing.

Sudden light burning into her eyelids, but she couldn't open her gritty eyes to see, nor her parched lips to speak.

Taste in her mouth, like metal, like blood.

Smell in her nostrils, rich and sweet, like the odour of her own body rotting.

It was silent, and then she heard a scream that came from far away, like an animal in a trap. The scream abruptly stopped, and it was silent once more, and that was almost worse.

She had been here before, in this dream. The same dull tang in her mouth and the same fetid smell in her nostrils and a mouth so dry she couldn't open it. She needed water, but she couldn't move her lips to ask for water.

Her skin itched and tingled. Her stomach hurt as if an animal was coiled inside her guts.

Very slowly, she moved a hand and placed it on her belly, over the top of a cotton gown, moved it up to her breasts, to her throat, to her face. Her skin was puffy on one cheekbone and when she touched it, throbbed slightly.

Very slowly, she opened her gummed eyes and at first it was

dark. After a time, she saw a square of light around the edges of the door and she could make out the shape of the room, square and empty: just four walls, a high window, a door, a bed.

She was in the bed, in the room, in a building somewhere, but what had happened before? She tried to find things that had a name and a shape, something to hold on to while panic rose and sank inside her and pain washed round her skull.

She was Nancy North, Nancy for her grandmother and North like the North Star and the North Pole. She was thirty-three years old. Her hair was pale brown, and her eyes were blue in some lights and grey in others. She had a small birthmark on her left buttock. She was five foot and four inches, and she was a chef.

No. She used to be a chef. In another life.

Into her mind came the image of her little restaurant, clatter of pans and steam rising, beautiful Japanese knives laid out, her olive-wood pestle and mortar. She thought of asparagus spears and eggs cool in her palm before she cracked them open, the sour bubble of yeast and the settle of sifted flour. She felt her cheeks becoming wet.

She didn't have a restaurant anymore. She had been ill. She had been ill, and she had lost everything and been locked away. Like before. Or perhaps she had never left. Perhaps it was the escaping that had been a dream.

But now the blankness had been breached and memories were starting to seep through. Nancy lay still and waited for them to gather in her and make sense.

Packing boxes. A body swaying in a doorway. Green boots with yellow laces. A frightened face. Nobody's safe. Fingers digging into her flesh. Mean faces, whispering voices. A mother screaming at her kitchen table. Someone trying to kiss her. A crying baby. A used condom curled up in her fist. A man taking grunting swings at a punch bag in the garden, again and again. Someone looking at her with pity and reproach. Darling Nancy. Please. You're a risk to yourself and others. Only trying to save you. Save me. Men in green scrubs at her door. Nancy North, please come with us.

Nancy sat up. Pain swung in her head like a wrecking ball. Her ribs ached.

Felix, she thought. It was Felix who had done this to her. Michelle had lied, and Felix had put her away. She was locked in the dark and he had sent her there.

Nancy struggled to make the jumble into a narrative. If it was a narrative, one thing leading to the next, other people would understand. They had to see that this wasn't about her being psychotic. This was about a young woman who had been killed. Nancy had been pulled into someone else's story. She knew Kira had been killed, because that was why she herself had been sectioned: someone was trying to make her look mad so that she wouldn't be listened to or believed. Her incarceration was the proof that Kira had been murdered and the murder was proof that she wasn't mad.

If she could only persuade people that she was being called psychotic precisely because she wasn't, then they would have to let her go.

That sounded wrong. It sounded a bit deranged.

She needed to get the narrative right because she couldn't be in this place a moment longer or she really would go mad and what they said she was, she would become. And she had to keep the rage and terror tamped down and concentrate on her calm, rational explanation. My name is Nancy North and I am not mad. People are trying to make me look mad because I know the truth. Except that was what mad people said.

*

In time, the single star faded, and the window lightened. There were sounds. The distant rumble of traffic. A bird outside the window. Brisk footsteps in the corridor. Nancy imagined all the corridors and all the rooms with the pane of glass in the door so that people outside could stare in. There was nowhere to hide. They wanted to get into her mind as well, peer at the secrets in there, all the foolish hopes and desires. She turned her face to the pillow and closed her eyes.

'Nancy. Nancy. Are you awake.'

Female voice. Northern. Kind – or at least not unkind.

Nancy turned and opened her eyes. She half sat, blinking and slightly dizzy. The worst of the headache had gone, just a heavy dull throb remaining. She felt raw and frail and puny.

She tried to say something. It came out as a parched grunt, but the woman understood and poured water from a jug into a beaker and handed it to her.

Nancy drank eagerly, water dribbling down her chin. She looked at her right wrist but her watch was gone. She remembered now how they had taken it from her when she came here. They had taken her necklace, her earrings, everything stripped away from her.

'Time,' she said.

'It's nearly nine o'clock. You've slept for hours.'

Nancy had no sense of having slept at all. She had been wiped out, drugged into a dreamless sleep that could have been minutes or years.

'Time for your medicine.'

She held out a small plastic container in which there were four pink pills.

'No,' said Nancy.

'They are just—'

'No way.'

'Doctor's orders,' said the woman. Her voice didn't seem quite so kind anymore.

'You're just trying to knock me out again.'

'The doctor will be here soon and will explain everything.' She moved the pills closer, almost under Nancy's nose. 'These will help you keep calm.'

'I don't want to be calm. I need to tell my story. It's urgent.'

'You can tell your story soon enough,' said the woman. 'We encourage patients to tell their stories. It's all part of the process of recovery.'

'I shouldn't be here. It's a mistake. They want to keep me quiet.'

'Nancy, we're here to make you better.' Now she was talking as if Nancy was a small child on the edge of a tantrum. 'You were very agitated when you came yesterday. Don't worry. We're all on your side.'

She rattled the pills encouragingly.

'What can I say to make you believe me?' Nancy stared into the woman's unyielding face. 'Nothing? Are you telling me there's nothing I can say or do to change this?'

'I'm just here to give you your medication.'

'I don't need medicine. There's nothing wrong with me.'

'A lot of people say that when they first arrive.' Her voice grew sterner. 'You know that we can make you take it, if you refuse to do so voluntarily? You don't want that, do you?'

'Give them to me,' said Nancy.

She took the container and hurled the pills across the room.

'That wasn't very sensible.'

THIRTY

Everything felt blurry, all the edges felt soft. Nancy wasn't sure whether time was moving very slowly or very quickly or whether it was moving at all. But the next thing she was aware of was the sound of footsteps and a key in the door and there were people around her dressed in green and white. She was grasped on both arms and both legs, so that she couldn't move.

'What are you doing?' she cried out.

'Turn her over,' said a female voice.

The room seemed to rotate. Instead of looking up at a fluorescent light screened with metal mesh, she was now face down against the rough surface of a mattress. Something hard, a button, was jammed against her nose. She could hardly breathe. Something heavy was pressing down on her back, someone's knee maybe.

The same female voice now spoke close to her ear.

'We don't like it when you fuck us around and you're not a good girl. It's very, very boring and we hate being bored. If you don't take your medicine, then we'll make you take it, and it might teach you a bit of a lesson.' Her voice became a little more distant but also louder. 'Okay, pull her trousers down.'

She felt hands on her waistband and her trousers, and her knickers were pulled down to just above her knees. She could feel the coldness of the air. She knew she was being looked at. She knew there were men in the room. Her mouth was jammed against the mattress, so she couldn't speak. She just screamed and groaned like an animal. There was a jab in her buttock and a sensation of cold spreading into her and her trousers were pulled up again.

She was pulled round and saw a blurry face looking down at her.

'You mess us around and we'll put you in solitary for a week. Got it?'

Nancy felt a tiredness so great that it was like a liquid she was submerged in. She drifted between a sleep that felt like being awake and a wakefulness that was like being in a dream. Gradually she became aware of her surroundings. She was in a room alone. The door was closed. Sometimes a little slat opened, and she saw eyes looking at her. The walls were a dirty green and they were bare except that high in the wall opposite the door was a small, barred window, too high for her to look out of or even to reach.

There was nothing in the room. A few times – she couldn't remember how many – a heavily built nurse led her out of the room and along a corridor and helped her onto a toilet. The door opened and she was given a tray with a plastic mug of tea and piece of toast covered with strawberry jam and an apple. Breakfast, she thought dimly, it must be morning. She had to sit on the bed with her back to the wall and balance the tray on her thighs. Even after she had finished, she was ravenously hungry, but the food did something to cover the horrible taste in her mouth, dry, sour and metallic.

The door opened again, and the nurse took the tray.

'You've got an appointment,' she said.

Nancy was led along a corridor lined with rooms like the one she had slept in. It felt partly like a high school, partly like a prison. The nurse led her through a common space where a group of people were watching a daytime chat show, then took a bunch of keys from her pocket and unlocked a door. The atmosphere felt suddenly different, like an office, newly decorated with pot plants and pictures on the walls. The nurse knocked on a second door and in response to a voice from inside, opened it, steered Nancy through and shut the door behind her.

THIRTY-ONE

Nancy looked around, blinking. She felt like she had escaped from her nightmare back into the real world. The room was both soothing and bright. Ahead was a window looking out on a large garden. She could see a lawn and a large beech tree. On one wall was a large photograph of a fox – brightly, fiercely red – on a frozen lake.

A young woman was sitting in an armchair. She was about Nancy's own age, with short brown hair, a freckled face. She was wearing jeans and a bright yellow sweater with sleeves that reached just below her elbows. She smiled and gestured at Nancy to sit on the sofa that was against one wall, facing the photograph of the fox.

'Are you okay?' she said. She sounded more like a concerned friend than a doctor.

When Nancy started to speak, she realised how dry her mouth was. Her voice was a croak.

'I've been sectioned. I've been restrained. I've been forcibly given medication.'

'I'm really sorry,' said the woman. 'I hope we can get this sorted out.'

'Who are you?'

'My name's Stef, Stef Cavendish. I'm a doctor here.'

'You said you were sorry. What are you sorry about?'

Dr Cavendish took a phone from her pocket and laid it on the arm of the sofa.

'Is it all right if I record our conversation? It's perfectly okay to say no.'

'I'd like you to,' said Nancy. 'I'd like there to be a record of what I say.'

'Good,' said Dr Cavendish and leaned over and tapped on the screen of her phone. She looked down at it. 'I think it's working.'

'Am I free to call someone?'

'Of course.'

'Can I call a lawyer?'

'Absolutely.'

'Now. This moment. Can I call someone now?'

Dr Cavendish smiled again.

'We can sort all that out. But first, I thought we could just have a chat about what's brought you here and then I can make a quick assessment.'

'What kind of assessment?'

'Are you clear about your situation?'

'Clear? I don't even know where I am. How can that be allowed?'

'You're in Oakwood Place.'

'I've never heard of it. What is it? Where is it?'

'It's a specialist mental health unit. We're in Kenton.'

'Kenton? Where's Kenton?'

'You were lucky to get a place.'

'I don't want a place. I just want to get out. I want to get back to my life.'

'That's what we all want. We want you to be back home as soon as it's safe.'

'I didn't say anything about wanting to be back home.'

Dr Cavendish showed a flicker of interest.

'What do you mean by that?'

Nancy hesitated. 'It's not important. This is difficult for me. I'm finding it difficult to trust people at the moment.'

'Why is that?'

Nancy gestured around her.

'Because I'm here. The people around me conspired behind my back and they made up things and exaggerated things and now I'm here and I'm not free to leave.'

'Can I suggest something?'

'Sure.'

'You're talking about your friends conspiring behind your back. I wonder if you might consider looking at it another way. Do you think it's possible that your friends and your neighbours were actually trying to help you behind your back? Being restrained under the Mental Health Act, as you have been, is only done under very special emergency circumstances. Basically, it means that there is an imminent possibility of the person being a threat to themselves or to someone else. I've read your report and it seems that more than one person had those fears for you.'

'They wanted to get rid of me. They wanted to shut me up.'

'Nancy,' Dr Cavendish said, almost in a tone of reproach, 'is that what friends do?'

'Who said they were my friends?'

'One of them is your partner.'

Nancy looked down at the floor before answering. On the terracotta-coloured lino floor was a richly patterned rug, a red square and a yellow circle on a blue background. She looked back up at the doctor.

'You know I've been in a psychiatric hospital before?'

'Yes.'

'And you know I've been put on medication, and I've taken it regularly and responded well to it.'

'That's what Dr Lowe says.'

'But once people know that about you, they look at you in a different way. Every odd thing you do, anything you say, if you get a bit sad, a bit angry, people think that might be a sign of you going crazy again. You're not allowed to be different.' She looked more sharply at the doctor. 'My boyfriend, Felix, you ask why he'd do something like this to me. I think he almost relishes the idea of "looking after" me. I think he's like one of those people who like the idea of having a cat but they want to keep it inside all the time, they don't want it to go outside into the world, they just want it for themselves.' She stopped herself and wondered if she had said too much. 'You probably think I'm being paranoid.'

Dr Cavendish leaned towards Nancy.

'Do you already think that I'm another of the people who are your enemy?'

'I don't know. Do you think I belong in here?'

'I would like for you not to be here.'

'That's not an answer.' Nancy spoke in as calm a voice as she could manage. 'Do I seem unsafe?'

Dr Cavendish made a dismissive gesture.

'Forget about all that,' she said. 'You don't need to try and convince me of anything. Forget I'm a doctor. Just imagine that we're two friends meeting for coffee and tell me everything that's been going on in the last few days.'

Nancy felt a sudden rush of relief. Perhaps this could all be over. All right, she said to herself. I'll stop trying to be clever. I'll just say it. So she started to describe all that had happened since she and Felix had moved into the Harlesden flat. She talked about the dislocation in moving to a part of London she didn't know. She talked about her brief, mild psychotic episode, the voices and the visions and the meeting with Kira. She talked of the shock of the death. She described the awkward meetings with the neighbours.

And it did really feel like she was talking to a friend who understood her. Stef Cavendish never looked shocked or disapproving. She nodded in sympathy, she smiled, she looked thoughtful, but she never interrupted or made comments, even when Nancy paused. Nancy didn't leave any of the awkward bits out. She was determined not to be evasive. She described how she had sneaked into Kira's flat; she described the row in the street, the used condom she had found, her growing certainty that Kira hadn't taken her own life but been killed.

'I'm not proud of everything I've done,' she said finally. 'I've made some mistakes. But this whole sectioning was being done by people for their own reasons. Michelle Strauss saying I threatened her and threatened myself, that was just completely made up from nothing. She's just doing that for her own reasons, and we have to find out what those reasons are. And I've got this feeling that Felix doesn't like the idea of me recovering and moving on with my life. I was planning to leave him, I was actually packing my bags, when I was sectioned. This is his way of keeping me. There. That's my story. What do you think?'

Dr Cavendish nodded slowly.

'Thank you,' she said. 'That was really helpful.'

'Good. Now, as we talked about before, I've got the right to contact people and I've also got the right to challenge my detention. I've done my part by being as frank with you as possible and now I'd like to make some calls.'

'Let's not get ahead of ourselves,' said Dr Cavendish.

'What do you mean by that? I just want to do what I have a right to do.'

'Our priority is your health and that comes before everything.'

'What does that mean?'

'For the moment, I want to make some adjustments to your medication, perhaps increase them a bit.'

'You mean the anti-psychotics that have been knocking me out for days?'

'It's a matter of restoring your equilibrium.'

'What are you talking about? Haven't you listened to what I've been saying?'

'I've listened very carefully and now I think we need to work together to control your psychotic episodes.'

'I've told you. I have controlled them. I'm not psychotic. I was sent here to stop me from speaking the truth.'

'As I say, we need to do this together. Recognising these delusions is the first step on the road to recovery and you need to show me that you are co-operating and the first way you can show this is by taking the medication that I prescribe to you.'

Nancy wanted to shout, she wanted to jump up and down, she wanted to shake this grinning woman who had been sitting opposite her and pretending to be her friend, but with the most enormous effort she spoke in a steady tone.

'I know about this medication. I probably know as much about it as you do, because I've taken it and you haven't. The point of it is to subdue floridly psychotic patients by making them almost unconscious. What I need to do is to phone people who will be sympathetic to me and explain the situation I'm in so they can help me.'

'What you need to do is to get better and the way you'll get better is by co-operating and taking your medicine. I've got your best interests at heart.'

'Forget all that,' said Nancy, more harshly now. 'All that

pretending to be my friend. I just want what I've got a right to. Give me a phone and let me talk to someone.'

'I don't think that would be helpful just at the moment.'

'I'm not going to take any medication. That'll turn me into one of the other zombies out there watching TV all day. Just keep me under observation and you'll see that I'm absolutely calm and lucid.' She noticed her voice had become very loud. 'Calm and lucid,' she repeated in what was almost a yell.

'Please don't shout. It doesn't help.'

'I'm not shouting,' shouted Nancy.

Somehow, without her noticing, Dr Cavendish must have pressed an alarm bell because the door was suddenly thrown open and Nancy found herself surrounded by uniforms. She tried to tell them that she could walk on her own, but she was hauled off her feet and carried out of the room, her head banging against the doorframe so that everything glowed in yellow spots. She started to shout, and she felt a blow in her stomach, accidental or deliberate, that winded her.

Back in her room she was thrown on her stomach once more. She heard someone laughing as her trousers were pulled down and felt the jab in her buttock and the grey softness descending.

THIRTY-TWO

'When I get out of here,' Nancy said to the next doctor she saw, a man this time, with a thin, nervous face and thin, nervous hands that he kept cracking, 'I'm going to make a complaint.'

'That's your right,' he said, in a deferential tone.

'I was forcibly injected. My phone has been taken away from me. The staff treat people like animals.'

'I'm sorry you feel this.'

'I am going to make such a stink. As for the people who put me in here, they'll regret it.'

Her voice cracked. She heard the false bravado in her tone. But the doctor leaned forward in his chair.

'That sounds like a threat.'

'That's because it *is* a threat.'

'You know that you are here under section two, which allows you to be detained for your own safety and the safety of others for twenty-eight days.'

'I know. I've lost count, though. How many days have I been here? Two? Three? How long do I have left?'

'That rather depends on you.'

'What does that mean?'

'If we still feel that you are at risk, or are putting other people at risk, then you can be detained under section three of the Mental Health Act.'

'Section three? What's that?'

'Under section three you can be detained for up to six months.'

'No.'

'Which can be extended.'

'But that's not right.'

'We want you to go home as soon as possible. But it does depend on you working with us on your recovery: taking the drugs, having insight into your condition.'

'You're saying you could keep me here as long as you want?' The words came out in a whisper.

'We can keep you as long as we feel it's for your benefit, and that you aren't a threat to other people's safety.'

'How can this be allowed? I'm a prisoner but I've not done anything wrong.'

'You're a patient. You need to stay here until you're cured, until you're safe.'

'I'll go mad if I'm kept here.'

The words hung in the air.

'You need to understand your condition and work with us so that you can recover,' said the doctor. He steepled his fingers together and regarded her with an expression she couldn't read. 'And that will take as long as it takes.'

She didn't know what day it was, what time it was, how long she had been in this place. She lay on her bed in a dazed huddle of wretchedness, her eyes half closed, and listened to the sounds coming from outside the door. Someone was crying. It was a terrible sound. Would nobody comfort her?

A door slammed. A woman laughed. She had an itch on her calf but felt too listless to reach down and scratch it.

When she woke once more, her head throbbed and the light coming in from the barred windows hurt her eyes. She could feel the sting from where she had been injected. She could smell herself, stale and unwashed. She looked down at what she was wearing: loose joggers, a mustard-coloured sweatshirt, bright striped socks that Felix had given her. She felt her mouth tighten into a grimace when she thought of Felix.

Nobody believed her. Nobody would listen to her. Out there, in the world, people she had turned to had betrayed her. In here, the nurses and the care workers, even the doctor with the nice smile and bright, enquiring eyes, treated her appeals for help as a symptom of disorder. The more she said that she shouldn't be in here, the more convinced they became that she should, she must. Every time she argued her sanity, she confirmed she was deluded.

She had to find someone who trusted and believed her and would be her voice. Someone who would fight for her and get her out. She swung her legs off the bed and sat up properly, pushing her hands through her matted hair. Who? Who would be on her side?

A few weeks ago, she would have said Bridie. She and Bridie had been friends for years, had stood by each other through hard times. But Bridie had contacted Felix after they had visited the would-be restaurant – and the thought of that little unloved space that she had planned to rescue made her chest ache – and told him she had been agitated. What was the word Felix had used? Grandiose. So she couldn't turn to Bridie. Perhaps Sam or Delia would help – but they had been there too, on that day of hope, and perhaps they had felt the same. Obviously not Felix. He was her enemy now, with his tender smile and soft, patronising voice. Calling her 'darling' and putting her in here.

The woman was still crying, though more softly now, a sound of defeat. Nancy stood up, slid her feet into the trainers under her bed, and went to the door. She half expected it to be locked, but it swung open and she found herself back in the corridor. She went into the common room, where the television was on. It was always on. Two women were sitting side by side, staring at the screen. One of them was barely more than a girl, with a pasty face and hair scraped back into a high knot. The other was middle-aged, with a sagging face and pale, cracked lips. They didn't look up at Nancy, just stared at the quiz show.

A nurse came in. She was large, with a shiny bob and apple cheeks.

'Hello,' said Nancy. 'I'm Nancy.'

'I know who you are.' The woman didn't sound as nice as she looked.

'Can I have my mobile, please? I need to make some calls.'

'Your mobile?'

'Yes. It's quite urgent.'

'I don't think so.'

'What?'

'You can't have it.'

'That's not true. I'm not a prisoner in here, I'm a patient. It's my right!'

'Right?' She smiled.

'Yes.'

'It's not a right, it's a privilege,' said the woman. 'Each ward has its own policy. Here, we remove all mobile devices until there's been a risk assessment.'

'Risk assessment? Why should having a mobile be a risk?'

The nurse shrugged.

'Lot of ways.'

'When will this happen?'

'Don't know. We're short-staffed at the moment. We can't even get light bulbs changed.'

'This is fucking crap.'

The young woman watching the television sniggered.

'Watch your language,' the nurse said.

'I need to make some calls. What am I supposed to do? Who can I complain to?'

'You can fill out a form.'

The nurse left and Nancy subsided into a chair. On the screen, two eager young men with identical bouncy hair styles were debating with each other whether the capital of Australia was Sydney or Melbourne, while a clock ticked loudly.

'It's Canberra, you twits,' said the young woman. 'Do you want to use my phone?'

'What?'

'You can use mine.'

'Really?'

'Just don't be caught with it.'

She held out her mobile in its shiny pink case and Nancy took it and pushed it into her pocket.

'Thank you,' she said. 'Very much.'

'Sure.'

Nancy went back to her room. She sat on the bed, with her back to the door, so nobody would be able to peer through the little aperture and see what she was doing. She keyed in the number and heard it ring.

'Hello,' said the man who answered, speaking in a loud and cheery voice. He worked from home nowadays, for the same marketing firm he had worked for when Nancy was born. 'Robert speaking.'

'Dad?' Nancy kept her voice low. 'Dad, it's me, Nancy.'

'Nancy?' His voice changed to one of concern and alarm.

'You have to help me.'

'What? Can you speak up?'

'There's been a horrible mistake. I'm in hospital, in a mental health unit.' She struggled to remember the name. 'It's called Oakwood Place. In Kenton. I don't actually know where Kenton is.' She could feel a sob forcing its way up her throat but made herself stay calm. Her father hated any shows of emotion.

'It's in West London. North-west. Near Harrow, I think. Anyway, it's all a mistake. There's nothing wrong with me. I need you to get me out of here.'

'Nancy,' said her father. 'We're very sorry indeed this has happened again. You'll be out soon.'

'No. Listen to me. You're good at things like this, Dad. That's why I've called you. You can get me out. Or find me a lawyer. Can you do that for me? Please?'

There was a brief silence before her father spoke again, and when he did it was in a level tone, as if he was trying to calm her down.

'I know it must be very hard for you, but it's for your own safety.'

'I get it,' said Nancy flatly. 'You've talked to Felix.'

'He came to see us.'

'Of course he did. Getting his story heard first.'

'He was very upset.'

'Poor him.'

'He feels terrible.' There was a pause. 'So does your mother.'

Nancy wanted to say that this wasn't about her mother, but she couldn't because in a way, of course, it was. That unspoken thing.

'I'm sorry about that,' she managed.

'We both thought you wouldn't do this again.'

'What does that even mean?'

'It means you have to take responsibility.'

Nancy felt anger rip through her.

'Like Mum does, you mean, when she gets ill.'

There it was. A silence followed. She could hear her father breathing, waiting for her to apologise. Nancy didn't speak.

'I don't know what you mean,' her father said at last.

'She has never once admitted to herself or to me that she has it too. I mean, whatever I've got, whatever makes me have these horrible episodes, comes from her. And you never have either.'

She thought of times when she was a child, when her mother had scared her with strange stories that she told with glittery-eyed urgency; times when her mother had been practically locked into her room by her father, meals carried in to her on a tray, large beakers of milk and slabs of over-cooked chicken breast, and strange sounds coming from behind the closed door.

'I need to go.' Her father's voice was cold.

'No. Don't go. Dad, please. Please listen. I'm begging you. I shouldn't be in here. I can't be. You need to believe what I say, not what other people say about me. You're my father. You have to save me from this.'

Tears were rolling down her cheeks down.

'Nancy, you need professional help so that you can get better.'

'But I was framed,' she said, and heard him sigh.

The last vestiges of hope left her. She ended the call and returned the mobile to its owner and pressed her face to the window, looking out at the world.

THIRTY-THREE

The second session with Dr Stephanie Cavendish seemed completely unlike the first. Her office had felt homely and re-assuring. Now it felt unreal, like a stage set. The photograph of the fox on the ice had felt glowing and warm. Now Nancy just felt the coldness of the ice, sucking the life out of everything around it. Stephanie Cavendish had seemed like someone who could have been her friend. Now she saw her as an opponent, trying to lure her into revealing secrets that could be used against her.

It felt so different that Nancy wondered if she was being paranoid. Was this what madness felt like?

'I was sorry that our last meeting ended the way it did,' said Dr Cavendish.

Nancy considered how to answer this. Was the doctor still trying to pretend that they were like two girlfriends chatting over coffee? It didn't matter. She knew what she had to do.

'Why were you sorry?' she asked meekly.

'Because you were angry, in pain and in denial.'

Nancy looked out of the window and then back again.

'I don't want to be any of those things. We started off on the wrong foot.'

'I'm glad to hear you say that.'

'I saw another doctor,' Nancy said.

'I know. Dr Tost. He told me about your session.'

'He said I could be moved from section two to section three and if that happens, I could be here for years. I could be locked up for the rest of my life. That can't be right, can it?'

Dr Cavendish gave her friendly smile.

'That sounds a bit over-dramatic. What we care about is your safety and the safety of those around you.'

Nancy tried to make herself smile back.

'Look at me,' she said. 'Do I look like a threat to the safety of people around me?'

'You threatened to kill someone.'

Once more Nancy had to stop herself shouting that this was completely untrue. Instead, she looked thoughtful and nodded her head several times.

'I want to get better,' she said. 'I want to leave here and start my life again. I suppose you want the same thing.'

'Of course we do.' That same smile.

'But how will you know when I'm safe to let out? What do I have to do?'

'That's a complicated question. Our conversations with you form part of our assessment. But what is more important is your behaviour overall, your ability to follow rules, to take your medication, to take part in the group therapy sessions. Above all, you need to have genuine insight into your condition. You need to take responsibility for it and work with us to help yourself. When we last met, you were telling me about how the man you lived with, your friends and your neighbours, had got together to make you look insane and get you sectioned. These are your friends and the man who loves you. Do you hear how that sounds?' Now Dr Cavendish wasn't smiling. 'I'm going to be frank with you. What I heard and saw at our last session was a woman who perceives everyone around her as an enemy and if she were released, there would be a very real danger that she would carry out the threats she has made.'

Nancy felt like she'd been punched in the stomach. She could barely speak.

'What do I do?' was all she could manage.

'Be good. Do what you're told. Show you can be a citizen and that you're facing up to the truth. It's really very simple.'

Nancy clenched her hands. She put an expression of contrition on her face. She looked the doctor in the eyes.

'I will,' she said with great earnestness. 'I want to be well.'

'It will take work and courage.'

'I know. I'm ready.'

'Don't worry,' said a voice.

Nancy had been lying on her bed, lost in thought, almost in a dream, and the voice had startled her. A nurse was standing in the doorway. He was one of the male nurses. Tall, with long black hair, tied in a pony tail. His lower arms were a sleeve of tattoos, signs and symbols and fantasy warriors. The name tag on his chest identified him as Mil Burns.

'What did you say?'

'You looked like you were worrying about something.'

'I was just thinking.'

'You didn't come to lunch,' he said. 'I came to check that you were all right.'

'I'm all right. I just wasn't hungry.'

'Do you want me to bring you something?'

Nancy looked round at him in some surprise.

'No. I'm fine. I'll make up for it at supper.'

'Is anything up?'

'I'm just trying to get things straight in my head.'

'What sort of things?'

Nancy swung her legs down onto the floor so that she was sitting instead of lying. She looked at the nurse once more. It felt a shock to be talked to in a normal tone.

'I had a meeting with one of the doctors.'

'Which one?'

'Dr Cavendish.'

The nurse grinned.

'Stef Cavendish. Yeah, she can be a bit of a challenge.'

'What do you mean by that?'

'She thinks highly of herself. Let's leave it at that.'

'I don't care if she thinks highly of herself. I just want her to think that I'm okay and that I can be discharged.'

'And how's that going?'

'Not very well. I think I'm seen as ...' Nancy stopped and searched for the right word. 'Unco-operative.'

'Yeah,' said Mil. 'I've heard a bit about that. You want some advice?'

'I think I could do with some.'

Mil pushed the door shut and came and sat down on the bed beside Nancy. She could smell his scent and also something medicinal.

'It's all a bit of a game in here,' he said. 'It's like being in the playground at school. It's all about being in the right gang or the right friendship group. You've got the cool kids and you've got the people who are picked on and left out.'

'I thought it was about curing people,' said Nancy.

Mil laughed. 'Mainly it's about getting through the day without having too many disasters. I've had my eye on you. You don't look as if you belong here.'

'That's right. I don't belong here.'

'As I say, it's all a game and if you want to get out of here, you've got to play the game. You've been rubbing people the wrong way, not taking your meds, not co-operating. All these people, they're only human, and if you make their job difficult, then they'll make things difficult for you.'

'I can see that,' said Nancy. 'I didn't mean to cause trouble. I'm going to try to be a bit more easygoing.'

'That's the spirit. What you need, in this place, is to have people in your corner. On your side. I mean, you're someone who'd have no trouble making friends. You're beautiful. Has anyone told you that? If not, they should have.'

He put his hand on her head and softly ran it down her hair. Nancy froze. She felt like a jolt of cold electricity was running through her body. His hand moved down until she felt it in the middle of her back.

'I'd like you stop doing that,' she said.

'I'm just being friendly,' he said. 'You know, what you'll discover, is that if you have a special friend in here, then you can get any help you want. I can do you a lot of good.'

She moved away from him and stood up with her back to the wall. He stood up as well and stepped towards her. He was tall, towering over her.

'As I say, I could be a good friend to you. I could also be an enemy and I can tell you that you really wouldn't want me as an enemy.' He lifted his hand to cup her face. She flinched and jerked away from him, and he laughed. 'Hey. You should just relax. You might even enjoy it.'

He dropped his hand and gripped her breast. She could smell his sour breath. He leaned in towards her. She waited until his body was up against hers and then, with all the force she could manage, she brought her knee up into his groin. He staggered with a howl and Nancy followed him, punching and scratching at him in any way that she could. Everything was a mist and suddenly out of this mist came a blow that caught her in the face and then she was flung back against the wall. There were screams and shouts and she wasn't sure whether they were coming from her or from someone else.

She heard him swearing at her and then the door was flung open with a bang, and she was being grasped and held down on the bed. Her eyes were blurry with tears, and she could taste blood in her mouth. She swallowed some of it and it made her cough and choke. She frantically tried to turn to spit it out but she was held immovable on her back. She thought for a moment that she would black out.

She heard his voice, panting.

'She went for me, the bitch. I came into her room to tell her about lunch, and she went for me. Scratched me and punched me. She's completely out of fucking control.'

'He tried to rape me,' she said. 'He tried to force me. He said he'd help me if I had sex and then he . . .'

She felt a hand over her mouth so that she could barely breathe. His face was right against hers.

'Are you listening? Are you listening? You cause me any more grief and I'll slam your face against the wall and no man'll ever look at you again. You get that?'

The hand was removed from her mouth.

'Did you hear what he said?' She looked around at the face hovering above her. 'He was threatening me. I want to report him.'

Another face appeared close to hers. A nurse, a woman this time. She was grinning, so Nancy could see that one of her top teeth was missing.

'Threaten you? I'm sorry, love, I didn't hear that. I think what you need is a day or two in solitary. And if you cause any more trouble, we'll make it a week. You get me?'

'If you let me go, I can talk calmly.'

'Let you go after what you did to our mate's face? Are you having a laugh? Right, guys.'

'I can walk.'

'If you keep talking, we'll shove a flannel in your mouth.'

Nancy was dragged out of her room and along the corridor. She saw the lights above her, the cracks in the ceiling, curious faces staring down at her as she passed. She heard a door clanking open and she was deposited on a bed. She looked around. It was a grey room with nothing but a bed, a toilet and, on the wall opposite the bed, a large window through which she could be observed. She was alone except for the female nurse.

'All right?' said the nurse.

'I want to talk to someone,' said Nancy. 'I want to talk to a doctor.'

'If you make a fuss,' said the nurse, 'we'll close the curtain and give Mil the key to your cell. Now, what was it you were saying?'

Nancy took a deep breath.

'I'm fine,' she said. 'I don't need to talk to anyone.'

THIRTY-FOUR

A nurse came to her cell. Nancy took the pills she gave her and washed them down with water, then opened her mouth to show that they were gone.

'That's a good girl,' said the nurse approvingly.

Nancy bared her teeth in a smile.

She took the pills the next morning as well.

She did sit-ups and press-ups.

She recited things to herself – snatches of half-remembered poems, the times table, holiday phrases of French and Spanish, anything to hold herself tethered to the world outside.

She ate the gluey sandwiches they brought to her, the plasticky bread sticking to her teeth. She even said thank you. When had she last eaten a proper meal? She couldn't remember. She must have been given food since arriving here, but the hours and days were just a grey sludge. The last meal she could recollect was in the flat – spaghetti with roasted tomatoes and feta cheese. She hadn't even made it herself. It had been given to her and she had eaten it dutifully, knowing she was being watched. It had been so long since she had cooked a proper meal, though since she was a child, cooking had been her passion.

Out of the blue, she had the clearest memory of first learning how to crack open an egg and separate the yolk from the white, letting the gloop of the white slide into a clean bowl while the yolk remained in the shell. Six yolks for custard. She loved making custard. Slow cooking. Dough rising into a pillow.

She put a forearm across her eyes and in the darkness let herself imagine the meal she would cook when she got out of here. It was winter. Something simple, warming. She would make a creamy, satisfying dhal with coconut milk and lime.

In her mind, she went through the steps: she sliced the onions thinly with her favourite knife; sizzled them in olive oil; roasted coriander and cumin seeds till their aroma was in her nostrils; crushed garlic, cut chillies into little rounds. She added the lentils, coconut milk and vegetable stock, and stirred, steam in her face. While it slowly cooked, she would make yoghurt flatbreads to mop it up, a crisp green salad, a glass of red wine in her hand. She would eat it alone, dreamily, only thinking about what it tasted like, letting the good flavours comfort her.

She slid into a deep sleep.

On the third day she was allowed back into her own room.

She sat in the common room and watched a programme about house improvements in a wash of drugged drowsiness. Her distress stood to one side. Her anger felt like a fire that had almost dulled to its embers. Almost.

There were other women there as well. The middle-aged one from earlier; one who rocked from side to side and bit her fingers; one with a mop of blonde hair and bright red nails who introduced herself as Gloria; one who couldn't sit in one place for long but went to stand at the window, staring out at the night. Nancy wondered if any of them was the one who had sobbed like an abandoned child.

*

She swallowed down her pills the next morning. The clock in the common room said it was ten past eleven, but it had said that last night as well. She played a game of Scrabble with the young woman who had lent her the mobile phone. She was called Josie and had vertical scars on her wrists. She was nineteen and had tried to take her own life on multiple occasions, the first when she was only fifteen. She had been sectioned four times before, twice when she was still a minor, and had been in Oakwood Place for two weeks and three days. She said it was by far the grimmest, nastiest place she'd been put in, and was notorious for its harshness. Everyone who came here was made worse, not better. Someone should do something about it but no one ever would. They had all become invisible.

She easily beat Nancy at Scrabble.

'My name is Nancy North.' Nancy sketched a smile at the seven women sitting in the circle. She felt self-conscious, tongue-tied, and had no idea what to say next. She tried to imagine herself talking to Helena, with her soft white hair and her deep brown eyes, but her head was humming and there were floaters in her eyes, adding to her befuddled sense that this experience was real and at the same time a horrible dream from which she might lurch awake. 'I've not been here long,' she added.

'You've made enough noise though,' said one of the women, sitting across from her. She had long dark hair in braids and a curved nose like a beak. The woman next to her gave a chuckle.

Nancy clenched her fists. Her nails dug into the soft flesh of her palms.

'Sorry,' she said meekly.

'I'm glad you're with us today, Nancy,' said the therapist.

Nancy would have known she was the therapist even if she hadn't already introduced herself at the door. She was quite young, probably in her late thirties or early forties, with a nimbus of soft black hair around her oval face, and she wore tapered trousers in a muted check, a grey flannel shirt, neat ankle boots. Her skin was smooth, her nails shone and she sat very upright. She had come from the outside and everything about her was clean, tidy, pleasing.

Most of the women in the circle sat in disarray, with their tatty clothes and slumped shoulders – and Nancy was among them. When she had climbed out of bed this morning, she had pulled on the same clothes that she had worn yesterday, given her hair a cursory brush before tying it back. She had seen her face in the mirror: tired, pale, bruised, fearful. A couple of the women were more smartly dressed and looked alert. But even they looked like inmates: perhaps the expression in their eyes. Perhaps the powerlessness that bound them all together.

'I thought it was a good idea,' she said.

'Would you like to tell us what brought you to Oakwood?'

Nancy looked at the therapist, so professionally friendly, and then round the circle.

'I heard voices.' She spoke flatly and kept her gaze fixed on the window. 'They weren't real.'

That at least was the truth.

The therapist nodded at her encouragingly, leaning forward slightly in a posture of availability. She wants me to spill my guts, thought Nancy. That's what this circle is all about – women sharing their torment and showing their pain. The doctor had called it having insight.

'I know I need to work hard to have insight into my condition,' she said in her robot voice. 'Only then can I move on.'

'Fuck that.' The woman with braids spoke in a loud voice, almost a shout. 'What did your voices tell you? Did they tell you you were Joan of Arc or something?'

'They told me I wasn't safe.'

That was true as well.

The woman beside Nancy put a hand on her arm. She had a face made of wrinkles.

'Nobody's safe, babe. Have you lived this long without knowing that?'

THIRTY-FIVE

She had a shower and washed her hair with shampoo from an oversized plastic bottle. It smelt of apples. She dressed in jeans, a clean shirt, a chunky cardigan, wondering who had chosen the clothes she had here. Felix? Mostly he had packed as if the weather was warm. There was even a checked dress in the case, and a grey linen jumpsuit with a pink belt that she hadn't worn for years. Most people here wore tracksuits, sweatshirts, things you could pull on with minimum effort.

She cleaned her teeth and stared in the speckled mirror at the face that stared back. Hollow cheeks, cracked lips, a bruise on her cheek, a scratch running from her jaw to her ear. How had that happened?

'Can I go outside?' she asked a care worker when she went into the common room, where the television played to no one. He looked like a schoolboy and had pimples on his forehead and gel in his hair.

'If you don't mind freezing to death,' he said.

She didn't have a coat or jacket, so she put a blanket round her shoulders and went out into the corridor.

It all felt unreal. Her feet tapping on the linoleum floor, shouts in the distance, someone talking to themselves behind a closed door, the exit slowly coming towards her as she walked.

The garden was a large walled enclosure with no means of escape. There were a few leafless trees, and some shrubs in a bed at the far end. The care worker was right. It was freezing. Her feet ached in their thin trainers, her cheeks stung, and her gloveless fingers throbbed. The sky was a dull white and as she walked a few flakes of snow fell.

Nancy didn't know what day it was. She had no sense of how long she had been here. She knew it was nearly December, or perhaps it already was. Christmas was coming. She had to be out before then. She had to be out before the next year started.

She walked in a loop around the garden, then heard feet crunching on the gravel path behind her and turned. It was the nurse with the missing top tooth who had grinned down at her after Mil Burns had assaulted her. She was tall and looked solid. Her shoulders were broad and her hands large. Her badge identified her as Beth Styles. Nancy remembered the nurse laughing, pushing her into the cell, threatening her. She remembered the feel of her hands and the smell that had come off her, sweat and perfume and breath that smelt of coffee. She pulled the blanket more securely around her, feeling weak and helpless.

'Hello,' she said.

Beth Styles made a noise.

'It's trying to snow,' Nancy continued. 'I wish it would. I love snow.' She turned her face towards the blank sky.

'Too cold to stand around,' said the nurse.

'I wanted to say that I'm sorry I made a nuisance of myself,' said Nancy. 'I know you have a hard job and people like me must make it even harder.'

Beth Styles regarded her suspiciously.

'Yeah?' she said.

'I wasn't in my right mind,' said Nancy.

'You were kicking off something rotten.'

'I know. I was angry. I said things I shouldn't have.'

The woman shrugged her heavy shoulders.

'We get used to it,' she said. 'It's part of the job, restraining people, ignoring things they shout at you, crying for help. You get used to it.'

Nancy stared at her, biting her chapped lips.

'That must be difficult,' she said at last.

'We do what we do.'

'Is it very upsetting?'

'Upsetting?'

'Seeing people in such distress.'

'Like I said, you get used to it.'

Nancy, Josie and the woman with long braids, whose name was Roxanne, decorated the plastic Christmas tree that had been put up in the common room. Nothing sharp, nothing metal; no long ropes of tinsel. Plastic baubles in pink, purple, red and green on loops of string.

'Very nice,' said Josie sarcastically, hanging one round her earlobe. 'Makes you feel properly festive, doesn't it?'

The therapist's name was Loretta Slater, but she told Nancy she should call her Lorrie.

'All right, Lorrie,' said Nancy. She smiled, folded her hands in her lap.

There were only five women in the circle this time.

'Who would like to begin?' asked Lorrie. Today she was wearing a green corduroy jacket over tight black trousers and had brushed her hair behind her ears.

Roxanne put up her hand.

'I had a terrible night,' she said.

Everyone waited.

'Terrible,' repeated Roxanne.

'Because you couldn't sleep?' Lorrie asked eventually.

'I was thinking about my little girl,' said Roxanne. 'Missing her mummy.'

And she began to cry. Nancy realised this was the woman she had heard before, sobbing as if her heart must break. She leaned forward, wanting to comfort her in some way.

'That must have been very painful,' said Lorrie.

Roxanne tried to answer, hiccuping and wiping her face with the back of her hand.

'Sorry,' she said eventually. 'It gets to me sometimes.'

'Of course,' said Lorrie. 'Of course it does.'

'If I could only see her. Just the once.'

'Can't you?' asked Nancy.

Josie, sitting next to her, kicked her foot.

'Social services took her,' she hissed.

Nancy sat back in her chair and closed her eyes. When she opened them again, another woman was talking about how the drugs made her feel.

'Groggy,' she said. 'Heavy.'

The other women nodded, and Nancy nodded.

'Kind of numb,' agreed Josie. 'Sometimes that's a relief though.'

Nancy took the opening.

'I agree,' she said. 'I know it's for our own good, but it can feel hard to think properly about all the things I need to think about.'

Lorrie nodded at her encouragingly.

'I'm only just beginning to understand that it was right I should be sent here,' said Nancy, looking from face to face. 'At the beginning, all I felt was a sense of betrayal. I thought I'd been trapped by the people I trusted. I was angry and wretched and self-pitying, and I didn't see how horribly hard it must have been for them as well. One of the things that happened when I was ill was that I lost all empathy for others. I feel ashamed of that.'

'Oh, fucking fuck,' said Josie. 'Really?'

Nancy ignored her.

'The pills calmed me down and gave me a chance to recover. But now I feel they aren't helping so much. It's like a great, thick blanket has been thrown over me.'

'Have you talked to the doctor about it?' Lorrie asked. 'Perhaps the dosage can be decreased.'

'Thank you,' said Nancy gratefully. 'I will do that.'

'What are you up to?' asked Josie.

'I'm working on getting better.'

'I know what you're doing.' She poked Nancy in the ribs with a forefinger. 'I won't tell.'

THIRTY-SIX

'Dr Tost and I feel you should have the use of your mobile,' said Stef Cavendish.

'Really? That's great.'

'I've told the nurse on duty.'

'Thank you.'

'Who will you call?'

'I don't know. I haven't thought about it.'

Who did she want to speak to? Nancy could only think of all the people she didn't want to speak to. Head of the list was Felix.

Helena, she thought. I could talk to her and she would listen.

'Perhaps your partner?'

'I was just about to say that. Yes. I need to talk to Felix. I need to say sorry.'

'Will that be hard for you?'

'Probably. I don't know if he can ever forgive me.'

'Do you think it would be more helpful to speak to him in person?'

'To Felix?' Panic filled Nancy like black smoke. 'You mean, in here?'

'Patients do have visitors.'

'I know.'

Yesterday, Josie had seen her mother and been quiet and sullen all evening.

'The thought makes you uneasy?'

'Do you think I should?'

'*Should* isn't the word I would use. It's not a moral obligation. You might find it helpful and part of the recovery process
to talk about what happened and tell him what you now feel
about his actions and yours. I know you were extremely angry
with him when you were first admitted.'

'I was. I blamed him. I thought he had betrayed me. I was
in such a state that I didn't see things from his point of view
at all. I didn't try and imagine what it must have been like for
him.' She met the doctor's gaze. 'Poor man,' she said softly, as
if talking to herself. 'All he's been through.'

'You can recognise that now?'

'Perhaps it's too late. I wouldn't blame him for never wanting
to see me again.' Nancy covered her eyes with a hand and spoke
in a low voice. 'I feel so terribly ashamed.'

'Shame is a very common reaction among the patients I see.
You were ill.'

'I still feel ashamed. Even if I was ill, I was responsible. All
the people I accused, the people I hurt. I can hardly bear to
think about it.'

'Perhaps you feel it's too early to see your partner.'

'No, no.' Nancy sat up straighter. 'I need to. I owe it to him
and I strongly believe it's part of the recovery. I need to face
up to what I did.'

'It would be a supervised visit,' said the doctor.

'You mean, someone would be there with us?'

'It would be me, or Dr Tost. It's just protocol.'

'You mean, you want to make sure I don't attack him or
something?'

'We want a safe, managed setting.'

Nancy thought of the little cameras in the corridor,

the apertures in the doors of the rooms, eyes everywhere, watching.

'Your partner should check with us before arranging anything,' Cavendish continued. 'As a rule, we don't work at the weekend.'

Nancy smiled. Stephanie Cavendish smiled back.

'Well done, Nancy,' she said.

'There you go.'

The pimply care worker slid the mobile across the surface. 'Bring it here when you need it charged.'

'Can't I just have my charger?'

'No way.' The young man grinned like it was a big joke. 'Ligatures.'

Nancy sat on her bed, her back against the wall, and stared down at the mobile in her lap. There was a sound that made her look up. She saw eyes staring through the little aperture in the door. They disappeared after a few seconds.

She turned the mobile on, tapped in the passcode, saw that she had dozens of messages and missed calls. She ignored them all. She had to do this now, in the same way that you have to jump off a high diving board before your nerves fail.

It rang several times, and then a breathless voice said: 'Nancy?'

'Is this a good time?'

'Yes, of course. Any time is a good time. Hearing your voice, it feels strange.'

'Are you at home?'

'I'm on my way back from work, walking up the road now.'

Nancy glanced out of the window and saw that it was dark.

'What time is it?' she asked.

'Nearly six o'clock.'

'What day? I've lost all track of time here.'

'Day? It's Friday.'

'Friday the what?'

'It's the second of December,' said Felix gently. 'You've been away for eleven days.'

Away. He made it sound like a holiday.

Nancy thought of the rolling darkness of the past eleven days; the muzzy, drugged, boundless horror of it, rough hands turning her, needles jabbing her, Mil Burns grabbing her, people laughing, doors slamming shut, keys turning in the lock, like a nightmare on a loop, repeating and repeating.

'Eleven days,' she repeated. 'Only eleven days.'

'Nancy,' said Felix. 'Darling Nancy, listen to me. You can't begin to imagine how terrible I feel about it all. I was desperate and I was very scared that something truly awful was about to happen. I didn't know what else to do.'

'I know,' said Nancy. She made her voice tender. Her mouth pulled back into an ugly grimace.

'I've been in hell,' he said. 'Worrying about you, going over and over what happened and trying to work out if I could have done anything different.'

She interrupted him.

'Can you come and see me?'

'You mean, in hospital? Of course. Say the word. I'll come any time. I'll come now.'

'You have to arrange it through the hospital.'

'I'll do that. I'll do that at once.'

'We can talk about everything then.'

'What shall I bring? Do you need books, more clothes, food? Just tell me.'

'Bring me my green jumper. And some cookery books.'

'Really? All right, if that's what you want.'

She heard his key turning in the lock. He was walking into the house. The door shut. She heard a voice. A baby crying. She could imagine the hall, the door that led to Kira's room.

'You sound better,' he said. She could tell from his footsteps he was walking up the stairs towards their flat. 'More rational.'

'I feel rational,' she said. 'But let's talk when we meet.'

'You don't hate me?'

'Of course not,' she said. She ran a fingernail along the bare skin of her arm and saw an angry scratch appear.

'I love you very much,' he said, his voice dropping so she could barely hear him. 'I've never loved you more than I do now. We can get through this together.'

Thirty-seven

He would come on Monday. It was just a matter of getting through the weekend. She did the rough calculation. About sixty-five hours. And half of that was numbed, medicated sleep.

On the Saturday morning, she ate porridge and drank tea at the communal table. The porridge was so overcooked and dry that she had to break it off in chunks. She could only swallow it if she drank the stewed, lukewarm tea at the same time. It was like eating damp cardboard, but she needed to put food into her body. Also, there was always a nurse somewhere around, watching, judging.

There was the temptation to stay in her room, pull the covers over her head, try to forget where she was and wait until Monday. But she couldn't lock the door from the inside, and she was more vulnerable on her own, without witnesses. Mil Burns or one of the other male nurses might visit her. She decided she'd be safer staying in the public spaces as much as possible. Also, she needed her docility and compliance to be witnessed. She was an actor on stage, playing out her recovery to anyone she could find to be her audience.

There was no library in the ward but there was a TV room and a pile of magazines. Some women were playing a board game while half-watching a documentary about a boat journey down the Amazon. Nancy leafed through magazine after magazine, reading about developments in the royal family, advice on the best dating apps to use, recipes for spring, couples therapy, electric cars. They were like messages from the messy, noisy world outside.

Briefly, just before lunch was served, there was a row when someone changed the channel and someone else changed it back. It was almost turning into a fight and Nancy knew that the right thing to do would have been to intervene and try to calm things down. That's what she would have done at any other time. But Nancy did some quick mental calculations of everything that could go wrong. One of the women might turn on her. Or there might be a fight and it would look as if she was involved or even as if she had started it. A nurse would arrive and think: there's that Nancy North, causing trouble again. It would go in the file. It would count against her. She just kept her head down and read an article about the best herbs to grow on a town balcony.

After lunch she walked outside. It was a bright sunny day and in front of the building it almost felt warm. She was careful always to stay in full view of anyone who might be watching. Looking around, Nancy realised for the first time that a hundred and fifty years earlier this must have been an elegant country home, with servants and cooks and gardeners. The lawns led down to mature oak and ash trees that had been arranged in the garden for just this view from the house. There had been hundreds of estates like this and now they had become schools or old people's homes or country house hotels or psychiatric hospitals. Here in the winter sunshine and clear air and the trees all around, Nancy had the brief, poignant feeling of what this place could have been: a comfort, a sanctuary. But it was already getting dark, turning cold, so she went back inside.

*

That night and the following morning were much the same. At the end of lunch, a male nurse she hadn't seen before came and sat next to her. He started telling her a long, involved story about when he had left the army and the various jobs he'd done and gradually Nancy got the sense that he was sitting too close. She could see from his tag that his name was Terry.

'You got a boyfriend?' he suddenly asked.

'Yes.'

'It must be difficult being separated from him.'

'He's coming to see me tomorrow.'

'That's nice. But it's not enough, is it?'

'I'm looking forward to seeing him.'

'You need someone to keep an eye on you in here,' the nurse said. 'Look out for you. Bit of TLC.'

'I feel like I've got a lot of people keeping an eye on me,' said Nancy, as calmly as she could manage.

It was nothing, she tried to tell herself. It was nothing worse than a hundred encounters she'd had like this in pubs and clubs and sitting on trains and planes. She didn't tell Terry to shut up and she didn't just walk away, but she didn't respond to his flirtation either. She steered the conversation into as neutral an area as possible, avoided eye contact and then, after what felt like enough time, she pushed her plate aside and stood up. Terry put a hand on her arm.

'Good to get to know you,' he said.

She just nodded and made her way back to the TV room. She opened a magazine and pretended to be deeply engrossed in whatever page was in front of her but instead she was thinking about her situation. Had the word got around that she was vulnerable? When someone sat next to her, Nancy didn't even look round. The less she engaged with anyone the better.

'I like these programmes,' the woman said.

Nancy continued to read – or pretend to read – her magazine.

'Don't you like them? Are you ignoring me? Don't you like them?'

Nancy tried not to look irritated. She put the magazine down and looked round. It was Roxanne from the group session and she was watching a nature programme. It was about gazelles.

'You see that one hanging back?' said Roxanne. 'The leopards are going to go for it. It's the weak one. They can smell weakness.'

The leopards did indeed go for the smaller gazelle and there was a desperate chase but in the end the gazelle managed to escape and return to the herd.

'They always do that in the documentaries,' said Roxanne. 'They like to give it a happy ending. It's bollocks, though, isn't it? Most of the time they get caught. Otherwise, the leopards would starve to death. They don't like to show that, do they?'

'It would be a bit grim, I suppose,' said Nancy.

'It's nature, isn't it?'

Nancy picked up her magazine again and pretended to look at the spring fashions in this eight-month-old magazine.

'Time for your meds, Roxy,' said a voice.

'No, that's all right.'

'Now don't mess us around, there's a good girl.'

'I'm feeling fine,' said Roxanne. 'The meds do my head in. I can take them later. I want to watch this programme now so fuck off.'

Nancy didn't look round. She continued to stare at the magazine. She knew what was going to happen and within a couple of minutes she heard the familiar rushing of feet and the shouts as a group of nurses seized Roxanne and forced her down onto the floor. Roxanne was pleading and crying. She was too big to lift and they had to drag her across the linoleum. Nancy couldn't stop herself. She raised her eyes from the magazine and as she did, so she met Roxanne's gaze, tear-stained, her cheeks red.

Nancy turned back to the magazine. She heard the nurses shouting and swearing at Roxanne and she heard them laughing as well, making fun of her. The sounds receded as Roxanne was dragged out of the room and along the corridor, but Nancy could still hear them. There was even a scream. What were they doing to her?

She felt her face burning in shame. She had always thought of herself as someone who would get involved, who would help people, even if it was a risk. There would have been no point, she tried to tell herself. If she had tried to intervene, the nurses wouldn't have retreated. Maybe it would even have made things worse.

That could have been true, but it wasn't the point. The point was that it might also have made things worse for Nancy herself. She felt as if she was back in the school playground failing to intervene with the bullies because the bullies might turn on her. She had made a decision to stay out of trouble and this was the result. She couldn't think of anything else to do, but she hated herself for it.

THIRTY-EIGHT

For a moment Nancy and Felix stared at each other like strangers. Nancy knew that she looked different. She was thinner, her hair was more unruly than ever, there were rings under her eyes. And Felix seemed awkward and out of place in this setting. He had dressed up for the meeting in a bright new white shirt and fawn chinos, as if he were going to an interview for a job in middle management.

The place where they met hardly felt like part of the hospital. Dr Cavendish had led Nancy to a reception room with two sofas and the sort of nautical pictures you might see on the walls of a country hotel. Large windows looked out on the garden.

Dr Cavendish introduced herself.

'I'm going to stay during your meeting,' she said. 'But I won't be involved. These first encounters can be stressful for everyone, and I just want to make sure everything goes smoothly. Please, just forget that I'm even here.'

She sat on a chair over by the window. She didn't have a notebook, but she didn't look away or get on with her own work either. She just sat with her hands in her lap.

Felix looked over, almost nervously, at Dr Cavendish.

'Can I hug her?'

Dr Cavendish looked enquiringly at Nancy. Nancy nodded and stepped towards Felix and they hugged. It felt clumsy and strange, like two children hugging, not quite knowing where to put their hands. Nancy closed her eyes. She could feel the familiar bulk, smell his aftershave. They stepped apart and sat on the sofa, a couple of feet apart.

'How are you doing?' Felix asked.

'It's been difficult,' said Nancy slowly. 'But I'm starting to feel better, I think.'

'You look good,' he said.

Nancy didn't quite know how to respond to this. She knew that she didn't look good. Anyway, she told herself, that was beside the point. That wasn't what this meeting was about.

'I'm so glad you felt you could come,' she said.

'Of course I came.'

Felix started to say something else but Nancy held up her hand to stop him.

'There's something I need to tell you, Felix. I've been thinking about it for the last few days.' She paused, composing herself, and then spoke slowly and deliberately, holding his gaze as she did so and feeling the doctor's eyes on her. 'What I wanted to say is that I'm becoming aware of how horribly difficult I made things for you, how badly I behaved and how much I have hurt you. When I was brought here, I've got to admit that I was angry with you. Very angry. It's been a slow and painful process to go through, but I've come to realise that you were doing your best to save me. It was necessary.'

She forced herself to keep looking directly at Felix. Don't look at Stef Cavendish, she told herself. Don't make it look as if that speech was really aimed at her, to get her approval.

'I've got to accept that I've got a mental problem and some-times – quite often, actually – other people can see it more clearly than I can. It must have been appalling for you and I'm really sorry.'

Nancy stopped and looked down at the floor. That was enough, she thought. Or was it too much? She suddenly had the fear that Felix and Dr Cavendish would start laughing at the obviously fake and overdone confession.

'I was just doing it for you,' said Felix. 'You have to realise that whatever I do, whatever you do, we're always on the same side, always a team.'

Nancy turned back to Felix, and he looked towards the doctor.

'She seems so much better,' he said. 'I thought I'd lost her, but now I feel like I've got my own Nancy back.'

The words, and the tone in which he spoke them, made Nancy almost physically sick, but she still kept her calm gaze on him.

'Can I ask you something?' he asked.

'What?'

'The things you said. About the poor girl who took her life, I mean.'

'Kira,' interposed Nancy before she could prevent herself. The 'poor girl' had to be named.

Felix frowned.

'Yes, Kira. You said terrible things.'

'I know,' said Nancy. 'I can hardly bear to think of it.'

'You said she didn't take her own life. You made wild accusations against people.'

'Yes.'

'But now you recognise that was wrong? That what it looked like was what it was.'

'What it looked like was what it was,' repeated Nancy submissively.

She thought of Kira's face as she had seen it on that dreadful day, wild with fear and distress. She thought of the body on its rope. She put a hand against her mouth for a moment, feeling nauseous.

'You have no suspicions any longer?' asked Cavendish, glancing from one face to the other.

'Of course not,' Nancy replied fervently. 'I was ill. Everything seemed suspicious. Ordinary things became dangerous. I felt everyone was my enemy.' She turned to Felix. 'Even you, Felix, which is a terrible thing to say. I even thought you were against me. Now I know it was my psychosis. And I feel so ashamed.'

She covered her eyes with a hand and took a few whimpering sighs.

'I understand,' said Felix. 'And I will make sure everyone in the house understands as well. They do already. Everyone is very sympathetic.'

Nancy took her hand away.

She was so horrified by the idea of the people in the house talking about her, feeling sympathetic towards her, that she didn't trust herself to speak.

Felix turned to the doctor.

'Do you think she's ready to leave?' he continued.

These were exactly the words she had been hoping to hear, but Nancy made the supreme effort not to seem too eager. She shook her head slowly, sadly. You never knew how Dr Cavendish would interpret this. If Nancy said she thought she was cured, Dr Cavendish might see this as a sign that she *wasn't* cured.

'I don't know, Felix,' she said. 'I'm not sure if I'm quite ready. I mean ...' She made herself hesitate, as if searching for the right words. 'I think I'm doing better and I'm taking the medication and I think it's settled me, but maybe I need to be absolutely sure.'

'You're never going to be absolutely sure, Nancy,' said Dr

Cavendish. 'It isn't like a broken leg. There's no simple cure. What we hope for is that you gain an insight into your condition, that you follow instructions and take your medication and that you feel able to resume your normal life.'

'Doesn't she seem better to you, Doctor?' asked Felix.

'I think that Nancy has made considerable progress. After a rocky start.'

'What does that mean?'

'It's only to be expected. People sometimes find it difficult to accept their situation. That's part of their illness. Acceptance is part of their recovery.'

'But now she does seem to be recovering.'

Nancy was burningly aware that they were talking about her as if she weren't in the room or as if she were a child who didn't understand grown-up language.

'Yes, I'm pleased with the way things are going.' Dr Cavendish smiled. 'But if you're asking if she can just walk out with you today, then the answer is no.'

Nancy felt a terrible lurch of disappointment, but she tried not to let it show in her expression.

'We need to have an assessment,' Dr Cavendish continued. 'Above all, we need to agree officially that Nancy is no longer a threat to herself or to others.'

'How long will that take?'

'A few days. We need to be certain.'

'I'm so sorry,' said Felix. 'I hoped I could take you with me.'

Nancy felt a dull, grey ache of disappointment. Still, she had achieved what she had set out to achieve. Now she just wanted Felix to leave her alone.

'I'm just glad you came,' she said. 'You don't have to stay any longer. You've done enough. If things go well, we'll be together soon.'

Felix leaned forward and kissed her. Nancy tried to keep the kiss soft and chaste. He stood up.

'I'll have everything ready for you,' he said. 'Everything perfect.'

'I know you will,' said Nancy.

Three and a half days later, Nancy walked down the corridor behind a nurse with her holdall, past all the doors with their apertures, past the public room where the television was playing to no one, past the reception hub where the nurse with the missing tooth was sitting.

Nancy tried to breathe normally and to keep her expression calm, but at every moment she expected a tap on the shoulder, a voice telling her it had been a mistake. Her stomach churned and her heart felt jittery with hope and dread.

'Off, are you?'

She turned and saw Mil Burns behind her. He was grinning at her. She looked at his long black hair that had threads of silver in it, his stupid tattoos of dragons and warriors, his knowing smile. Heat rose in her like bile.

'I am,' she said.

She didn't smile but she didn't shout or snarl either.

'You'll be back. A woman like you.'

She didn't reply. The nurse unlocked the door and pushed it open. Nancy stepped out of the ward.

Terry was there, the nurse who had asked her if she had a boyfriend. He was blocking her way. She took a step towards him and for a few seconds, he didn't move, just stared at her. She stared back, saying nothing though a scream was rising in her. Then he nodded and stood aside.

'See you,' he said.

'I don't think so.'

She wanted to run, but she made herself walk at a steady pace. She followed the signs towards the exit.

Nobody stopped her, nobody called her name, and after what seemed like an age she was at the revolving door and could see the outside world, a car park, a road beyond it, a bus going by, people on the pavement in their heavy winter coats, a plane overhead angling off to somewhere warm.

She stepped into the door, pushed it forward, came out the other side. Briefly, she allowed herself to look back at the building, its stained brick walls and rows of windows. Perhaps Josie was at one of them, her face grey as it had been this morning when she'd said goodbye to Nancy and Nancy had held her hand and told her to be in touch when she got out. The brave hopelessness of her.

Then two hands landed on her shoulder and she froze.

'Nancy. Babe.'

She turned and he kissed her – on her forehead, then her lips. He took her bag and wrapped one arm around her, pulling her close. His eyes were shining.

'I'm going to look after you now,' he said tenderly. 'I'm going to keep you safe and sound.'

PART THREE

Thirty-nine

Maud passed Danny Kemp in the corridor. He was dressed in a close-fitting black suit that Maud thought looked too tight on him but which he was obviously well pleased with, and his hair was brushed back from his forehead.

'Guess where I'm going,' he said.

She studied him.

'A funeral.'

'Kira Mullan's funeral.'

'The woman who took her own life?'

'Yup. All the way to fucking Derbyshire. But that's me. I like to show how much I care.'

'I hope it's a good funeral.'

'And you know that woman who said we should investigate further?'

'Yes.'

'The one you said we should listen to?'

'I remember.'

'She only went and got herself sectioned. Shut up in a mental home.'

'I'm so sorry to hear that,' Maud said gravely.

His face reddened.

'You never even met her. She wasted police time.'

'Not that much time.'

*

Felix opened the passenger door and leaned over to do Nancy's safety belt up for her. The interior smelt of pine.

'It's my mother's car,' he said. 'She sends her love, by the way.'

Nancy smiled at him. As far as she remembered, she hadn't uttered a word yet, but he didn't seem to mind. He put the key in the ignition, started the engine, then took her hand and gazed at her.

'You look so frail.'

Little spots of rain pattered on the windscreen.

'I bought us some coffee,' said Felix. He handed her a large cardboard cup. 'It should still be hot. And there's a cinnamon bun if you're hungry.'

'It won't take very long to get back to the flat, will it?'

'We're not going back to the flat. Not right away.'

He released the handbrake and eased out of the parking space.

A small part of Nancy was relieved – she had a horror of the whole house, of the faces she would see, of Kira's closed door, of Michelle and Dylan paying a visit, of how everyone would look at her, speak to her. But the sooner she went back, the sooner she would be able to leave again. This time she would leave for good.

She just needed to do it right, so that nobody would be able to stop her. She was free, but she still felt unsafe, as though she had only been granted a temporary reprieve and that at any time she could be recalled if she put a foot wrong. She had been let out of the hospital because she had gone along with a collective version of her story that cast her as deluded. If immediately on release she reverted to the other Nancy, the one who believed Kira had been killed, who thought her neighbours had tricked her, and who urgently needed to leave Felix, what would happen?

'I worried about going back there at all,' Felix said. 'After everything that happened. But we've paid for the next quarter. Will you be able to bear it?'

'Yes,' said Nancy.

'And I was thinking it might even be good for you, to meet the people you thought were plotting against you and see how much they are on your side.'

'I guess,' said Nancy.

It was tiring, being this sweet and docile woman.

'Michelle brought a cake and some flowers round.'

'How kind of her.'

She was thinking of how tomorrow after Felix left for work she would pull the big case from the top of the wardrobe, pack a few clothes, retrieve her passport, be gone.

'Of course I've taken tomorrow off as well, so we have three clear days together.'

Not tomorrow then, she thought. Three more days of smiling and lying and being servile. She could do that.

'Amazing,' she said.

The car turned onto the main road. Nancy pressed her face to the rain-streaked window and looked at the receding hospital. Her heart was still thudding: perhaps it would take a long time before she was free of the terror.

'Where are we going?' she asked.

'It's a surprise.'

She slid a glance at Felix, his large competent hands on the steering wheel, the smoothness of his freshly shaved cheeks, and the little smile that was twitching his lips. He was content.

'Will you have some coffee?'

'Please.'

She handed him one of the cardboard mugs of coffee and he

took a hasty sip before handing it back. She took a mouthful of her own; it didn't taste quite right, something metallic about it. That would be the drugs.

'I can't believe you're here,' said Felix. 'After everything.'

Nancy could scarcely believe it either; it was as if she was in a dream and at any moment might wake to see Mil Burns leaning over her.

'This will be our new beginning.' Felix's tone was fervent.

'Yes.'

'You're very quiet.'

'I'm feeling in a bit of a daze.'

He put a hand briefly on her thigh and her flesh shrank, her soul shrank.

Three days.

The rain was strengthening, the windscreen wipers made hasty arcs on the window. Vans and cars ahead of them were dirty smudges in the wet greyness. Felix hunched forward in the seat, frowning in concentration.

They passed under a large bridge of thundering traffic and now seemed to be leaving the density of the city behind them. There were open spaces, light industrial units, a line of great pylons marching into the fog.

Felix was saying something about plans for Christmas Day, only seventeen days to go, about the new year.

'Where are we?' she asked.

'Nearly there. I might need the sat nav in a moment.'

They turned off the road, down another, smaller one, and he pulled over into a layby and took out his phone, keying something into it.

'Just a few minutes now.'

'Can't you just tell me?'

She almost allowed herself to sound cross.

They drove slowly down a small country lane. Felix nearly ran over a dead badger.

He slowed down and turned up a rutted driveway that ended at a narrow red-brick house, an enormous ploughed field behind it.

'I don't understand.'

Felix turned off the engine and faced her.

'Paying almost my entire salary to live in that poky flat isn't good for you. London isn't good for you; all the pressures of city life. I should have recognised it before. I blame myself.'

'What are you talking about?'

Felix pointed. There was a For Sale sign half-hidden by the hedge.

'I've put an offer on it,' he said, smiling triumphantly at her. 'Yesterday I heard it's been accepted.'

'What?'

'Don't worry, my parents have lent me the deposit. We can have a house of our own, Nancy. Two bedrooms and a box room and our own little garden. I can commute to London if we buy a cheap car to get me to the station. We'll actually save money. You can have some peace and quiet and recover.'

'You did all this while I was at Oakwood?'

'The owners are expecting us. I told them you wanted to see it as well.' He leaned in closer. 'Are you pleased?'

'It's a bit of a shock.'

'I know it will take time for you to adjust. You think of yourself as a city girl. But look what the city has done to you.'

He got out of the car and by the time he was opening her door, was soaked, his hair plastered to his skull.

Nancy got out, into a deep puddle. Rain ran down her neck.

'What's that smell?' she asked.

'There's a farm along the road. It's better than the smell of traffic, isn't it?'

Nancy preferred the smell of traffic.

They walked through the mud to the front door and rang the bell, which set off a musical chime. The woman who answered was about their age; she was carrying a bawling baby that reminded Nancy of Olga and Harry's daughter, Lydia. From inside, they heard a screaming and crashing sound.

'That's Joey having a tantrum,' the woman said wearily. 'Can you take off your shoes?'

They took off their shoes. They looked into the living room, where Joey was indeed having a tantrum, flinging wooden bricks and miniature cars at the wall, his face huge and purple with rage. They examined the kitchen, whose window looked out onto the unyielding ploughed field, and the downstairs toilet. They went upstairs and took in the master bedroom with a side cot attached to the bed, the small bedroom decorated with dinosaurs, the very small box room piled high with junk, the bathroom.

'What do you reckon?' asked Felix as they climbed back into the car. For the first time that day, his face was anxious.

'It's a lot to take in.'

'Think of it in the spring, when everything is green and fresh. There are some lovely walks near here and the village is only a mile up the road. It's got a shop and a pub. We could go and have a drink there now, if you fancy it, get a feel for the place.'

She looked at him, then nodded.

'That'd be nice,' she said.

In the Green Man, which was cosy and pretty in a very English way, with a fire in the grate, Nancy had a ginger beer and a packet of crisps. Felix had a half of a local ale. He raised it to her and they clinked glasses. He smiled. She smiled back.

Then he looked away.

'About the house.' He was speaking in a mumbled rush. 'There's no rush, you need to get well, but if we ever decide to have a . . .you know.'

He broke off.

'Felix,' said Nancy gently, imagining screeching and throwing the ginger beer into his face. 'The house is perfect.'

'Really.'

'You're right. London hasn't been good for me.'

'You don't mind I went ahead without consulting you first?'

'You couldn't consult me. I was ill. You've done all this for me, and I won't forget it.'

FORTY

On the drive back, Nancy half slept, and half pretended to sleep. When she opened her eyes, she saw the beginnings of London: warehouses, petrol stations, supermarkets, scrubby fields. She immediately felt better, as if she was coming to a country where she was comfortable.

She was aware that Felix was glancing at her, looking back at the road, then glancing at her again.

'What is it?' she asked.

'I'm just thinking.'

'What about?'

'I was worried,' he said. 'You know that everything I've ever done has been because I love you and I want what's best for you. You know that, don't you?'

'Of course, I do. It can be difficult sometimes. But, really and deeply, I know that.'

'You look so calm. I was worried that you might be angry.'

'Angry about what?'

'About everything. Everything that's been going on.'

'Being angry was part of my problem,' said Nancy. 'I think I've learned, or I'm starting to learn, that the people around me were trying to help, even if it didn't always feel like that. It's not about being cured. It's about managing things, keeping a balance. I think I can do that now. I'm just looking forward to getting my life back. I just want to do the normal things, being at home, getting back to work.'

Felix visibly hesitated before answering. He gave a cough.

'About that. I rang your work up and had conversation with a woman there called . . .' He paused. 'Is it Jane?'

'Jill.'

'Jill, that's it. I talked to her and explained the situation and said that once it was over you'd probably be needing some rest, so you'd be away for a while.'

'Well, I'm back now and I think it would be good for me to get straight back to work.'

As Felix replied to this, he didn't look round as he had been doing before. He just stared ahead at the road.

'I'm not sure that'll be possible.'

'Why not? I feel fine. It would be good for me to work. And I need the money.'

'I'm sure you're fine. You seem so much better, although of course you will need to be careful. But I rang your work and this woman Jill who I talked to said that she'd need to hire someone else. I suppose that's the problem with small companies.'

For a moment, Nancy felt she wanted to scream or lash out or jump out of the car, even though it was going at seventy on the motorway. Once she had suppressed all those impulses, she just wanted to ask: why would you do that? But she pushed her nails into the palms of her hands and waited before speaking.

'I thought it would be a help,' she said meekly. 'It would be a way of getting my life back on track.'

'Your life *is* on track, my darling. We just need to keep it that way. You've had too much to deal with. I think that's what set you off. I want to do everything I can to protect you from that.'

'But when do you think I'll be ready?'

'We'll know,' said Felix in a reassuring tone. 'But not now. You should let yourself be looked after.'

'What about you?'

'What about me?'

'You should be able to live a normal life. You shouldn't have to spend so much of your time looking after me.'

'You let me worry about that.'

When Felix unlocked the flat and Nancy stepped inside, she felt a sudden rush of panic. She was hit by the memory of what had happened when she was last there, being restrained and dragged out screaming. It wasn't even a memory. She was there and it was happening all over again. She could hear the sounds and smell the smells. Felix started to ask her something but she interrupted him.

'Wait,' she said. 'Give me a moment.'

She rushed into the bathroom and shut the door and locked it. At first she leaned over the toilet bowl. She thought she was going to vomit but she took a few deep breaths and the feeling subsided. She took all of her clothes off. Everything smelt of the hospital: her clothes, her body, her hair, everything. She stood in the shower and made the water as hot as she could bear. She washed her hair and then found a flannel and scrubbed every bit of her body that she could reach. She rinsed herself off and then washed her hair and her body all over again until her skin felt raw. The smell was still there, but Nancy knew that it was in her head. It would take days, weeks, to go away.

She left the shower running until she felt the temperature start to drop. As she switched the water off, she heard voices. Someone else was in the flat. She looked down at her discarded clothes in dismay. She rapped at the door.

'Felix, could you bring me something to put on?'

She dried herself and stood wrapped in her towel, waiting, until there was a knock on the door. She opened it just a few inches. Felix pushed her blue dressing gown through the gap. She pulled it on and felt it cling to her damp skin. She opened the door and stepped into the living room. Michelle and Dylan were sitting on the sofa. There were glasses of red wine in front of them on the coffee table. Both of them smiled at her.

'Welcome home,' said Michelle. 'We brought mince pies. And wine. It felt right for the season.'

Dylan stood up and walked towards Nancy. He looked at her and put his hands on her shoulders. She felt like an animal being checked over in a meat market. He looked back at his wife with a grin.

'She looks all right, don't you think? She maybe needs a bit of fattening up.'

Nancy was conscious of her dressing gown against her damp body. She felt naked under their gaze. Michelle looked at her husband and Nancy saw her give the faintest shake of her head, an expression of mild, weary exasperation. Nancy thought of a mother watching her little child misbehaving again.

'Shall I pour you a glass?' said Michelle.

'Nancy shouldn't really drink,' said Felix. 'Doctor's orders.'

'Of course. That's so stupid of me,' said Michelle. 'Shall I make some tea?'

'That's all right,' said Nancy. 'I'm going to put some clothes on.'

Nancy went into the bedroom, closed the door and leaned against it, as if she could keep the rest of the world out, just for a few minutes. She calmed herself. It was okay. She could do this. She threw off her dressing gown and started to get dressed. When she had pulled on knickers and a pair of black jeans, there was a knock on the door.

'Just a moment,' she said.

The door opened and Michelle stepped inside. She pushed the door closed behind her.

'I'm getting dressed,' said Nancy, folding her arms over her naked breasts.

'Don't mind me,' said Michelle cheerfully and sat down on the bed.

Nancy was in such a state of shock that she was unable to speak. Only a few people had ever behaved like that, hanging around while she was getting dressed as if it didn't matter. That was what lovers and best friends do, not the woman who had lied to get her sectioned. She turned her back to Michelle and rummaged in a drawer.

'It's good to see you looking better,' Michelle said.

Nancy finished dressing, finally pulling a heavy sweater over her head. It felt like protection. She faced Michelle once more.

'Better?' said Nancy, slowly, almost as if she were testing the word to see what it meant. 'My life's better. There's no doubt about that.'

'I did what was best for you,' Michelle said. 'You need to understand that.'

'I do understand. The doctors told me what you said about me.'

'It wasn't just me. Everyone was worried about you. You're lucky to have a partner like Felix, who cares for you so very deeply. You're lucky to have a doctor like Harry as a neighbour; he gave me good advice. And . . .' She hesitated. 'I know that Dylan can be a bit much, sometimes. He's not exactly politically correct. But he was worried about you. We acted the way that friends and neighbours should act.'

Nancy felt like shouting at her. She didn't doubt that Felix had instigated it or that Harry and Dylan had been involved.

But the bar for being sectioned is high. Michelle had claimed that Nancy was an imminent threat – to Michelle's life and to her own life. That had been why she had been in custody and assaulted and forcibly injected.

'It's been difficult,' she said. 'But I get that now.'

'I'm so glad. What are your plans for the future?'

Michelle smiled as she asked that question, but Nancy saw that behind the smile there was an almost ferocious curiosity.

'I want to get completely better,' said Nancy. 'And I want to get on with my life.'

'That's a really good idea. Such a good idea. Will you be getting back to work?'

Nancy shook her head.

'I've got plans.'

'What sort of plans?'

'In a previous life, long, long ago, I used to run a restaurant. I am thinking of doing that again. That should occupy most of my spare energy.'

Michelle's smile now looked genuine.

'I'm so glad. Shall we join the others? You need to try one of my mince pies.'

Almost as soon as the two of them had entered the living room, there was another knock at the door. Felix opened it, and Harry and Olga came in. Olga ran across and embraced Nancy. She smelt of sour milk and her body was bony and sharp, but she was the only person Nancy was glad to see.

'We were happy to hear that you were back,' Olga said. 'It must have been so distressing.'

'It wasn't great,' Nancy said.

'I can't imagine it,' said Olga.

'I hope you'll never have to find out. Where's Lydia?'

'Harry's mother's staying with us and we've got an evening

without looking after her. I feel like I've been let out of prison. And look.' Nancy saw that Olga was holding a small paper bag. 'Mince pies. Because it's almost Christmas. They're from the delicatessen down the road. They're really good.'

'That's very kind.'

Olga asked for a plate for the mince pies and then gave a yelp of horror when she saw the ones that Michelle had brought and started apologising.

'Don't be silly,' said Michelle. 'Yours look wonderful.'

While the others were talking and laughing, Nancy sat on her own to one side. She just wanted some quiet. She wanted to sleep. She saw that Harry had sat down next to her. He was holding two mugs of tea and he placed them on the small table in front of them.

'It's good to see you back,' he said stiffly, not meeting her eyes.

'Michelle told me that you helped with having me sectioned,' she said, coldly. 'I suppose I should thank you for that.'

He flushed crimson.

'That's not true,' he said. 'I don't know why she would say that.'

'Nor do I.'

'Look.' He was speaking urgently now, leaning towards her. 'She said that you had made an explicit physical threat, and she asked me what she should do. I said that in the last resort, someone who is a risk to others or themselves might have to be sectioned. That was as far as it went.'

'Right.'

'You might not believe me but it's true.'

Nancy looked from him to the group of people at the other side of the room. Felix was watching her. She turned back to Harry.

'I do believe you,' she said gently. 'And in fact, I'm grateful to everyone.'

'Grateful?'

'I was not in my right mind. I needed to be helped and I do understand how that was hard for everyone. Especially Michelle. And Felix of course. It's been particularly awful for him. I don't know how I'll ever be able to repay him.'

She smiled across at Felix and he smiled back.

'I'm glad you see it like that,' said Harry.

'I do.'

She stood up. Everyone was looking at her.

Three days, she thought. Three more days.

FORTY-ONE

Maud walked back to her flat after work, even though it was filthy weather. She didn't mind the cold and the wet. She almost relished the wind scouring her face and the sting of the rain. It felt purifying after the station, where the air was stale and overheated and the atmosphere often toxic. That day, she had found a new recruit weeping in the toilets.

'I don't know how you stand it here,' she had said to Maud.

Sometimes Maud didn't know either.

'What's happened?' she asked.

'It's not just one thing, it's day in and day out, the way they look at me, or laugh behind my back or try and show me up.'

'That's hard.'

'Nobody would dare push you around though.' She blew her nose hard, then studied her face in the spotted mirror to make sure her eyes weren't red.

'Come to me next time you have trouble,' Maud had said.

She was soaked through by the time she was approaching her flat, which she didn't yet think of as home and probably never would. It was on the third floor of an apartment block, and the best thing about it was its small balcony which in the spring and summer had geraniums on it that her father grew and gave to her. Pelargonium geraniums were his unlikely hobby and passion.

There was a figure hovering by the communal entrance, and

she slowed, narrowing her eyes. Even in the rain and darkness, she was sure she recognised it.

The figure turned as she approached.

'Hello, Maud,' said Silas.

Silas with his black hair and his blue eyes that crinkled when he smiled. He was smiling now, but she didn't smile back.

'What are you doing here?'

'Nice to see you too,' he said. 'I wanted to talk to you.'

'After a year of silence?'

'Yes.'

'You could have called or left a message.'

'I did, but you didn't answer. I phoned the station and they said you'd left. And here I am.'

'How did you know where I live?'

'Is it a secret? As a matter of fact, I asked your brother. Terry.'

'What do you want? I thought you were living in Denmark or somewhere.'

'I was. But I've come home. I want to talk to you.'

'What about?'

'Can I at least come in? It's freezing out here.'

Maud hesitated, then nodded.

'Okay. But not for long. I've work to do.'

'You're not making me feel very welcome.'

She gave him a look but didn't answer, turning her back on him to unlock the door. They went up three flights of stairs without talking, then she opened the door to her flat and they stepped inside.

'Nice,' he said, looking around.

'It's not really.'

'You still have that linen apron I gave you.'

'It's only been a year and a half, Silas.'

'Are you going to offer me a drink?'

'Why don't you get yourself a beer from the fridge, or there's wine in there as well. I've got to get out of these wet clothes.'

She left him and went into the bedroom, where she stripped off her clothes and pulled on old jeans and an oversized cream-coloured cotton jumper. But he would recognise that as well, so she took it off and replaced it with a green shirt. She ran her hands through her wild wet hair and refused herself even a glimpse in the mirror. What did it matter?

'What do you want to talk to me about?' she asked as she re-entered the living room which was also the kitchen.

'Can't we have some small talk first?'

'I've got work to do.'

Silas held out a can of beer, but she shook her head, so he pulled the tab off and took a mouthful, then sat down on one of the chairs. Maud sat opposite him.

'Have you missed me?'

Maud's expression didn't alter. She looked at Silas, who she knew intimately and who was also a stranger. She had loved him unequivocally and thought that he had loved her too. They had lived together for years, had bought a flat together, shared a friendship group, planned a future, started trying for a baby – and at that point he had left her. He had said it wasn't the right time for him, he wasn't ready, and he had disappeared from her life, leaving possessions to be divided, a flat to be sold, a life to be picked up and put back together again, piece by piece.

Had she missed him? At first, she had missed him so much that she had felt scraped thin by loss. Her whole body had hurt with it. Her heart had felt like a throbbing bruise. Memories were wounds.

She had dealt with the separation by throwing herself into work and into her friendships, and then by starting the law

conversion course that was her exit strategy from the Met. She
had had a few flings, but nothing that came remotely close to
commitment. Bit by bit, Silas had receded.

'I've survived,' she said coolly.

'You always were a class act,' he said. 'And I was a fool.'

Maud stood up and went to the fridge, taking out a can of
beer and pulling the tab, watching the spume of foam curl up
out of its mouth.

'I want to say sorry,' said Silas. 'I behaved like a shit.'

Maud didn't reply, just took a gulp of cold, bitter beer.

'I panicked,' said Silas. 'I wasn't ready.'

'You told me that at the time.'

'I made a mistake. I realise that now.'

There was a silence. Maud remained standing. She took
another mouthful of beer.

'Aren't you going to say anything?'

'What do you want me to say? There's no going back, Silas.'

'Do you mean it's too late?'

'Did you think I'd be waiting for you? That you could come
back after all this time and say you're sorry and that you made
a mistake and I'd fall into your arms?'

'Of course not.'

'I don't know you anymore. You don't know me. It's over. It
was over the day you packed up all your stuff while I was away
on the Charlotte Salter case and left without even having the
courage to say goodbye.'

He left. Maud made herself a cheese omelette, which she ate
with a glass of red wine while reading through the notes she
had made. She sat up till late, trying to concentrate, trying not
to think of anything except this tunnel she was pushing her way
through like a mole, determined to find a way out.

FORTY-TWO

That night, Nancy went to bed early, claiming exhaustion. She wasn't exhausted; she was quiveringly alert, full of a restless anticipation. She lay in the dark and listened to the sounds of Felix clearing up: dishes clattering, a tap running, music playing. At one point, she heard him singing along.

He eventually came softly into the room. She was curled up on herself, her face pressed into the pillow and her eyes closed, but she could feel him standing beside her for what seemed like ages although it was probably no more than a minute. She made herself breathe peacefully and at last he moved away, and she heard him pulling off clothes, and then he climbed in beside her with a sigh of contentment. He put a warm hand on her back, moved it up and down in a soothing motion. She murmured and shifted away from him, feigning deep sleep. She felt him settle beside her and soon he was snoring slightly, a small rumble that she had once found endearing and comfortable, but now made her want to scream.

Be calm, she told herself. She breathed in and out on the words. Be. Calm. She tried to let her limbs relax. She thought of Michelle smiling at her, Dylan looking at her, Harry being concerned. She thought of Felix ringing up work and making sure she wouldn't go back there, that she had no income and no independence. How much money did she have in her account? She couldn't remember, but it wasn't very much.

That didn't matter. She could find work, any work would do, preferably in a cafe or restaurant. She felt that she was still standing on the rim of the nightmare she had been in. Felix could contact the doctors again. Michelle could. And then, perhaps, they would take her again, jab her with needles, shut her in a windowless room, tell her she was mad until she was mad.

Friday. Saturday. Sunday. She would act frail and docile. In the darkness she felt her lips curl into a sneer: how easy it was to fool Felix, after all. How could he believe that she, who had always been stubborn and cross, had become this defeated little creature?

Michelle was another matter. Michelle had lied about Nancy. She knew Nancy knew that. Nancy knew she knew.

Why had Michelle lied? Nancy thought of the way Dylan had looked at her that evening, and the way Michelle had looked at Dylan looking at her.

But she mustn't think like that. That was all behind her. Kira was dead and although Nancy was certain that someone had killed the young woman, there was nothing she could do about it. She was done with being a ludicrous amateur detective; done with trying to find out who had murdered her, done with remembering the howls of Kira's mother as she sat in Nancy's kitchen. She needed to save herself now.

Three days. They stretched out like a desert, but she would get through the time, tired and passive.

She felt Felix turn and shift beside her; he moved closer, and she felt his warmth, his breath on her shoulder, and moved away. Everything about him revolted her: his strong body, his large hands, his thick blonde hair, his smile, his frown of concern. Whenever he touched her, her flesh shrank and it was hard not to jerk away from him. At least she wouldn't have to let him have sex with her. She was convalescent, after all: that was what he kept telling her.

She pictured herself on Monday morning, kissing Felix goodbye, waving him off, running to the bedroom and packing a small bag: passport, laptop, a few shirts, underwear, toothbrush. She could be out in minutes. She let herself imagine running out of the door and down the road, wind and rain in her face; she would run so fast nobody would be able to catch her.

Where would she go? She couldn't contact anyone in advance, in case they saw it as their duty to tell Felix. Perhaps she couldn't go to any of her friends, not at first, not until she knew she safe.

She felt very alone. But being alone was all right. Being alone was being free.

FORTY-THREE

'What shall we do today?'

They sat drinking tea together. Felix had produced almond croissants and fresh orange juice from the fridge and laid them ceremoniously on the little table. There had been enough for six people. Nancy had pulled apart a croissant, eaten a few shreds.

'I thought I could have a walk,' she said.

'Really? It's foul out there.'

'I don't mind.'

'I'll come with you.'

'You don't need to.'

'I'd like to.'

She smiled at him. He smiled back. Her head banged.

'Lovely,' she said. 'I need fresh air.'

They walked to the little park in the drenching rain.

'Christmas very soon,' said Felix. 'Nine days.'

Where would she be at Christmas, she wondered, and who would she be with?

'What shall we eat on the day? Just you and me, I thought. In the circs.'

'Oooh, let me think.'

'I can cook.'

'That's nice of you.'

He took her hand.

'Just think,' he said. 'This time next year, we'll be in our own little house in the country.'

'Wow,' said Nancy. 'Amazing.'

She slid him a glance. Was she overdoing it? But no, he seemed entirely unsuspicious. She felt a bubble of laughter rising in her.

On the way back, they passed a chemist and Nancy stopped.

'There are things I need to get.'

'Make me a list. I can buy them later.'

'I'll do it now.'

'Let me give you some money then.'

'I'll use my card. Go on ahead. Get out of your wet clothes.'

'There are a few things I need as well.'

They went into the shop and Nancy put shampoo, tampons, hand lotion, shower gel and toothpaste into her basket. She unslung her backpack and fished out her wallet, but Felix was beside her, holding out his card to the cashier.

'It's my stuff,' said Nancy, pushing his arm away. 'I'm paying. Even though I seem not to have a job any longer,' she added, unable to stop herself. She rifled through the wallet. 'Where's my card?'

'It doesn't matter, let me.'

'It should be in here.'

'Well—'

'I always keep it in here.'

Felix tapped the payment device with his own card.

Nancy picked up her toiletries and slid them into the backpack, and together they left the shop, back into the driving rain.

'If I can't find it, I need to report it missing and order a new one.'

'It's not missing.'

'What?'

'I cut it up.'

'You cut it up,' she repeated slowly. 'You cut up my card?'

'Yes.'

'Why would you do that?'

'Don't be angry. Because I was told that people in your situation can spend money wildly. They can ruin themselves. It's like a symptom.'

'Was that based on medical advice?'

'I wanted to save you from yourself.'

Nancy considered the words. To be saved from yourself. It was an interesting concept, she thought. To rescue the self from the self. She looked at Felix, his hair plastered to his skull, his face wet with rain, his expression part pleading and part self-righteous.

'You should have asked me,' she said at last.

His expression relaxed a fraction.

'I thought we should set up a joint account,' he said.

She hated everything about this. But the suggestion already seemed related to her past life.

'A joint account is a good idea,' said Nancy. 'But it does feel odd to have no access to money in the meantime.'

'I can give you what you need.'

No card. No access to money. No income of her own.

'Let's go back,' she said. 'Before we freeze to death.'

As they neared the flat, they saw Seamus coming up the stairs from the basement flat, holding a small umbrella that wasn't keeping him dry. He gleamed with health and cheerfulness, everything about him a bit too much: his lips too red, his hair too glossy, his eyes too bright. Nancy could smell his musky aftershave.

'Nancy!'

His smile wavered, then strengthened. His eyes flickered from her face and away. Nancy couldn't tell if he was embarrassed, ashamed or guilty: this was the man who had tried to kiss her and then claimed that it was she who had come on to him. It had been read as yet another sign of her unstable state.

'You're back. I'm so glad to see you. You look good. Great. Doesn't she, Felix?'

'She does,' said Felix, and put his arm around Nancy's shoulder, pulling her towards him assertively so that she almost toppled.

Water dripped from the spokes of the umbrella onto Seamus's face.

'Will I see you both this evening?'

'This evening?' asked Nancy.

'There's a Christmas party up the road. They have it every year. It's okay. A bit middle-aged.'

'I don't know,' said Felix. 'It depends on how Nancy's feeling. She might not be up to a party yet, and I'm obviously not going without her.' His arm was still tightly around her. 'I thought you might want a quiet evening at home.'

'I'd like to go,' she said.

'Really?' Felix nodded at Seamus. 'In which case, see you there.'

'Great.' Seamus raised his umbrella in salute and loped off.

FORTY-FOUR

Nancy put on headphones and tuned in to her Spotify playlist. It didn't quite drown out Lydia's shrieks, nor the hammering noise coming from the bathroom, where Felix was trying to mend the malfunctioning shower. She picked up her phone: she had put off looking at all the WhatsApp messages and Instagram notifications that had been pinging onto her screen.

But after about ten minutes, she put the phone down again, feeling slightly sick. Friend after friend had been in touch, sending her their condolences, saying they quite understood that she needed time to recover but they were there for her, even cancelling arrangements she had made with them because they knew that it was early days. There were multiple voicemail messages, but she couldn't bear to listen to them.

She went into the bathroom, where Felix was on the floor, squinting at a pipe.

'I think I've found the source of the problem,' he said cheerily.

'Did you contact my friends about what I was going through?' she said.

He twisted towards her.

'People were worried about you. I had to say something.'

She bit her lip.

'I thought maybe I should be the one to do that.'

'It was no trouble,' he said.

Nancy imagined kicking him in the face as he lay there.

'I think you may have given the impression that I'm still sick,' she said.

Felix sat up and regarded her.

'I know you're much better. I'm happy about that. But you've been through a huge thing. Don't you think that you need to learn from what happened? For your sake and mine, don't rush back into your hectic way of life, out most nights, trying to fit everything and everyone in, hardly any time for us. You risk it starting all over again.' He adjusted the spanner, then looked her intently. 'And you really don't want that, do you? You don't want to end up back in hospital.'

'No,' said Nancy slowly. 'I don't.'

Felix smiled at her and then lay back down again.

'The trouble,' said Maud, looking critically at the fish pie she had ordered, 'is that the kind of men I like don't like police officers.'

She was thinking of the way that man Stuart had visibly shrunk away from her when they had first met. She wasn't sure why it had got under her skin so much: after all, she was used to the way people reacted to her job. Though they had never directly challenged her, Silas's parents had been disapproving of her profession. The only time they thawed towards her was when she became briefly famous for exposing failures inside her own force.

She hadn't seen Stuart for the past two weeks. He hadn't come to the classes and she found herself wondering why. Perhaps he had dropped out, like several of the others, and she wouldn't have to see him again.

She was sitting with two of her brothers in a pub in Shoreditch, and one of them, Terry, had asked her warily if she was seeing anyone. Her initial reaction had been to bat the question away with a kind of cool amusement, but she looked at his kind, weathered face and relented. Maud knew her father and her four brothers talked about her, worried about her being single, childless, contrary, unsettled, a detective and her own worst enemy. At the rowdy family get-togethers, she came alone and unattached, played with her nephew and nieces, often made an excuse to leave early.

Terry was her oldest brother, and he was a roofer like their father: Frank O'Connor & Son fixed roofs and gutters throughout East London and into Essex. Terry had a wife and three daughters. The next brother, Brian, had a son and two dogs. The younger brothers were twins; one of them was going to be a father in the spring; the other had just moved to Romford with his partner and talked about starting a family.

'And the other trouble,' she continued, sinking her fork deep into the potato before she found any fish, 'is that I don't seem to like police officers either.'

'There must be some nice ones,' said Brian.

'There must,' said Maud dubiously. 'Somewhere. And the third trouble,' she added, 'is that being a detective has rather put me off men in general.'

'That's not good,' said Terry.

'I know.'

'Do you ever see Silas? He rang me, you know.'

'Silas and me are never going to get back together, if that's what you're imagining.'

'I wasn't.'

'Also,' she said, 'when would I find time for a relationship at the moment?'

'You work too hard.'

'I like working. I like solving things, hearing all the different contradictory stories, making connections, piecing together all the bits and finding the picture. It's just everything around the real task I'm not keen on.'

In her head, she heard the laughter of the men in the station a few hours ago about a sex worker who'd come in with an accusation against one of her clients. Knowing, ribald laughter that had made her want to set fire to the place.

'But do you manage to have fun?'

'Yes,' she said, smiling at her brothers. 'I have fun.'

FORTY-FIVE

Nancy dressed in her velvet jumpsuit and black boots, put on a touch of make-up and red lip gloss, let her hair loose.

'You look nice,' said Felix.

'Thank you.'

'But you might be cold.'

'I'm fine.'

'Anyway, we won't stay long.'

They walked up the road together, hand in hand. The rain had stopped but a cold wind blew against their faces.

'It might snow,' said Felix.

'That looks like Michelle and Dylan,' said Nancy, pointing at the figures ahead of them.

'Probably. I think the whole road gets invited.'

Sure enough, when they got inside the little house, which was already crammed with people and noisy with talk, Nancy saw that not only were Michelle and Dylan there, so too were Barney and Seamus, standing with a blonde woman and laughing at something she was saying. Her heart sank.

She took hold of a glass of mulled wine and breathed in the lovely smell of cinnamon and cloves. Felix put a hand over the top.

'Should you?' he asked gently.

'I'll just have a sip,' she said.

'Well, it's up to you. Be careful.'

'Yes, Felix,' she said.

And she was: very, very careful. She would tiptoe through these days, not put a foot wrong. And then she would vanish from Felix's life and people would wonder how she could leave such a kind and loving man, who had sacrificed so much for her. She patted him on the shoulder.

'You don't need to worry about me,' she said.

She talked to a woman who used to be in a circus, a drunk man who said her hair was the colour of summer rain, an entwined couple who invited her to their wedding though they didn't know her name. She talked briefly to Barney, whose speech was slurred and who held her hand and gazed at her as if she held the key to the universe. She avoided Harry, who looked tired and grumpy and had obviously come straight from work. On the stairs on her way down from the bathroom, she talked to the man who owned the house. He was wearing a pink shirt and a Santa Claus hat and was sweating profusely.

'I'm Jonathan,' he said. 'Jonnie.'

'Nancy. Thanks for this.' She gestured at the room of people.

'We've not met before, have we?'

'I've only lived on the road for a few weeks.'

'People come and go,' he said. 'Blink and you miss them. We've lived here for eleven years, more than almost anyone. Not as long as Michelle and Dylan, of course. Have you met them?'

'Yes.'

'Terrible what happened in the house next door to them. Did you hear about it?'

'Yes, I heard.'

'You never know what's going on in other people's lives, do you?' Jonnie wiped his brow, then flinched at a glass breaking.

'Did you meet her?'

'Yes. In fact, she was here this time last year. Nice girl.'

Woman, thought Nancy, but just nodded.

'Very lively,' added Jonnie. 'I thought she was a bit over the top, to be honest. But then, you know, out of the blue she told me and my wife that she got horribly homesick. I think she was a bit pissed by then. She got quite teary. Said she loved London but she missed her mother and home cooking and she even sometimes missed the rain. Like a child, she was, when she was talking about it. I thought to myself that maybe all the flirting and giggling was an act, a brave face she put on. Then, all of a sudden, she was smiling and laughing again, and when someone put on music, it turned out she was a great dancer.'

Nancy made a sound at the back of her throat. She thought of Kira being homesick, of Kira dancing and laughing, of Kira gazing up at her in terror, of her hanging in the doorway.

'I wonder what he made of it,' said Jonnie.

'Who?'

'That fellow there. They seemed pretty close. I think they left the party together.'

He was pointing. Nancy followed the direction of his finger.

'Barney?' she asked.

'No. The fellow he's talking to.'

As if feeling their gaze on him, Felix looked up and for a moment, their eyes locked.

He crossed the room to them. Nancy heard Jonnie give a small grunt.

'Time to go,' Felix said, putting a hand on her arm.

'I'm having a nice time,' said Nancy.

'You don't want to overdo it. She's been unwell,' he added to Jonnie.

Jonnie looked from Nancy to Felix, his brow furrowed.

'I didn't mean . . .' he began.

'I know.' Nancy smiled at him. 'It's fine.'

'What were you talking to Jonnie about?'

'Nothing much. The road and how it's changed.'

'That's London,' said Felix. 'People get pushed further and further out. It's one of the reasons it'll be good to leave.'

'Did you go to their party last year?'

'Me? Not that I remember. Why?'

'Just wondering.'

They walked down the road together, Felix holding her hand again and their steps in time. It was very dark. The moon was almost full; the stars seemed to fizz when Nancy looked up at them.

So, a year ago, Felix had been to the party and left with Kira. He had quite often visited the flat when his friend lived there. He had met the other occupants of the house and he had never denied he had met Kira as well, so why pretend otherwise? It couldn't be simply because he had thought Nancy would be suspicious if he was friendly with a young woman. She had loads of male friends; she wasn't a jealous person. In fact, she had always wanted Felix to go out with his own group more.

'Home,' he said.

A nasty little flat in a house full of people who Nancy disliked or distrusted.

'Lovely,' she said, and he turned the key in the lock.

FORTY-SIX

It was Saturday morning and Nancy was scrolling through recipes on her mobile. A Christmas ham, Christmas vegetables, Christmas cocktails, Christmas recipes for people who were tired of Christmas.

Felix leaned close to her as he refilled her coffee mug.

'Any ideas?' he asked.

'What?'

'I see you're looking at recipes. Has it given you any ideas?'

'I don't know.' She moved her phone away so he couldn't keep on peering at it. 'Maybe.'

'Months ago, I had the idea that we might go away for Christmas. Find a place on the coast. Or even go abroad. Next year, perhaps.'

'Yes,' said Nancy slowly. 'Now's probably not the right time.'

'Anyway, there's something to be said for having a quiet time to ourselves. We can go for a walk somewhere in London. Along the river. There'll be nobody around. We can have a drink in a pub and then come back for a nice meal.'

Nancy imagined the Thames path on a bright cold Christmas day, walking through Greenwich or round the Isle of Dogs. Standing with a beer and packet of crisps, looking across the water. It was the sort of thing that loving couples did. As she thought about it she suddenly felt it as a beautiful memory she had been deprived of in a life she would never get to live.

'That sounds perfect,' she said.

Felix sat opposite her.

'If it's going to be a Christmas at home then there's one thing we need. What's that?'

Nancy's sense of irritation returned. Why did he have to keep asking her questions? It was as if he was constantly testing her, giving her a chance to pass or fail. If he had something to say, he should just say it.

'I don't know. What?'

'A Christmas tree.'

'It's probably too much trouble, just for us.'

'Don't say that, Nancy. It wouldn't be Christmas without a tree.' He gulped down the remains of his coffee. 'I'm going to the market to buy some decorations and then I'll get the tree. Want to come?'

'I'm still feeling a bit tired,' she said. 'If that's okay.'

'It's perfectly okay. We don't want to rush things, do we?'

She had been a 'we'.

'No,' she said. 'We don't.'

Felix took his jacket from the hook and put it on. He wrapped a scarf round his neck.

'Anything you want me to get you?'

'I can't think of anything.'

When he had gone, she sat and stared at nothing for several minutes. In other times she would have been the one who suggested going out to the market and then maybe following it with brunch somewhere. She would have bought flowers for the flat and some interesting vegetables to do something with for dinner. She would have called friends round for an impromptu meal.

Abruptly, she stood up.

She couldn't buy flowers, couldn't call up friends and invite them round. But she could go outside, breathe fresh air, think things through. She pulled her jacket on.

Out on the street, she turned away from the direction that Felix would have taken towards the market. A cluster of people were standing on the pavement by the entrance. There were five of them, all about her own age. They weren't quite a group. Nancy could see that there were two men together, a man and a woman, and a woman on her own, and they looked like they were waiting for something to happen.

Nancy tapped the lone woman on the shoulder. She had a round face and spiky dark hair.

'Excuse me,' she said.

'Are you here for the viewing as well?'

Of course, Nancy thought to herself: Kira's flat. It was being rented out again. She was surprised it at taken this long.

'Quite a group,' said Nancy, nodding at the other two couples.

'I'm sure there'll be others,' said the woman. 'There's not much on the market at the moment.'

For a moment Nancy felt an awful temptation. But she told herself, no, absolutely not. She had herself to worry about now. She was planning her own escape from the house and that was difficult enough. Above all, the landlord had already caught her in the flat once. Two more people had arrived. They didn't seem to be together. Nancy turned to go and almost collided with a young man, immaculately dressed in suit and tie. His hair was brushed back and held in a small bun. His face almost gleamed.

'Hi, everybody,' he said. 'My name's Ian and I'm here to give you the tour of this highly desirable property.'

There was a murmur of greeting from the group.

'Isn't the landlord coming?' Nancy asked.

'He couldn't make it,' said the man. 'But I can answer all your questions. And anyway, this flat speaks for itself.'

Go in, said the voice. *You know you want to.*

'No, I don't want to,' said Nancy.

The woman looked at Nancy curiously. Nancy felt embarrassed for a moment but then told herself it didn't matter.

If you don't, you'll always wonder.

Ian pushed his way through and unlocked the front door with a flourish. Nancy hesitated at the back of the group and then felt as if she had fallen into a river and was being pulled along by the current, as if it was happening to her against her will. She was curious, compelled. She couldn't stop herself.

Once the group was inside, Ian stopped before opening the flat door.

'You'll already know how handily placed we are for transport and for the shops,' he said, while Nancy fumed with impatience, listening out for possible footsteps coming down the stairs. He opened the door and stood aside to let them all move past him inside.

Nancy gulped as she stood inside the flat once more. She had made the decision. But she would be as quick as possible and then she would leave.

'How did you know?' a voice said next to her. Nancy looked round and saw that it was the woman she had approached.

'Know what?'

'That he wasn't the landlord?'

Nancy was taken back. Why did this woman even want to know?

'I've met him,' she said.

'Is this all a fake then,' said the woman, gesturing towards the other people. 'Have you been promised the flat already?'

'No, nothing like that.' Nancy moved away as if she had suddenly seen something she needed to check out. She noticed Ian looking at her. Had he heard what she had said? He looked away again. It was probably nothing.

She took a moment and looked at the flat. It looked bare, shabby and abandoned. Only the winter sunlight making wavy patterns on the bare boards gave it a sense of possibility. There were the few items of furniture she had seen before – the pine table with a burn mark on the middle, the bench sofa and the wing-armed chair, a low stool, a fraying rug, faint square marks on the grubby walls where pictures had hung. The plug sockets were loose, the fridge was obviously rusty, the window-panes were in bad shape. Smudgy black marks and obvious signs of damp showed that Goddard hadn't even bothered to give the rooms a deep clean or the walls a lick of paint before renting it out again.

The two men were looking out of the window into the small garden. The other couple were in the kitchen. What would they think if they knew what had happened here?

She walked across to the spot. She felt like there should be a radioactive force where Kira had died. It should scorch her. But there was nothing, of course, except Nancy's own feeling of shock and desolation. She looked up at the beam. Nothing. Probably there had never been any evidence that would have been useful, but everything was gone now.

She looked down and then she saw something, just a wisp, between the floorboards. She knelt down and tried to take it between her thumb and first finger. She couldn't. The crack was too small. She thought for a moment and then took the keys from her pocket. She selected the thinnest of them and worked it into the crack between the two floorboards and worked it upwards.

She had it. She took it between her fingers.

'What are you doing?'

She stood up and found herself facing Ian.

'I'm checking the floorboards,' she said.

'Everything's in good order.'

'Really?' said Nancy.

She couldn't stop the question sounding slightly sarcastic.

Ian raised his eyebrows.

'Don't just take my word for it. You can ask the landlord yourself. He just texted me. He'll be here in a minute.'

Nancy was almost impressed with her response. She thought at first that her legs would give way under the shock at the sheer disaster of what she was facing. But she didn't. She remembered what she was holding between her fingers. With her left hand she took her wallet from her pocket and managed to flip it open. She released what her fingers were holding. She snapped the wallet shut and slid it back in her pocket.

'Thanks,' she said to Ian. 'I'll be off now.'

'Are you interested?'

'I've got lots to think about,' she said, urgently needing to get to the exit.

'I'm sorry,' said Ian. 'Did I get your details?'

Nancy ignored him.

She opened the door and William Goddard was standing there, a huge form blocking her path. He was fumbling with his key, and it took a moment until he looked up and faced her, a further moment for him to look utterly confused.

'It's you,' he said, and then his tone grew louder. 'What the hell are you doing here?'

The situation was such a nightmare that Nancy felt weirdly calm. She was able to think clearly. He's confused, she thought, he's angry. Just say something, anything, that sounds calm and normal.

'I heard you'd be here,' she said. 'I wanted to talk to you.'

He looked so surprised by this that he found it difficult to speak.

'What about?' he asked finally.

What about? Nancy felt like a drowning swimmer desperately trying to find something to cling on to.

'The damp in our ceiling. I keep trying to call you.'

He frowned. It wasn't true, but Nancy knew that he was a bad landlord, and she knew that bad landlords spent their time not replying to their tenants.

'I'll send someone round,' he said.

Nancy just mumbled something and inched past his bulk, out into the hall.

'Nancy,' said a voice, and she turned to see a large, bushy green tree moving towards her.

'You were quick.'

Felix put the tree down and stepped from behind it.

'What are you doing down here? Are you going out? I thought you needed a rest.'

'I just . . .'

'I gather your ceiling has damp,' said Goddard, who was still standing in the doorway of Kira's flat. He made it sound like an accusation.

'What?' Felix looked confused.

'I've never noticed that,' said a woman's voice, and Nancy saw that Michelle was there as well, largely obscured by the tree.

'We can discuss it later,' said Nancy firmly and headed for their door.

'I bumped into Michelle in the market,' said Felix. 'She helped choose the tree.'

'We've splashed out on loads of decorations.'

Michelle held up a carrier bag filled with glinting baubles.

'The tree's bigger than I expected.'

'It's a good shape,' added Michelle.

'Shall we have coffee?'

Felix unlocked their door and pushed the bushy tree through. Needles scattered everywhere.

'Lovely,' said Michelle.

'I might lie down,' said Nancy.

'Michelle's been very helpful. Why don't you put the kettle on?' It sounded like an order. 'Do we have biscuits?'

'We have lots of mince pies,' said Nancy. 'I'll warm some up.'

She went into kitchen alcove and turned on the kettle, then filled the kettle with water. She found the tin of mince pies.

'Shall I put those on a small baking tray?'

Michelle moved towards a drawer as if she owned the place. 'That's—'

Nancy stopped. The used condom. She had forgotten all about it. Now, in a flash of horror, she saw herself, all those weeks ago, rummaging round in Kira's garbage bag, and then she saw herself standing just like this with Michelle, and surreptitiously dropping it, in its plastic bag, into the deep drawer of baking utensils.

She jolted sideways and stood in front of it just as Michelle's hand reached out.

'It's fine,' she managed to say.

'Come on, Nancy.'

'I'll do it.'

'Very well.'

Michelle waited.

'When the oven's warmed up.'

Michelle gave her a curious smile.

'It's okay, you know.'

'I'm sorry?'

'You don't need to worry.'

'What?'

Bubbles of sweat were pricking on Nancy's forehead.

'I threw it away,' Michelle said.

'What are you talking about? I don't even . . .'

'I threw away the surprise package I found in there,' said Michelle calmly. 'Don't be anxious. Felix doesn't know. It's just between you and me.'

'I don't know what you mean . . .' Nancy's voice stuttered to a halt.

'You can get out a baking tray and we can have those mince pies with our coffee.'

With an immense effort, Nancy turned and slid open the drawer. She pulled out a baking tray, her eyes searching for the bag and not finding it. She wiped her forehead with the back of her hand.

Michelle stepped forward and took the tray from her other hand.

'Poor Nancy,' she said.

FORTY-SEVEN

'What were you doing downstairs?'

Felix was standing too close to her. Nancy made an effort not to step away.

'Nothing really.'

'What did he mean about damp? We haven't got damp?'

'Some sort of misunderstanding. He must have been thinking of Harry and Olga.'

'Is everything okay between you and Michelle?'

'Why do you ask?'

'I know she feels terrible about you being sectioned. It wasn't easy for her to come and tell me what you had said to her.'

'She doesn't seem to feel that terrible.'

'I knew you were still upset with her.'

'I'm not upset.'

'And you're angry.'

'I'm not.'

'You seem a bit angry.'

Nancy contorted her mouth into a smile. She could feel her blood pulsing.

'I'm not angry, but if you keep on telling me I am, then I probably will be before long.'

He held up his hands.

'Okay. Let's decorate the tree.'

'Great idea,' Nancy said.

'We have to start with the lights.'

Felix took a roll of lights out of their plastic wrapping and carefully unwound them.

'I bought them when you were in hospital,' he said. 'In hope.'

He pushed the plug into the socket and turned the switch. Nothing happened. He turned the switch on and off: still nothing. He crouched down and examined the wire, muttering.

'That's irritating,' said Nancy mildly. 'Maybe we have to do without lights this year.'

She took a yellow metal bauble out of the bag Michelle had left and hung it on a branch.

'What do you mean, do without lights? I only bought them a few days ago. They weren't cheap and they've never been used.' He seemed to make up his mind and stood up, coiling up the rope of lights. 'I'm going to return them.'

'Now?'

'Yes.'

'Where did you get them?'

'I saw a shop selling Christmas things on my way back from work. Fifteen or twenty minutes, less if I walk fast.' He looked at his mobile. 'I'll be back before one. You can have lunch waiting and we'll decorate the tree this afternoon.'

'I don't mind waiting till Monday.'

'We're doing it today. That was the plan.'

He pulled on his jacket and left in a demonstrative hurry. Nancy went to the window and watched him go, breathing out a sigh of relief. It felt like a small gift to have this unexpected time to herself. She would look at her things and decide what she was going to take, make sure her passport was where it should be.

But as she was thinking this, she saw Michelle and Dylan pass under her window, away from their house. They were both wearing waterproof jackets, gloves and scarves and Dylan was carrying a small backpack. They looked as if they were setting out on a wet winter walk.

This is your chance, said the voice.

'No,' said Nancy, almost in a moan. She wanted to put her hands over her ears, but she knew the voice wasn't real. It was inside her.

She knew she mustn't. She absolutely mustn't. All she had to do was to wait out the rest of this day and tomorrow, and she would be free. Nothing else mattered. Kira – poor, homesick, gregarious, hopeful Kira – didn't matter anymore. She was dead. The case was closed. Nancy had done her best, and her best had nearly wrecked her.

Nancy stood at the window. She thought about her time in the hospital. She couldn't go back there. She thought about Kira, staring wildly at her by the door, asking for her help, and about Kira's mother screaming in pain. She thought about Kira's body swinging on the rope.

The blue rope.

She thought of Dylan's scratched nose the first time she had met him, the day Kira had died. She thought of the way Michelle looked at him, of the way Michelle now looked at her, of how Michelle had got her sectioned – with Felix's help of course.

You have to know.

Nancy resolutely ignored it.

You'll always wonder. It'll drive you mad.

'No,' said Nancy out loud.

Think of Kira.

Nancy looked down at Michelle and Dylan's garden, with its little shed at the end.

She went to her bag and took out her purse. She opened

the purse and took out the thin nylon strands she had pushed inside. Blue strands. Strands from the rope, from when it had been cut? What else could they be?

She returned the strands to her purse. Felix was out of the house for a minimum of half an hour. Michelle and Dylan looked like they would be gone for hours.

Oh no you don't, she urgently instructed herself, even as she strode to the kitchen door, yanked it open, and before giving herself time to think, went down the metal steps into the garden.

There wasn't much of a separation between their patch of earth and the yard that the ground and basement flats had access to, just a disintegrating wall that was more symbolic than practical. But the fence between their house and Michelle and Dylan's was a robust wooden lattice on top of a low brick wall, with bare rose stems and other climbing plants twined into it from their side. Nancy gave it an experimental push, but it stood firm. There were no gaps between its sections. She looked back at the house, scanning the windows, and then, before she could lose her nerve, pulled a rickety table across. It was green and slimy and covered in bird shit.

She clambered on top. She scissored one leg over, hooked a foot through the lattice work, and launched herself. Her jersey caught on the fence. She heard it tear and she heard the fence creak and give way. Then she was thumping to the ground on the other side, landing on a spiky green bush, rolling over onto soil and then gravel. A spike of pain went through her shoulder. She was lying spreadeagled, her feet stretched out and her cheek pressed into the sharp pebbles.

She felt slightly sick and stayed where she was for a few moments, getting her breath back, then stood up and wiped the mud off her face with a sleeve of her torn jumper. She examined the fence, which she had pulled apart in her fall so that there was now a gap. One of the roses had been torn off the lattice and broken at its base.

Now what? She eyed the shed at the end of the garden. It was padlocked but the padlock looked pretty flimsy. She saw a small rock near the base of a little tree and picked it up. She rapped it against the padlock. The padlock did not fly apart as she had hoped. She banged it again, several times, and harder. The sound rang out in the cold air, and Nancy eyed her surroundings nervously, anticipating a face staring at her from a window.

This, she told herself, was both reckless and useless. She should just leave now.

But she walked round to the side of the shed and found a window that was dark with grime. She tugged its small handle, and it swung open. Nancy thought she could just about clamber through it, but when she tried to pull herself up, pain shot through her shoulder. She dragged a little wrought-iron bench across and clambered onto it. It swayed as she stood on it but held fast. And from there it was easy to squeeze through the window and into the dark shed, feeling cobwebs stick to her face as she did so.

She landed on something soft. She squinted in the gloom and saw she was standing on a bag of compost. She stood down from it, among a cluster of objects that were hard to make out. There were things that belonged to a garden shed – a strimmer, a spade, a box full of trowels, secateurs, garden twine and gloves, a precarious tower of plastic pots, a large watering can, several saws of different sizes. There was a chair with no legs, a bicycle wheel, an old window frame, multiple large pots of paint in stacks. There was something large in the darkest corner that when Nancy put her hand out to touch it, moved. It was Dylan's punch bag.

Nancy was looking for a coil of rope. There were two shelves high up on the wall and she reached up to feel what was on them. A series of small paper packets with sharp corners fell on her face, some scattering seeds all over her. There were empty jam jars, plastic containers of rose food. No rope.

Nancy knew that even if the fibres she had picked up from Kira's flat came from the rope used to hang Kira, and even if Dylan was the owner of that rope, it was a slim chance that he would have kept it, and if he had kept it, had put it in this shed. She was only looking in here because it was possible to look here.

Just as she was thinking she should give up and climb out, she heard a sound. There were voices in the garden.

FORTY-EIGHT

Before she could stop herself, she pulled the little window shut and then realised they might have seen that. There was nowhere to hide. She squatted on the ground and put her arms around her head, trying to control the shallow gasping that was coming from her.

If they found her, they would call the police. Or the doctor. She would be back in custody and this time it wouldn't be just for a few weeks. She cursed herself as she crouched there in the dark. What had she done? Why had she done it? Was this what it was like to be mad? Was Felix right about her? Why else was she in here, among the dead flies and old plant pots, looking for clues that probably didn't exist to a death that nobody but her thought was a crime?

For a moment, she heard a faint insistent whispering. *Mad*, it seemed to say. *Crazy.* Voices coming from nowhere, people who weren't there.

She squeezed her eyes shut.

'Where do you want me to put it?' Dylan was saying.

That was real at least. He sounded cross.

'I thought it could go where the camellia used to be.'

Michelle's voice sounded horribly close. They must be standing about three feet from the shed.

'Do you want me to plant it now?'

'Why not?'

He'll need the spade to dig a hole, thought Nancy. She imagined it, the key in the padlock, the door swinging open, and Nancy curled on the floor, hiding her face. The thought was so ghastly she almost called out to them, just to get it over with.

'Because it's raining.'

'It's more drizzle than rain.'

'I call this rain.'

'It's up to you,' said Michelle in her pleasant, modulated tone that made it clear she thought he was just prevaricating.

'What's happened to the rose?' Dylan said. 'Look. It's been snapped.'

'That's my Himalayan Musk. And the fence is damaged.'

'Shit. That's all I need. I bet it was that fucking Seamus. He comes out here and smokes weed.'

Nancy waited for them to notice the bench up against the shed. The effort of breathing quietly hurt her chest. There were things moving on her scalp. Spiders, she thought.

'I'm going to have a word with him.'

'It could have been anyone,' said Michelle.

'I hate having a household of tenants next to us.' Dylan was getting angrier as he spoke, working himself into a temper. 'You don't look after a place unless you own it. With their loud parties and rubbish everywhere and look at the state of their garden. Not to mention having a madwoman as a neighbour.'

'You think she's mad, do you?' Michelle's voice was still low and pleasant.

'You're the one who said so. Paranoid and crazy. Anyway, you just have to look at her to know she's not right. Those glittery eyes and the way she watches people.'

'You watch people,' said Michelle. There was a slight pause. 'Or rather, you watch women.'

'What are you talking about?'

'Don't pretend: this is me, remember. I've seen the way you look at Nancy.'

'That's crap.'

'She's very pretty, in an unconventional way, if a bit unkempt.'

'Don't tell me you're jealous!'

'Don't be ridiculous. I'm just saying, Dylan, that you should be careful. Because you looked at Kira that way as well.'

There was a sudden silence. When Dylan spoke, his voice was a growl.

'You're going too far.'

'Am I? I'm glad to hear that. I can't always be getting you out of scrapes.'

'You stand here, wanting me to plant this bloody bush in the rain, and insult me at the same time.'

'Plant it later then.'

'Don't worry. I intend to.'

There were footsteps on the gravel. A door opened and shut. After a few seconds, Nancy uncurled herself and stood up. Her legs shook and she felt dizzy with the aftermath of her terror. But the whispering had gone.

Now she needed to get out of here without them seeing her. She tried to remember from when she had been in their house if the shed was visible from the kitchen. Probably. How long should she wait? When was the most likely time for the kitchen to be empty? She had no idea – and anyway, if she waited much longer, Felix would come home and find her gone.

She decided to make her escape at once, and before she could argue herself out of it, had climbed back out of the window, onto the little bench and into the garden. She dragged the bench over to the fence, climbed up and pulled apart the damaged latticework sections to make a gap wide enough for her to climb through. The rose tore at her skin and she could feel blood trickling from under one ear.

She jumped and landed heavily, scrambled to her feet, peered over to see if she could shift the bench back a bit, but was unable to. Pulled the fence closed as best as she could.

'Well, hello!'

She spun round to see Barney.

'Hi,' she said.

'Jesus!' He was staring at her in amazement.

'What?'

'Has something happened?'

'What do you mean?'

'You're bleeding. And covered in mud and something green as well.' He took a step closer. 'You look really rough. What've you been up to?'

Nancy put a hand to her face and tried to brush away some of the dirt.

'Gardening,' she said.

'Really?' Barney stared dubiously at the cracked paving stones, the nettles and weeds, the obvious lack of any gardening implements or sign of weeding and clearing.

'Yes, really.'

'Are you sure you're all right?'

'Yes.'

'You don't seem all right.' He was standing up against the dividing wall now, a foot or two away from her. 'You can tell me, you know, I'm on your side.'

'I must go and shower.'

She started back up the metal steps and as she did so, Michelle came into the garden she had just exited.

'Nancy?' she called. 'Can I have a word?'

Nancy didn't answer, nor turn her grubby, blood-smeared

face. She ran up the remaining steps and opened the door into the kitchen. Hearing the key turn in their entrance door, she charged into the bathroom, locking the door behind her.

'I'm back,' called Felix.

'Just having a shower.'

'The water won't be hot.'

'Never mind,' she said.

She turned to face herself. No wonder Barney had been startled: her hair was wildly matted, her face was smeared with mud and green mould, there was a bruise on one cheek and blood trickling down her neck. Her jumper was torn beyond repair.

She took all her clothes off, releasing earth and gravel and numerous plant seeds onto the floor, then stepped under the shower. Felix was right: the water was not hot. But she washed herself thoroughly, shampooed her hair, then wrapped herself in a towel and scooped up all her clothes. Her skin was covered in goosebumps.

'Hi,' said Felix as she came out.

'Any luck with the lights?'

He pointed. A twinkling rope of lights was plugged into the sockets.

'Brilliant.'

'What've you done to your cheek?'

'Oh, that. Just bumped into something.'

'When you're dressed, we can have lunch, then decorate the tree.'

'I haven't actually got anything ready yet.'

Felix frowned.

'What have you been up to?'

'This and that,' said Nancy.

FORTY-NINE

Felix said he was going out to get some food, a few other things. Did she want to come along?

'I'm still feeling a bit tired,' Nancy said.

'We need you to get better.'

As soon as the door closed, she phoned her bank. She pressed a number and she found herself on hold. As she listened to a piece of piano music that she recognised but couldn't name, she wandered round the flat, wiping surfaces, rearranging objects and occasionally looking out of the window for Felix. If he returned, she would have to hang up and try again the next time he left the flat. Five minutes went by, ten, fifteen and she started checking the street more and more often.

She started swearing at herself and swearing at her bank and then went to the window and saw Felix at the end of the street with two bulging tote bags. She was about to terminate the call when it was answered.

'I need a replacement bank card,' said Nancy.

'No problem,' said the voice cheerfully. 'Are you having a good day?'

'I'm sorry, I'm in a hurry.'

'No problem. First, I'm going to take you through security.'

She had to provide her address and her post code and her mother's maiden name and her contact telephone number.

Finally, she explained that she wanted a new debit card.

And no, she didn't want it sent to her address. Could she collect it in person from a branch? A pause. She looked out of the window. Felix was walking up to the front door. Yes, she could collect it from a branch. She would need to bring two forms of identification. Now, for the address of the branch. Nancy heard Felix's footsteps on the stairs. She fumbled for a pen, dropped it, picked it up and wrote the address on an envelope. The door opened.

'Thanks,' she said and broke off the call.

'Who was that?' said Felix.

'Nobody.'

'Nobody? It sounded like somebody to me.'

'Of course it was somebody,' said Nancy. 'I meant that it was nobody important.'

'Who?'

Was this really happening? Was she really having to justify herself? She thought desperately of something that would make Felix stop.

'It was one of those calls where they ring you and say they've heard you've been in an accident and that it wasn't your fault. One of those dodgy insurance companies.'

'Yes,' said Felix slowly. 'I know what they are.'

Nancy couldn't tell from this whether he was mollified or didn't quite believe her.

It didn't matter, though. It was Saturday. Monday was the day.

But there was one more task remaining. As Felix was putting the food away, Nancy scrolled through the contacts on her phone. She was looking for the right sort of person, a person who wasn't also a friend of Felix's, preferably someone who didn't know about her recent psychiatric problem. She needed someone who she had lost touch with but not someone she had fallen out with or had lost touch with so long ago that it would be embarrassing. No ex-lovers. And they had to live in London.

She scrolled down, silently saying no, no, no to herself and then she stopped at a name she hadn't even thought about for a year or more. Megan Hutchens. A few years back she had been part of a group that used to meet occasionally for a drink or for coffee. Nancy had thought they were about to become proper friends and then Megan suddenly left her job and went travelling abroad. But Nancy had heard from someone that she was back. Yes, she'd be worth trying.

Nancy just needed five minutes on her own, but it proved hard to get five minutes on her own. She thought of going into the bathroom and locking the door, but the walls of the flat were so thin that Felix would hear that she was talking to someone. In the afternoon, Nancy, in desperation, said that she wanted to go out for a walk and get some fresh air.

'I'd love that,' said Felix.

'If it's all right,' said Nancy, 'I'd really like to go on my own. Just to clear my head.'

'It's not all right,' said Felix with a smile, as if he thought Nancy had been joking and he was joining in. 'I'd really like to go with you. There are things we need to talk about.'

Nancy considered trying to insist but she knew that Felix wouldn't give way.

When they were out on the street, Felix took her hand. It didn't feel romantic to Nancy. It felt more like she was a dog on a lead.

'Are you all right?' he said.

'I'm fine.'

'You don't have to be defensive.'

'In what way was I being defensive?'

'Well, like that. You're talking in a defensive tone.'

Nancy felt as if she was a fly caught in a web, getting more and more entangled in the sticky threads.

'I don't know what to say. You asked me a question and I answered it.'

'It wasn't a real answer. It feels like you're shutting me out.'

'I'm not.'

'I'm not being angry,' Felix said. 'It's because I care about you. I wonder about your state of mind. When you're cutting yourself off in that way, it makes me wonder if things might be going wrong with you again. I wonder if that's something we should think about.'

Nancy murmured something unintelligible in response. She wanted to avoid saying anything that would provoke an argument or that would make Felix suspicious.

'You know that I'd do anything to make you all right and keep us all right as a couple. Anything.'

'Yes, I do know that,' said Nancy with absolute sincerity.

It worked out more easily than she had expected. Just before they were going to have supper, Felix said he was going to have a shower and change into something more comfortable. As soon as Nancy heard the water, she retreated into the kitchen, as far from the bathroom as it was possible to get, and she rang Megan Hutchens. Please don't have moved, she said to herself. Please don't be on holiday. Please answer the phone.

She did answer the phone and for once everything worked out as Nancy had planned. Megan was delighted to hear from Nancy. She'd been meaning to get in touch. When Nancy gave the briefest of explanations of her situation, she was immediately sympathetic. When Nancy asked if she could stay with her for a few days, she said of course and sounded as if she meant it. Was tomorrow possible? The sooner the better, said Megan.

Tonight, if Nancy wanted. If she wanted to come during the day, Megan would leave a key with her neighbour, who worked from home. And she lived in West Hampstead, which wasn't even that far away.

When the conversation ended, Felix was still in the shower. He couldn't have heard anything. It was perfect.

FIFTY

Maud was skating. Every December, she went with a group of friends to one of the ice rinks that sprang up round London. This year, it was at Somerset House. The evening was cold and clear. The large, decorated Christmas tree glittered, and the moon was almost full. Floodlights shone on the glimmering oval of ice which people were zig-zagging around, some gracefully, others in a blundering rush that usually ended in a fall.

Maud had learned as a young child. She'd had lessons every Saturday afternoon at the Lee Valley rink and even entered local competitions. She rarely skated now, but she still had an agile, confident gait and she loved the crisp sound of her blade cutting into the ice, the paradoxical sense of control and freedom, concentration with the feeling of being in a dream.

All of a sudden, a figure ahead of her lurched, half spun, arms akimbo, and came crashing to the ground. Maud came to a crisp halt and looked down. A face stared up at her.

'Maud?' said Stuart.

'Hello.'

'What are you doing here?' He was still lying outstretched on the ground, his soft brown hair messy, his cheeks glowing.

'Skating,' she said, and he grinned up at her, seeming quite happy to stay where he was.

She held out a hand and pulled him to his feet, where he tottered slightly and grabbed on to her.

'I'm not very good at this.'

'It takes practice.'

'Will you show me?'

She took him by the arm and slowly they made their way round the rink, past her friends and his. They didn't speak, except for her to tell him how to push with his skate, how to balance and hold the glide.

'Thank you,' he said when they'd completed the circuit. 'In about ten years, I'll have got the hang of it. How come you make it look easy?'

'I learned as a child. Then you never quite forget – like riding a bike.'

'I'm not really an arsehole,' he said.

'Good to know.'

'Do you want a drink?'

'Now?'

'They're selling mulled wine.'

'All right.'

They stepped off the ice and teetered across to the kiosk where Stuart bought two paper cups of mulled wine. Maud bent her head to breathe in the cinnamon and cloves and allspice. When she lifted it again, she saw Stuart was watching her.

'What?' she asked.

He looked embarrassed.

'You look different.'

'In what way?'

'Less stern.'

'Do I look stern?'

'At the evening class, anyway.'

'You haven't been for a bit.'

'No. I had flu and then last week, I got a puncture on my

way and it would have been almost over by the time I arrived. Did I miss much?'

'The introduction to contract law.'

He groaned.

'You'll catch up.'

One of her friends called to her from the rink, beckoning.

'Can we do it again?' Stuart asked, seeing she was preparing to go.

'What, skate?'

'Meet.'

'I'd like that,' she said.

Then she rejoined her friends, and Stuart watched her as she flew round the ice, slender and strong, her curly blonde hair rippling, her face alert, a frown on her thick brows but a tiny smile on her lips.

That night, in bed, Felix nuzzled against Nancy and started rubbing his hand slowly up and down her spine. She pretended to be asleep.

The following day, she said that she had a banging headache. She stayed in bed all day, the curtains closed, and every time Felix came into the room she closed her eyes and breathed evenly. He would stand by the bed for several minutes. Her skin crawled when she thought of him staring down at her. Rage and fear shifted heavily inside her. It took all her will to keep lying there, unmoving, her face wiped clean of all expression.

But she just had to wait it out. Tomorrow she would be free.

FIFTY-ONE

At a quarter past eight on Monday morning, Felix opened the door of the flat and then turned.

'Do you need any money?'

Nancy didn't actually need any money. She had her Oyster card. And in the past few days, she had squirrelled away bits of cash in an inside zip pocket of her jacket. She had almost fifty pounds. She could make that last until she collected the debit card. But it might seem strange not to ask for anything at all.

'I could do with some,' she said. 'I might need to buy something.'

Felix took his wallet from his jacket and extracted two notes. Nancy saw that they were both twenties. He looked at them and then put one back in his wallet and replaced it with a ten. He handed them to her. When she had taken the money and put it in her pocket, he continued to watch her. Was he waiting for her to say thank you? She couldn't bear to. The idea made her almost physically sick.

'Have a good day,' she said.

Once he was gone, Nancy knew that there was no real hurry. It would be seven or even eight hours until he returned. But she felt almost superstitious about something going wrong. She pulled out a canvas bag from under the bed and quickly crammed it with everything she would need to get by for week or two. She wished she could take more but that would have needed several bags and she didn't want to attract attention. Someone might get suspicious and tip Felix off.

She had thought about leaving without a word but then that would give Felix the excuse to call the police and get her into trouble again. Perhaps he would do that anyway. She picked up an old envelope and wrote on the back:

I'm going away. Don't try to contact me. I'll be in touch about collecting my stuff.

N

She placed it prominently in the middle of the table. She looked around. There was nothing left to do. She picked up the bag and walked out of the door.

She opened the door and stepped out onto the path where she almost collided with a woman coming in. She was carrying a large picture, half wrapped up in a bath towel. Nancy heard the woman say hello in a strange, almost surprised, tone. She knew the woman, but for a moment she couldn't think where from.

'What are *you* doing here?' the woman asked.

The question was unexpected and, almost without thinking, Nancy replied that she lived in the upstairs flat. The woman looked baffled.

'I don't get it,' she said. 'I'm just moving in. How can you be here as well?'

'I live upstairs.' As Nancy said the words, she recognised the woman. She had met her during the viewing of the flat.

'But if you already live here,' the woman began, 'what were you doing . . . ?'

'It's complicated,' Nancy said. 'I needed to talk to the landlord.'

'Well, anyway, I'm your neighbour now. My name's Sadie.'

'I'm Nancy.' She looked at the eager, flustered face of the woman. 'You're renting the flat?'

Sadie grinned.

'I hope so. I've paid the deposit. I got a bit worried when I saw your face. I wondered if there'd been some kind of mix-up.'

'You're moving in today?' Nancy said, trying to change the subject.

'That's the plan. I haven't got much stuff with me. I'll bring the rest on the weekend.' She seemed to be considering something. 'Nancy, would you like to come in for a coffee?'

'I'm really sorry,' said Nancy. 'I was just on my way out. I'm in a real hurry.'

'Are you going away?'

She gestured to the bag Nancy was holding.

'Yes, for a few days.'

'Some other time then,' said Sadie. 'When you're back.'

'Yes. Some other time.'

Nancy heard the door close behind her. She walked a few cautious steps, half expecting someone to stop her . She was free.

Then she stopped. Something had struck her. She had met Sadie at the same spot she had met Kira. She tried to push it away, but the image of Sadie's young, eager face kept coming into her mind. This woman was moving into the flat where Kira had died. Had been murdered.

Keep walking, Nancy told herself. Walk away. Sadie won't be in any particular danger. There's no reason why she should be. And anyway, this is no longer any business of yours. You got involved once before, you did what you thought was the right thing and it ended with you being in a mental hospital. If it happens again, they'll put you away and you'll probably never come out. Let someone else do the right thing.

She took another few steps and then stopped.

She thought of Kira asking her for help. She thought of Sadie, eager and friendly.

'Fuck, fuck, fuck, fuck, fuck,' she said.

An old woman approaching, looked at her, aghast. Nancy hadn't realised that she'd spoken the words out loud.

'Sorry,' she said, but the woman shook her head disapprovingly.

Nancy hesitated. The bus stop was in the wrong direction and the bag was cumbersome. She went back into the house.

'Hi again. I thought you were on your way out,' said Sadie, who was struggling with her keys.

'Forgot something,' said Nancy.

She entered her own flat, left the bag by the door where she would collect it on her way back, and ran down the stairs and out onto the street.

It would be her one last act of defiance, before she was gone for good.

PART FOUR

FIFTY-TWO

That Monday morning, Maud was on the phone in the middle of an argument when she became aware that a colleague was standing in front of her, trying to get her attention. She turned her back on him, but he moved in front of her, brandishing a file. She tried to wave him away, mouthing that she was busy, but he held the file in front of her face. When she finally put the phone down, he was still standing there.

'Did you get it sorted, ma'am?' he said.

'No, I didn't get it sorted.' She looked at him suspiciously. 'What are you doing here? Why are you waving that file around?'

The young detective smiled.

'You know how I went on that course about how to deal sensitively with women?'

'I did not know that,' said Maud. 'Did it do any good?'

'I think it did. Because I've got a woman in my office at the moment. In the old days I'd have just kicked her out or charged her with wasting police time. But now that I've been on this course and I've learned that we've got to be social workers and social psychologists as well as coppers, I want to check in with you before I kick her out or charge her with wasting police time.'

Maud sat back in her chair.

'All right then. Check with me. What's the problem with this woman?'

'You mean, what *isn't* the problem with her? It's Kemp's case actually, but he's on annual leave and anyway, he'd just tell me to get rid of her. A month ago, a young woman killed herself.'

'Yes,' said Maud. 'I remember.'

'Hanged herself in her flat. Case closed. But this woman came in claiming it was murder. It turned out that she was a full-on psychotic. Seeing things, hearing voices. We took a statement and looked into it out of politeness. You know, co-operating with the public. The next thing we heard, she was in hospital.'

'I heard that too.'

Maud remembered Kemp's look of triumph when he told her that the woman had been sectioned.

'Now it seems that she's talked her way out of it and she's back in here saying it's murder again.' The young detective seemed to be considering things. 'She's nice-looking, mind. I want to deal with it sensitively. Maybe I should take her number and talk to her about it over a drink after my shift.'

Maud looked at the detective impassively. Detectives said things like that to her to see how she'd react. If she got angry, they would laugh and say that they were only joking. Except that Maud knew that sometimes they weren't joking. Sometimes they did get the numbers of women who came in to report crimes.

She took the file from his hand.

'I'll talk to her,' she said.

FIFTY-THREE

Nancy looked up as the door opened again, expecting to see the young man with a broad face and irritating smirk. Instead, a woman came into the room, shutting the door quietly behind her. She seemed about the same age at Nancy herself, perhaps slightly older. Nancy didn't really know what she expected a detective to look like, but it wasn't like this: the woman who came swiftly towards her was slim and upright, of medium height. She was dressed in a rust-coloured corduroy jumpsuit, belted at the waist, and sturdy black boots. Her hair was tangle of blonde curls, loosely tied back, and her face, startlingly pale, looked slightly asymmetric. She had several studs in her ears, a large mouth and clear eyes that she fixed on Nancy, a slight frown creasing her forehead.

Maud's first impression of the woman who Kemp had dismissed as crazy was of a quivering kind of energy. She was small and slight, with large eyes, high cheekbones, a fall of pale brown hair that she kept pushing at impatiently with her fingers. Maud saw she had bitten her nails to the quick. She wore jeans and a moss-green jumper that she had rolled up to the elbows so that Maud could glimpse a small abstract tattoo on the soft skin of her inner arm.

'Ms North,' she began gently.

'Nancy. I'm Nancy.'

'Nancy, my colleague tells me . . .'

'He just thinks I'm mad,' Nancy said impatiently. 'He wouldn't even hear me out, just kept leering at me and saying I should try and keep calm.'

Maud had glanced at the file before coming in. Much as she disliked Kemp, it had seemed he was right, and that Nancy North had conjured up wild suspicions out of a kind of paranoia. Her plan had been to steer this woman away as kindly and courteously as she could. The woman in front of her was clearly desperate, but there were many other desperate people.

'As I understand it, the situation is this. Kira Mullan was found dead on Monday the fourteenth of November. The investigating police and the coroner decide that she took her own life. But you believe that she may have been murdered. This is based on a brief meeting you had with her, a very brief meeting, on the day she died. You said she seemed distressed.'

'Scared,' said Nancy. 'She seemed scared. I think she was asking for help.'

'I understand that you were also in the middle of a psychotic episode.'

'A very mild episode, but yes, and that's why nobody takes me seriously. But it doesn't make me wrong.'

'You see the problem though.' Maud tapped on the file with a forefinger. 'There's no actual evidence.'

'I felt the same,' said Nancy. There was a faint tremor in her voice. 'That's why I wasn't going to do anything more. But then a new woman moved into Kira's flat this morning and I looked at her and I just couldn't leave it. I couldn't. I tried to.'

'You know I've got to say this, Nancy, but you've just recovered from illness.'

'I was sectioned again,' said Nancy. She had made a great effort to be calm. 'After I'd talked to the police and been dismissed as paranoid and psychotic, the neighbour from next door told my partner, Felix,' – Maud saw how Nancy's lip curled as she said his name – 'that I had threatened to injure or kill myself or someone else. That's the key thing. If you're an immediate threat, that's when they lock you away. Felix told my doctor, and I was dragged off to a mental health ward. I spent weeks there.'

'I'm sorry.'

'I'm not asking for sympathy.' Nancy took a deep breath. 'Felix calls me reckless and perhaps he's right. I'm sure I can be difficult, and it's true I have an illness, or a condition at least. But it's under control. I went to my doctor, adjusted my medication and I was okay. But you know, once you've had a mental diagnosis, every time you're a bit impulsive, a bit passionate, if you just raise your voice, people think it's happening again. Everything's a symptom. When Michelle, our neighbour, said that, it was enough to have me put away, but it wasn't true. It was an outright lie.'

'Why would she do that?'

'I don't know. Maybe she wanted me out of the way.' She shook her head. 'I know, I know. Even to myself that sounds paranoid. I don't have solid evidence, but it just feels all wrong. I know Kira didn't kill herself. I met someone who had a crush on her who said she had been happy just before. And everyone's been lying. Felix said he didn't know her and then it turns out he knew her quite well. Seamus – he lives downstairs – says I made a pass at him when it was actually the other way round. And who do you believe, the handsome gym instructor or the crazy woman? I heard Michelle tell Dylan – her husband, who's a fucking shit by the way, and who had a cut on his face the day Kira died – that she had seen the way he looked at Kira and that she couldn't always be getting him out of trouble.'

Nancy could see the disappointment on Maud's face.

'I know. It's not enough. I tried to find something that was. I broke into Michelle and Dylan's garden shed to look for the rope.'

'What? I'm not sure you should be telling me this.'

Nancy shook her head impatiently.

'It doesn't matter. I needed to see if there was a rope that matched the fibres I found between the boards in Kira's room.'

'Did you break in there, as well?'

'I sort of pretended to be a prospective tenant. I wanted to see if there was a matching rope in their shed. It was stupid. I nearly got caught.'

'Stupid is one word for it,' said Maud. 'Criminal is another.'

'I know. You see, people have been calling me mad, and I think I almost have become mad. I can't seem to let go. It's hard to describe. When I saw Dylan and Michelle walk by on the road outside and this idea of searching in the shed came into my mind, it was as if I was listening to two voices: the sane and logical voice, telling me not be a self-destructive fool, and the other voice, insisting. Just like now, when I had to come here, for one last go.'

'When you say voices . . .' Maud began cautiously.

'I do mean voices.' Nancy's eyes were fierce. 'I'm not going to lie about it. I've come to the end of everything now. I know how I must sound to you. I know what everyone thinks of me. In a way, I think that about me as well. It's like something that's going on inside me and outside of me as well. Dissociation, is that what they call it?'

She put a hand up and clutched her hair.

'What's wrong with me? Why can't I let things go like other people do? Maybe it was something about Kira. When I met her that afternoon, it was as if she was calling out to me. But maybe everyone's right and I'm deluded and sick.'

Maud didn't know what to say. She looked at Nancy's troubled face and wanted to help her, but she couldn't think of what to do. When Nancy spoke again, she sounded calm and resigned and sane.

'When I was in the hospital, it was like a crazy game. I had to say that I believed I had been mad in order for them accept that I was sane and let me out. Coming here is a terrible risk. Felix is just waiting for me to step out of line. He watches over me. Every time I raise my voice, he narrows his eyes and looks concerned. If they send me back, I might be there for years.'

Maud knew what she needed to say to Nancy. She needed to tell her to concentrate on saving herself, getting her life back together, but she couldn't find the words. She played for time by leafing through the files, glancing at the dry information about the nature of Kira's death, the cursory interviews with people in the house and with Kira's boss, the details of her last phone calls and messages, on to photos of the body before it was cut down, then on the slab, the coroner's report, the interview with Nancy herself.

Nancy waited. For the first time in weeks, she had the sense that someone was dispassionately looking at the case, sifting through facts, neither patronising nor dismissing her as someone whose mind was troubled and whose words could therefore not be trusted, but were merely the wild utterances of a woman who heard voices and saw faces that were not real. She didn't go as far as to hope that Maud would take up the cause, but she believed she would at least be rigorously fair.

Maud was just flicking through the awful photographs one last time when she stopped. She felt a lurching feeling. Oh no, she thought. She looked at one photograph more and more closely.

She wanted to close the file and be done with it. She wanted to get back to work. She wanted Nancy to get back to healing herself and repairing her life. And now this.

'What?' said Nancy.

'Take a look at this photograph.'

Maud swivelled it round towards her and Nancy stared at the stark image. The noose around Kira's horribly lengthened neck, her body slack and heavy, her face dark, her eyes open, those green boots with their yellow laces. She blinked and looked away.

'I know it's distressing,' said Maud. 'But what can you see? Apart from the body.'

Nancy made herself look again.

'Clothes scattered around,' she said. 'An overflowing wicker basket, a guitar, an overturned stool.'

She peered at the objects that were out of focus, the small pine table, the bench-like sofa and dark grey wing-armed chair. There was the wind chime she had seen on the day she had crept in there after the cleaners, the candles and throws and little things Kira had used to brighten the dingy space.

'The stool,' said Maud. 'Tell me about it.'

'What?'

'Tell me what you see.'

'It's just a stool. Three legs. Small.'

'Imagine it standing the right way up. How tall do you think?'

'I don't know. I'm not good at that sort of thing. Eighteen inches?'

'That sounds about right. And how far are Kira Mullan's feet from the ground?'

'More than that, I think.'

'It'll need to be checked, but much more.'

'But if that's true, then . . .'

Nancy stopped, her eyes wide and shining with sudden hope.

'It has to be checked, of course. But if true, it indicates that she couldn't have stood on the stool.'

'Does that mean it was murder?' Nancy asked.

Tears were running down her cheeks.

'It means that it needs investigating,' Maud said. She considered this. 'My colleagues are not going to be happy. Danny Kemp is going to be very unhappy.'

'What happens now?'

'We'll need to talk to you further.'

'I've left the Fielding Road flat – well, I'm in the process of leaving it. That won't matter, will it?'

'I've got your details. Are you leaving London?'

'I'm going to be in West Hampstead for a bit. What about the other people in the house? Will they need to know?'

'Yes, they'll need to know.'

FIFTY-FOUR

When Maud had finished, Chief Inspector Craig Weller looked displeased.

'You want to be careful, Maud.'

'What do you mean?'

'Kemp was in charge of this case, and he was satisfied. Policing isn't just about going into old cases and stirring things up.'

Maud had many things she felt like saying. She could say that she thought policing was about solving crimes. She could say that if an investigation had been handled badly, then it needed to be done again, properly. But she knew that she had got as far as she had partly by not saying what she felt like saying.

'I just think that this death deserves some more investigation.'

'From what you've told me, your only witness is a woman who's just come out of a psychiatric hospital.'

'She's not a witness. She's just a woman who brought this to my attention and what she told me sounded credible.'

Weller sniffed dismissively.

'This thing about the stool being too low. It feels a bit thin to me.'

'In what way?'

Weller thought for a moment.

'Off the top of my head, if the stool was too low, she could have put some books on it and stood on those.'

'That's worth considering,' Maud said. 'I'd just like to point out that I've checked the photographs of the scene, and I couldn't see anything that could have been used in that way.' She gave a slight nod. 'Of course, the scene might have been interfered with. The first people on the scene may have moved things. As I say, it's worth investigating.'

'Investigating,' he said, as if the word had an unpleasant taste. 'It was Kemp's case; if anyone's going to be doing the investigating it should be him.'

'He's on annual leave. And I'm just winding up the case I was working on.'

'Hmmm.' He glared at her. 'And how will you proceed?'

'First of all, of course, I need to call Kira's mother and warn her we're looking again at her daughter's death. And then I'll look at the case with fresh eyes. Bearing in mind this new evidence.'

'I'm saying this for your own good, Maud. You don't want to get a reputation as an officer who goes around second-guessing her colleagues. They might start to think you're not a team player.'

'I thought I'd just ask some questions, see if there's anything to investigate. If there isn't, then there's no harm done.'

'Except for some time wasted.'

Maud swallowed hard.

'If you don't want me to do this, you can just tell me.'

'I'm not here to micromanage you,' he said. 'I'm just trying to watch out for you.' He smiled. 'You might say I'm taking a fatherly interest in your career. Just keep me informed.'

As Maud left, she felt it had gone much as she had expected. Her boss had given her permission, but it had been reluctant permission. If it turned out badly, it would all be down to her.

FIFTY-FIVE

Nancy left the police station almost giddy with a relief that she hadn't felt for weeks, months. She had done the right thing and now it could be dealt with by a professional – a fabulous woman with snaky blonde hair.

Now she could return to the flat, get her things together and start her new life.

She was lighthearted as she ran up the stairs and let herself into the flat for the last time. But as she was stooping to pick up her bag, she realised that there was something strange. She felt it the way she felt that rain was coming, even when the sky hadn't turned black.

Felix was sitting on the sofa. He had left that morning for the office, but he was here. Sometimes he worked from home, but he wasn't working, and he wasn't reading. He was just sitting.

'I thought you were at the office,' she said, stepping away from the bag so he didn't notice it. Perhaps he already had.

'Yes, I know.'

'Did something happen there?'

'Nothing in particular.'

Nancy was finding it hard to read his mood. He wasn't obviously angry, but he wasn't affectionate either. He was just calm.

She walked across to the kitchen table and put her hand flat across the note she had left. It had been so visible that it was hard to believe Felix hadn't already read it. She crumpled it into a ball and pushed it into her pocket. She filled a tumbler with water and drank it.

'When were you going to tell me?' Felix asked.

Nancy felt as if a cold electric shock were running through her. Oh. They were going to be having this conversation after all. She suddenly felt that her legs were trembling and might even give way under her. She returned to the main room, found a wooden chair and sat down on it facing Felix.

'About what?'

'Don't play games.'

'I'm not playing games. If you want to ask me a question, then ask me a proper question and I'll answer it.'

'Have you been to the police?'

'The answer is yes. And how do you even know to ask that question?'

Felix gave a little laugh that made Nancy feel almost physically sick.

'I'm sorry, but you don't get to ask the questions. I just want to make this clear so that we know what we're talking about. Did you go to the police about Kira's death? Again.'

'Yes.'

'After all we've gone through.'

'It's me that's gone through things, not you, but yes. Now I've answered your question, maybe you can answer my question. How did you know? Have you been following me?'

'It might have been a good idea if I had been following you but no, I wasn't. Someone told me.'

'You weren't following me, but someone else was.'

'It was someone who was concerned about you. Although they weren't exactly following you.'

'I know who that is,' said Nancy bitterly.

The two of them just stared at each other for several seconds.

'I don't quite know what to say,' said Felix. 'I really don't.'

'There's nothing you need to say,' said Nancy, trying to stay calm. 'I'm a grown woman who's tried to behave like a good neighbour.'

'Nancy, Nancy, Nancy,' said Felix soothingly. 'This is me you're talking to. Not an enemy.' He stood up. 'Shall I make some coffee?'

'I'm fine,' said Nancy.

'I'll make some anyway. It'll be good for us, while we talk.'

Nancy sat on the chair, as if frozen to it, while she heard the kettle being filled and the clatter of cupboard doors shutting. After a few minutes, he came back from the kitchen with two mugs, a cafetière and a little jug of milk on a tray. He placed it on the table and poured the coffee and handed one to her. She took it, almost numbly.

'What I can't understand,' he said, as if no time had passed since he had last spoken, 'is why you didn't discuss this with me before going to the police.'

'It didn't need discussing,' said Nancy.

Felix sipped at his coffee and looked at her thoughtfully.

'I don't think you quite realise the situation you're in,' he said.

'I think I do.'

'You've just come out of psychiatric care and one of your main symptoms was your paranoid fantasies about this tragic girl. They let you out because you seemed to accept that you had been imagining things, making them up out of your sickness. You've caused disruption to everyone here. You've wasted police time.'

'The detective I've just talked to doesn't seem to believe that I'm wasting her time.'

'We'll see about that. Maybe this detective doesn't know you as well as I know you. She certainly doesn't care about you, the way I do. And have you thought about Kira's family? What do you think it'll be like for them when the police start stirring everything up again?'

'I have thought about them,' said Nancy. 'I think about them every day.'

He laughed and shook his head.

'You know what's doing my head in. I'm going back over the last days and I'm thinking about all the things you've said that just aren't true. My first reaction was to feel betrayed and angry. You lied to your doctors to avoid treatment. You lied to me, so that I would back you up. But I'm not angry. I'm worried that your symptoms are starting all over again. I think we might need to see someone about that before it gets worse.'

Nancy was still wondering how to answer, whether she even needed to answer, when the doorbell rang. Without taking his eyes off her, Felix got up and walked over to the door. Nancy heard a crackly voice and Felix pressed the button to let the person in.

FIFTY-SIX

He opened the door and waited expectantly. Nancy had risen and stood behind him. There were footsteps and two people entered. One was Maud. With her was a younger man, tall, with pale red hair, a bony face, wide-apart, surprised eyes and an ill-fitting suit. He had the expectant look of a teenager arriving at his first job interview. Maud was wearing a distressed grey jacket over her jumpsuit, which made her look more like a builder than a detective. She nodded at Nancy, but spoke to Felix.

'I'm Maud O'Connor.' She held out her identification and gestured at her companion. 'This is my colleague, Mark Forrester.'

'I'm sorry if I look surprised,' said Felix. 'I hadn't realised until a few moments ago that Nancy was going to go to the police.'

Maud looked puzzled. 'Is that a problem?'

'I'm worried that this might all be a waste of your time. I keep hearing that the police don't have time to investigate crimes in London, and I'm a bit surprised to see you here about this.'

'Why are you surprised?'

'I thought it had all been settled. I thought the police had already investigated Kira's tragic death.'

'I'm not sure how much of an investigation there was,' said Maud, looking around the flat, as if it interested her.

'I think you may have misunderstood the situation here.'

'Really? In what way?'

'I hate having to say this, but I'm worried about my partner.' He gave a meaningful glance towards Nancy, who scowled furiously. 'She's in a very vulnerable situation. She's been having some severe mental disturbances and we've been trying to get through this together. She's been having delusions. They became serious enough that she has spent some time in hospital. She's only just been discharged, and I'm concerned that going to see you in the way that she has is a sign that the delusions are starting again.'

'I am here, you know,' said Nancy.

Maud smiled at her, then turned back to Felix.

'I have talked to Nancy, and she seemed reliable to me.'

'Reliable?'

'Yes.'

'With respect, you're not a psychiatrist and you don't know her the way I do.'

'You're right,' said Maud. 'I'm not a psychiatrist. For my sins I'm a police detective, and maybe I can just ask a few questions.'

'You're sure you're not making things worse for a vulnerable person?'

'Oh, for fuck's sake, Felix,' said Nancy.

'We'll be as sensitive as we can. Is it all right if we talk here?'

'Why do you want to talk to me?'

'You both lived in the same house as Kira Mullan.'

'It's just routine,' said Forrester.

They were the first words he had spoken. He blushed.

'Sit anywhere,' said Felix.

Forrester sat on the edge of a chair and took out his notebook. He poised his pen, at the ready. Felix took the sofa, sitting back and folding his arms.

'I suppose you'd like me to leave,' Nancy said to Maud.

'I'd like you to stay.'

Nancy didn't sit next to Felix. She took her wooden chair and moved it against one wall and sat there. Maud sat on the sofa and turned to Felix.

'I just want to get the arrangement of this house clear in my mind. You and Nancy moved into this flat recently.'

'Yes.'

'How recently?'

'A couple of months ago.'

'We moved in on Saturday the twelfth of November,' said Nancy.

'Thank you. Did you know anyone in the house?'

'Nancy didn't, but I did. We got the flat because a friend of mine was moving out. And through him, I knew Seamus and Barney. They live in the basement.'

'Did you know the victim?'

'If she *was* a victim.'

'You seem quite committed to the idea of her not being a victim.'

'I just don't like to see the police wasting their time.'

'That's very public-spirited of you, Mr Lindberg. Did you know Kira Mullan?'

'I would have seen her around.' Felix looked across at Nancy. 'Nancy has been through a very traumatic time. It's been bad for her, but it's also been bad for those around her. She's needed a lot of looking after. One day she might come to realise what people have done for her.'

There was a silence that Maud didn't break for a long time. She simply looked at Nancy, who was gazing straight ahead, and then back at Felix.

'Did you know Kira?' she said finally.

'No. But she lived downstairs. I'm sure I saw her coming and going.'

'Actually, you did know Kira,' said Nancy.

Her words were like a stone dropped into a well. The four people in the room seemed suspended for a few seconds in the silence that followed. Nancy looked at Maud, not Felix, but she could feel his gaze on her as if it was a tangible weight.

'You knew her,' she persisted, though it was hard to speak the words out loud.

'Oh, Nancy!' Felix put his hand up to his eyes. 'My darling one.'

'Why do you say that?' asked Maud, ignoring him.

'Because someone told me. He said that Felix and Kira were at a party together last Christmas, and that they left together.'

Maud turned to Felix.

'Mr Lindberg?'

Felix leaned towards her. He looked handsome and sad.

'The kindest thing I can say is that Nancy is misremembering or misinterpreting what this person may or may not have said. As I've explained, part of her illness manifests itself in paranoid suspicions about other people.' He stared at Nancy and gave her a tender smile. 'Even though you never have reason to be jealous of me. I'm loyal.'

'It was Jonnie who told me,' said Nancy, who felt giddy with the euphoria of not pretending. It was like a teetering edifice, held together by fear and lies, was falling down around her; even though she might get crushed, there was a thrill in its collapse. 'From number 73.'

'You're doing it again,' said Felix in a low but carrying tone.

'I can see this is a difficult subject,' said Maud, while Forrester wrote down the address in his notebook. 'Let's move on for the time being.'

'Hang on,' said Felix. 'I just want to clear up this accusation my partner has made.'

'You mean, it isn't true?'

'I mean, maybe I spoke to Kira at a party. It was a year ago. People were drinking. I could have spoken to any number of people. Maybe we happened to leave the party at the same time, but that's all. I don't want you to fall into the same trap that Nancy has fallen into, and make nasty inferences from an innocent meeting.'

He kept glancing at Nancy, his face gentle and his eyes cold. She held his gaze and wouldn't look away. Something about the detective gave her a new confidence.

'I'll do my best not to fall into any trap,' said Maud. 'But to continue: Kira Mullan lived downstairs. Your two friends live in the basement. And a married couple live across the hall from you.'

'Harry and Olga and their crying baby.'

'On Saturday evening, there was a party in the basement flat that Kira went to. Did you also go?'

'Briefly,' said Felix. 'But it was very crowded, and I didn't really know anyone, so I didn't stay long.'

'What time?'

'I don't know. Around ten, I suppose, after we'd had the supper I'd made and then I'd cleared up. I only stayed an hour or so.'

'Did you see Kira?'

'No, or maybe I did without realising it. As I say, I barely knew her.' He threw an angry glance at Nancy. 'And it was rammed.'

'That would mean you came home at about eleven?'

'Yes. Nancy was fast asleep. I unpacked a few things and then went to bed. I was tired. It's been a tiring time.'

'Can you take me through your movements on the Sunday?'

'I told the police all this before.'

'Now I'd like you to tell me.'

He took a deep breath.

'I was here all morning. Trying to get some kind of order into the place. I wanted to make everything nice for Nancy. I did almost all the packing myself and now I wanted to do most of the unpacking as well. I don't think disorder is good for her. I've done my best to protect her from that.'

Nancy felt like a coiled spring. She forced herself to remain sitting in the wooden chair, her eyes fixed on him. Felix picked up his coffee, which was now cold, took a sip and grimaced. Maud didn't react, simply waited for him to continue.

'Then she left. I didn't know where she was going. I see now I should have insisted I went with her, but ...' He shrugged. 'Anyway, about ten minutes later, maybe a bit more, I went out myself.'

'What time would this have been?'

'About two forty-five, I guess. I can't be sure. I went to the big DIY place about half a mile from here. Britten's. I needed a few things – nails, some screws and wall plugs, Polyfilla, stuff like that.'

'Britten's, you say. Do you have a receipt?'

'Probably.'

'If you could find it, that would be useful.'

'Now?'

'When we've finished talking. You can give it to Mark here.'

Forrester bobbed his head.

'Why do you need all of this, anyway?'

'I am trying to fill in all the gaps,' said Maud. 'Get a clear picture of the day.'

'All right. I went from Britten's to meet a mate for a beer. Gary Overton.'

'Gary Overton,' repeated Forrester, writing it down.

'I can give you his details.' Maud nodded. 'We had a drink up the road from Britten's, and then we came back here for a bit. Nancy was home by then, but she was in bed, and I didn't want to disturb her. Sleep is an important part of her recovery,' he added. 'Then Nancy woke up, Gary left – I think he was a bit embarrassed because she was clearly in a bad way. Some people find mental health issues hard to deal with. Shortly after that, people came round for a drink.'

'Who?'

'Michelle and Dylan from next door. Seamus. Barney. And Harry. Not his wife. She was looking after the baby. When they left, we had supper, pottered around a bit, then went to bed.'

'You were there when the body was discovered the following day, right?'

'Not exactly. I came home from work, late afternoon I guess, I'm not sure of the exact time but that must be on the police records, and there was this commotion going on at the entrance of Kira's flat.'

'Who was there?'

'Michelle, Seamus, Dylan, or maybe Dylan arrived when I did. It's a bit of a blur. And then she arrived.'

'She?'

'Nancy.' He stared at Nancy. She stared back. 'Nancy arrived and went haywire.'

'I did not go haywire. I wanted to see the body because I could see the boots, and they were the boots that the woman I'd met the day before was wearing. But you wouldn't let me.'

'Nancy, Nancy,' Felix said helplessly.

'You and Dylan hauled me upstairs like a sack of potatoes. I was angry. Being angry is not being haywire. Being suspicious is not being paranoid. Wanting answers is not a sign of paranoid delusion.'

'When did you last see Kira?' Maud asked Felix.

'No idea.' He gestured helplessly. 'Maybe at the party the night before. I heard she was there but I don't remember seeing her.'

'And not that Sunday – the thirteenth of November?'

'No.'

'You're quite sure?'

'Yes.'

'And you still say you didn't really know her?'

'Yes.'

'Thank you. If you could dig out that receipt, my colleague here will be back to collect it.'

She stood up and Forrester followed suit.

'Nancy is not a reliable witness,' said Felix, also getting to his feet. He looked very tall and solid next to Maud, who was slender though sturdy, with her pale nimbus of curls and her dark brows. 'I want you to bear that in mind. She's ill. I don't like to think what this might do to her.'

Maud looked at him steadily, as if she was considering him. His cheeks gradually flushed.

'Would you agree to a DNA test?' she asked. 'It's a very simple swab.'

The muscles around his mouth tightened.

'I assume you're asking both of us.'

'I'm asking everyone.'

'Just a formality,' said Forrester.

'If it's necessary.'

'Good. A colleague will arrange it shortly.'

'By the way, there was a used condom,' said Nancy.

Her voice rang out. Everyone turned to look at her. Even

Maud, whose face was usually composed, seemed momentarily startled.

'In a bin bag full of Kira's rubbish. I found it.'

'For fuck's sake,' said Felix. 'You see. You see what you're dealing with here?'

Nancy continued talking in a slightly husky voice to Maud.

'I took it because I thought it might be a clue.'

'It might be,' said Maud. 'Where is it?'

'I hid it in the drawer with the baking stuff. But Michelle took it.'

'You know this how?'

'She told me.'

'This is unbelievable,' said Felix. 'You can't be taking any of it seriously. It's a farce.'

'We can let ourselves out.' Maud turned to Nancy, who still sat by the wall. 'I'll be in touch with you soon, she said, looking at her steadily. 'Take care.'

FIFTY-SEVEN

'That was awkward,' said Forrester in a carrying whisper as they closed the door to Felix and Nancy's flat.

Forrester had only joined the unit eight weeks ago, and Maud wondered how he would deal with life in the Met. He was big-boned and awkward, his eyes wide apart, his shoulders hunched to disguise his height. He was anxious to please and his enthusiasm hadn't yet been rubbed away. She had seen him with his peers, trying to join in the joshing and banter, but always one step behind. Either he would learn to be one of the gang or he wouldn't. She wasn't sure which was worse.

'What did you make of them?'

Forrester furrowed his brow.

'I feel sorry for him.'

Maud thought of Nancy sitting tensely in the chair, her eyes bright with fear and defiance. She thought of Felix, his exaggerated gentleness and air of martyred patience.

'Don't you?' Forrester asked.

'No, I don't. You sort those DNA swabs. Him, her, everyone else we talk to in the house.'

She knocked on the door of Harry and Olga's flat and heard shuffling footsteps before the chain slid across the bolt and the door swung open. She found herself face to face with a large, red-faced baby. Holding the baby, looking too small for the task, was a tiny woman. She was wearing a shapeless dress and slippers, and her hair was tied tightly back from her narrow face.

'Hello?'

'I'm sorry to bother you. Are you Olga Fisk?'

'Yes.'

'I'm Detective Inspector Maud O'Connor. We were wondering if we could have a word.'

'What's this about?'

'We're here about the death of Kira Mullan.'

Olga furrowed her brow. 'I thought that was all over.'

'Can we come in?'

Olga moved away from the door and the two detectives followed her into the flat. It was smaller and darker than Felix and Nancy's, with no door out to the garden. There were baby things everywhere – little garments hung over the radiator and the backs of chairs, a changing mat on the floor, an overflowing basket of dirty clothes and towels and muslins next to the washing machine, a buggy against the wall, bottles in the sink along with unwashed dishes. On the table was a pile of medical textbooks. There was a slightly rancid smell in the air of sour milk and wet clothes.

'Sorry for the mess,' said Olga. 'The washing machine's broken and the landlord doesn't fix it. And the roof, it keeps leaking.' She gestured upwards.

'That's hard,' said Maud, wondering how three people could live in this tiny, damp flat.

'Harry's got exams. That's my husband.'

'Which must make it even harder. How old's your baby?'

'Lydia. She is three and a half months.' She jiggled Lydia on her hip, then pressed her lips against the downy crown of her daughter's head.

'Is your husband here?'

'He's at the hospital. Why do you want to speak to him?'

'We're talking to everyone in the house. We want to speak to you as well.'

'He's here all day tomorrow, before doing nights. What do you need to know?'

'Can you remember what you were doing on the Sunday that Kira was last seen?'

Olga nodded. 'I told the other officers,' she said. 'Can't you look at what I said then?'

'I'd like you to tell me,' said Maud.

'All right,' she said reluctantly. 'Harry and I were here all morning. We were both tired. Lydia had been awake a lot and there had been the noise of the party as well, all night. I tried to keep Lydia quiet so Harry could revise. In the afternoon, he looked after Lydia for an hour or so while I met a friend for coffee in the new place by the cinema. That was sometime after three. I met my friend a bit after half past three. Sometimes,' she added, 'I have to get out of here, get away from her.' She looked apologetically at her baby, as if she could understand. 'I love her of course, but being a mother – it can eat you alive. There are days I feel I am disappearing. Then I have to remind myself who I am. Harry understands that.'

Maud nodded.

'Did he look after Lydia here?'

'No. He left when I did and took her out in the buggy. She sleeps in the buggy. And then after I'd had my coffee, I went to meet him, and we walked back together. We were here after that until six, when he went to have drinks with the neighbours. I was here with Lydia.'

'Neither of you went out apart from this?'

'I went to the corner shop with Lydia mid-morning, half past ten or eleven, for milk and then walked round the block, but it was nasty weather; we didn't stay out. And Harry went for a ten-minute walk after lunch to clear his head.' She saw Maud's questioning look. 'That was at about two thirty, something like that. Before three, anyway.'

'And you didn't see Kira?'

'No.' Olga stroked her baby's plump cheek. 'The last time I saw her was the day before.' Tears filled her eyes. 'She said she would babysit.'

'That was nice of her.'

'Yes. I didn't know her well, but I think that she was a nice person. She was always friendly and cheerful, and she was kind to me. It's hard to believe—'

'That she took her life?'

'Yes.' Olga held the baby closer. 'It's very sad.'

FIFTY-EIGHT

'What have you done?' said Felix, as the door to their flat clicked shut.

'I've done what was right.'

'What happens now?'

'What happens,' said Nancy, making herself speak clearly and meet his eyes, 'is that the police look into Kira's death. It's in their hands now.'

'That's not what I meant.'

'What did you mean?'

'What do you expect me to do?' Felix looked at her calmly.

'You can go back to work, for a start,' she said. 'You've taken enough time off as it is.'

'Not today. Not for a while. I think I've been too trusting. I'm staying here.'

Nancy stood up.

'You can stay here if you want. I'm going for a walk.'

'It's cold out there.'

'I need fresh air. I hate being cooped up.'

'I'll come along.'

'I'd like to be alone.'

'I've seen what happens when you're alone. Creeping out, going to the police, deceiving me.'

'This isn't about you, Felix.'

'No. It's about you. About your . . .' He searched for the right word, found it, spoke it in almost a whisper. 'Your *imagina-tion*. And about how safe you are to be left alone.'

'All right. I won't go out.'

'We'll go together. Once you've unpacked your bag.'

After their visit to Olga, Maud had been intending to knock on the door of Seamus and Barney's flat. But back on the street, at the top of the steps that led down to it, when she saw a barrel-chested middle-aged man with a broad forehead, jutting chin and collar-length hair unlocking the door of the neighbouring house, she changed her mind.

'Mr Strauss?' she called.

'Yes?'

'Could I have a quick word with you? I'm Maud O'Connor and this is my colleague, Mark Forrester. We're investigating the death of Kira Mullan.'

Dylan froze, his hand on the key. His face darkened.

'She killed herself. That's all done.'

'We're taking another look,' said Maud.

'For God's sake, is this what you lot do? I had a phone stolen a few weeks ago. What did the police do? I'll tell you, nothing. A friend of mine got his bike taken and even though it was tagged, the police couldn't be bothered to look into it. But you're poking around in a case that's been settled.'

'I'm sorry,' said Maud. 'Can you tell me why this is obviously such a problem for you?'

His expression changed from angry to confused. He passed a hand across his brow.

'Sorry,' he said at last. 'I didn't mean to fly off the handle. You have a difficult job. I guess everyone has just been rattled by what happened. Of course, you can ask me anything you want. Come in.'

They followed him into a large, light-filled living room, paintings on the walls, books on the shelves, everything in its right place. Maud tried to picture the other house, and figured this must be the equivalent of Kira's entire flat, though she hadn't seen that yet.

'Coffee? Tea?'

'No, thank you,' said Maud.

'I'm fine,' said Forrester, taking out his notebook and bouncing it up and down on his knee.

'How can I help?'

'We're just putting together a picture of the Sunday that Kira was last seen alive.'

'She was only seen by Nancy North. Maybe it was just her imagination.'

'When did you last see her?'

'Me? I have no idea. I saw her quite a bit, of course, though not to talk to. I don't work,' he said. 'I was made redundant last year, and I'm at home a lot. My wife works part time.'

Maud nodded. She wondered how a man like Dylan Strauss would deal with being unemployed while his wife was still earning.

'I'd see Kira come and go. I used to meet her in the street. Every so often I'd help carry her shopping.'

'You didn't go into her room?'

'No,' he said. 'Not that I remember.'

'You don't remember whether you ever went into her flat?'

'That's what I said.'

'You didn't see her on Sunday the thirteenth of November?'

'I've told you. No. Not that I remember at least. Michelle and I were out most of that day. We left mid-morning to go to lunch and then an exhibition in town. We got home about half past four and then an hour and a half later went to drinks at Felix's place. I think Felix had invited Kira, but she never turned up.'

'You were out most of the day, with your wife, and you didn't see Kira?'

'That's it. I'm not much help, I'm afraid.'

'But you were on friendly terms with her?'

'I didn't know her well, but I always thought she was well-meaning. I sometimes used to worry about her.'

'Why?'

'She was always going out in the evenings, dressed up to the nines. She looked like she knew how to look after herself but I'm not sure she did.' He paused, let his eyes rest on Maud's face. 'You don't think she killed herself? Is that what this is about?'

'Tying up loose ends,' said Forrester.

'You look clever enough,' said Dylan. 'You don't want to be pulled into that woman's weird world.'

'Are we still talking about Kira Mullan?'

'I'm talking about Nancy. Don't get me wrong, I feel sorry for her. But she's not well. She thinks we're her enemies. We just did what we had to. I saw what she was like when they took her away. She was like a wild animal. And this whole fantasy about that girl being murdered and making wild accusations. It's just ridiculous.'

'And the cut on your nose?'

'What?'

'Did you have a cut on your nose that Sunday?'

'It's her, isn't it? You're listening to bloody Nancy North, again.' He stopped and realised that the detectives were waiting for an answer. 'If I had a cut, which I don't remember, it would have been from gardening or shaving or something like that.'

'Shaving your nose,' said Maud.

'Gardening, then. Anyway, I don't remember a cut.'

Coming out of the Strausses' house, Maud saw a couple in the distance. She stopped for a moment, narrowing her eyes, and recognised Nancy and Felix. He was looking at her. She was paying him no attention.

FIFTY-NINE

Barney Samuels turned out to be a talker. He talked to fill silences, and he talked because he had grievances he wanted to air and thoughts he wanted to share, and because, Maud thought, he was someone who felt he wasn't properly listened to.

Maud listened to him intently, and as she did so, she watched him. He was short – with a short man's compensatory posture, legs apart, chest pushed slightly forward – and had a wide boyish grin that he used rather too often. His wry way of putting himself down seemed defensive.

Barney told her what he had done that Sunday in some detail: he had been horribly hungover after their party, had drunk a great deal of coffee, eaten some cold pizza and tried to do a bit of clearing up, but abandoned the attempt. 'I thought I'd wait till Seamus got back,' he said. 'After all, it was his party more than mine.'

At midday, he had left the flat and gone to his parents' house in Lewisham for Sunday lunch. 'Pork,' he said, 'with apple sauce, roast potatoes and red cabbage.' He had returned at about half past four, had a short nap, and then gone to Felix and Nancy's for drinks. That evening, he and Seamus had been together, cleaning the flat, playing a video game.

'Did you see Kira that day?'

'No. The last time I saw her was at the party, one or two in the morning, I guess. She was a bit wasted. But then, so was I.'

'Did you talk to her?'

'Just in passing.'

'How would you describe her mood?'

'She seemed quite chirpy.'

'Chirpy?'

'Chatting away, drinking, giggling. I don't know. I didn't really pay much attention.'

'She didn't seem down or troubled by anything?'

'Not that I could see. She was a party animal, Kira was. But to be honest, I stayed away from her.'

'Why was that?'

Barney flashed her his rueful grin, but it dissolved and his face turned sour.

'She had made it pretty clear she wasn't interested.'

'Do you mean, interested in you?'

'Yeah. I mean, it wasn't anything much, but after she and Seamus broke up – not that that was much either – I thought it was worth a try.'

'You propositioned her?'

'If that's the word. Anyway, she turned me down.'

'When was this?'

'A few days before the party,' said Barney.

'How did you feel about that?'

'I'm kind of used to it. Seamus is the one women like. They fall for him. He doesn't always treat them well, but that doesn't seem to put them off.' He shrugged and spread his palms. 'Mind you, Kira didn't let herself get pushed around. She chucked him.'

'When?'

'A week or so before that Saturday night at ours, I think. I'm not sure. It wasn't a big deal. But he isn't used to being dumped.'

Maud nodded.

'Men,' said Forrester. 'Why do women put up with us?'

'I have no idea,' said Maud.

'Like Michelle and Dylan,' said Barney.

Maud made a small, encouraging sound, praying that Forrester wouldn't intervene.

'I mean, she knows he's cheated on her.'

'How do *you* know?'

Barney grinned.

'You know, things he's said. He jokes about it. She sort of does as well. She calls him a rogue, that sort of thing. It's like she goes along with it, like it's a stupid hobby he has.'

'But you haven't actually seen him with anyone.'

'Well, I wouldn't, would I? I'm not spying on him.'

Maud thought about what Nancy had told her of Michelle and her part in having her sectioned.

'How well did Michelle and Dylan know Kira?'

'Michelle knows everyone. Finger in every pie. She has keys to all the flats. She has them for safe keeping and when people are away, she checks up on things, waters plants, collects mail, stuff like that. I think she likes to know what's going on. I assume she did the same for Kira as well.'

'You're saying that the Strausses had everyone's keys.'

'I think so. She had ours at any rate, and I know Felix gave her a set. I don't know about Harry and Olga. Have you met them?'

'I've met Olga.'

'Poor thing.'

'Why do you say that?'

'Cooped up in there with a crying baby and an overworked husband who shouts at her. I mean, we sometimes hear him, even down here. I don't know what it's like for Felix and

Nancy. What Felix has to deal with! What with the baby crying and Harry shouting next door, and then living with someone who's not in her right mind. He must be a saint.'

'Mmm,' said Maud neutrally.

'She pounced on Seamus, you know.'

'I heard that,' said Maud.

Barney's eyes were suddenly bright. He looked pleased.

'According to Seamus. Who likes to think he's irresistible. Imagine if two women turned him down in a matter of weeks. Can I ask you something?'

'Yes.'

'Why are you in the police? I mean, you don't look like a detective.'

'What do detectives look like?'

'Good point.' He laughed. 'Not like you, anyway. Why?'

Maud got up, smiling at him.

'I said you could ask. I didn't say I'd answer.'

'Thank you for agreeing to see me like this.'

Nancy sat on the bed with the door shut and her laptop angled towards her. She could hear Felix vacuuming in the main room, imagine him nosing the machine into the corners with a determined expression on his face.

'Hello, Nancy,' said Helena gravely, her face grainy on the screen, half in shadow. 'I'm sorry about what you've been through. We have a lot to talk about.'

'That's an understatement,' said Nancy, trying to smile.

'Where would you like to start?'

'I wish I could see you face to face.'

'We can arrange that.'

'This'll have to do for now.'

'How are you?'

'I'm feeling like a prisoner,' said Nancy in a whisper.

Helena waited. If only Nancy could look into her soft brown eyes, she would feel a bit better, as if someone understood her.

'I was never mad,' she said. 'It's hard to tell you everything that's happened. I wake in the night and I'm there again. In the hospital. I hear the sounds of people crying; I know there are eyes watching me in the thick darkness. It's as if something is crouching, waiting to pounce. I'm so scared, I almost want to die, just to get it over with. The horror of it. And the horror is still there, it's not safely in the past; it's like a door into pitch blackness and if I don't take care, I'll be sucked through it again and it will slam shut. If I tell you, Helena,' she said, more quietly, 'that I'm very frightened of . . .'

The bedroom door swung open and Felix came through, pushing the vacuum cleaner.

'Don't mind me,' he said, bumping it against a wall and then reversing. 'Pretend I'm not here.'

SIXTY

'Hi,' said Stuart in a stage whisper.

He was late and had squeezed his way past a couple of other people in order to sit next to Maud.

She nodded at him and turned her attention back to the lecturer.

'Contract law is the legal body that encompasses the origination, enforcement and enactment of all legal contracts. A contract is essentially an agreement between separate parties initiating mutual obligations enforceable by law.'

Stuart was scrabbling in his leather messenger bag for a pen. Maud slid over one of hers.

'Companies and consumers both use it almost every day. Does anyone have an example of how they themselves have depended on it today?'

'Did you get my message?' Stuart hissed as hands were raised.

'Yes.'

'You didn't reply.'

'Sssh.'

'There are four basic rules of contract law,' the man was saying. 'Offer. Acceptance. Intention to create a binding legal relationship. Consideration. We will take these in turn.'

Stuart and Maud sat side by side, Maud taking notes in her meticulous cursive, Stuart occasionally making hasty scrawls amid his doodles.

'Well?' Stuart said as the lecture came to an end and the class were gathering their things together and pushing back their chairs.

'Yes.'

'Yes?'

'Yes, I'd like to go out for a meal with you on Thursday.'

'Great. And how about a drink now?'

Maud thought of the work she needed to do on the Kira Mullan case. She was tired, but full of a restless energy that she often felt at the start of a new investigation, her brain working away and trying to make a shape out of the fragments. She looked at Stuart, and once again felt a slight uplift, a sense of coming alive again after so long in the dull aftermath of her grief about Silas.

'One quick drink,' she said.

He was easy to talk to, smart, funny. They didn't talk about previous relationships, nor about their work, though they discussed the other people on the course and which bits of the law they found tedious. They swapped snippets of information about their lives. He came from Dorset; she from East London. He was one of two; she had four brothers. His parents were both alive, though his father had heart failure and was probably on borrowed time; her mother had died when she was a teenager and her father had brought the family up single-handedly. He hated Christmas; she hated making New Year resolutions. He hated flying and she hated enclosed spaces.

'Another,' he said, pointing at her glass.

'One drink meant one drink.'

'Okay. We'll see each other in a couple of days.'

'Actually, we'll see each other on Wednesday: it's the last class of the term.'

'I've got to give this Wednesday a miss,' he said.

'Thursday then.'

They went out onto the street.

'I've got my bike,' he said, pointing.

'I'll say goodbye.'

'Maud.'

'What?'

'I just . . .Shit. I'm out of practice.'

'That's all right,' said Maud, and put her arms round him and kissed him on the mouth, then pulled back.

'Night,' she said, and walked away with a smile on her face that he couldn't see.

A few moments later, he biked past her.

'Your rear light's not working,' she called.

He raised a hand and waved.

SIXTY-ONE

It was past eight in the morning, and Felix was still in his dressing gown, freshly shaven and his hair damp from the shower. He sat across the table from Nancy and buttered a piece of toast.

'Aren't you going in to work this morning?'

He looked up briefly, then put marmalade onto the toast and took a small, crisp bite, crunched it for several seconds, swallowed.

'No,' he said eventually. He took another bite, wiped his mouth with a square of kitchen towel, took a sip of tea. 'I'm working from home for the time being. I've cleared it with my boss, who is being very sympathetic. Aren't you going to ask me why?'

'All right. Why?'

'I am not going in to work because I don't trust you. I don't trust you not to lie to me and I don't trust you not to do something stupid and harmful. Do you know how near I am to calling your doctor and telling him what you've done?'

Before she had time to stop herself, Nancy opened her eyes wide and pincered her thumb and forefinger so they were almost touching.

'This near?' she said, instantly wishing she hadn't.

'Are you laughing at me?'

'No, of course not. I was just – oh, I don't know. Don't look at me like that.'

'Do you know how much you've hurt me, Nancy? Do you have any idea of what I've done for you, what I've given up?'

'Why don't you just leave me then?'

'I love you,' he said. 'And I'm responsible for you now. You don't realise it at the moment, but you need me, Nancy. You're standing on the edge of another disaster. You understand that, right?'

'Right,' she said.

'And it's true.' He held up his thumb and forefinger. 'I am that near.'

He bit into the toast again. Crunch crunch crunch. There were crumbs on his chin, a smear of butter on his upper lip.

'Do you know what we haven't done for a very long time?' he asked.

'What?'

'Not since Friday the eleventh of November, to be precise.'

'Very precise.'

'That's a long time to go without any sex.'

'Lots of things have happened,' she said.

'Not even a proper kiss,' he said. 'As if you don't desire me anymore.'

'The drugs,' she said. 'They change things.'

'Sure,' he said. 'And I've been very sympathetic. But I think it will be a way of rebuilding trust. I'll be gentle, Nancy. You can tell me what you want me to do. And we can we have the whole evening, the whole night.'

He smiled at her. She smiled back. He finished his toast.

She would not, could not. Not ever again. Not even a kiss. Not even to save herself from wreckage.

Maud looked at the front of the house. It was an elegant Georgian facade opposite Ealing Common. Very nice. Very expensive. He lived in better style than his tenants did. She walked up to the glossy dark blue front door and pressed the bell. She heard a chime from inside. There was a pause and footsteps approaching. The door opened, revealing a large, bald man, dressed in a lilac-coloured tracksuit that didn't look as if it was used for much actual sport.

'William Goddard?' she said.

'The office rang,' he said. 'I know who you are.'

'Good,' said Maud.

But she took out her identification anyway and showed it to him. He leaned forward and examined at it.

'Detective inspector,' he said.

It wasn't clear whether this was a statement of fact or an expression of doubt.

'Can I come in?'

Goddard seemed to be seriously considering whether the interview could be conducted out on the doorstep.

'I haven't got long,' he said. 'I've got work to do.'

He led Maud through an elaborate hallway, black and white tiles on the floor, a curved staircase in front of them. Maud smiled as she thought that the whole of Kira's flat could fit into this one entrance hall.

'Is something funny?' Goddard asked.

'Big place,' Maud said.

'I've got four children. They're away at school at the moment but when they get back for Christmas, the house'll feel a lot different, I can tell you.'

'Boarding school?' said Maud. 'Business must be good.'

'You sound like that's something to be ashamed of.' He led Maud into a vast living room decorated entirely in white: oversized sofas, a white fluffy carpet, a vast mirror over the fireplace. 'I got all this through sheer bloody graft.'

He gestured Maud towards one of the sofas. It was very soft, and she almost sank into it. She had to perch on the edge to feel safe.

'We're having another look at the death of Kira Mullan.' Maud waited for Goddard to reply but he remained impassive. 'Do you have any response to that?'

He just shrugged.

'You just do what you have to do.'

'I've been talking to your tenants, looking at the files. There are a lot of mentions of you. People talking about the damp and things not being fixed that need to be fixed.'

Goddard gave a loud sigh.

'Are you another of those people who moan about landlords like everything is our fault? I've got no interest in discussing this with you. The tenants are always bloody complaining. What I do is follow the rules. If they think I'm not, then they can contact my solicitor.'

That would be a tort, Maud thought to herself, almost amused by her new legal knowledge.

'My point was that your dealings with your tenants can be a bit combative, a bit angry.'

Goddard clamped his hands on his knees.

'I'm always fair,' he said. 'Whatever the provocation.'

'What about Kira Mullan?' Maud asked. 'What were your relations like with her?'

'You've been talking to that mad woman in the house, haven't you?'

'I've been talking to everyone.'

'Do you know what she did? She bloody snuck into the flat when someone left the door open and she got caught. And then she snuck in again, pretending that she wanted to rent it. If I were you, I'd have a look at that fruitcake. You know how they talk about the murderer returning to the scene of the crime?'

'Why do you think it was murder?'

He was taken aback for a moment.

'You said it was a murder inquiry.'

She hadn't said that, but she let it go.

'What did you make of Kira Mullan?'

'Nothing much. She was a tenant, like any other.'

'You don't seem to like your tenants. You say they make false complaints. Was she like that?'

He hesitated.

'Not that I remember,' he said.

'Did she ever complain or ask for something to be repaired?'

'I'd have to check the records at the office. I can't recall anything in particular.'

'What was she like when you met her?'

'I've got twelve properties I'm dealing with. I can't remember every time I talk to one of them.'

William Goddard was saying absolutely nothing. But Maud had learned one thing: he knew how to talk to legal authorities. Don't take the risk of being caught in a lie. Never say no, unless there is absolutely no risk in saying it. Instead say, *I can't remember, not to my recollection, I'll have to check.*

'Now, the keys to each flat: how many copies do you give each tenant?'

'One,' he said without hesitation. 'But of course, they can get more cut if they want.'

'And to the front entrance?'

'One Chubb and one Yale. I think they often forget to Chubb it though.' He tutted.

'And Kira's keys – did you retrieve them after her death?'

'Yes.'

'Just those, or were there multiple copies?'

'Just those. To the best of my recollection.'

'Do you know if anyone else had keys to her flat at the time of her death?'

'No.'

'Except for you, of course.'

He looked at her for a beat and then nodded.

'Obviously,' he said. 'I'm the landlord. I have to have access to the properties.'

'And did you often use them?'

'You mean, let myself into the flats?'

'Yes.'

'It's normal practice to go round when they are at home, with prior warning.'

'That's not really an answer.'

'I don't recall,' he said. 'It would not be my usual behaviour is all I can say. I like to give my tenants privacy, and that is what I do unless they are in breach of their contract with me.'

'I told your office that I would need a set of keys for Kira's flat. Do you have them?'

'One of my employees will be there to let you in,' he said. He looked at his watch. 'They might already be there.'

'Thank you.'

'Is there anything else?'

'What were you doing on Sunday the thirteenth of November?'

He stood up.

'I've got to go to the office now. When I'm there I can check my work diary.'

'Do you work on a Sunday?'

'Sometimes,' he said, but his colour was high and she could tell he was angry.

'I was hoping you could tell me now,' said Maud. 'To the best of your recollection.'

'It's better if I check,' he said. 'I wouldn't want to mislead you.'

SIXTY-TWO

The ground-floor flat where Kira had once lived was poky and unprepossessing. Little had been done to it to freshen it up for its new tenant. There were damp marks on the walls, signs of silverfish in the bathroom and peeling skirting boards. The fridge was rusty and the window frames in need of repair. The new tenant, Sadie Emerson, had obviously not finished unpacking, but Maud was struck by how few possessions she had, and how bare the flat would still look after she had done. A perching place, temporary and inhospitable. She thought of the cosy flat she and Silas had briefly owned together, and an almost physical longing went through her.

She moved slowly from room to room, trying to get a sense of it. Forrester followed in her wake, stopping when she stopped and looking where she was looking. Everything that had belonged to Kira was gone, all traces of her cleared away. Maud stood under the girder and looked up. It was from there that the young woman's body had hung, in full view of the hall once her door was opened. She thought of the image, the slack body, the blue rope, the green boots.

From her battered leather satchel, Maud removed the police photo of Kira's room after the body had been cut down. The chaotic heap of clothes on the floor, the armchair and bench sofa, the upturned stool. Where was the stool? She went into the bedroom and found it beside the bed, a pot of face cream and an eyeliner on its surface. She took out her tape measure and measured it, then smiled in grim satisfaction.

'Seventeen inches,' she said to Forrester. 'Write that down. And ask one of the crime scene investigators to make an exact calculation of what height would have been needed for Kira to hang herself. They'll be able to work it out from the photos. Get Matthew Moran if he's available.'

Forrester wrote down the figure.

'What would be ideal,' said Maud, talking more to herself than to him, 'is for there to be no doubt. We don't want anyone claiming that Kira could have stood on tiptoes.'

She remembered Nancy talking about the blue fibres she had collected and squatted on the floor, searching, finding nothing. She made a note to retrieve them from Nancy.

She stood and turned to go, but hesitated, her hand on the doorknob. There was something snagging in her mind. What? Like the remnants of a dream, it slid from her.

She went up the stairs, stopping briefly in front of Felix and Nancy's flat. She could hear voices from inside, but not the words. She thought about Nancy. She was like an electric circuit, energy always coursing through her, a fluctuating, dynamic system. But yesterday, in the flat, when Maud had talked to Felix, that vitality had been switched off. She had sat quite motionless in a hard-backed chair near the wall and her face had been blank as a stone.

Maud turned away and knocked instead at the door opposite, which immediately swung open.

'Dr Harry Fisk?'

The man had sandy hair and his freckles stood out on the dull paleness of his face, which looked stiff with exhaustion. Behind him, Olga was pacing up and down the narrow room with the baby held against her breast, shushing and cooing while the baby whimpered and occasionally broke out into a high wail.

'That's me. You're the detectives?'

She started to retrieve her ID but he waved it away.

'I was expecting you. But can we go somewhere else? I've barely had any sleep. It's past my bedtime, but Lydia won't settle.'

'There's a cafe down the road.' She turned to Forrester. 'Perhaps you can go to the basement flat and tell Seamus Tyrell to expect me in an hour. Then return to the station and talk to Matthew Moran and write up the notes. Oh, and chase up Goddard's movements for the Sunday.'

Forrester looked slightly crestfallen, as if Maud was leaving him out of a game he had been looking forward to playing.

'I'll buy you coffee,' Maud said to Harry. 'Unless that will keep you awake.'

'Nothing will keep me awake. Except my daughter.'

She bought them both cappuccinos. She waited in silence while he drank the coffee in large mouthfuls, wiping the foam from his upper lip, and ate the pastry as if he was starving, dabbing up the last flakes with a finger. Then he sat back with a sigh.

'That's better. Thanks. I feel almost human again.'

'I don't know how you do it.'

That wasn't exactly true. Maud herself often stayed awake most of the night, either for work or keeping up with her studies.

'You get used to it,' he said. 'It's not too bad. And I know I've got the best job in the world. It's just with a new baby.' He shrugged. 'Olga does her best to keep Lydia out of the way when I'm on nights, but that's hard for her. I feel bad that I'm not around enough, supporting her.'

'You don't have family who can help?'

He shook his head.

'Not so much,' he said. 'They live a long way from us.'

'It's a lot to deal with,' said Maud, thinking of what Barney had said about Harry – how he shouted at Olga so loudly that even in the basement flat they could hear his voice.

'But you're not here to talk about me. It's about Kira. You think she didn't kill herself.'

'I'm not sure,' said Maud neutrally. 'I just want to clarify a few details.'

She opened up her notebook. Harry sat up straighter.

'How well did you know her?'

'She's just someone I said hello to on the stairs.'

'Did you ever socialise with her?'

'No.'

'Did you ever go into her flat?'

'I took a delivery for her once, and there was another time when she asked me about a leaking pipe. She said the landlord wasn't answering any of her calls or emails. Which wasn't surprising because he never contacts us unless he wants to get more money out of us.'

'When did you last see her?'

He frowned.

'I'm sorry, I can't remember.'

'Not on Sunday the thirteenth of November?'

He shook his head.

'I'm sure I didn't see her then.'

'Did you go to the party downstairs?'

'Not exactly.'

'What does that mean?'

'It's a bit embarrassing. I went for about one minute, to complain about the noise. It makes me sound like a grumpy old man. But if she was there, I didn't see her. It was very crowded and dimly lit.'

'Can you tell me what you did on the Sunday?'

'Obviously I've thought about it, given what happened. The idea of us being there in the house acting normal with her going through that.' He shook his head slowly. 'In the morning I revised. I've got exams coming up. I think Olga went out briefly to get a few supplies, but otherwise she was there as well, with Lydia. The weather wasn't great, and I think we both felt a bit cooped up. In the afternoon, I took Lydia out for a walk, and Olga went to meet a friend.'

'What time would that have been?'

'I'm not sure. I guess we left the flat together at about three, three fifteen, and I walked around to get Lydia to sleep. Olga joined me and we walked back together, which took about fifteen minutes I think.' He stopped and took his phone out. 'Look, I think I've got something.' He tapped away at his phone. 'I've got about ten thousand photos of Lydia. Including this one.'

He handed Maud the phone. She saw a selfie of Harry, a sleeping Lydia and a stressed-looking Olga.

'I can even see the time you took it,' Maud said. 'Three fifty-eight.'

She handed the phone back.

'We would have been back at about four fifteen or four thirty.'

'Nothing else?'

'No. Except I went once round the block after lunch, to clear my head. We'd been kept awake by the party and I was feeling muzzy and unable to concentrate.' He grimaced. 'I was a bit short-tempered. I probably wasn't that nice to Olga.'

'You left the flat together at about three fifteen, and came back to the flat together an hour or so later?'

'Yes.'

'Then?'

'I was there revising until I went across to Felix and Nancy's for a drink. I didn't stay long. I could hear Lydia crying and I felt bad about leaving Olga alone again.'

Maud turned the page of her notebook.

'Can I ask you about Nancy North?'

'Nancy?' He looked startled.

'Yes. Apparently, as a doctor, you believed she was in danger of harming herself or others and therefore should be sectioned.'

'That's not right. Michelle came and asked me for my advice and all I said was that *if* Nancy was genuinely in danger of harming herself or others, then being sectioned would be an option her doctor would have to consider. That's not the same thing at all.'

'No.'

'I would never give a medical opinion based on someone else's anecdotal evidence.' His pale cheeks were flushed. 'I'm not an expert in mental illness. That's not my area.'

'All right,' said Maud.

'I think she blames me and I can see why if she thought I had a hand in it. But I didn't. I feel very sorry for her. She's had a rough time. You think that Kira Mullan was murdered.'

'I didn't say that.'

'Whatever. If she was murdered, that means Nancy was right all along and none of us took her seriously. That must have contributed to her feeling of paranoia.'

'Sometimes paranoia is justified,' said Maud.

'Maybe everyone's a bit paranoid. Presumably you're talking to all of us because we are under suspicion, or that's how it feels. Which seems pretty bloody insane to me. I mean, look at us. We're—' He floundered to a halt.

'Ordinary people?'

'Yes.'

'And you think ordinary people don't do terrible things?'

'No,' he said with a sigh. 'We can all do terrible things. Me included. Of course I know that. It just feels crazy, that's all. I mean, Seamus is a bit of a dick, but he's mostly hot air. Barney is having trouble finding what he wants to do in life, but wouldn't or couldn't harm a fly. Felix is having enough to do with looking after his partner.'

'And you?'

'Me? I'm worn out and I have debts and a wife and a little baby who depend on me. And I lose my temper sometimes.' He glanced at her. 'As I'm guessing you've been told.' He smiled. 'I was going to say that I'm a doctor but then you would have told me that Dr Crippen was a doctor.'

Maud got up. 'Time for you to get some sleep.'

SIXTY-THREE

She didn't immediately leave herself. She had a bit of time to spare and as it was nearly lunchtime, she bought a roast vegetable wrap and some more coffee. She sat in the lovely warmth of the cafe, while outside the sky was a stony grey and people walked past in their thick coats and gloves, heads lowered against the wind.

Half an hour later, she was back at the house, but this time she took the metal steps to the basement flat. Seamus knew to expect her, and she was surprised when he opened the door dressed in a puffer jacket, a scarf around his neck. He smiled at her; he had strong white teeth.

'Are you the detective?'

'I am. And you must be Seamus Tyrell.'

'Yes.'

Maud took him in: tall, broad-shouldered, with dark hair, a slightly florid complexion and bold, bright eyes. Barney had said his flatmate liked to think himself irresistible, and Maud had a particular aversion to men who believed they were charming.

'You look like you're on your way out.'

'I'm meeting a client at the park for a workout.'

'Were you not expecting me?'

'I thought you could ask me whatever you want to ask me as we walked.'

Maud looked at him coolly and he glanced away.

'Sorry,' he mumbled, abashed. 'I can tell them I'm running late.'

'It's okay,' Maud said, because it was: people often talked more freely when they weren't sitting face to face with you. 'We'll walk.'

He shut the door and they set off down the street, the wind in their faces so she sometimes had to strain to hear what he said.

'How well did you know Kira?'

'Not that well.' He slid a grin at her. 'We had a fling for a few days, but that didn't mean I knew her. Though of course,' he added, hastily rearranging his expression to look sorrowful, 'it made it harder for me when she died.'

'When did you have this fling?'

'It ended about a week before she, you know, took her life in that tragic way.'

'What did you feel about her death?'

'Sad,' he said. 'Shocked. Very sad and shocked. Of course.'

His stride quickened, but Maud kept up with him. She wanted to see his face.

'Shocked and sad.' The words sounded like a newspaper headline.

'Obviously I felt terrible. I wondered if I could have done anything. Or if it was because she was upset, you know, that it had ended.'

'You say you ended it. The fling with Kira.'

'It was never a big deal,' said Seamus. 'It just happened and then, unhappened. You know how it goes?'

He smiled at her again, inviting complicity.

'Can you describe her?'

'I'm not very good at that sort of thing: medium height, great hair.'

'Her character.'

'Oh,' he said. 'Feisty. Fun.'

Maud kept her face expressionless, in spite of the spurt of irritation she always felt when men describe women as feisty.

'When did you last see her?'

'At our party. She was there for a few hours. She seemed fine, chatting, drinking, dancing, laughing. But I didn't really talk to her or anything.' He slid her a glance. 'I was otherwise occupied.'

'With another woman?'

'It made me wonder if that might have set her off. It might have tipped her over the edge.'

'I should tell you that I'm not certain Kira Mullan killed herself.'

Seamus slowed his stride.

'Barney said you were just tying up loose ends.'

'Did you have a key to Kira's flat?'

'No.'

'But you have been in her flat?'

'A few times.'

'You didn't see her on the Sunday after the party?'

'I wasn't around. I was at the gym most of the day. I'm a fitness instructor. You can check.'

'Yes.'

'I only came back shortly before the drinks thing at Felix's. I felt pretty hungover, but not as bad as Barney.'

'Were you still on good terms with Kira?'

'As I said, it wasn't a big deal.'

'You say you were the one who ended it.'

'I moved on, yes.'

'I've heard another version.'

'What do you mean?'

'That she ended things with you.'

Seamus turned his wind-flushed face to her.

'Is that what Barney said?'

'Is it true?'

'He's just jealous because he fancied her and didn't get any-where. It's kind of a habit with him and me.'

'But is it true?'

'Why would I lie?'

'A man might feel humiliated,' said Maud. 'He might re-frame it.'

He stopped dead and she did too.

'She did not dump me,' he said.

But Maud thought there was panic rather than anger in his voice.

'What about Nancy North?'

'Her? What's she been saying?'

'It's what you've been saying that interests me.'

'Sorry?'

'You told her partner, Felix, that she'd made a pass at you.'

'That's right. And if you've heard anything different, well, you know what state she's in.'

'According to you, I shouldn't believe your flat mate and I shouldn't believe your neighbour,' said Maud thoughtfully.

'Here's the park and there's my client waiting. I'll say goodbye.'

He moved away and Maud let him go.

SIXTY-FOUR

Michelle knitted. Her fingers moved swiftly, and the thin needles clicked; the ball of yarn uncurled. Maud, sitting in the Strausses' pleasant living room, watched her as she spoke. She had a clever, owlish face, round glasses, greying hair cut elegantly short. She wore elegantly baggy trousers, a loose linen shirt. Everything about her was neat and calm. Maud thought of how different she was from her husband, Dylan, with his shoulder-length hair that needed washing, his stubble and rumpled clothes. She remembered what Barney had said about Dylan's philandering and wondered if it was true.

Yes, Michelle said, she had known Kira reasonably well. Click click click. She had been in her flat a couple of times, and Kira had been here.

'She once came for dinner. She said how she was homesick and missed family mealtimes.'

Michelle had a voice that managed to sound slightly ironic at all times, a faint question mark at the end of her sentences. Maud could imagine her giving lectures, or in a seminar, eyebrows raised, courteous but mildly intimidating.

'Can you describe her?' Maud asked, as she had asked Seamus.

The needles paused for a few seconds as Michelle gave this her consideration.

'She was rather guileless,' she said. 'She sometimes seemed

even younger than she was. She was eager to please. I got the sense that men misread that. I think her lively manner probably concealed a shyness. She told us she often drank too much because it helped her get over her anxiety in social situations. She probably took lots of drugs as well,' she added, 'but I don't think she was going to tell me and Dylan that, because she saw us as horribly old and respectable.'

'And you're not?' Maud asked, and Michelle cast her an amused look before bending over her needles again. 'Respectable, I mean.'

'Dylan's an old hippy,' said Michelle. 'But you've met him.'

Maud thought about what Nancy had overheard from her hiding place in the Strausses' garden shed: Michelle telling Dylan she had seen the way he looked at Kira and that she couldn't always be getting him out of trouble.

She hesitated, then asked:

'Were your husband and Kira also on friendly terms?'

A friendly, amused glance.

'I believe you want to know about the cut on my husband's nose. Which I don't remember, but then, he's always injuring himself. He's the clumsy sort. Dropping things, scratching himself when he's gardening.'

Click click click.

'Yes, he told us he probably did it gardening.'

'There you are then. And in answer to your question, Dylan was on neighbourly terms with Kira, just as I was.'

'And you? Are you an old hippy?'

Michelle gave a chuckle.

'Do I look like one?'

'How did Kira seem during her last week?'

'If you mean, did her behaviour in retrospect suggest she was thinking of ending her life, no. Absolutely not. But I don't think

I talked to her during that period, although I'm sure I must have seen her coming and going.' The shrewd raised glance again. 'You don't think she killed herself, do you?'

'When did you last see her?'

'I don't know. Not the day she died at any rate. You want my movements. I can't add much to what Dylan must have told you. We left here mid-morning to have lunch and then go to an exhibition at the South Bank. We got home around four, four thirty, and then an hour and a half later went to drinks at Felix's place.'

'What exhibition?'

'Ceramics in contemporary art, at the Hayward. I was more impressed than Dylan.'

'Do you have keys to Kira's flat?'

'Of course. I have keys to all of the flats in that house. And to a few other houses as well. As you've probably been told, I'm the street busybody, and it's a very neighbourly street. We have a WhatsApp group and a party once a year and in general try to look out for each other. It makes sense for me to have keys. We can take deliveries for people, water their plants, let them in when they've lost their own keys which happens quite often, especially with Barney. I work part time, but Dylan's here most of the time.'

'Do you still have Kira's key?'

'Yes. Do you want it?'

'Maybe. Did you ever use it?'

'Several times.'

'But not recently.'

'I can't remember when I last did. Some time ago.'

'There's something else.'

Michelle went on knitting, not looking up.

'I expect you want to ask me about Nancy,' she said.

'Yes. You were the one who told her partner, and Dr Fisk as well, that she threatened you and also said she might do harm to herself.'

'That's right.'

'Nancy says you made that up.'

'I know.' She paused to unkink the diminishing ball of yarn. 'It's been an upsetting time for all of us here, first Kira and then Nancy's wild assertions, and then the way she has turned me into her enemy, someone out to get her. Why would I put myself through all of that? I made every effort to be friendly with her, welcoming.'

'Did she ever do anything to upset you?'

'Apart from saying I had lied about her, no. I was sorry for her, but not as sorry as I was for Felix.'

'Or to upset your husband?'

'Not that I know of.'

'She has told us that you removed a used condom from a drawer where it was hidden; she had taken it from a bin bag full of Kira's rubbish.'

She wrinkled her face in distaste.

'When Nancy was in hospital, I did my best to help Felix a bit. He was very upset. I cleaned things up in his kitchen when he was at work one day. I made him some biscuits too, a bit of home comfort. And that's why I found that disgusting thing. Of course I threw it away. What would you have done? I had no idea where it came from.'

Suddenly Michelle laid down her knitting and leaned forward, taking off her glasses. She seemed suddenly older and less impregnable.

'I didn't lie about Nancy,' she said. 'And honestly, for everyone's sake including Kira's poor mother, I don't think you should reopen a case that was closed because of what one troubled person tells you. You need more than that poor woman's suspicions.'

'I was right about Kira,' said Nancy, sitting on her bed, propped up with pillows, her computer on her lap. 'The detective believes me. Kira was killed.'

She tried to read her therapist's expression, but she was just an image on a small screen whose eyes she could not meet.

'I need to get away,' she continued, in a low voice so that Felix wouldn't hear. She knew he was out there, like a prison guard. 'But I'm frightened.'

SIXTY-FIVE

Outside on the pavement, Maud remembered something. She walked to the house and pressed one of the bells. She heard a crackly voice.

'It's Maud O'Connor,' she said.

The crackly voice got louder.

'I'm sorry,' she said. 'I can't hear what you're saying.'

The voice continued. Maud just pressed the bell again and when she heard a click, she pushed the main door open. She walked up the stairs, to where Felix was standing at the open door of his flat, looking at Maud with an icy expression.

'Has something happened?'

'I'll keep you in touch if there's anything you should know.'

'I assumed since you are here again unannounced, there must be something important you wanted to ask.'

Maud looked at Felix with a new interest. In her experience people usually felt nervous when they met police officers. They felt somehow guilty even if they were completely innocent. They would respond by going silent or starting to babble. But Felix didn't seem intimidated at all. He was angry and a little contemptuous. Maud wasn't quite sure what to make of it.

But she only said with a stern courtesy, 'I'm here to see Nancy.'

'Nancy,' said Felix, very loudly.

He didn't take his eyes off Maud. It sounded like he was shouting at a dog that had strayed too far.

'You could just tell me where she is.'

'You can't simply walk in on her. She's in the bedroom. She may not be in a state to be seen.'

The bedroom door opened, and Nancy emerged. Her face looked pale.

'What's up?'

'I just wanted a word with you.'

She looked round at Felix, signalling that she wanted to talk to Nancy alone. He frowned.

'When you interviewed me, you didn't have any problem with Nancy being there.'

Maud continued as if Felix hadn't said anything.

'Can we go into the bedroom?'

Nancy led Maud through and shut the door behind her. She leaned on it as if the extra weight were needed to keep it shut.

'Making him angry doesn't really help,' she said.

'I wasn't trying to make him angry,' said Maud. 'I wanted a moment to ask if you're all right.'

'Is that why you came here, to ask that?'

'No, I came about the blue fibres from the rope that you found. Have you still got them?'

Nancy opened a drawer in a chest, rummaged through it and then closed it and opened another one.

'I've got it somewhere. Yes, here.' She held up a plastic food bag containing the strands. 'I thought I should put it in something to protect it. I don't know whether it will be admissible as evidence.'

'It doesn't need to be admissible to be helpful,' said Maud, taking the bag and pocketing it. 'You didn't answer my question.'

'What question?' said Nancy.

'How are you?'

Nancy didn't answer immediately. Instead, she turned away and walked to the window and looked through it.

'Is there something else you want to tell me?' Maud asked.

Nancy looked back at Maud with a new alertness in her expression.

'As I'm sure you have seen, I need to leave,' she said. 'Would it be all right if I went with you, right now?' She smiled. 'I don't mean go with you to the police station or anything like that. I just mean go with you out of the flat until I'm well away.'

'I think that's a good idea,' Maud said.

'It won't take long. I'll just throw a few things into a bag.'

'Take as long as you need.'

It took barely any time: after all, she had done it before. She pulled her bag from under the bed, and within five minutes she opened the door, letting Maud through first.

Felix was standing in the middle of the living room, obviously waiting for them. Both women separately wondered if he might have been listening at the door.

'You took your time,' he said and then saw that Nancy was carrying her bag. 'What's going on?'

'I'm leaving,' said Nancy.

Felix stepped sideways to stand between the two women and the front door.

'That's ridiculous. You can't just walk out like that.'

'I can.'

Felix looked at Maud.

'Is this something to do with you? I can tell you, if it is, then I'm going to be talking to your superior.'

Maud smiled at that.

'Talking to my superior? What do you think Nancy is, four years old?'

'I'll tell you what Nancy is,' said Felix icily. 'She's a severely vulnerable woman who has twice been hospitalised as a protection not just to other people, but to stop her from harming herself. She was recently hospitalised because she threatened to kill a neighbour and then kill herself.'

'Could you please move out of our way? Or are you actually trying to physically stop us?'

Felix took a step forward and, even though she was a police detective, Maud felt a sense of threat.

'Do you realise what you're doing?' he said to Maud.

'Nancy asked me if she could leave with me when I left.' Her voice was calm. 'I think she felt that if she tried to leave on her own, she might be at risk. Judging from your response, I can see what she meant.'

'You didn't answer my question.'

'I didn't think it was a real question.'

'Well, it was. Nancy is not well and she's not safe. I've spent much of the last few months looking after and keeping her from harm. Once she leaves this house, if she does something to someone or something happens to you, then it'll be down to you.'

There was a silence. Nancy looked at Maud. Was she about to be abandoned?

'Will you move out of our way?' said Maud.

'I'm very tempted not to.'

'That would be an extremely bad idea.'

'Where are you going?' Felix asked in a less angry tone.

'You don't need to worry about that,' said Nancy.

'I do need to worry about it. I want to be sure that you won't just be wandering the streets.'

'I won't be.'

Felix gave a strange chuckle.

'You've worked it all out behind my back.' He turned to

Maud. 'How much do you know about Nancy? When she was in the hospital, she told a string of lies to get out. She told them what she thought they wanted to hear. As you can see, she's also been lying to me. When she comes to you with this story about a so-called murder, why do you think she's suddenly telling the truth?'

Maud hadn't wanted to engage him in conversation; she simply wanted to get out of there. But she couldn't resist saying something.

'You're talking about the woman you've been living with,' she said. 'Someone I suppose you were in love with. And she's standing right in front of you.'

'Someone I *was* in love with? How dare you? I'm still in love with her. Nobody could have done more for her than I have.'

'She's here,' said Maud, still calm but raising her voice. 'Don't talk about her like she's your dog.'

'All right,' said Felix and, almost theatrically, he turned towards Nancy. 'You have an illness, Nancy. It's as much of an illness as if you had diabetes or cancer. If you try to pretend that it doesn't exist, then it will destroy you.'

Nancy turned to him. Her voice was clear and strong; her face was almost radiant.

'You're part of my illness, Felix,' she said.

Felix turned to Maud and pulled a face as if to say: see what I mean? He looked back at Nancy.

'Where do I forward mail?'

'I'll sort something out. Anyway, I don't get much mail here.'

She pushed her way past Felix, who stood back, raising his hands as if he was allowing the two women to pass.

When they were out on the pavement, Maud turned to Nancy.

'What do you do now?'

'Give me just one minute.'

Nancy took her phone from her pocket and made a call. She turned her back as she talked; Maud could only hear a few apologies. When Nancy turned to her again, she was obviously relieved.

'I've got a friend in West Hampstead. She was the person I rang when I was planning to leave before, when I came to the police station and saw you. I think she was a bit puzzled about the delay, but she's still fine about me staying with her. It'll just be for a few days until I find somewhere myself.'

'Good.'

'Can I ask one more thing? Could you walk with me to the bus stop and wait till the bus arrives? Just to make sure.'

'Do you really think he's a threat to you?'

Nancy looked at Maud almost in surprise.

'I know he's a threat to me. He had me put away in a mental hospital.' Maud started to say something, but Nancy interrupted her. 'Don't say he was doing it out of concern for me. You saw the way he was with me.'

Maud smiled.

'I wasn't going to say that, and I did see the way he was with you. I think you've done the right thing.'

'What were you going to say to me then?'

'I was going to say that Felix was correct about one thing. You have been ill, and you do need to take care of yourself.'

Nancy took her hand from her pocket. She was holding a pill bottle, and she gave it a shake.

'Don't worry,' she said. 'I'm not going to stop taking my meds.'

'I've got a car,' said Maud. 'I'll drop you.'

'It's quite a way from here. I'll get a bus.'

SIXTY-SIX

'So,' said Matt Moran, 'do you want the short version or the long version?'

Moran was a tall, slightly gangly man with fading brown hair that usually flopped over his brows, but which today looked as if he had attacked it with a pair of scissors, leaving an uneven fringe. He was wearing a thick jumper covered in a zig-zag pattern and with a hole in one elbow, and comfy-looking cords.

'The long version, of course,' said Maud.

'Good.'

He took his laptop out of its protective cover and laid it on the desk, pulling up a chair so they could look at it together.

'We will start with the drop,' he said, as the computer came to life. 'I have diagrams.'

'I do love a diagram.'

'First of all, though, here's a chart with the data. From the autopsy, Kira Mullan was 165.2 centimetres in height – that's taking into account the stretching that naturally occurs with a hanging. You will have noticed how the neck is longer.'

Maud nodded.

'The heel of her boots, which I have not actually measured, but have estimated from the photographs . . .'

'Estimated?' said Maud. 'Is that accurate enough?'

'This is me,' said Moran in an affronted tone. 'Of course it's accurate. The estimated height of the heel is about 3.5 centimetres, which brings her up to 168.7 centimetres. The stool is 43.18 centimetres. The photographs show that Kira's body was hanging from a beam 248.5 centimetres above the floor, which is 205.32 centimetres from the stool. The rope,' he continued, 'measured, to the nearest few millimetres, 53 centimetres from the knot at her neck to the beam, 53 centimetres. Okay?'

Maud's face was screwed up in concentration.

'I'll take your word for it,' she said.

Moran double clicked on the next file.

'You can see the diagram.'

'I can see it. What does it mean?'

'That this woman could not have used this stool to hang herself.'

'Even on tiptoes?'

'Even on tiptoes.'

'That's good,' said Maud. 'I mean it's terrible, but it's what I needed.'

'I've also looked at it from a different angle.'

'What does that mean?'

'I am not a pathologist, and I don't want to be disrespectful of the idiot who carried out the post-mortem.'

'Don't hold back.'

'Obviously the body has now been cremated. But from the photographs, it seems evident that Kira Mullan died of ligature strangulation rather than hanging. Those little red dots around her eyes – they're called the petechiae, if you're taking notes – are a tell-tale sign. They don't generally occur in a hanging except in an incomplete one where the weight is partially supported. Which as we know was not the case. In my view, Kira Mullan was strangled, and then hung from the beam, presumably using the same rope, though of course that's not demonstrable.'

'Wow,' said Maud.

Moran closed the laptop.

'Really, it's a very straightforward case.'

'Your short version is that Kira Mullan did not hang herself.'

'Yes.'

'This will keep Weller quiet for a bit.'

'I'll send you the PDF.'

'Fantastic. Thanks, Matt.'

'No problem. It was fun.'

SIXTY-SEVEN

'Did you organise the DNA swabs?'

'They're on it.'

'Remember to chase them though.' Maud pushed a few corkscrews of hair behind her ears. 'Let's see what we've got. I want us to have the clearest possible picture of Kira's last movements, when people saw her, talked to her, heard from her; what her mood was like. Stop me if there's anything you think I'm missing or if an idea occurs.'

Forrester nodded and sat forward in his chair, jiggling his left knee slightly. Maud looked up from the file she was consulting.

'On Saturday the twelfth of November, Kira makes an appearance at Seamus and Barney's party. Apparently, she is carefree and lively, but no one we've talked to seems to have actually said a word to her.'

'Do we know when she left?'

'Good question. No, we don't. It's as if she was there, but not there.'

Maud took a sip of water and continued.

'On Sunday the thirteenth of November, between around ten thirty in the morning to early afternoon, Kira visits her boss, Viv Melville, in a place called The Cornerstone, where Kira had worked for the past ten months. She is apparently in an agitated state, but won't say why – the police take this as corroborative evidence of her troubled state of mind.'

She looked up.

'Anything strike you?'

Forrester licked his top lip nervously. He didn't reply.

'It's stating the obvious, I guess,' said Maud. 'But she was happy when people saw her at the party and distressed by the next morning. What happened?'

'Yes,' echoed Forrester. 'What happened?'

'The next sighting we have of Kira is outside 99 Fielding Road at about three that afternoon. Nancy says that Kira was very distressed or scared.'

'Or both,' said Forrester.

'Then at three fifteen, according to phone records, there's a missed call from Viv Melville, and half an hour later, at three forty-seven, Kira sends a WhatsApp to her mother, telling her she loves her – again, the police take this as evidence to support their theory that she took her own life.'

Forrester made a tutting sound. Maud frowned and continued.

'After that, nothing more is heard from Kira, and nobody reports seeing her. Her body is discovered the following day, in the early evening, hanging from the steel girder in her flat, a stool kicked over at her feet. Clothes are scattered everywhere. The pathologist estimated that she had been dead for at least twenty-four hours and probably for more – in other words, she was not alive after about six, six thirty, on the evening of Sunday the thirteenth of November. There is no sign of a forced entry.'

'She died between three forty-seven and six or six thirty?'

'That's right.'

Maud took another sip of water. She didn't really need Forrester for this, but speaking it aloud clarified her thoughts.

'We need to find out what people who had access to the

house and her flat were doing during that window. That is, the other residents of 99 Fielding Road, the landlord William Goddard, and Michelle and Dylan Strauss.'

Forrester didn't speak. Maud saw that he seemed dissatisfied. 'What?' she asked.

'Why are you assuming that Kira was killed by someone who had access to her flat?'

'That's a good question. The answer is that I'm not assuming that, but I am starting with them for two reasons. One is that there was no sign of a forced entry, no one noticed anyone else in the house, and it's fairly likely it was someone who could come and go without being noticed.'

Forrester started to object but Maud ignored him.

'You're right, that's not enough. The other reason is that Nancy North was sectioned at the time she was refusing to accept Kira killed herself. That meant she was out of the way. It also meant that even when she wasn't out of the way, she wouldn't be believed.'

'You think the two things are connected?'

'I do,' Maud said.

'Even though Nancy isn't exactly reliable?'

'I think she's pretty reliable. I know she's had delusions but she's been reliable about the delusions, if that makes sense.'

'I suppose so.'

'Our next question is, who had the opportunity?' Maud paused to get her thoughts in order. 'Nancy North says she left the flat at about half past two, when Felix was there, saw Kira at about three at the entrance of the house, when she was returning. She then went to her flat, had a sleep, and woke to find Felix and his friend in the flat. This fits with what Felix has told us: that he was there when Nancy left, left himself before three to go to pick up things for the flat—'

'I've got the receipt,' put in Forrester. 'It's like he said.'

'Good. And then he met a friend for a drink and came back with him late afternoon, when Nancy was still asleep.'

'Gary Overton confirms this. Which means he's in the clear.'

'Harry and Olga Fisk were together all morning,' said Maud. 'Harry went out for a few minutes early afternoon, and then the two left the flat together and came back together.'

'But they weren't together in between that.'

'True. Harry says he took Lydia for a walk while Olga had a quick coffee with her friend. You should check how long it would have taken him to get back to the flat, and then return to the cafe to meet her.'

'With a buggy, remember. It's probably more difficult to kill someone with a crying baby in tow.'

'And they both say it was about a fifteen-minute walk. The timing probably doesn't work but we should check it. Seamus says he was at the gym almost the entire day. You can check that as well. They probably have CCTV at the gym.'

Forrester nodded and wrote in his notebook.

'Barney says he was at his mother's most of the day, which also needs to be verified. And I'll look into Michelle and Dylan's story, which is that they were at lunch and then at an art exhibition.' She sat back. 'And then everyone turned up for drinks at Felix and Nancy's flat.'

'By which time Kira was probably dead,' said Forrester. 'Or she died when they were all gathered.'

'Did you get Goddard's statement?'

'I did. Apparently, he and his family spent the day with his brother and his family in Essex. I haven't been able to get hold of the brother yet.' He nibbled the end of his pen. 'But if it's true—'

'Yes?'

'If it's true then it looks like nobody on your list could have killed Kira. Except one person, of course. Nancy North.'

Nancy sat on the sofa, barefoot, holding a mug of green tea and looking across at Megan Hutchens, who was curled up in an armchair with her own mug. They had been catching up. Megan had spent a year and a half travelling around South America and now she was back working as a supply teacher.

'What about you?' Megan asked cheerfully, when she had finished. 'Why were you looking for a place in such a hurry?'

Nancy gulped. She had already decided that she should be as frank as she possibly could. But once she came to it, it suddenly felt difficult to say the words out loud. As she described meeting Felix, her illness and her first spell in hospital, then he death of Kira and being sectioned and getting out of hospital and going to the police, she couldn't avoid seeing the growing expression of bemusement on Megan's face, her smile slowly fading. It sounded fantastical to herself as well, as if someone else was talking, someone who wasn't entirely to be taken at her word.

When she had finished, Megan didn't speak at first. She just looked down at her tea.

'It's gone cold,' she said. 'I forgot to drink it.'

She leaned forward and put the mug on the little table in front of her.

'You can see why I contacted you. I'm so grateful.'

'Don't be stupid. It's . . .' Megan stopped herself. 'I've got about a million things I want to say. I don't know which one to say first. This boyfriend . . .'

'Felix.'

'Yes, Felix, were you frightened of him? I mean, physically frightened?'

'I don't know about physically. I needed to get away from him.'

Nancy glanced down at her mobile, checking for the hundredth time that he hadn't called or messaged. Nothing. She didn't want to hear from him, was intending to block him when he tried to contact her, but she didn't understand the silence. What did it mean? What was he thinking, doing, planning?

'Does he know where you are?'

'No. And I don't want him to know. I just want him out of my life.'

'London's a big place. I suppose you'll be quite difficult to track down.'

'I just want to get my life sorted and get a job. I really owe you, Megan, I'll pay you proper rent.'

'Don't be silly. Just stay here as long as you need to.'

'Hello, Mum,' Nancy said. 'It's me.'

'Is something wrong?'

'No. I just thought—'

What had she thought? Why did she think she could rescue her mother, when her mother did not want to be rescued?

'I just thought we could talk about things,' she said lamely. 'I don't know why we never have. It shouldn't be taboo. Or I could come and see you. You should know that I've left Felix and when I tell you—'

She stopped, listened to the silence.

'Mum? Are you there?'

Her mother had ended the call.

Nancy laid her mobile on the bedside table and lay back in bed. One thing at a time, she told herself.

*

Maud lay in bed, tired but not sleepy. Thoughts churned. Strict tort and notions of right; her empty fridge; her weekend plans on hold; Stuart lying on the ice looking peaceful and smiling up at her; that horrible house full of people who all had alibis and something niggling away at her; Nancy North walking out of her flat, bag slung over her shoulder, head held high. 'You're part of my illness,' she had said to Felix, and Maud had wanted to cheer.

In the dark, she smiled. She liked Nancy North: her spirit, her stubbornness, her courage and her recklessness. She wasn't going to let her down. This is why I'm a detective, she thought. I can do this.

Miles away in West Hampstead, Nancy also lay in her bed, curled up on herself. She was cold and tired, but she was free. She had escaped. She would never see Felix again and she would banish him from her memory, not let him have any hold over her. She thought of how she had felt, walking out with the detective beside her and sensing him behind her, ominous; the way her heart had hammered so hard it was almost painful. But she had done it. Tomorrow she would find a job, any job. It was nearly Christmas, and she knew that pubs and cafes would be desperate for help, especially help from someone who knew the ropes. She would take her pills, get in touch with friends she could trust, rebuild her life from the rubble, brick by brick. The main thing was that she was safe again. Her fear was just the memory of fear now. The hope felt like ice melting. It hurt. She wanted it so badly: life.

Sixty-eight

The following morning, Maud arrived early at The Cornerstone, a bar and cafe in West Kilburn, about two miles from 99 Fielding Road. It wasn't yet open, but she could see a woman moving round in its dimly lit interior, shifting chairs. She knocked and the woman lifted her head, then came to the door and unlocked it.

Viv Melville was a woman in her late middle age, with strong shoulders, greying dark hair, dark eyes, a pouchy, lined, lived-in face.

Maud held out her ID. The woman nodded.

The Cornerstone had two dimly lit rooms that were crowded with an assortment of unmatching benches and chairs, a couple of sagging armchairs and sofas, lots of hanging plants, posters advertising long-ago gigs, speckled mirrors and a resident wire-haired terrier who growled, licked Maud's hand and then subsided again. The only concession to Christmas was a string of white lights wrapped around the central pillar.

'Coffee?'

'That would be great.'

'What kind?'

'Flat white, if that's easy.'

She took off her thick coat and unwrapped her scarf, then sat at a table and opened her notebook, watching as Viv Melville pulled levers and the machine gurgled and steamed.

'There you go.'

'Thanks.' Maud took a sip. 'This is just what I needed.'

'You're here about Kira?'

'Yes.'

'Why?'

'We've reopened the case.'

'You don't think she killed herself?'

'I know she didn't,' said Maud.

Viv Melville sat opposite her, solid and calm. 'How can I help you?'

'Tell me a bit about Kira first. How long had she worked here?'

'About nine months. She started off just part time but by the end she was pretty much full time. She was great. Not always on time.' Viv Melville gave a little remembering smile. 'But always so apologetic. And when she was here, she worked hard and never complained, and the customers loved her. She was very chatty. Interested in everyone. Made people laugh.' She looked at Maud. 'She was a nice young woman.'

'Was she usually cheerful?'

'She was homesick. She cried easily, like a child. But she was never gloomy, and she cheered up quickly as well. If you're asking if she ever seemed depressed, the answer's no.'

'Did she talk about her personal life?'

'Sometimes she laughed about scrapes she'd got into with men. I got the impression she had a fair few casual flings. The last time she worked here, on the Friday evening, she said she'd just spent a lovely day with someone.'

'With a man, you mean?'

'Yes.'

'A sexual relationship?'

'Definitely.'

'What makes you sure?'

'It was obvious. She was excited, and also a bit dreamy. She kept looking at herself in the mirror. She said it was early days, but she had a good feeling about him.'

'You don't know who he was?'

'She didn't say.'

'No clues?'

'No. Except he was apparently going to be away for a few days but had promised to call her when he returned.'

Maud made a note on her pad.

'On Friday she was happy.'

'Very.'

'And then you saw her again on Sunday. Can you tell me about that?'

Viv drew a deep breath.

'She was completely different. She turned up at the cafe at around ten thirty.'

Maud wrote down the time and drew a circle around it.

'She wasn't working that day and I knew she was going to a party the night before. I was surprised to see her. The place was rammed. Lots of people come for brunch on Sunday mornings; the queue sometimes goes round the block. I saw at once that she was upset. Sobbing. I took her into the back.' Viv Melville gestured with her head to the door leading from the second room. 'For a while she just wept. I couldn't get any sense out of her. Every so often it would seem like she was stopping, only to start up again. A couple of times I left her just to check on how Finn and Robbie were coping and deliver a few plates to the tables.'

'Did she say anything?'

'At first all she could manage were a few apologies. *Sorry sorry sorry, you're busy.* That kind of thing. She gradually calmed down a bit. I made her a cup of tea and she drank it and blew her nose and said she shouldn't have come. I asked her what had happened, and she just said she didn't know what to do. I asked her: do about what? But nothing made much sense.'

'Can you remember anything specific she said that would cast light on her mood?'

Viv Melville shook her head.

'You only remember her saying she didn't know what to do?'

'I think – I don't know.'

'What?'

'I think she said she was ashamed.'

'Ashamed.'

'Yes. Or scared. Or maybe both. Ashamed and scared.'

'Nothing else?'

'No.'

'Ashamed and scared and she didn't know what to do.'

'Maybe there were other things she said, but she was gulping and sniffing and sobbing, all snotty, and she was crying so much she couldn't take a breath. I just kept hugging her and telling her it was okay, she was all right, I was here for her. That kind of stuff. Useless stuff,' the woman added.

'What time did she leave?'

'Shortly after one thirty, I think. I made her have something to eat. Fried mushrooms on toast, she always loved that. It used to be her regular snack after we finished work in the evenings. She said she felt better. That she'd be okay now, that she knew what to do.'

'And what was that?'

The woman shrugged helplessly.

'I don't know. I wish I did.'

'You said at the start that you could tell at once Kira was upset. What did she look like?'

'Awful. Like she'd hardly slept, mascara smudged all over her face, unbrushed hair. Her eyes were red and her face was swollen.'

'Swollen in what way?'

'I think from crying. But I don't know.'

'Were there any signs of violence?'

'No. I don't think so.'

'What was she wearing?'

'Wearing? I don't know. I can't remember.'

'She went to a party the night before. Was she still in party clothes?'

'Oh no. I remember thinking that I'd never seen her dressed scruffily. Normally she was quite glammed up when she came to work.'

'Trousers? Jeans? A dress?'

'Trousers, I think. The only things I know she was wearing were her green boots.' A little smile played round Viv Melville's mouth. 'She loved those boots. She saved up to get them.'

Maud nodded, thinking of the photo of the dead woman, her dangling body, the green boots with their yellow laces.

'Do you know where she was going after she left here?'

'No. But she was going to come and stay with me that night.'

Maud was startled.

'She was going to stay with you?'

'Yes.'

'You didn't tell the police that.'

'I think I did. I'm pretty sure.'

'Did you offer, or did she ask?'

'She asked me as soon as she arrived. She had a few over-night things with her, underwear and her toothbrush. Of course, I said she was welcome.'

'You're saying Kira was planning to stay, but then left again.'

'I think there was something she needed to do. That was the impression I got. It was all a bit of a jumble, and I kept having to check on what was happening in the cafe. She said she'd be back in a few hours.'

'You don't know what she had to see to?'

'No.'

'She didn't mention any names?'

'I don't think so.'

'But it was understood she'd return here later.'

'Not here. To my flat, which is about fifteen minutes' walk. We close at five on Sundays and she said she'd come after that.'

'Were you surprised she didn't turn up?'

'I assumed she felt better. I was a bit annoyed she hadn't bothered to let me know. I tried calling her, but there was no reply.' She grimaced. 'Of course there wasn't any reply. Actually, I called her earlier as well, to remind her to let me know when she was coming, so I'd be there to let her in. But she never picked up.'

'What time?'

'I'm not sure. Mid-afternoon.'

Maud sat for a few moments, staring at the scrawl of her notes.

'Is there anything else you can remember?'

'I don't think so.'

'You've been very helpful.'

'I wish that was true.' Viv Melville looked down at her large, strong hands, which were plaited together in her lap. When she looked up, her face was sombre. 'I was fond of her. She was very touching. Someone killed her.' She paused. 'Will you get them?'

Maud met her gaze and then nodded.

'Yes, I think I will,' she said.

SIXTY-NINE

'Did you think we wouldn't check?'

Michelle and Dylan were sitting together on their sofa. Michelle was upright, her knees drawn together. Dylan was lying back, his arms crossed, his feet stretched out. They both stared back at Maud without speaking.

'Did you think I would just trust you?' said Maud. 'I've had to spend half a day going through this footage and then writing a report about it. I don't feel very happy about that.'

That morning, after visiting Viv Melville, Maud had sat in a drab windowless office somewhere under the Hayward Gallery. The files were already set up for her on the screen, and she used the cursor to speed through the morning. The gallery filled with people scurrying around like high-speed insects, dizzyingly entering and exiting. It was a relief to slow them down at 13.29, which was when she had decided she would start, just to be safe: the Strausses had said they'd had lunch before going to the ceramic exhibition. Sometimes the room emptied entirely, sometimes it filled up and she had to stop the film to check the people one by one. Every time a couple entered the space, she studied the image more closely.

'What do you think I saw on the gallery's CCTV for Sunday the thirteenth of November?' Maud asked Dylan and Michelle now. 'Or more to the point, didn't see?'

'I think you're going to tell us,' said Michelle.

She didn't seem flustered.

'At fourteen twenty-three, I saw you, Michelle, entering Gallery Two. You were followed by a tall man in an anorak, an elderly couple and a woman carrying a baby in a sling. You were not followed by your husband.'

'People don't always go round art exhibitions hand in hand.'

'I looked at the footage from all the other galleries. It was a laborious process. I followed you from room to room, from file to file, and you were always alone.'

'Is this the point where we should ask to see a lawyer?'

'You can ask to see a lawyer at any point. But as you can see, this is an informal interview. If that doesn't suit you, we can make it formal. I could interview you under caution or I could even arrest you.'

'That's ridiculous,' said Dylan. 'Arrest us for what?'

'Perverting the course of justice. That would be a start.'

'It was a stupid thing to do,' said Dylan, and he cast an angry glance at Michelle. 'I'm completely innocent of any crime, of course, but I didn't have an alibi for the Sunday. Michelle went to the exhibition, and I didn't. I'm not interested in gazing at old vases. They all look the same to me. I just stayed at home.'

His face was flushed. Michelle, on the other hand, remained composed.

'Why would you have needed an alibi, when it was assumed that Kira had taken her own life?'

'It felt awkward. We got anxious,' said Dylan.

'A woman who lives next door apparently takes her own life, and you pretend you were miles away at the time.'

'It sounds stupid.'

'It is stupid.'

'I wholeheartedly apologise for what we did; it was foolish and wrong,' said Michelle. 'But you've got it the wrong way round: if we had for one second suspected that Kira hadn't killed herself but been killed, then of course we wouldn't have—'

For a moment her nimble tongue deserted her. She searched for the right word.

'Lied,' said Maud.

Michelle dipped her head.

'And yet even after you knew we were reopening the case you didn't come forward.' Maud turned to Dylan. 'Did anyone see you here?'

'No.'

'What did you do?'

'I'm not sure. I just pottered about. I may have watched some TV.'

'What did you watch?'

'I don't know,' said Dylan irritably. 'I can't remember.'

As he spoke, his wife was staring blankly in front of her. She gave no sign of hearing what he was saying. Maud turned to her.

'What about you? Why did you collude with your husband in his false statement even after you knew it was murder? You provided him with an alibi you knew to be untrue.'

'You've just said the words yourself. He's my husband.'

'You didn't give the reason I expected,' said Maud.

'What did you expect?'

'I expected you to say that you defended him because you knew he was innocent.'

'That goes without saying,' said Michelle.

'It did go without saying,' said Maud. 'Because you didn't say it.'

'It didn't need saying.'

'Really?'

The Strausses were seated beside each other but they didn't touch hands or exchange glances. They didn't even seem aware of each other.

'I think I know why you threw away the condom you found at Felix and Nancy's flat,' said Maud.

Dylan jerked his head up.

'What the fuck? Condom?'

Michelle did not reply, simply tightened her lips.

'Are you going to answer?'

'It wasn't a question,' said Michelle. 'I didn't think it needed an answer. I throw lots of things away.'

Maud sighed.

'I'm doing you a favour by coming here and talking to you like this. If you're going to be difficult about it, then we can do it in a police interview room with witnesses and a recording and you can bring a lawyer if you want. Once we do that, the pressure's on me to start getting results and that would mean charging you.'

'What's this about a condom?' asked Dylan.

'Do yourself a favour and shut up.' Michelle didn't bother to keep her voice down.

Dylan sat up straighter.

'We've said everything we could possibly say. I told a silly little lie to stop things becoming complicated and my lovely wife backed me up, like any wife would.'

He put a hand out, and put it on Michelle's thigh. She pushed it away with an expression of obvious disgust. Then she turned back to Maud.

'You want the truth? All right, I'll tell you the truth. When Dylan and I met, we didn't believe in . . .' She gestured with her hands as if she were trying to seize the right phrase. 'Tying each other down. It felt very easygoing and modern. In the early days, I had my own affairs from time to time. It doesn't seem right to call them affairs. Encounters. That would be a better word. But I got tired of that. It just became boring ...'

'Michelle, for God's sake ...'

'I'm answering the detective's questions, Dylan. I'm performing my civic duty.'

'Humiliating yourself is not performing your civic duty.'

'I'm not humiliating *myself*,' said Michelle. She was speaking to her husband now but she was looking straight at Maud. 'What was I saying? Yes. I got bored with it, but Dylan did not get bored with it. Was it ever exciting? I don't know. I told myself it was. But I just got used to being at parties and watching Dylan doing his version of what he thought was flirting. You know the thing, getting a bit too close, touching a bit too much, laughing too hard at their jokes.'

'Oh, for fuck's sake ...'

'I didn't think it was anything to be ashamed of. We've always been civilised about it. If I thought that a middle-aged man behaving like this was a bit pathetic, then I didn't say it out loud.'

'Why are you telling me this?' Maud asked.

'I was just providing some background before I answered your question. Yes, I did throw away that condom in the way I've been throwing things away and covering them up and pretending not to notice them for years.'

Dylan broke in.

'Would it make any difference if I said that that bloody condom had nothing whatever to do with me?'

Michelle continued as if he hadn't spoken.

'I know what's behind your question. You're wondering whether I did that because I believed that he had sex with that poor girl and killed her and I wanted to cover up for him.' She stopped and seemed to think about this idea as if it was something new. 'I saw Dylan talking to her sometimes, accosting her outside the house.'

'I never bloody *accosted* her.'

'She was pretty and friendly, and I knew he fancied her.'

'I did not fancy her!'

'Do I think he fucked her? I know he would have done it if he had had the chance. Would she have let him? Maybe. He can still look a little bit attractive when he makes the effort.'

'I'm not interested in his infidelity,' said Maud. 'Except where Kira is concerned.'

'You want to know if I think he killed the girl.' She looked round at her husband and then shook her head slowly. 'When I look at it dispassionately, I think Dylan has the rage but not the coolness required to cover it up successfully. I'm not sure that he could have managed to conceal it from everyone, me in particular. I know him very well.' She turned to Dylan. 'Don't you think that's right?'

Dylan had turned a deep, unhealthy red. His face seemed to have swelled in size and his jaw looked bigger than ever. His eyes seemed to bulge.

'I'm not sure I believe you.' Maud's voice cut through the ugly atmosphere, cool and clear.

They both turned to her and she saw the expressions on their faces. Michelle looked cold and contemptuous, Dylan hot with impotent rage.

'I've told you the truth,' said Michelle.

'And yet you went to considerable efforts to have Nancy North sectioned.'

'This again.'

'Yes.'

'Nancy North suffers from psychotic delusions.'

'No,' Maud said sharply. 'She wasn't deluded. Kira Mullan was murdered. You tried to keep Nancy quiet. She thought you were her friend and you lied about her.'

'You thought it was me,' Dylan broke in. 'You thought I'd murdered Kira.'

Michelle seemed to come to a decision.

'Interesting use of the past tense,' she said with an ugly smile.

Maud kept very still, saying nothing.

'Why not?' Michelle said, composed now. 'You push yourself at women who aren't interested in you. You drink too much. You get angry. Sometimes you can't control your anger.' She turned to Maud. 'You've probably had enough of this. Perhaps you can let yourself out.'

'What interests me,' said Maud, 'is if you feel like this about your husband, why do you try to protect him?'

'Good question.'

SEVENTY

'Hello!' called Nancy, opening the door with difficulty because the keys she had got cut that afternoon were stiff in the lock. 'I'm back. Where are you?'

'In the kitchen.'

Nancy carried two bags bulging with shopping into the small kitchen, where she found Megan standing at the sink, washing dishes.

'I've bought us supper,' said Nancy. 'I'll cook. And some provisions.' She started unpacking the bags, putting satsumas and nectarines into a wooden bowl, two bottles of wine into the fridge, along with a wheel of soft cheese, several bags of salad leaves, vine tomatoes, bulbs of fennel and a tub of miso paste. 'I'm going to bake something as well,' she said exuberantly. 'I'm back to cooking. I've got a job in a restaurant in Dalston. Quite near where I used to live. Nothing fancy, but it will do for now. I start tomorrow.'

'Good,' said Megan, but she didn't turn round from the sink. She kept on washing dishes, piling them up on the draining board.

Nancy stopped pulling shopping out of the bags.

'Are you okay? Sorry, I've just marched in here as if I own the place. Is something up?'

Megan washed the last dish, then turned. She wiped her hands methodically on a tea towel. She still wouldn't meet Nancy's eye.

'I've changed my mind,' she said abruptly to the window.

'What?'

'I made a mistake. You can't stay here.' She glanced at Nancy's bewildered face and then looked away. 'You have to leave.'

'You mean, leave your flat?'

'Yes.'

'I don't understand.'

'I know it's short notice.'

'You want me to go *now*?'

Megan started drying the dishes, paying great attention to her task.

'It's best.'

'But what have I done?'

'You haven't done anything. I just can't have you here.'

'What's happened? Please tell me, Megan.'

Megan was fiercely twisting a drying-up cloth inside a jug.

'For God's sake, Nancy,' she said. 'It's my home. I said yes on the spur of the moment and now I've decided it won't work. That's all.'

Suddenly Nancy understood. The room suddenly felt darker and colder.

'It's Felix, isn't it?'

Megan put the jug into a cupboard and turned round. There were spots of high colour in her cheeks.

'I don't want to talk about it.'

'He's got to you. What did he say?' Megan didn't reply. 'Whatever he told you, it's not true.'

'It's my decision,' muttered Megan.

Nancy opened her mouth to say something and then changed her mind. There was no point. All her previous high spirits had drained away; she felt utterly flat and dejected.

'If that's what you want. I haven't got much to pack. I can be out of here in a few minutes. Keep the food and the wine. And here.' She laid her newly cut keys on the table.

'Where will you go?'

'That's not really your problem, is it?'

'And that's it,' said the lecturer, a wispy man with a wispy grey beard and hexagonal spectacles perched on the edge of his narrow nose. 'We won't meet again until next term.'

Maud left swiftly and walked all the way back to her flat through the dark, blustery night, thinking hard. She needed to sit with her Moleskine notebook and write down all the thoughts that crowded her brain.

Poor Kira, she thought. She knew that she was nearly there.

That night, Nancy stayed in a bed and breakfast in Kilburn. It was a dingy, neglected house just off Kilburn High Street, with a sign in the window advertising vacancies, barred windows, a smell of fried fish in the hall, a narrow staircase whose bannisters were missing several struts. A house for strangers, loners, people who had fallen through the safety nets, people who had nowhere else to go, people whose next stop was the street.

The woman who showed her the room was taciturn, and the room itself was cold and comfortless. But Nancy had barely any money left on her card, and she couldn't afford much else. And after all, she told herself, as she sat on the metal bed, it was for one night only. Tomorrow, she would think about what to do, where to go. For now, she just needed a place to sleep.

She was hungry, and she went back onto the high street. She hovered on the threshold of an Indian restaurant, but in the end just went into a corner store and bought a pack of crisps, a can of ginger beer and a bar of chocolate. She ate the crisps and a piece of the chocolate in her room, washed down her pills with ginger beer. She listened to pattering noises coming from the ceiling, which sounded to her like rats, and she tried not to think. But thoughts wouldn't let her alone. They were like bats swarming in her brain, dark and ragged.

What had Felix told Megan? More importantly – and it was only now that this occurred to her – how had he known where she was? The reason she had turned to Megan and not any of her closer friends was that Felix barely knew of her existence; he certainly didn't have her contact details. Megan must have contacted him, she thought – but why? Had one of their mutual friends warned her against Nancy?

She looked at her mobile, scrolling through all the unread messages. Nothing from Felix. That should have been good, but it didn't feel good. It felt scary.

She felt horribly alone. She didn't know who to trust, which meant that that for now she couldn't trust anyone. She would have to work this out on her own. She went down the corridor to the bathroom, trying not to look at the stains in the toilet or the hairs in the sink. She cleaned her teeth and washed her face. She returned to the room and stood at the window, staring out at the night.

She would not give in to the sense of fear that was rising inside her. After all, she had persuaded Maud O'Connor to believe her and reopen the investigation into Kira's death; she had got away from Felix and would never see him again; she had found a job in a restaurant. From these, she could rebuild her life.

She couldn't sleep though. All night long, her heart beat like a drum, and when she dreamed, her dreams were full of freight trains rattling and screeching along their endless tracks.

SEVENTY-ONE

Maud arrived at work at half past six the next morning. She put the bagel in front of her, eased off the lid on her cardboard cup of coffee, switched on the computer. She had woken at five with the niggling sense that there was something she was missing, something she hadn't seen.

She pulled up the photos of the crime scene, sat back, took a mouthful of her coffee and then a bite of bagel, and studied the images. She had looked at them often enough, and she would have said she could describe everything that was in them. The body hanging like a rag doll above the chaos of the room. The stool lying on its side, too low as it turned out to do the job, the absence of any other solid objects that could have added height, the chaotic jumble of clothes strewn around the room.

Maud zoomed in on them: underwear, skimpy dresses, bright shirts, a young woman's wardrobe. Why were they tossed around like that? The mess looked frantic. Had Kira done it, or someone else, and if it was someone else, why? Maud answered her own question. They had been looking for something. What?

She clicked forward to the body on the slab. The body: how quickly a person becomes an object, a site of clues. She looked at the slight facial congestion and protruding tongue, both marks of hanging from a low height; at the furrow round the neck where the rope had been. She thought of Kira's mother seeing her daughter like that.

She had been happy on Saturday and sad on Sunday and had never seen Monday.

Maud moved back and forward between the photos until they almost lost their meaning. What had been bothering her?

She stopped. There: that was it, that was what she had been looking for without knowing it. In one of the photos of the room, right on the very edge of the frame so that it looked like a trick of light, a thin, vague strip of shadow, was a dark shape. She leaned forward and gazed at it: a slightly slanted line, like a narrow wedge. What was it?

She sat back and ate her bagel, drank her coffee, all the while staring at the image. A little smile appeared on her face.

'Morning.'

She turned to see Forrester. He had cut himself while shaving and his face was pink and naked.

Maud pointed at the screen.

'What do you make of that?'

He stared hard, his eyes flickering from object to object.

'That in the corner. It's only in one of the photos, which is why I missed it.'

'It could be just a shadow?'

'It can't be a shadow. That's not the way the light is falling.'

He wrinkled up his face.

'I think it's a mobile,' said Maud. 'The edge of a mobile, lying on the floor.'

'Is that a good thing?'

'It's an interesting thing.'

Maud heard a familiar sound and realised it was her ringtone. She looked at the caller ID and answered.

'Hello, Nancy.'

'Sorry to bother you. I told you I'd keep you informed of my movements. I thought you should know I'm not at the address I gave you.'

'What's the new one?'

'I don't have one. I'm on a bus, on my way to look at a couple of places in Dalston.'

'That's a fair way.'

'I want to put distance between me and that house. And it's my bit of London.'

'Everything all right?'

There was a small pause.

'I got a job in a restaurant.'

'Well done.'

'I lost a friend, though. Anyway, I'll let you know when I have a place.'

Maud sat in silence while Chief Inspector Craig Weller read the report on his screen. Occasionally he made little grunting sounds and murmurs. They felt like responses of some kind, but Maud couldn't understand them. When he finished, he swivelled round.

'I expect you want me to say that I'm sorry and that you were right.'

'I haven't said anything like that.'

'I didn't say you said it. I said it's what you were thinking.'

Maud couldn't quite believe that she was having to defend herself against what Craig Weller had decided she was thinking and for a moment she struggled to find a response.

'I've just sent you a report on the investigation,' she said finally. 'All I was thinking was that you should be kept informed.'

'There's no need for the defensive tone,' said Weller. 'If you'd shown yourself to be more of a team player, then maybe there wouldn't be that feeling about you.'

'What feeling?'

'That you're not a team player.'

'So,' said Maud, trying to change the subject in as calm and polite a way as she could, 'the report.'

'Yes. A murder inquiry. We'll need to set up a full team.'

'I wanted to discuss that.'

'Don't worry, Maud, don't worry. You'll be in charge. Until Kemp gets back from annual leave at any rate. He led on this.'

Maud kept her expression neutral.

'That's not what I meant.'

Weller looked suspicious.

'Then what did you mean?'

'I don't think we should set up a team. I'd like to carry on as I am.'

'Are you about to make an arrest?'

'I don't want to say anything just now. But I think it'll be a couple of days, maybe three.'

'It's that neighbour, isn't it?'

'Just a couple of days.'

'What's the problem with having a full team?'

'If we start all that, we'll waste a day choosing them, setting up the office, getting everyone up to speed. I don't need them.'

'It's the way we do things, Maud. What makes you think you're special?'

'I'm not special and I've got nothing against that way of doing things. But I'm almost there. If I'm wrong, then I can put a team together in a few days.'

'By which time you'll have wasted a few days.'

'We're always being told we're short of staff. I thought it would be a relief.'

'Not for a murder inquiry,' said Weller sharply. 'But I take your point. You'd better not mess this up. A woman's been murdered. We're supposed to show that we take something like that seriously.'

'Well, I'm a woman. That may count for something.'

Weller narrowed his eyes, as if he suspected that she was being sarcastic.

'All right,' he said. 'Go away.'

SEVENTY-TWO

'I've arranged to go to Hathersage this afternoon, to talk to Kira's mother. I'd like you to come with me,' Maud said to Forrester. 'Have the car ready by one.'

She wondered if she needed to cancel Stuart, who she was supposed to be meeting at eight, but decided that she would probably be back well before that.

Forrester started to ask a question, but Maud was already keying in Nancy's number.

'I'd like to ask you something,' she said.

'What?' Nancy asked.

'It'd be better in person.'

'Okay. But I'm in Dalston right now, looking at grotty bedsits, and then I'm due at the restaurant. I can't be late on my first day.'

'I'll come to you, if you can spare me half an hour.'

'Could you come to the restaurant? If I get there early, there won't be anyone around.'

'I can be there in an hour or so.'

The Pen was near the underground station, in an obscure back street and hemmed in by a warehouse on one side and a baker's on the other. It didn't open until half past twelve; the metal shutters were still down, and no lights were on. There was no bell. Maud rapped hard at the door and waited, and heard footsteps, then the rattling of the locks.

Nancy was wearing cotton trousers and a white apron. Her hair was pinned firmly back, no stray wisps escaping. She looked ordered and purposeful.

'This looks like a nice place,' said Maud, stepping into the dim interior.

'It'll do for the moment,' said Nancy.

'Did you find a place to stay?'

'It's grim, but I won't be there long. At least I'm not in Fielding Road.'

'You've had no contact with Felix?'

'No.'

'Something's bothering you.'

'I don't want to go into it right now.'

Nancy turned on the lights, and the room lay clear: wooden tables with benches, a bar running along one side, the double door at the back standing open to show the kitchen, where there was already a pan on the hob, steam curling from the lid. Sprigs of holly decorated the bar and lights ran along the shelf of bottles.

Maud gestured at a table in the window, and they sat opposite each other. She leaned down and slid a plastic folder of photographs from her case but didn't remove any.

'Have you found something?'

'I wanted to go through things with you one more time.'

'I've said everything I know.'

'I want you to go back over your meeting with Kira. Everything you remember.'

Nancy nodded. She screwed her eyes shut, as if she was summoning up that day. She opened them again and began to talk, not looking at Maud, but out at the narrow street glistening in the rain.

'It was very brief, a few seconds. I was turning into the house, and she ran into me, dropping things.'

'Hang on. Were you still on the pavement, or on that little bit of path leading to the front door?'

'I'm pretty sure I was on the path.'

'Did she run into you from behind or in front?'

'Why does that matter?'

'If you can't remember, I totally understand.'

Nancy screwed her eyes shut once more.

'I think from behind. I was turned sideways and she kind of hurtled towards me, into my shoulder. The door didn't open or close. I assume she must have been behind me.'

'She was going towards the house?'

'I guess so. I'd never thought of it like that.'

'Go on.'

'She looked rough. Matted hair, mascara down her cheeks. I remember she smelt of sweat and tobacco.' Nancy frowned. 'As if she'd been up all night and not washed since then.'

Maud nodded, leaned a bit closer.

'I told her it was all right, or something like that. And she said that it wasn't.'

'It wasn't all right?'

'Yes. And then she said, "but please". I'm sure of that. Because I felt she was asking me to help her.'

'But please,' repeated Maud. 'You're absolutely sure?'

'Yes.'

'It wouldn't have been anything else?'

'What else?'

Maud didn't say anything. Nancy looked back at the street, where a ragged pigeon was pecking at something.

'"Please",' she repeated.

'I was thinking about it,' said Maud. 'I was wondering if she might have said "police".'

'Police?' said Nancy. 'It's hard to remember. I don't know.

It's possible. Could she have been asking me to get the police? Shit. Did I let her down?'

'No,' said Maud. 'You didn't let her down. You were just a stranger in the street, with problems of your own. Did she say anything after that?'

Nancy forced herself back into the clamorous nightmare of that afternoon. She concentrated so hard, she felt she was almost standing on the path, face to face with Kira Mullan.

'She said, "no more" and "get away". I think she did. It was hard to make out the words. Hard to know what she was saying and what was in my head.'

Maud nodded.

'What do you think that meant?'

'I thought it meant that she was going to get away, or even telling me to get away,' said Nancy.

'Then what happened?'

'I helped her pick up some things she'd dropped.'

'What things?'

'Her wallet, some underwear, toothbrush and toothpaste, deodorant I think.'

'The things you take when you're going to stay somewhere overnight.'

'Yes,' said Nancy. 'Just like me.'

'Yet you think she wasn't leaving the house, but going back in. How was she dressed?'

Nancy rubbed her hands over her face, trying to keep her thoughts clear.

'I don't remember. Nothing that stood out, except she was wearing these cool green boots with yellow laces. That's how I knew it was her, later, when I saw the body.' Nancy's voice cracked. 'And then she told me to take care.'

'Take care?'

'Yes.' Nancy pressed her fingers into her temples. 'Are you going to tell me anything?' she asked almost fiercely. 'Are you going to let me know what's going on?'

'I'm thinking about what you've told me.'

'I haven't told you very much.'

'You have. For example, you've told me that Kira was packed for staying somewhere else. But when you met her, she wasn't going out of the house, she was going into the house.'

'Does that matter?'

'It's interesting.'

Maud opened her plastic folder and slid the photos across the table, fanning them out in front of Nancy.

'You've seen these before,' she said. 'When we last talked, I was thinking about the stool. Now I'm interested in these clothes. Why are they scattered like that?'

'I don't know.'

'If she'd simply been going through her wardrobe, would they would be thrown around like that?'

'Maybe she was looking for something.'

'Or someone else was looking for something?'

'The murderer?'

'It's a possibility.'

'Looking for what?'

'That's the question.' Maud pressed the tip of one finger against the dark shape at the edge of the photo. 'I think this is her mobile,' she said.

Nancy wrinkled her nose. 'Is that important?'

'I believe so. Why was it lying in that particular position, right near the door?'

'It fell out of her pocket when she was hanging?'

'No. That doesn't work; it's too far from the body.'

'Or she dropped it?'

'Maybe.'

'What are you thinking?'

Maud smiled and stood up.

'I'm thinking that it's time to leave you in peace.'

SEVENTY-THREE

Maud flashed her ID at the woman at the desk.

'Can I have a word with Seamus Tyrell?'

'He's with a client.'

'I won't keep him long.'

The woman sighed and pushed herself out of the chair. A minute later, she returned with Seamus, wearing shorts and a singlet, biceps gleaming with sweat. He glared at her.

'This isn't exactly convenient,' he said. 'And now half the gym knows there's a police officer asking me questions.'

'What was Kira wearing at your party?'

'How the fuck should I know?'

'She was there. You saw her.'

'I don't know. A dress, maybe. Something short. Lots of leg. Or maybe trousers and a slinky top.'

'What colour?'

'Colour?'

'Yes. Colour.'

'I didn't notice.'

'Bright? Muted?'

'Is that what you pulled me out to ask me?'

'Yes.'

'Then you were wasting your time and mine.'

*

'What was Kira wearing at your party?'

Barney looked as if Maud had woken him up from a midday nap. His eyes were puffy and his joggers and fleece creased. He hadn't shaved for several days.

'I don't know.'

'Dress? Skirt? Trousers?'

'Maybe.'

'Maybe trousers?'

'Maybe any of those three.'

'Nothing you can tell me?'

'Sorry.'

A woman would be more likely to know. Maud rang the bell of the Strausses' house and stood back, hoping for Michelle, not Dylan. She was in luck.

'What do you want to know? Haven't you done enough?'

'One question. I know you weren't there, but do you have any idea what Kira wore at Seamus and Barney's party? Maybe you saw her going in.'

Michelle looked baffled.

'Yes,' she said.

'Yes, you saw her, or yes, you know?'

'I know what she wore. She bought it that Saturday afternoon, and we met by chance on the street as she was coming home. It was a skimpy little garment; what do they call it? A sheath. Green and sequined and not much of it. She was very pleased with it.'

'Thank you.'

'That's all?'

'That's all.'

SEVENTY-FOUR

'This is nice,' said Forrester, as flinty hills rolled past them, leafless woods, rushing streams and grey stone buildings. 'One day I'd like to live somewhere like Yorkshire.'

'Derbyshire.'

'When I'm settled and have a wife and kids,' he said complacently. 'I wonder what houses cost up here.'

'Much less than in London, that's for sure.'

'What about you?'

'You mean, would I want to live somewhere like this? No.'

'You want to stay in London?'

'Yes. Turn off here.'

Maud had to admit that Hathersage was an almost ridiculously lovely village, nestled in a shallow valley and surrounded by gritstone edges and sweeping moorlands beyond. Ruth Mullan didn't live in its historic centre, but on the edge, in a modern bungalow that had a view of the church.

Forrester drove up the driveway in a splutter of gravel, and before they had come to a halt, the front door opened and Ruth Mullan stood there. She was quite tall and had long, greying hair and a face that was pouchy, with a grey pallor to it. Maud knew she was in her fifties, but she looked ten years older, as if grief had prematurely aged her. She didn't come out to meet them, but beckoned them in, wrapping her arms around her to keep off the cold.

'Come in,' she said. 'To where it's warm.'

They stepped into the hall, which smelt of pine disinfectant. Everything was shinily clean. The wood floor glowed. The living room was also immaculate, cushions plumped up on the sofa, every surface polished. On the mantelpiece over the wood-burning stove was a gilt-framed photograph of Kira.

'I'm very sorry that you've lost your daughter,' Maud said.

Ruth Mullan nodded in acknowledgement. Tears stood in her tired eyes.

'Me too,' said Forrester.

The door opened and a young woman stood there. She was so like Kira that for a moment it was as though a ghost had entered the room.

'This is Connie,' said Ruth Mullan. 'Kira's sister. These are the detectives, Connie.'

Connie ducked her head at them, scowled.

'I'm really sorry about Kira,' Maud said to her.

'Do you want some tea?' Ruth asked Maud and Forrester.

'If it's no bother.'

'I'll make it,' said Connie.

'She's at university, doing a masters,' said Ruth Mullan as her daughter left the room. 'But she's lost the heart for it. She's very angry. With the dog, with me, with Kira, with everything. She hasn't cried yet. She didn't even cry at the funeral.'

'Have you been offered help?' said Maud.

'Yes. Are you going to tell me?'

'Tell you what?'

'What happened to Kira.'

'That's what we're trying to establish.'

'But you're sure she didn't do it herself?'

'Yes. This must be hard for you to hear.'

Ruth Mullan shook her head fiercely, and her long, limp hair swung around her face.

'What's worse? Thinking your daughter took her own life, or thinking she was killed?' Her eyes glittered. 'Is it terrible to say I'm almost glad she was killed? Because then I don't have to think she was in despair and I could have saved her, but I didn't.'

'It's not a terrible thing to say.' Maud paused, then said: 'She sent you a WhatsApp on her last day alive.'

Ruth Mullan nodded, blinking away tears furiously.

'She told you she loved you.'

Again, a wordless nod.

'Was that characteristic?'

'She was very affectionate. Guileless. That's what one of her teachers called her. She got herself into scrapes, but she always meant well.' She blinked. 'Sorry. The message. Usually she sent lots of emojis as well. Hearts and smiley faces and champagne bottles, you know.' She put out a hand and gripped Maud's arm. 'You'll find out who did it?'

'Yes,' said Maud, with a firmness that made Forrester glance at her in surprise.

'How can I help?'

'We want to look through the things you collected from her flat. Have you kept them?'

Ruth Mullan led them out of the living room, down the corridor past the kitchen where Connie was noisily making tea, banging mugs and slamming cupboard doors, and into a small bedroom whose window looked out onto the moors.

'This is Kira's room,' she said.

The curtains were drawn back to let in the winter light. The bed was made up, and there was a dressing gown hanging on the back of the door and slippers under a wicker chair. A wind chime, similar to the one that had been in her London flat, hung from the ceiling.

Ruth Mullan pointed at the four loosely knotted bin bags on the floor, and next to them a wicker basket that Maud had seen in the photos, and a guitar.

'It's all there.'

'You've not unpacked anything?'

Tears stood in Ruth's eyes again and she rubbed them away with the back of her hand.

'I was waiting. Till it was easier.'

'Is this everything that was there?'

'Everything. Will you have to take it all away again?'

'Not if you don't mind us having a look through it here.'

Ruth Mullan looked down at the bags and shook her head.

'I'll leave you to it,' she said. 'Will you put things back in the bags?'

'Of course.' Maud turned to Forrester. 'Can you get the kit, please?'

Maud slid on plastic gloves, squatted and opened the first bin bag. It was full of bed linen and towels, and also a balding teddy bear with only one button eye. She carefully folded them again and replaced them. The second bag was bulkier, splitting at its seams, and it contained a mish-mash of objects: that wind chime, a few mugs wrapped in newspaper, some books and magazines, a capacious make-up bag stuffed with cosmetics, an assortment of deodorant, body and hand lotion, shampoo for dry hair, several bottles of perfume, a hair dryer, a hair straightener, and multiple pairs of shoes: trainers and boots and sandals with thin, precarious heels.

'What are we looking for?' asked Forrester.

'Her phone, for a start.'

The phone, without a charger, was in the third bag in a felt case that also contained her laptop. She took the phone out and tried to turn it on, but it was dead.

'Bag it,' Maud said.

She went into the living room and asked Ruth Mullan if she knew if her daughter had a PIN to unlock her phone once the battery was charged. The woman looked at her as if she was talking nonsense and shook her head.

'I don't know.'

Back in the bedroom, Maud started removing clothes, garment by garment, from the remaining bags. Kira had owned a lot of them. Most of them were flamboyant: a yellow jumper, a pink mohair one, a red satin shirt, a red dress with a plunging neckline, a couple of pairs of jeans, tee-shirts with happy mottos on them, 'Here Comes the Sun' or 'Choose Love'. The wicker basket was stuffed with hats and scarves and, under them, underwear and a little drawstring bag of jewellery. Maud looked at everything and put them to one side.

'Not here,' she said.

'What isn't?' asked a voice behind them.

Connie came into the room with two cups of milky tea, which she put on the bedside table, slopping liquid over the brims.

Maud looked up at her.

'A dress.'

'Which dress?'

'One she'd just bought, a sheath, green and sequined.' An idea occurred to her. 'You haven't seen it, have you?'

Connie shook her head. Her voice sank to a whisper.

'Don't tell Mum or she'd go mental, even more than she is already, but I did take a few things of Kira's for myself.'

Maud nodded.

'Is that bad?'

Maud shook her head.

'We always shared clothes. Kira loved clothes. I wanted to have things that belonged to her. You know.'

'Yes.'

'A shirt. A necklace. Her favourite jumper. But nothing like that.'

'You're sure?'

'Yes. Why do you want it?'

Maud hesitated before she answered.

'We think it was one of the last things she wore.'

'Why does that matter?'

'I don't know if it does.'

'Her PIN is 140999 by the way.'

Forrester wrote the number down.

'Her birthday?'

'Yep. There's nothing much there, though.'

'You looked at it?'

'Of course I looked at it. I kept on going through it, if you want to know. It made it seem like she wasn't really dead. Wouldn't you have done the same if it was your dead sister?'

'Probably. Did you use it at all?'

Connie shrugged.

'I forwarded some photos of her and me together to my phone. And I nearly sent a WhatsApp to a guy called Ollie who was messaging her all the time, wanting to hook up. But then he suddenly stopped, so I didn't. Does it matter?'

'No.'

'I keep seeing her,' said Connie abruptly.

'Your sister?'

'Yes. Does that kind of thing happen to other people?'

'I think it does, sometimes. Grief takes people in all sorts of ways.'

'Do you think there's something wrong with me?'

'Nobody should lose their sister at your age. That's what's wrong.'

'I dream about her. Every night I dream about her, and sometimes she's in trouble, but sometimes she's just normal, as if nothing's happened to her. Sometimes we're arguing about stupid things, just like we used to. I wake thinking she's still alive and then have to remember all over again that she isn't and I'm an only child and my mother is slowly going mad and it's all fucking horrible.'

'It is,' said Maud.

'It's odd,' she said to Forrester five minutes later as they were pulling out of the driveway in the gathering gloom, 'that the dress has disappeared.'

'I suppose so,' he said vaguely. Then: 'Was it wise to tell the mother we'd find out who did it? How can you be so sure?'

'Because,' said Maud, 'I know who did it.'

She looked at the time on the dashboard. She was going to be late for Stuart.

She arrived back at her flat after seven and only just had time to have a quick shower and pull on her jumpsuit and her sturdy biker boots before racing out again. Her hair was still slightly damp when she arrived, eleven minutes past eight, at the little Vietnamese place Stuart had chosen.

'Sorry,' she said, sliding into the seat opposite his.

'At least you haven't stood me up.'

'It's been one of those days. I had to go to Derbyshire.'

'Pottery county,' he said. 'I've been thinking about you.'

'I was seeing the mother of a young woman who died.' She studied his expression. 'I don't want there to be an elephant in the room,' she continued. 'You work in advertising and I think I can cope with that. I'm a detective in the Met: that's what I do. If you can't deal with it, I might as well leave right now.'

'Don't do that.'

'I know what people think of the Met.'

'Are they wrong?'

'Only because it's worse than they imagine. They just hear the stories that make the news. It's a toxic culture. Sometimes I agree with the people who say we should get rid of it and start again.'

'How can you bear it?'

Maud considered. A waiter came and handed them both menus.

'I sometimes think I can't. Or I shouldn't,' she said slowly.

'But?'

'But I'm good at it,' she said. 'I know I am. I do my job well and carefully. The case I'm working on now, one of my colleagues screwed up, he didn't care enough and he just didn't see evidence that was staring him in the face. But I'm on the point of solving it, and I think things will be a little bit better because of that. If I left because I was worried about compromising my precious integrity, that wouldn't have happened.'

Stuart nodded, his brow furrowed.

'Sometimes I'm angry,' Maud said, 'and sometimes I'm exhausted and feel defeated by it all. But in the end, it comes down to this: I'm a good detective.'

'I bet you are,' said Stuart. 'Let's order.'

'I already know I want sesame noodles. And broken rice.'

'Have you been thinking about me?'

Maud had been thinking about Kira Mullan and Nancy North, about the occupants of 99 Fielding Road, about a condom and a dress, a cracked phone and those watertight alibis, about the name that she now held in her mind.

She just smiled and touched his hand.

An hour later, they stood in the dark street together. He kissed her and his lips were cool and tasted of chilli and ginger and beer. She put a hand against the nape of his neck and he ran his fingers through the wild tangle of her hair.

'Shall we go to my place?' he whispered. 'Or yours?'

Maud stepped back.

'Not tonight,' she said.

'When can we meet again?'

'Soon,' she said.

Because soon this case would be over and she would be free for a while, until the next one got into her brain and fizzed away there.

'What are you doing on Saturday?'

'Seeing you?'

SEVENTY-FIVE

William Goddard didn't look pleased.

'Can I come in?' said Maud.

'Isn't there some legal requirement that you have to tell me in advance if you want to interview me?'

'I'm just here to get some information.'

'Am I legally obliged to answer your questions?'

Maud had to bite back a reply to this. This was the William Goddard who wouldn't fix a leaking roof or an exposed wire or a crack in the wall until he was legally forced to and, because he had lawyers and his tenants didn't, he never was forced to. There was a lot that Maud would have liked to say to Goddard and a lot she would have liked to do to him, but she needed information and, just now, that was more important than anything.

'We could have a discussion about what you're legally obliged to do,' she said. 'And discussions like that can turn a bit nasty. I just want to ask a few questions.'

'I've got no problem with that,' he said, in a softer tone. 'I just don't like being pushed around, that's all.'

Yes, thought Maud. For Goddard, every conversation, every interaction, was about power. If you weren't dominating, then you were being dominated.

As he led her into the house, he pointed out the details of the work he'd recently had done: the marble tiles, the bronze door handle.

'Hand-cast,' he said. 'It's more expensive but it's worth it. You can feel the craftsmanship every time you turn a handle.'

He made coffee for the two of them from an industrial-size espresso machine. He slid a large French window sideways, and the two of them stepped out onto the patio that faced a long garden. He pointed at the huge tree at the far end of the garden.

'It's a hornbeam. It's a hundred and fifty years old.'

'I wanted to ask about the flat,' said Maud.

'I've told you everything,' he said dismissively.

'I don't exactly mean the flat. I mean the contents, the stuff that was left behind.'

'Her family came and took all of that.'

'I've talked to them already. But there's always stuff that gets left behind.'

'Don't I know it?' said Goddard. 'You wouldn't believe the crap I've had to deal with over the years.'

'What did Kira's family leave behind?'

Goddard gave a sniff.

'Just odds and ends. A washing-up brush, some tumblers, knives and forks.'

'What about clothes?'

'There were a few things left in drawers. Socks, tee-shirts, just random stuff.'

'What did you do with it?'

'What do you think I did with it? I put it in a bin bag and threw it away.'

'Absolutely everything?'

He looked at her suspiciously.

'What do you mean? You reckon I helped myself to something I shouldn't? I can tell you that there was nothing worth stealing.'

'What about a dress?'

'I don't remember any dress.'

'Do you want me to describe it for you?'

He looked suddenly angry.

'If I didn't see a dress then there's no point in describing the thing I didn't see.'

'I'm not making any accusation. If you took the dress, I'd just like to see it.'

'I didn't take the fucking dress. Is that all?'

'Almost. Did you have the flat professionally cleaned?'

'A couple of women went in there and did a basic clean.'

'Not a thorough one?'

'Why are you asking that? What business is that of yours? It's usually the job of the old tenant to make sure the flat is in a presentable condition.'

'Which clearly wasn't possible in this case.'

'It was a crime scene. I thought the police wouldn't want it disturbed.'

'A crime scene,' said Maud. 'That's an interesting thing to say.'

'Why's it interesting? You're a detective investigating a murder.'

'I'm leading an inquiry that's been reopened. But when you found a new tenant for the flat, there was no inquiry.'

'I don't get it. Are you criticising me for *not* cleaning the flat properly?'

'Who's criticising anyone? I was just asking a question.'

'Well, the answer to your question is that – what with everything that was going on – I didn't have the time to get the flat deep-cleaned. I think the young lady was happy to move in.'

'And did the cleaners throw things away?'

'I told them to get rid of any rubbish they found. I assume that's what they did. You can ask them if you want, but I can assure you there wasn't anything left except old magazines, gone-off food, empty beer cans, things like that. No dresses.'

'Good,' said Maud. 'That's all I needed to know.'

'There should be a law about it,' said Sadie Emerson.

She and Maud were standing in the main room of what had once been Kira's flat and was now Sadie's. She looked exhausted.

'What do you mean?' said Maud.

'They should have to tell you in advance if something has happened. I can't sleep. I actually think the flat's haunted. When I'm lying in bed, I hear creaking in the walls and in the floorboards.'

'I think that happens in old houses. There's always movement.'

'That's easy for you to say. You don't have to live here. I imagine her walking around the flat in her bare feet.'

'I was wondering if she'd left anything behind. Clothes, perhaps.'

Sadie pulled a face.

'Course not.'

'Nothing at all?'

Sadie shrugged.

'There were a few things in the bathroom cabinet, in drawers.'

'What sort of things?'

'Oh, you know, stupid stuff. Like the things you stick between your teeth, whatever they're called. I threw it all away. It just gave me the creeps, the thought that she might have touched them.'

'But no clothes. I'm interested in a dress. Can you try to remember? It's important.'

'I don't need to try. If there was a dress, of course I'd remember it. If I'd found a dress, I'd have given it to her family. Or I'd have burned it, just to make sure it was gone.'

'But when you were cleaning, behind cupboards . . .'

'I haven't really cleaned properly and I'm not going to. I'm moving out as soon as I possibly can. I'm going to try and sublet this place.'

'Will you tell the person you sublet it to?'

Sadie flushed red.

'As I said, it's easy for you to say that.'

SEVENTY-SIX

The Pen was crowded that Friday lunchtime – regulars were joined by people who were at the end of their working week and those who were already on their Christmas break. From the kitchen, Nancy could hear the hum of voices and the chink of cutlery on plates. Behind her, Angie washed dishes and sneezed. The fridge rumbled. This, thought Nancy, was where she could lose herself.

Two days in, and she was already getting the hang of how to keep the little restaurant running smoothly. There were only a handful of simple meals, and most of her work was done in the mornings: making the brownies that were The Pen's signature pudding, preparing the thick tomato sauce that would, when an egg was broken over it, become shakshuka, peeling onions and garlic, making up large quantities of chilli oil, slicing cucumber very thinly and marinating it in soy and rice-wine vinegar. By the time customers began to arrive, all she had to do was grill the halloumi, fry the oyster mushrooms or lower noodles into boiling water.

The noise was thinning; it was nearly three and the restaurant was gradually emptying. Soon she, Angie and Carter the waiter would sit down together to eat a simple lunch.

The door of the kitchen swung open and the manager, who was also the owner, put his head through. He was large and shiny-faced and good-humoured until anything went wrong, when he had a tendency to turn purple and bellow.

'All good?'

'Good,' said Nancy. 'Any more orders?'

'You're pretty much done for now. Come here for a moment. I need you for something.'

Nancy followed him out into the restaurant, which only had a few diners left in it, and he pointed.

'Someone wants to compliment the chef.'

He practically pushed her in the direction of a table for two by the window and Nancy, wrapped in an apron and her hair scraped back, found herself looking at a man's back.

'Here's the chef,' said the manager. 'You can tell her yourself.'

She knew before the man turned. She took a step back.

He rose from his seat. He smiled.

'That was a delicious lunch,' he said. 'I wanted to tell you myself.'

Nancy tried to reply, but her mouth was dry and her vision blurry.

'Do you have a few moments?' Felix asked, still very pleasant and formal.

'No,' said Nancy.

'Of course you do,' said the manager, putting his large hand on her shoulder and pressing her down. 'You're off duty now until this evening.' Then he hissed in a low tone as Nancy sank into the chair opposite Felix, 'It doesn't hurt to be polite.'

'Thank you.' Nancy forced out the words.

'She only started yesterday,' said the manager. 'In time for the Christmas rush.'

'Amazing,' said Felix, wiping his mouth on the paper napkin.

'Is this your first time here? I don't recognise you.'

'First but not last,' said Felix. 'I must come back again. Maybe I'll become one of your regulars.'

The manager beamed and left them. Nancy made to rise but Felix put a hand on her arm.

'I'd like a chat,' he said.

'There's nothing to talk about.'

'There's lots to talk about. If you don't want to, I can't make you. But I'm not sure how your boss would react if he knew about your history. Someone who hears voices, has paranoid delusions, has recently been sectioned and is violent and abusive might find it hard to get work.'

'I can't believe you're doing this.'

'I just want to talk.'

'What do you want to talk about?'

He leaned towards her, his elbows on the table.

'How are you, Nancy? I've been worrying.'

'Fine,' she said.

'Really? I hope you won't mind me saying, but you still look a bit frail.'

'I'm fine,' she repeated. 'How did you find me?'

'Taking your meds? I worry that without me to remind you, you'll forget, and then – well, we both know what would happen then, don't we?'

She didn't reply. Dread was a bitter taste in her mouth, a thumping heart, a shrill whine in her brain, as if a cicada was trapped in there.

'And eating regularly?' he continued.

'Is that why you're here? To ask if I'm taking my meds and eating properly?'

'And how's your new best friend, that detective?' Felix asked.

'I need to go now.'

'How's the investigation?' He leaned in even closer. She could see the flecks in his irises and the pin pricks of his stubble. 'Ask her.'

'I'm asking you.' He looked away from her and smiled towards the manager who was standing at the bar watching them.

Nancy suddenly felt the dread dissolve and in its place was an anger that was pure and good. She leaned in so that their faces were nearly touching.

'I think she believes it's someone in the house,' she said slowly and clearly, watching his smile tighten until it was an ugly line. 'Or next door.'

She turned to the manager.

'The gentleman would like his bill, please,' she said and got to her feet. 'I'm pleased you enjoyed the meal.'

She walked away from Felix without looking back, not into the kitchen but into the Ladies, where she pulled off her apron and vomited until her stomach was empty.

SEVENTY-SEVEN

On the other side of London, Maud was sitting at her desk with Kira's fully charged mobile. She took off her oversized suit jacket, tied her hair more firmly back, then checked the PIN that Connie Mullan had given her yesterday: 140999. Kira's birthday: she'd been only twenty-three. Maud ran her forefinger thoughtfully across the crack on the screen, then entered the number. The phone came to life, pings and beeps coming from it, messages appearing.

Later, Forrester could go through everything, the WhatsApps, Kira's Instagram account, her photos. Now, Maud was interested in the last moments of the young woman's life.

She scrolled past the messages that had been sent after Kira was dead – *What are you doing tonight? Where are you? How was the party? Give me a call* – until she got to the one that Kira had sent to her mother at 3.47. *You're the best mother – love you lots.*

Maud chewed her lower lip thoughtfully: the police had read this as corroborative evidence that Kira had taken her own life.

Before that message was notification of a missed call at 3.16 from Viv Melville, from The Cornerstone where Kira used to work. Kira hadn't called her back.

Maud scrolled through the phone calls that day, then the different messages. She scrolled forward, past the day of

death, and saw that there were multiple calls and messages
from someone called Ollie. She jotted the number down on her
notepad, promising herself she would call him later.

She looked briefly at the photographs. There were none from
that Sunday. The last one was from Saturday late afternoon,
a selfie of Kira in her sequined sheath dress. She looked young
and glowing with health, with a peachy complexion and a soft,
dimpled smile. Twenty-four hours later, she was dead.

The little message sent at 3.47 was the last record of Kira
being alive. Three-quarters of an hour before that, Nancy had
collided with her at the entrance of the house. Maud considered
those forty-five minutes, almost feeling the cogs in her brain as
they turned and clicked into place.

She opened Settings on the phone and then the Privacy
option. For people like Kira, who didn't worry about things
like that, it was really the lack-of-privacy option. As she tapped
the phone, Maud felt like she was entering room after room
until she reached the one that Kira had never visited. She probably didn't know it existed, but it said a lot about her.

At a quarter to four that Sunday afternoon, Kira had been
at Mill Gate Road. Maud could see the exact spot on the map
from where the message had been sent. She stood up, slid on
her jacket and then her long quilted coat and woollen hat. She
left the station without anyone noticing her go and walked
rapidly along the streets. In the distance she could hear the
rumble of freight trains. The cold wind made her eyes water
and her skin sore.

Soon she was standing in a cul-de-sac, the criss-crossing
expanse of tracks just beyond her behind a high metal fence.
It was already starting to get dark. A train rattled past, wagon
after rusty wagon, the shriek of metal. At last it was gone.
She took her own phone and tapped in 99 Fielding Road as a

destination. It was sixteen minutes' walk from where she was standing.

'So,' she said to Forrester, perching herself on her desk, holding a mug of coffee with both hands. 'That three forty-seven message.'

'Yes?' He looked eager.

'A misdirection.'

'I don't get it.'

She smiled at him, almost dreamily, and he furrowed his brow, waiting for an explanation.

'Are you going to tell me what you're thinking?' he asked at last.

While she was starting to answer, she felt a presence beside her and looked round. A young officer was hovering.

'There's someone who wants to talk to you.' he said.

Maud shook her head impatiently.

'I'm in the middle of something. There must be someone else who's free.'

'She asked for you by name,' said the officer. 'She seems in a bit of a bad way. But I can tell her to go away, if you want?' He grinned. 'If you hear a bit of wailing from downstairs, don't pay any attention.'

'No,' said Maud sharply. 'Bring her up.'

Nancy picked up the mug of tea she had been given with both hands. She tried to raise it to her lips but had to put it back down because her hands were shaking.

'It's all right,' Maud said. 'Take your time.'

'He found me,' Nancy said. 'Felix came to my work – he came to my *work* – and he threatened me.'

'Tell us exactly what happened.'

With stumbling and repetitions and questions from Maud and Forrester, Nancy described what had taken place at the restaurant.

'It's doing my head in,' Nancy said, when she had finished. 'First he got to Megan. She didn't admit it but I know that he must have. Why else would she suddenly have made me leave?' She tapped Maud's desk with her forefinger. 'I was careful not to leave any hint of where I was going. I chose Megan because she was a friend from a time before I met Felix. They didn't know each other. But he managed to find her and get to her in some way. And then there's my job. London's the size of a bloody country. I thought I'd disappeared and that there was no way he could find me but there he was, sitting at a table with his smile and saying he'd tell my boss.' She raised her hands and gripped her head. 'It's like he's got inside my skull. He knows where I am, he knows everything about me. I don't know what to do. I came here, but I don't know why. There's probably nothing you can do either.'

Maud looked at Nancy with concern. She hadn't seen her quite like this before.

'That's not right,' she said.

'The one thing I wanted to say is that if Felix is the person you want for Kira's murder, then you'd bloody well better get a move on because if he's going down, I think he'd like to take me down with him.'

'Where is he now?'

'Felix? At work, I guess.'

'Where's that?'

'In Shepherd's Bush. I don't know the exact address. The company's called Court7. You can Google it.'

'I'm going to leave you here with my colleague,' Maud said.

Forrester looked puzzled and a little irritated.

'Are you going to make an arrest?'

'I can't talk about that right now,' said Maud. 'While you wait, you can do something for me.'

'Yes?'

'Go through Nancy's phone. Take it to a techie if there's any difficulty.'

'Why?' Nancy asked.

'I might be wrong, but I believe Felix has tampered with it.'

'Oh,' said Nancy faintly. Then: 'Of course. Why didn't I think of that? The bastard. The fucking bastard.'

'Could you open it for me and let me have a look?' Forrester said.

Nancy tapped her passcode in to her phone and passed it to him.

'I'll call you soon,' Maud said to Forrester .

He was tapping at the phone and didn't seem to hear what she was saying.

'I know how he did it,' he said.

'What?' said Maud. 'Already?'

'You know the Find My iPhone feature?' he said to Nancy.

'Kind of. I think I've heard of it.'

'Did you share it with Felix?'

'Of course not. I barely knew it existed myself.'

'Well, he's been added to the contacts. You and him.'

'Does that mean he'd know where I was?'

'He'd know where your phone was.'

'Can you disable it?' said Maud.

Forrester smiled.

'Yes, I can disable it. I'll need to do some more checks, though. There may be some hidden stalkerware.'

'Stalkerware?' said Maud. 'I hate that that word even needs to exist.'

She looked around and saw a young uniformed officer she'd
worked with recently.

'Hattie?' The woman looked round. 'Can you come with
me? It'll only be about an hour.'

'Where are you going?' Nancy asked.

'I'll call you.'

SEVENTY-EIGHT

The office of Court7 was an advertisement for itself, a riot of concrete and brightly coloured metal tubing and sheet glass.

'Wow,' said Hattie.

'Yes, I know,' said Maud.

'What am I here for?'

'I just need someone in a uniform. Someone who can look serious and disapproving and not say anything.'

'I can do that,' said Hattie cheerfully, just glad to get out of the station.

They walked through the heavy glass doors up to the reception desk. Behind it was a young woman with immaculately styled hair looking at them with a smile that turned to puzzlement when she saw Hattie's uniform.

'I need to see Felix Lindberg,' Maud said.

'I'll tell him you're here.'

'No,' said Maud. She took out her badge and held it in front of the receptionist. 'I don't want you to tell him I'm here. I want someone to take us to where he is and I don't want him to be warned.'

'He might be in a meeting.'

'It doesn't matter. If he's in the building, I want someone to take us to him.'

The receptionist looked troubled, indecisive. Finally she picked up a phone and spoke into it, turning away so her words couldn't be heard. A minute later a security guard appeared. The receptionist got up, walked round to the front and whispered to him, pointing upwards. He nodded. He looked at the officers.

'This way,' he said.

They emerged from the lift onto an upper floor, a large open-plan office. The guard led them through the desks. This was why Maud had brought a uniformed officer. If she had been alone, in her normal work clothes, nobody would have paid any attention. But everybody noticed the uniform. Conversations stopped; people openly stared with obvious curiosity.

Maud saw Felix before he saw her. He was leaning across a desk in conversation with a woman in a grey suit, a screen in between them. Felix was dressed in canvas shoes, dark brown cords and a green patterned shirt. He was relaxed and assured and at home and, weirdly, just at that moment Maud could see what had attracted Nancy to him.

He saw the expression on the face of the woman he was talking to and turned. His face went very red.

'What the hell are you doing here?' he said, in a hiss, as if he hoped to escape attention. But the room was silent, and it was obvious that everyone was looking, aghast and fascinated.

'I'd like a word.'

'You can't just turn up like this, unannounced in the middle of my office.'

'You mean, embarrass you at your place of work?' Maud said neutrally. 'I wouldn't want to do that. It'll just take a minute.'

'I don't need to talk to you.'

'You think so?'

'All right. We've got a free space.'

Felix led them across to one side of the office and entered a meeting room. He closed the door behind him. The buzz of the office had stopped but the walls were all transparent. He stood with his back to the door. At least his colleagues wouldn't be able to see his response.

'I'm going to make a complaint about this,' he said in a calmer voice.

There was a black-topped table surrounded by chairs. Maud and Hattie sat at the far side with their backs to the window, facing Felix.

'I've talked to Nancy,' Maud said.

'I'm concerned about her safety,' said Felix.

'So am I. When she left your flat, she was very careful to conceal where she had gone. But you found her new accommodation and you also found her new place of work. It took a few minutes with her phone to solve that mystery.'

'This sounds like the sort of conversation I should be having with a lawyer present.'

'It might come to that but just now, as I said, I'm concerned about her immediate safety. This is just a conversation for the moment. I want to help Nancy, but I may also be helping you. People used to think it was romantic or cute when a man wouldn't take no for an answer from a woman. And the law couldn't do much about it. But that's changed. I'm here to warn you. It is at the very least arguable that you have committed an offence under the 1997 Protection from Harassment Act.'

'That's ridiculous,' said Felix. 'I've got a complete right to talk to the person I've lived with for the past couple of years. She's unstable and vulnerable and I need to make sure she is all right.'

'I wouldn't use that argument in court. Talking to someone who doesn't want to see you, talking to people who know them, following them, those are all potential forms of harassment or stalking.' He started to say something, but she shook her head. 'Stop. I don't want to hear anything from you. If we do this again it'll be with a lawyer present. I'm here to give you information. If you make any further attempt to contact her or people around her, or if you do anything that might cause her anxiety, I will charge you. For your information, the maximum sentence for the basic charge is six months in prison. But if the offence is aggravated, involving threats of violence or causing serious alarm to the victim, then the maximum sentence is ten years.'

'You're going to regret this,' said Felix, still more calmly.

Maud turned to her colleague.

'Are you paying attention?'

'I am.'

She looked back at Felix.

'One of the key aggravating factors is if the harassment was systematically planned. I already know that your name has been added to Nancy's contacts on the Find My iPhone app.'

'She must have done that.'

'She didn't.'

'Don't take her word for anything.'

'If we find that Nancy's phone has been further tampered with, and it is being looked at as we speak, then we have our aggravating factor.'

'You came here, to my office, just to make a point, is that right?'

'Have I made it?'

'You've ruined my day, if that's what you mean.'

'Was that for real?' said Hattie.

They were back on the pavement outside the Court7 office.

'Which bit?'

'About charging him with stalking?'

'I'd like to,' said Maud. 'But I've got other things on my mind.' She took out her phone and dialled Forrester. 'Well?' she said, when Forrester answered.

'You were right. He's installed stalkerware. Or at least, stalkerware has been installed by someone.'

'No surprise there. How's Nancy?'

'Angry.'

'Good. She can go now. And you, meet me at the Fielding Road flat.'

'Sometimes,' Nancy said to Helena, 'being paranoid is just being realistic.'

They were meeting in person again, no longer as flattened-out versions of themselves on a screen. Helena had agreed to see her at such short notice because Nancy had said it was an emergency. Now she felt bad that Helena had given up her time. She realised, and was shocked she hadn't seen this before, that Helena was old. Although her face was calm as she sat in her familiar chair, her hands folded in her lap, Nancy thought she looked tired.

'I've been thinking,' Nancy continued, 'about my voices.'

'Tell me.'

'They often tell me to be scared, or to run away, and they were right.' She frowned. 'They were right, I was right; like I knew and didn't know. The voices were telling me to acknowledge something. Why did it take such a long time for me to do it? For two years, I've been living with a man who has been trying to control me. He didn't like half my friends. He didn't like me going out without him. He liked me being ill. He got me sectioned and when I came out of hospital, he started tracking me, stalking me. Or maybe he was already doing that. I was in a prison.'

'But now you've got free.'

'Yes. Although sometimes it feels as if he is still there, in my brain, in the way I feel scared if I hear footsteps behind me or wake in the night with a thudding heart.'

'This will take time, Nancy.'

'Time and work,' said Nancy. 'I know. I'm ready for that.'

SEVENTY-NINE

They didn't go in at once. Instead, Maud led Forrester away from number 99, past Michelle and Dylan's house, towards the high street.

'Where are we going?' Forrester asked.

'I need to check something.'

They got to the high street and turned right, walking past boarded-up shops, a bookie, a twenty-four-hour greengrocer, a nail parlour, a barber, a money-lending outfit, and a place apparently selling only old-fashioned umbrellas and telescopes.

'Here,' said Maud, stopping outside a pound shop. The pavement outside was stacked with small stepladders, wheelbarrows and rakes, plastic storage containers, hard-bristled brooms, wheelie cases chained together, bags of compost, plastic Christmas trees, even children's buckets and spades although it was December.

Maud looked at it with satisfaction, then stepped inside. The shop was separated by narrow aisles of shelves that were piled high with a miscellany of objects. There were batteries and wigs and food whisks and tools; dolls, fishing rods, treats for dogs, plastic flowers, tinsel, many, many Christmas decorations. There seemed to be no logic to how they were arranged.

Maud and Forrester made their way up the first aisle, though they had to reverse when a woman with her buggy came from the other direction. They turned the corner and Maud stopped.

'Look,' she said, pointing.

On the bottom shelf, next to a basket full of nails and screws, were several coils of blue rope. Maud picked one up and examined it.

'It looks the same,' she said.

She went to the man wedged behind the counter, surrounded by scratch cards, cans of fizzy drinks and behind him a variety of vapes and packs of cigarettes. He was reading a newspaper.

'This rope,' she said, holding it up.

'Five pound forty,' he said. 'Cash for anything under a tenner.'

'Can you remember if anyone came in here on Sunday the thirteenth of November, and bought one like this?' He stared at her. 'I'm a detective,' she said, bringing out her ID.

'That's a month ago. Course I don't.'

'Do people buy rope like this often?'

'People buy all sorts of stuff.'

'Do you have CCTV?'

'No.'

'Do you keep a record of what's bought?'

'No.'

Maud pulled out her wallet and extracted a ten-pound note. 'I'll take this rope,' she said.

A few minutes later, Maud and Forrester stood in Kira's old flat. Maud had asked Sadie to leave for a while, to get a coffee. For a time, she just stood there, as if she was meditating. When she spoke, it was to herself as much as to Forrester. Going over things again and again.

'Think of Kira,' she said. 'She should have been running away but when she bumped into Nancy she was coming back. It was that important. And think of the clothes tossed all over the floor.'

'Could it just have been Kira, looking for the dress, if that's what was being looked for – and it's a big if – and not finding it?'

Maud shook her head.

'If she'd gone back, if it was that important, I think she'd know where it was.'

'Or if it was the killer who was looking for the dress, he – or she – might have found it and taken it away and destroyed it.'

Again Maud shook her head, more slowly this time, still thinking it through.

'Maybe,' she said. 'We can't know. But those clothes on the floor, that doesn't seem like normal searching. You know when you look for something and don't find it and then you start hunting in the places you've already looked?'

'It's just a guess.'

'If you like. I'm guessing that Kira came back for the dress because it was her one weapon. I'm guessing she hid it somewhere and the killer didn't find it and nobody else has found it. Which means it's still here. Or at least, I hope that's what has happened.'

'Everything you say is based on a hope and a guess.'

'It's based on the evidence.'

'Or not.'

Maud smiled. Forrester was in an unusually hostile mood. She wondered what the other detectives had been saying about her. She wondered what Forrester had said back.

He gestured around the room.

'It's not a big flat. Where would you hide something here? What do you want to do? Take the floorboards up?'

'It may come to that,' said Maud. 'I hope not.'

'Where do you want to start?'

Maud stared around her, frowning.

'The only thing to do is go through the flat inch by inch, looking for places where she could have pushed a dress. Behind the lavatory cistern, that kind of place. You start in the bathroom; I'll do the bedroom. Then we can search in here.'

They both pulled on gloves. Forrester disappeared into the small bathroom. Maud heard him give a muted yell as he bumped into something. She went into the bedroom.

She searched methodically, moving slowly through the room, crouching to look under the bed, reaching up to see if there was anything on top of the wardrobe – there was, but only a broken flip-flop, a running cap and many dead flies. She opened the wardrobe door, moving aside the few dresses and shirts of Sadie hanging there, then moving the shoes to make sure nothing had been bundled up at the back and overlooked.

'Not behind the cistern,' called Forrester. 'I'm taking the panels out from the bath to see if she hid it there.'

'Careful you don't damage anything,' called Maud as she heard a bang and something ripping.

She opened each of the pine chest's drawers, dipping her hand behind each one in case the dress was secreted in a cavity. Then she pulled the chest away from the wall. There was a little ventilation grid and she crouched down to examine it. It was insecurely screwed into place and it was easy to remove it and feel inside for a dress. Nothing, except dirt and mouse droppings. She took off her soiled gloves and put on a new pair.

'Nothing,' called Forrester. 'They have a real problem with silverfish though.'

They met in the main room.

'You take the living area,' said Maud. 'I'll do the kitchen bit.'

In a narrow cupboard, there was a small, rusty boiler that needed a service. She searched on top of it and tried to slide her fingers behind, but there was no room for a dress. She took the mop and old vacuum cleaner out of the cupboard and then a bundle of plastic bags. She got Forrester to help her edge out the greasy oven and found nothing but clotted dust balls, more flies, more mouse droppings. She did the same with the fridge, the washing machine. The landlord had been telling the truth when he said the flat hadn't been deep-cleaned.

She squatted down to examine the cupboard under the sink. Behind her, Forrester was lifting cushions on the sofa and peering down behind the radiator. She took out a cracked bucket, several cloths that urgently needed to be thrown away, an empty bottle of floor cleaner, a nearly empty bottle of white spirit, a spray can for silverfish and other household bugs, fabric stain remover, bleach. There was nothing there.

'I think these might come off,' said Forrester, squatting beside her and jiggling at the narrow wooden board that ran along the floor under the sink.

'I don't think they will,' said Maud. 'Have you looked in those high storage cupboards?'

She put her hand into the grimy space behind the pipes, moving it to the left and the right. Her fingers touched something.

'Nothing here,' said Forrester.

Maud's hand closed on plastic. As she drew it out, she heard a very faint chink. It was a white bag with red handles, folded up on itself. Her eyes gleamed. She sat back on her heels and carefully opened the bag.

She was aware of Forrester, kneeling beside her.

'It can't be,' he said.

Maud drew out the dress. Green, minute and shiny, its sequins glinting.

'We found it. You were right! You were fucking right.'

Maud let the garment hang from her fingers for a few

seconds. Then she let it fall back into the bag and got to her feet.

'This is a job for Matt Moran,' she said.

'How long will it take?'

'Eight hours minimum, if it's treated as a matter of urgency. But it's already quite late. By tomorrow morning, I think. We'll come back then.'

'Tomorrow's Saturday. I'm playing football.'

'I can see you on Monday, if you want.'

'I can cancel.'

Before calling it a day, Maud called Ollie's number, but he didn't answer. She left a brief voicemail. Ten minutes later, he called back.

'Yes?' he said. 'You want to talk to me about Kira.'

'I do.'

'Why?'

Maud hesitated.

'Where are you?'

'Right now, I'm leaving work. Near Paddington,' he added.

'Do you have time to come to the station in Harlesden?' said Maud. 'For a quick chat.'

He arrived thirty-five minutes later, out of breath as if he'd been hurrying.

'Thank you,' said Maud as he was shown into her room. 'This shouldn't take long, but I thought it better to do it in person.'

He nodded.

'You were friendly with Kira,' said Maud.

'Yes.'

'What was your relationship to her?'

'I liked her,' he said frankly. 'I mean, *like* liked.'

'Did you know her well?'

'No. I first saw her at The Cornerstone when I met up with friends there for a drink. She served me and we chatted. I went back a few times, because of her. Then I asked her on a date.'

'When was this?'

'The date? Thursday the tenth of November,' he answered readily. 'I stayed over after, and we spent most of Friday together.'

'At her flat?'

'Yes.' He looked down at his hands, which were plaited together in his lap. 'It was lovely,' he said.

'And did you see her again?'

'No. She had to go to work that evening and the next morning, crack of dawn, I went away for a few days. A stag do in Barcelona. I called and messaged her when I got back, but she didn't reply. I thought she'd changed her mind about me, but it didn't seem in character for her not to tell me straight out. I looked in at The Cornerstone and she wasn't there, and I went to where she lived. That's when someone told me she was dead. I couldn't believe it. I wondered if the woman wasn't quite reliable – she kept telling me to go to the police but not mention her. I didn't go. I mean, what was there to say?'

'Did you use a condom?'

He flushed.

'Yes,' he said. 'That is, a few actually.'

The mystery of the condom was resolved, thought Maud. Not evidence of any kind of crime, but of a happy sexual interlude spent with a man who was keen on her. She was glad to tie up this loose end, and glad too that Kira had had that.

EIGHTY

Maud and Forrester walked up Fielding Road together in silence. After the greyness and drizzle, the morning was cold and crisp, the bare branches of the plane trees silhouetted against a sharp blue sky.

When they reached the house, they both stopped for a few seconds, readying themselves. Maud nodded at Forrester, and he pressed the bell. They were buzzed in without being asked for their names.

The door of the flat opened a few inches and a segment of a face showed.

'Yes?'

'Is your husband here?'

There was a pause. The door opened further, and Olga stood before them, still in nightclothes, her hair hanging round her face.

'He's on night shifts again. Someone was ill and he's doing their shift. He'll be back soon, I think.'

'We'll wait for him.'

'In here?'

'If that's all right.'

Olga stood aside. They could see the baby in a bouncy chair in the kitchen, and the remnants of Olga's breakfast on the table.

'Coffee?' she asked. Her hands were knotted tightly together.

'No, thank you.'

'Why do you want to see him?'

Maud didn't reply. She drew out a chair and sat at the table, looking down at the baby, who for once wasn't crying. Suddenly, Lydia smiled up at her, a smile that crinkled up her entire face. Maud put out a finger and touched her cheek softly.

'It's him, isn't it?'

The way Olga said it, it was more of a statement than a question.

The room was quite silent. Maud could feel the tick of her heart, the throb of her blood in her veins.

'Why do you say that?'

Olga took a step forward, putting one hand on the table to steady herself. Her eyes were bright, and her cheeks flushed, as if she had a fever.

'We need to ask him some questions,' said Maud.

'You don't need to lie to me,' said Olga.

She drew up the cotton sleeve of her pyjama top. There was a red weal on her wrist.

'He did that?'

'And other things. He gets angry. He's tired. I'm tired. Lydia cries. He says he can't escape from it all, that he's living in a prison.'

'And he takes it out on you.'

'More since that girl died,' said Olga simply. 'When I saw you at the door, I knew.' But she shook her head as she spoke. Her eyes glittering. 'I'm a coward,' she said harshly. 'I think I always knew. But how do *you* know?'

Maud hesitated, then made up her mind.

'You're right. When your husband comes back, we're going to arrest him for the murder of Kira Mullan. Harry wasn't a suspect at first because Kira apparently sent a message to her mother. At the time she sent it, Harry was with Lydia on his way to meet you and there is no way that he could have got back to the flat after that, with Lydia in tow, killed Kira, and then returned to you.'

Olga nodded.

'But in fact Kira died before that message was sent. We believe that Harry met her when he was taking that walk around the block at about three that afternoon, to clear his head. That was when Kira was returning from seeing a friend. I think she had made up her mind to go to the police about what had been done to her the night before. She must have told Harry that and told him she had the evidence to prove it.'

'Prove what?' Olga's voice was a croak.

'What do you think?' said Maud steadily.

She saw Olga's small face stiffen. Lydia gave a gurgle and Olga bent down and lifted her, cradling her, but still staring at Maud.

'Go on,' she said.

'It doesn't take long to strangle someone. There was just enough time for Harry to go to the pound shop up on the high street, buy a coil of rope, and intercept Kira at her flat. And she had just enough time to hide the evidence that she'd come back to collect before he killed her. There were clothes flung everywhere, but not the dress that she was wearing when he raped her. She had only bought it that afternoon, ready for the party. His DNA on it must have come from that night.'

'His semen,' said Olga flatly.

'Yes.'

Olga kissed the top of Lydia's head, murmured something to her in Polish.

'Then he took her mobile,' continued Maud, 'went back upstairs, and half an hour later, the two of you went out together with Lydia in her buggy. He left you to have coffee with your friend and he wheeled Lydia to the little cul-de-sac at the junction of all the railway tracks and sent a WhatsApp to Kira's mother.'

'Hang on, how would he have opened Kira's phone?' Forrester asked.

'I've thought about that. I believe he must have held it up to Kira's face as she was dying, and then it was a simple matter of keeping it alive when it was in his pocket. It's the kind of callousness that fits with his subsequent behaviour.' She turned to Olga once more. 'When you and he came home again, he simply posted the mobile through Kira's letter box. There's a crack across the top of the screen where it fell onto the hard floor.'

'Clever,' said Forrester.

'You say *must have*,' said Olga. 'You say *he must have done it*. You mean he could have done it. This is not proof.'

'You sound like a lawyer,' said Maud.

'He'll have a lawyer,' said Olga. 'I'm saying what the lawyer will say.'

'I hadn't quite finished,' said Maud. 'Harry didn't just have one phone with him. He had two phones. He had Kira's phone and he had his own phone. All we need to do is wait for him to come home and look at his phone. Then we'll know if the two phones were in the same place.'

There was a long silence and Olga just stared at Maud.

'What if he didn't have his phone with him?' she said.

Maud turned and looked at Forrester who looked suddenly alarmed, thinking it might all have gone wrong. She looked back at Olga.

'But he did have his phone,' she said. 'He showed me a photo he had taken of the three of you. It really proved he was where he'd said he'd been. I think that was the moment I knew he'd done it. I didn't know how, and I didn't know if I would be able to prove it, but I felt he was being too clever. He was almost rubbing my nose in his perfect alibi.'

Another long silence.

'I think,' Olga said slowly, 'I need to go to the toilet. Could you look after Lydia?'

'I'm sure you're not going out of the room to phone your husband and tell him to dispose of his phone,' said Maud. 'A man who has hurt and bullied you. But I'd better come with you just to make sure. My colleague can look after a baby for a few minutes.'

Forrester looked mildly alarmed by the prospect.

Olga didn't go to the toilet. They didn't speak and for twenty minutes, Maud, Forrester and Olga waited in silence. The tap dripped. Lydia, bunched up in her mother's arms, became slack and heavy; her eyelids flickered and closed.

Then they heard footsteps.

The key turned softly in the door.

EIGHTY-ONE

Maud was sitting at her kitchen table, eating a piece of buttered toast and drinking tea. She was tired, the energy of the past days draining away from her and leaving her pensive. A case had been solved; a man had been charged with murder. But she didn't feel exultant. It was such a sad story, such a familiar one.

Her phone rang and she saw it was Craig Weller. She was so startled that she had to compose herself before she answered.

'Is something up?' she said.

'And hello to you too,' Weller said.

'I was just surprised.'

'I want you to come in.'

'What? Now?'

'We're going to have a press conference.'

'On a Saturday afternoon?'

'Just get here as soon as you can.'

Maud had a quick shower and changed into clothes that seemed more suitable for a detective appearing at a press conference. She tied her hair back and put on lip gloss. She picked up the letter she had written and put it in her jacket pocket.

Twenty minutes later, she was being led into Weller's office. On the way over she had toyed with the idea of asking what was the point of this. A press conference on a Saturday afternoon was what you did when you wanted to bury a result, not boast about it. She decided there was no point in mentioning it. It was already arranged. There was nothing to be done, and it didn't matter now anyway. But as she stepped inside the office, she saw that Weller wasn't alone. He was with DI Kemp, and they were laughing together, as if in the middle of a shared joke. They looked round at her.

'Good to see you, Maud,' said Weller affably. 'I hope you weren't at the football.'

'No, I wasn't at the football.'

'Football's probably not your thing.'

'I play it rather than watch it.'

'Really?' said Weller, raising an eyebrow. 'Good for you. Women's football used to be a bit of a joke when I was growing up, but you see it on the TV now.'

'About the press conference,' said Maud. She looked at Kemp. 'I thought you were on holiday.'

'I am.'

'Danny's kindly agreed to come in,' said Weller. 'After all, he was in charge of the inquiry at the beginning.'

'What inquiry?'

'The Kira Mullan murder inquiry, of course.'

'I didn't know there *was* a Kira Mullan murder inquiry. I mean, until I started it.'

Craig Weller laughed. He seemed in an unusually benign mood.

'That's really a sort of philosophical point,' he said. 'What I mean is that the inquiry that culminated in the current charges being brought against Harold Fisk started with Danny here in charge.'

'It's actually Harry,' said Maud. 'It's not short for anything. Harry is his actual name.' She turned to Kemp. 'I see you're wearing your funeral suit.'

He laughed in an unfriendly way.

'It's also my conference suit.'

'Exactly.' Weller's expression became more serious. 'An announcement like this is really about how we project ourself as a department. What we want to show is that we're a team. It's all about teamwork.'

'Quite,' said Kemp. 'Teamwork.'

'I'm thinking of the department, Maud,' said Weller, 'but I'm also thinking of you. I don't want you to always be seen as stirring things up, as telling your colleagues how to do their jobs.'

'I don't understand,' said Maud slowly, who was, in fact, starting to understand. 'I'm just going to announce that a man has been charged with a murder. That's all we're allowed to say, isn't it?'

'About that,' said Weller. 'I totally want you to be there. I want the whole team to be there. But I think the right thing would be if Danny did the actual presentation.'

Even though she was shocked, Maud felt she should have been more shocked.

'Do you know the details of the case?' she asked, as calmly as she could manage.

Kemp laughed.

'I looked through the file. It was all straightforward really, wasn't it? Still, we should have a drink some time to celebrate. Get the lads together.'

'Did you ask Forrester?' said Maud.

'Ask him what?'

'To come to the conference. As part of the team.'

'No, I didn't,' said Weller, frowning. 'I thought I'd give him the time off. It's not like there'll be that many people at a conference late on a Saturday afternoon.'

Maud thought of asking why they were holding it on a

Saturday afternoon, but she didn't because she already knew the answer. Late Saturday afternoon was likely to be too late for the Sunday papers and by Monday it would be a tiny item somewhere inside that nobody would pay attention to. It wasn't a very glorious case for the department, a murder that had been missed and then solved by the wrong detective. Better just to forget about it.

It wasn't the first time that Maud had been on the brink of resigning. She could almost taste the words in her mouth. It would be easy, such a relief. She looked at Weller and then Kemp, and she understood that they would not try and make her stay; they would even be pleased. She was a difficult woman, never a pushover, not one of the team of lads. She wouldn't turn a blind eye.

She waited a few moments, watching them watching her, then swallowed back her bitter words and nodded pleasantly.

'I won't be coming to the conference either,' she said.

Weller's frown deepened.

'You don't think you've been given enough credit? That's not going to look good.'

'Not at all. I've got a date.'

'A date?'

'Yes.'

'Surely that can wait.'

'You always talk about work-life balance. I'm sure Danny will do it very well. Just remember that Kira Mullan was a woman, not a girl.'

EIGHTY-TWO

Stuart put the two dry martinis on the table. They were in a bar in Westbourne Grove, all bare boards and steel beams and the walls stripped back to the brickwork.

'I told them to make them very dry, the way you said.'

'Good.'

'That means stronger, right?'

'Yes, that's right.'

They picked up their drinks and took a sip and both flinched slightly.

'Wow,' said Stuart. 'That's something.'

'It's what I need. I'm going to have two at least. I want to get a bit drunk this evening.'

'How's your case going?' said Stuart. 'Caught anyone yet?'

'We arrested a man this morning.'

'Bloody hell. I didn't think the police caught anyone anymore.'

'He's been charged. There'll be a trial.'

'But he did it?'

Maud gave a faint smile at this.

'I couldn't possibly comment. But the CPS won't go ahead unless they think they've got a good case.'

'You should be out celebrating.'

'I am out celebrating.' She picked up her glass. 'This is my celebration.'

'I'm honoured,' said Stuart. 'As long as you've charged the right person. And he's not a member of an oppressed minority group.'

'He's a doctor. He did the murder to cover up the fact that he'd raped the victim. And yes, he's the right person.'

'That's a lot,' said Stuart. 'I'm . . .' He started to speak and then stopped and looked searchingly at Maud. 'It must have been distressing.'

'Some of my colleagues,' said Maud, thinking of Danny Kemp with his eyes like boiled sweets and his nasty smile, 'forget that the people who are abused, or raped, or murdered, are human beings. They're just clues. It's probably how they cope with the deprivation, the chaos and the cruelty that they see every day. But that's what would make me leave the Met – if I became like them. I never met Kira, but I know she was young and kind-hearted and happy, and that her mother and sister are wrecked by her death. If that doesn't distress me, then I've crossed over, become like the people I'm trying to catch.'

She took a large swallow of her drink and felt its fire inside her.

'That's great,' she said.

Stuart took a more cautious sip of his.

'Mmm,' he said. Then: 'I have a son?'

'You have a son?'

'Alfie. He's three years old.'

Maud waited a beat, looking at her drink.

'Do you have a partner?' she asked.

'No, Maud,' Stuart said. 'I do not.'

He took her hand, held it to his mouth, kissed it.

'How often do you see him?'

'Every other weekend.' He reached for his drink again and

knocked it over. 'Fuck.' He grabbed a handful of napkins and wiped the table. 'I'll get another one and one for you.'

Maud watched him go. She finished her martini, feeling her edges blur, the chattering in her brain subside. She was lost in thought, and at first, she didn't notice the man coming to the table and sitting down.

'Surprise, surprise,' said a voice and she looked up and saw that it wasn't Stuart. Felix leaned across the table and spoke in an undertone. 'You fucked me over,' he said.

'I think you'd better leave,' said Maud.

Felix smiled. 'I happened to be in a bar, and I saw someone I recognised and walked over to say hello. Is that a crime?'

'You did not happen to be in a bar. Leave.'

He leaned even more closely towards her.

'You fucked me over and you made me look like a fool.'

'Fine,' said Maud. 'Now fuck off.'

He smiled again.

'Things can happen. That's all I'm going to say. Things can happen. Just wait and see.'

He lifted his right hand and jabbed at Maud's chest with his forefinger.

'What's going on?'

Felix looked round. Stuart was standing there, holding two new dry martinis.

'Shove off,' Felix said.

'That's my seat.'

Felix stood up and pushed against Stuart, spilling the drinks. Stuart looked too astonished to respond. Felix pushed against him again, then hit him. Stuart staggered back, one of the glasses falling to the floor and breaking.

Maud looked around desperately, but she could only see the cutlery on the table. She saw Stuart flexing his arm, as if he was going to throw an inexpert punch. Except he had a glass in his hand. She knew what that could do.

'Stop,' she said in a loud voice.

She took a fork from the table and stood up and as Felix turned to her, jabbed it into his neck, hard, and held it there so that he shuffled back until he was standing against the brick wall. She knew how much stronger he was than she was, and she pushed the fork a bit harder. Her face was close to his, as if they were about to kiss. She didn't know what people were doing around her. She spoke to him in a whisper.

'I can push this right through your throat, and it'll be self-defence. So. Are you going to fuck off right now?'

He nodded, unable to speak.

'Right now?'

Another nod.

She slowly withdrew the fork, away from his line of sight. He might think it was a knife. She thought he still might try something, but he didn't.

'You'll wish you'd never done it,' he said very quietly, then turned and walked out.

Maud turned to Stuart.

'What was that?' he said.

'Maybe we should leave.'

Outside on the pavement, Stuart was still in a state of shock. Maud linked arms with him.

'Let's go to my place,' she said. 'We can have another drink there. First, I've just got to make a quick call.'

EIGHTY-THREE

Nancy was pulling a tray of baked camembert stuffed with cranberries out of the oven when her mobile vibrated in her pocket. She ignored it. A few moments later, it buzzed again, insistent, and she put the oozing rounds of soft cheese on a worktop and pulled it out to glance at the caller ID. It was Maud.

'I know this must be the worst time to call.'

'Yes.'

'Have you seen Felix?'

A jolt of alarm went through Nancy.

'No. Why?'

'He's in an ugly mood. He might turn up. Just be on your guard.'

Felix didn't turn up, and Nancy tried to put the fact of him out of her mind, welcoming the Saturday night rush. She had escaped him, but still he was like an infection in the blood. Every time she thought of him, it was as if he had achieved a small, ugly victory over her. At the end of her shift, she ordered an Uber even though it was only a ten-minute walk, and when she got to her bedsit she looked up and down the street, imagining shadows in the alleyways and doorways, or crouching behind the skip full of earth and rubble next to the building she lived in. But there was no one there, just a van passing by, a couple of drunk teenagers holding onto each other for support, a fox among the dustbins.

The place she was renting was two flights up a flight of narrow stairs. The lights didn't work and she fumbled her key in the lock before managing to get the door open.

It was a cold, unlovely space. There was barely room for the bed with its lumpy mattress and the pine chest of drawers, and the tiny balcony under the window was like a category error. The bathroom was a cubicle with a malfunctioning shower and a toilet with a basin, and the kitchen consisted of a single hob oven, a fridge that made strange noises, and a table that folded out from the wall. There was no storage space, but then Nancy had nothing to store. All her things were still in the Fielding Road flat, and she had no intention of returning there. She only had the single bag of clothes she had taken with her on the day she had left with Maud. She'd picked up some tee-shirts and underwear from Primark.

But it didn't matter. She was beginning again, and she felt a curious pleasure in that. She would do it better this time. She had a quick shower, enduring the water that dribbled and spat from the shower head, first tepid, then scalding, cleaned her teeth, pulled on pyjama trousers and a tee shirt. She boiled the kettle and filled the hot water bottle she had bought the previous day. She made sure the chain was pulled across the door and the windows were bolted shut. The view from the bedroom was the one thing she liked about this tiny space: it looked out over a patchwork of rooftops and chimneys and glimpses of people's yards and gardens. As she drew the curtains, Nancy glanced down at the street that was dimly puddled by the lamps. Nothing.

She climbed into bed. The night was full of noises. Traffic, the far-off noise of a party that would probably go on until morning, the screech of an animal.

She took a few sips of water from the glass by the bed and told herself she was safe. She thought she wouldn't sleep, but she could feel sleep pulling at her, drawing her under, into the comfort of forgetting.

Maud and Stuart walked from the bus stop swiftly and went up the flights of stairs to Maud's flat. Inside, they kissed. Maud took off his coat and scarf and hung them on the hook, then her own.

'This way,' she said.

He was nervous at first, but she wasn't. It had been too long, mouth against mouth and skin against skin, hands in her hair, her name in her ear. She felt that a part of her that had lain dormant was coming back to life again. She was unpeeled, defenceless, full of exultation.

After, they lay close but apart, flung out on the bed.

'Who was that guy?' Stuart asked at last.

'A self-righteous creep,' said Maud. 'But dangerous.'

'I've never actually hit anyone,' said Stuart. 'I'm terrified of physical violence.'

'Good.'

'Can I stay the night?'

Maud, lying on her back with her eyes half closed, tipped her head to look at him.

'All right.'

'We can have breakfast in the morning.'

She sat up, swung her legs out of the bed.

'First, we're going to have that second drink. The night is young.'

EIGHTY-FOUR

Nancy dreamed there were people shouting. She dreamed that her mouth was full of cobwebs and furry moths, and she had to fight for her breath. She half woke, befuddled and far too hot. She kicked the hot water bottle out of her bed. Her closed eyes were stinging, and she began to cough, wracking coughs. Breathing made it worse, made it hurt more.

She sat up in bed, fighting with the duvet that had wrapped itself round her, opened her eyes, and it took her too many precious seconds to understand that the room was full of smoke, her lungs were full of smoke, her eyes were raw with smoke.

The frame of the door was searingly bright.

She heard the sounds. Licking, crackling, roaring from the other side of the door.

She picked up the pillow, tipped the water from the tumbler over it and held it to her mouth. She made for the door, then turned back. She couldn't go out there, into that furnace. The heat was growing. She coughed and retched. The door was rippling, blisters forming and popping in the varnish.

Nancy stumbled to the window and yanked it open. She knew that as soon as the fire forced its way into this room, then the air from outside would feed it and make it fiercer, but it was the only way out. She looked down and saw faces on the pavement looking up, the open O's of their mouths. They were all looking at her.

Nancy was a body in crisis, hacking and gasping, panic torrenting through her veins, eyes streaming, chest and throat closing as if she must suffocate in herself. But there was a small, cold part of her that stood to one side, seeing herself framed in the window as the small crowd below must be seeing her.

And it was this calculating part of her that singled out a particular face tilted up towards her. It was not appalled; its mouth wasn't open in horror. It wore an expression of calm, curious scrutiny.

Felix was down there. He was watching her die.

Their eyes met. He smiled, gave a little nod.

The nod was like a bucket of beautiful clear water. In one movement, Nancy reached down, grabbed her mobile, found the camera, and took a photo of him. He saw her doing it and flung up his hand to cover his face, but it was too late.

Then she clambered out of the window and onto the flimsy balcony, which creaked underneath her. She could feel it giving way and sense the rusty screws and hinges easing loose from the bricks. She leaned forward and flung her mobile towards the group beneath her, away from where Felix stood. She saw a woman catch it.

Then she fixed her eyes on the skip full of soil. The frail balcony gave a final heave. Behind her, the door burst open in a clamour of roaring flames.

'Jump,' the voice in the dark said. 'Jump for your dear life. Jump as if you could fly.'

Nancy put her foot on the rim of the balcony and as it gave way, she pushed off with all her strength and all her hope, her arms open wide, her mouth wide in a cry of longing, her lungs full of blessed air, her eyes full of open sky. Free.

EIGHTY-FIVE

It was a beautiful spring evening; the light thickened, and the first stars showed, a pale shaving of moon. As Maud O'Connor and Stuart Nemsky walked along the road together, their fingers occasionally touched. They didn't talk. Maud looked straight ahead, but she could feel his eyes on her.

'My bus stop is just ahead,' she said at last. 'We should say goodbye here.'

'I miss you already,' he said. 'I'll be on the other side of the world from you. When I'm awake, you'll be asleep and dreaming.'

He was taking his son to New Zealand, where one of his aunts lived, for three weeks.

'You'll have the best time,' she said. 'Especially with Alfie.'

'I'll be home soon.'

She kissed him on his lovely mouth, and he put his hands in the wild tangle of her hair and pulled her closer.

'Don't forget me,' he said.

'How could I?'

She turned and left, walking briskly away, not looking back. As she rounded the corner, she put one hand in the air in a gesture of farewell.

And suddenly she knew it really was farewell. It had been nice. It had been more than nice. She had desired and she had been an object of desire. There had been the closeness, exploring each other's bodies, the letting go, and then the intimacy of talk, teasing, sweetness. Someone to be excited by, comfortable with, have fun with. Wasn't that enough? Wasn't that what everyone wanted?

No, it wasn't enough. Silas really had been the one for her, but it had all gone wrong somehow. Stuart was funny and attractive; he'd been good for her, and she hoped she'd been good for him, but she knew that there was something missing and she wasn't going to settle for that. Better to be alone, better to be free.

She wasn't going to ghost him. She would have to tell him, and soon. She was already composing the message in her head: Dearest Stuart. This is a painfully difficult message to write . . . Her chest ached.

Maud walked from the bus stop to a small building on the untrendy edges of Stoke Newington, its window frames freshly painted and a tub of flowers at the entrance. The shutters were ajar and the room inside looked empty, but the door opened before she could knock.

'Please come in.'

Nancy was formal, slightly shy. There were burn marks on her cheek that would never go away, though they would fade, and while the cast on her leg had come off, she still limped. But she wasn't thin any longer. Her face was rounder and softer. She looked healthy. There were freckles on the bridge of her nose.

Maud entered, sliding off her canvas jacket and looking around appreciatively. It was a small space, with only room for a few tables, but it was clean and bright and open to the kitchen, where stainless steel fridges glowed and pots and pans hung from a rail along the wall. To one side of the kitchen, a door opened onto a yard where someone had evidently been levering up the cracked tiles.

'Are you all right?'

Nancy was looking at her attentively.

'It's nothing,' said Maud. 'Just someone I was thinking about.' She made herself smile. 'This looks nice.'

'If all goes well, we can have the yard as an overflow space in the summer.'

'You must have worked flat out.'

'Not just me. I've gone into partnership with Sam and Delia, who were with me at the old place. And my parents put down the deposit. Guilt money,' she added. 'It's been very useful.'

'And how are you?'

'Me? I'm well.' She threw a half-humorous glance at Maud. 'Felix didn't get bail.'

'I heard,' said Maud. 'I think he's going to discover that arson is a really big deal.'

'I feel I drove him mad,' said Nancy. 'I feel responsible, in a way.'

'Don't you dare.' Maud gestured around her. 'You've got enough to feel responsible for.'

Nancy took a white apron from one of the drawers and tied it round her waist.

'Are you ready?' she asked.

'Ready.'

'We're going to offer almost no choice at the restaurant – and it's all going to be fresh, local and seasonal. Tonight. I'm going to cook what I will cook for the opening on Friday.'

'What's on the menu?'

'We'll start with a few little nettle, sheep's cheese and butter gnocchi. And after that, some poached sea bream served with steamed spring vegetables.' She looked suddenly anxious. 'Does that sound all right?'

'It sounds amazing. I usually live off pasta and takeaways.'

'You don't mind nettles?'

'I've never eaten nettles. I'm not sure I've eaten gnocchi either, for that matter.'

'Take a seat. I've got some white wine in the fridge.'

Maud sat at the table nearest the kitchen. Nancy lit a candle and poured her a glass of wine. Maud sipped at it and watched as Nancy cooked.

With Nancy, Maud had always had the sense of mobility, restlessness, a flickering but incessant energy. But now, although her hands were deftly moving between tasks, the young woman seemed composed. She rubbed the cooked flesh of potato through a sieve, separated egg yolks from their whites using the cup of her hand and dropped them into the potato flour, grated cheese into the mixture. At the same time, it seemed, she chopped vegetables so quickly that Maud could barely track the movement of the long blade, roasted seeds, scattered spices into a large pan of boiling water. All the while, she was tasting, adding salt and black pepper, frowning, nodding judiciously, and even finding time to offer Maud more wine.

It was quiet in the room, just the click of the knife against the surface, the gentle bubble of the stock. All the different tiny tasks seemed to flow together, and Maud, watching intently, found it oddly comforting.

It was like a form of meditation and as she sat there, things seemed to fall away. The rape and death at 99 Fielding Road, the fire that Nancy had barely escaped from, the intoxicating affair with Stuart and the knowledge that it was coming to an end and she would soon be alone again, all of these things seemed like fading dreams. What was real was here, was now: the glow of the candle on the wooden table, the smell of garlic and ginger in the air, the young woman a few feet away wrapped in an apron and bent over her task, utterly focused, at home with herself after all the horror she had endured.

The first course was plated up. Nancy turned to Maud.

'The fish will only take a few minutes,' she said. 'Let's have this first.'

She put two steaming little dishes on the table, took off her apron, poured them both more wine. Then she took a seat opposite Maud. They both picked up their forks, smiling at each other.

'Thank you,' said Nancy.

Tears were running down her cheeks.

Maud smiled, though she too was full of intense emotion.

'I was only doing my job. Now then: let's eat.'

Acknowledgements

It takes many people to bring a book into the world, and with each book we write, the list of people to whom we owe thanks grows longer – and our anxiety that we might inadvertently leave someone off that list more acute.

We are forever grateful to our fabulous agents. Sarah Ballard of Curtis Brown is always our first reader, our champion, our anchor, our advocate. Huge thanks as well to Sam Edenborough of Greyhound Literary, and in the US Joy Harris of the Joy Harris Literary Agents. We know how lucky we are to be looked after by you all.

We are so glad to be part of the Simon & Schuster family, and to be supported and looked after by the team there. In particular, we are grateful to Katherine Armstrong, Suzanne Baboneau, Ian Chapman, Jess Barratt, Joe Christie, Mathew Watterson, Hayley McMullan, Louise Davies, Genevieve Barratt. And many thanks as well to the dynamic, hospitable group in Australia, above all Anna O'Grady and Dan Ruffino.

The wonderful team at HarperCollins in the US have watched over us. Thank you to Emily Krump, Tessa James, Christopher Connolly, Paige Meintzer.

Our admiration and gratitude goes to all the people who work on the front line with such commitment and optimism and unflagging love of books: the booksellers, organisers of literary events, people who work in libraries and those who set up book groups.

And thank you to our fellow crime writers: the kindest, most supportive and generous-hearted group of people you could ever hope to meet.

Finally, we salute our large, chaotic, joy-giving, porous and ever-growing family: children, grandchildren, siblings, nephews and nieces, and one remaining parent. Thank you all.